Praise for The Bottom Rail

The Bottom Rail is a Southern novel that makes *Tobacco Road* read like a Sunday School lesson. Lindsley's innate ability to portray Southerners is in evidence throughout the book as the Carter family climbs up and down the rails of Lindsley's metaphorical ladder.

The Bottom Rail supplies the reader with everything from murder and serious bootlegging to 1946 Georgia politics, as dirty as it gets. The pages almost turn by themselves.

Move over Ersine Caldwell and make room for Susan Lindsley.

Cappy Hall Rearick, Southern Humorist and Columnist
Author of *The Road to Hell is Seldom Seen*

The Bottom Rail captures the gritty essence of the rural South in the immediate wake of World War II in this panoramic tale of love, betrayal, lynchings, chain gangs, moonshining and murder. It's an "Old South" you won't forget.

H. W. "Buzz" Bernard,
Best-selling author of *Eyewall, Supercell* and *Plague*

Susan Lindsley's award-winning novel *The Bottom Rail* takes us back in time and place (the rural South) to the world of Harper Lee's *To Kill a Mockingbird*—only this time the story is told from the point of view of the Ewells, represented by the Carter family. Abandoning their stills in the Appalachians, the Carters migrate to Georgia during the Great Depression to get a new start as farmers. But they discover early on that bootlegging is far more profitable than farming as long as the sheriff refuses to raid their stills. The family includes bootleggers, cattle thieves, lynch mobs, murderers, and a one-armed war veteran who manages to wrest power from the county commissioner by stealing an election in precisely the way the commissioner himself would have stolen it if he had been given the chance. The Carters may be uneducated, racist law-breakers, but they are never dull. They are lusty, loyal to one another, and always resourceful. Although they arrive in Georgia as the bottom rail of the title, they manage to end up as top rail by virtue of determination, ruthlessness, lawlessness, and the basic intelligence of one of their own—Virgil—who finds a way to power in spite of the odds, some self-imposed, against him and his family.

Susan Lindsley writes with a sure hand, conveying not only her love of the South, despite its historic flaws, but also the language nuances of its rural areas. She portrays its people, black and white, complete with both beauty spots and warts, with honesty and affection. Her story is compelling, drawing the reader from one event to another, from a love scene to a lynching to a (literal) shotgun wedding, with clarity and brutal candor. Once you begin to read, you won't put it down.

June Hall McCash,
Winner, Georgia Author of the Year
for novels *Almost Eden* and *Plum Orchard*

The Bottom Rail

This book is a work of fiction, and all characters are products of the author's imagination. Any resemblance to real people, living or dead, is purely coincidental.

ISBN-13: 978-0-9859255-4-3
ISBN-10: 0-9859255-4-x

First printing, November, 2013

Cover artwork by Deborah Cidboy, website debsrealm.com

Additional cover design by ThomasMax.

Author's website: yesterplace.com

Published by:

 tm

ThomasMax Publishing
P.O. Box 250054
Atlanta, GA 30325
Website: thomasmax.com

The Bottom Rail

By Susan Lindsley

ThomasMax
Your Publisher
For The 21st Century

Acknowledgments

Two artists joined me in producing this novel: Deborah Cidboy designed and painted the excellent cover, and Pat Blanks sketched the cat saddle shown in the "Words about Words" at the end of the story. Thanks, gals! You're super artists.

I owe a debt of gratitude to those who supported my efforts with this story. Several pairs of eyes helped me find and solve problems— Thulia Bramlett, Trish Bass Riner, and Pat Blanks.

Without the on-going encouragement of my life-partner Gail Cabisius, this book would never have found its way to paper.

Special thanks are due my three fellow writers who reviewed an early manuscript and praised my story—June Hall McCash, Buzz Bernard, and Cappy Rearick.

Lee Clevenger, my publisher, honored me greatly by selecting my manuscript as winner of his "You Are Published" contest.

Thank you, all.

Introduction

When farmers depended on split-rail fences, the upper class mended them by putting in a new rail. Lower class farmers took the less costly route—moving the bottom (rotten) rail to the top and replacing it with the still-solid top rail.

"The bottom rail done got on top" has been a rural expression stating that a poor white has moved up the ladder financially or politically, and has also started up the social ladder.

NOTE TO THE READER

This story is laid in the 1930's and 1940's, a time of "non-politically correct" language, a time of harsh relationships and prejudices that often resulted in violence. I have used the language and terminology, as well as some of the dialect, of that period. I do hope that no one is insulted by this usage. I use it not to cause pain or insult but only to keep the story as close as possible to the conditions of the time; if I were politically correct (in terms of the twenty-first century) the entire story would ring false.

If you are offended today, please keep in mind that many white folks were also offended those many years ago. Unfortunately, bigotry never seems to die out.

For Pat and Pat
Our 70-year friendships get older,
but stronger, every day

A Word from the Publisher

You are reading a book that won the ThomasMax "You Are Published" annual contest at the Southeastern Writers Association's annual conference and workshop, an event held for nearly four decades on beautiful St. Simons Island. This is Susan's second time to win this contest. Her non-fiction entry: *Margaret Mitchell: A Scarlett or a Melanie?* was a previous winner. Lightning can strike twice in the same place.

It's ironic that the things in this book that are now offensive to many would have been shrugged aside as, "Well, that's how it was back then" not so long ago. But if you go back to the time period of this book's setting, there would be umbrage also -- for completely different reasons. I won't elaborate; I'll let you, the reader, figure out that one.

If you are a writer, I urge you to attend our annual workshop and conference. We have instructors from many phases of the industry. We always have at least one, sometimes two, novel instructors, and often feature classes on poetry, non-fiction (general or specific topics), writing inspirational works, writing for young readers, writing short fiction and a host of other topics. These topics and the instructors rotate annually. We also will have an agent from a major literary agency to whom attendees can pitch or discuss their projects. In addition, we have contests (the ThomasMax contest results in a book deal, but most of our contests have cash prizes) and *free* evaluations by instructors in up to three different manuscript categories.

The 2014 event will be held June 13-18. Our host will again be Epworth-by-the-Sea. You can find out more about our annual event by visiting our website, southeasternwriters.org.

When we judge contest entries, we have no idea of the author's identity. So when I discovered the author of *The Bottom Rail* was Susan Lindsley, I was delighted. Susan's past winner has been relatively successful sales-wise. She has also self-published some works with our company . . . and I consider her a close personal friend. But I reiterate, we at ThomasMax had no clue as to her identity when judging the contest entries. All other SWA contests are judged similarly to prevent any personal prejudice.

We hope to see you in 2014 or at one of our future annual events. It's the greatest "bang for the buck" writers' training you will ever receive.

--- Lee Clevenger, President, ThomasMax Publishing

PART I: SUMMER 1931

Chapter 1

The baby girl did not want to be born. Sounds and motions penetrating into the womb told her what life offered. She curled tighter into herself, clutching safety with a fierce determination that could eventually be her undoing.

Although unaware of the long, hot days of July, she sensed the outside world. The constant jolting and bouncing, the squeal of wagon wheels begging for oil, the rattle of trace chains, and the voices that rose and fell with tension penetrated to disturb her comfort. She did not know her family had fled the Great Depression, crop failure, and the mountains in hopes of finding a future somewhere farther south in Georgia. She knew only that she wanted to stay in the darkness and warmth, to hide forever from the noises, to keep the soft padding that offered some protection from the bumping.

The jolting and noises stopped, and soon the heavy voices faded away. Then she felt only the regular beating of Penny's heart and heard only the slush of her mother's blood and the irregular growling of her belly. Silence came to her from the outside, silence and an infrequent, soft murmur that she found soothing.

Penny sat against a tree, her knees pulled up against her extended belly and her body slumped forward to ease her back, and rested her face on her knees. "I shore be a-hoping they git us one-a them-there chickens."

Ellen, her older sister, said, "I shore kin use something besides corn bread and tomatoes. How you doing?"

"Oh, Gawd, Ellen. I jest want this here baby to git born. Seems like I kain't git over this-here up-chucking even now. All that snuff Ma gave me ain't heped but a little bit."

"I never had the up-chucks like you. Didn't last me but a couple months. You shore are gitting skinny."

Moonlight broke through the cloud cover to reveal a small meadow, three wagons with a brace of mules hitched to each, their bits slipped so they could eat what grass and weeds the July sun had not burned brown. A small fire, built for low flame and little heat, burned in the middle of the meadow, and a black pot filled with water sat beside it.

"They git a chicken, maybe you'll feel like some broth," Ellen said.

From the edge of the field, Penny stared into the flames as if seeing her future burning away.

Ellen called to the two children who tumbled in the shadows. "Come on back here so's I kin see you. Soon's your pa gits back, we'll have us-ens some chicken."

Penny's husband Sam and his two brothers had walked off right at dark, headed back down the main road toward the shanty they passed at sundown when several chickens flew up to roost in a chinaberry tree near the road. Jack, the oldest, decided at least one of the hens would be in their pot for supper.

Long leg shadows moved back and forth in the light as their only lantern swung with Jack's stride. On bare feet, they walked silently through the night.

Gus, the youngest, whispered, "Hope that nigger ain't got no scattergun."

"Hesh up, Gus," Jack said.

"How come? We still got a ways to go. They ain't nobody to hear us talking."

"That ain't it," Sam said. "Don'tcha go talking about us gitting shot. We gotta git some food, especially with Penny sick. She gitting as gaunt as the mules."

A shadow moved from the woods to their right, came into the road, and looked their way, its eyes gleaming, reflecting the lantern. The men froze, and the fox turned away, fading into the brush as silently as its shadow.

They sighed. "Leastways it ain't got the rabies," Jack said.

"Yeah."

"Iffen it'd had a chicken, I'd shot it, though," Gus said.

"I told you to leave that-air gun at the wagons. We got no call to be shooting. We jest be needing a chicken."

"Yeah, I know, Jack. I jest got to thinking what if a dog does come out after us?"

"If he had any dogs, they'd have come after Buster when we went by today. He ain't got no hound," Jack said.

Gus moved ahead of the others, and they walked in silence for a few minutes.

"Hey, cut that-air lantern. I see houselights," he said.

Jack raised the bail, lowered the wick, and blew out the light. To let their eyes adjust to the half-moon light that filtered through scattered clouds, they stood in the night's whisper of breeze through the grass and the constant call of crickets.

The moonlight showed three men dressed in overalls, without shirts. They could have passed for triplets, with the same sharp features, lean faces and dark hair that curled over their deep-set, black eyes.

As Gus pulled cigarette makings from his overalls pocket, Jack's hand grabbed his.

"You light a Lucifer and we got another five minutes-a waiting."

Gus shrugged and said, "Sorry. I warn't thinking."

"I kin see pretty good," Sam said. "Kin y'all?"

"Yep. Les git moving. Leave that-air shotgun here with the lantern. We'll pick 'em up on the way back."

Jack placed the lantern near the ditch, and Gus laid the .12 gauge carefully by it. "I don't feel right, leaving my shotgun out here this-away."

"You shoulda left it in the wagon like I told you to. We gonna git back long afore anybody comes by. Les go."

They strode down the road but, to keep their night vision, they did not look toward the lamplight in the shanty window.

"I kin see that chinaberry tree," Gus whispered. "It ain't more'n spitting distance across the ditch."

"Sam, you and me'll make a foot-step for Gus, seeing he be the littlest. And be kerful crossing the ditch," Jack said.

They hunched their backs as if doing so would keep them from being seen and quickly scooted across the ditch. With the chinaberry tree between them and the house, they walked upright toward it.

After making a cat saddle, Sam and Jack squatted, and as soon as Gus stepped onto their hands and gripped their shoulders, they stood erect. Gus stayed crouched as he released his grip on Sam and stretched that hand up, but he could not get his fingers close enough to grab the hen. As he turned loose his hold on Jack's shoulder and rose to his full height, he began to wobble and lunged for the hen, but only brushed her leg as he started to fall. She squawked and flew. Jack and Sam tried to keep their hands steady, but couldn't, and Gus, desperate to break his fall, grabbed the now empty branch. As he fell, he pulled it down, popping it with a loud crack.

Chickens cackled and flapped across the yard; Gus yelled as he hit the ground; the shanty door slammed open, and a shadow stood black against the lamplight, a shotgun rising.

Jack yelled, "Run."

The scattergun fired as Sam and Jack scrambled across the ditch and Gus still wallowed around on the ground. The figure in the door yelled, "Git outta here, you chicken thief. I got chullen to feed. You come back and I won't be shooting over your head. Git outta heah!" He fired the other barrel.

Sam and Jack ran, jumped the ditch, and left Gus sprawled as they disappeared down the road. Gus scrambled on all fours to the ditch and across it. Once on the road, he took off in a hard run, and a few yards down the road he caught up with his brothers.   They stood together a moment, hands resting on knees, trying to catch their breath. Gus sat down in the middle of the road.

"You okay?" Sam asked.

"Yeah. I gotta sit a minute. That there ground's hard. You both run off and left me. I could-a got shot."

They all sat, cross-legged, and Jack began to laugh.

"You shore did squeal like a stuck pig when you fell."

"You wouldn't know. You was too busy running."

Sam reached into a pocket and pulled out a tobacco plug and his pocket knife. He opened the blade, thin from years of sharpening on stone, and sliced himself a chew before he passed both knife and plug to his brothers. As he dropped his knife back into his pocket, Sam said. "We best be gitting to the wagons. The women-folk'll be in a fret."

Worried over his shotgun, Gus took the lead by a step as they jogged down the road. He spotted the lantern from the moonlight reflected in the smoky glass. They did not light it. Gus grabbed his firearm, and they kept up their trot all the way back to the meadow.

*   *   *

When Ellen and Penny heard the gunfire, they jumped up. Penny almost lost her balance and had to lean on the tree.

The two boys ran to their mother. "Is somebody shooting at

Daddy?" Virgil, the larger boy, asked.

Ellen dumped the pot of water on the flames and stirred the steaming ashes with a stick to be sure she had put the fire out. "Git over to the wagon, boys," she said. "We be moving soon's the men git back."

"They ain't gonna have no chickens," Penny said. "I jest hope one of 'em ain't got shot." She sighed with her exhaustion and walked to one of the wagons. "I gotta lie down some, Ellen."

She leaned on Ellen's shoulder as she stepped onto the wheel hub and into the wagon. Buried in old hay that smelled of spilled whiskey, urine, and dogs, crockery jugs lined the sides of the bed. A diapered child slept under the wagon seat, a month-old infant beside him. Penny carefully stretched out on her back and pulled her knees up so her feet were flat on the wagon bed.

"I kin stand this tonight, El. Reckon kin you git any rest?"

"I'll be fine, Pen. I gotta put the boys back there with you, seeing there ain't any room anywhere else." Ellen's voice rose a little. "Virgil, you and Bobby git them puppies up here right now."

They crawled under the wagon and came out, each clutching a hound puppy. As Ellen took the pups, the boys crawled under for the others. The mother dog came out after her puppies and watched as they disappeared into the wagon.

"Git in," Ellen told the boys, and they scampered up, to sit beside Penny.

Ellen adjusted bridles and slipped bits into mouths to prepare the teams to move out. Before she finished, the three men trotted out of the darkness.

Ellen noted the empty croaker sack. "Y'all awright?" she asked.

"Yep. Les git moving."

"You ain't got no chicken?"

"We be lucky we got ourselves. That nigger didn't miss by much. And he had hisself a shotgun. And I fell outta the tree."

Jack laughed.

"You shoulda seen him, Ellen. We was half-way back here while Gus wallowed around on the ground, squalling worsen them chickens."

"You gitting shot at ain't funny, Jack," she said. "What'd I do iffen you got yourself kilt?"

"I ain't gitting kilt. Quit fretting so."

"Where's Penny?" Sam asked.

"In Gus's wagon. She laying down."

"Hump."

The men hurried to finish the last of the bridling, climbed into wagons, and clucked the mules into motion. The wagons rattled across the meadow and down a narrow lane through the woods. A few minutes later, they bumped across the ditch onto the main road, where they turned southeast into a night silenced by their approach.   Lightning bugs courted, their flashing lights like stars sprinkled through the darkness, and in the distance a barred owl asked them, "Who cooks for you?" Crickets, shrilling at each other, quieted as the wagons approached. Somewhere ahead a chuck-will's-widow called.

Less than a mile down the road, they passed a house showing only one light, but giving off the fragrance of fatback and greens that teased their empty stomachs. The wagons rolled on through the night and the July heat.

Chapter 2

By afternoon, Penny sat beside Sam on the wagon seat, a board ripped from the side of a barn to replace the spring seat. Even a pad of hay stuffed in a croaker sack didn't cushion the seat for Penny in the final days of her pregnancy. Sam refused to sit on anything but the hard board.

Red dust rose from beneath the mules' feet and the wagon wheels to settle like a red coat on everything. The mules plodded, their harness loose after days of pulling had dropped their weight. Bones shaped the rough hides, like rocks turned up in plowing. Harness sores attracted flies that their tails seldom bothered to flick away. Once in a while, a driver would rake a switch at the insects.

When Penny squashed a horsefly on her arm, the blood mixed with the dust, and she used the hem of her feedsack dress to wipe it off. More dust than blood decorated the skirt tail.

She used her belly for an arm rest when she was not grasping her back at the waistline and squeezing while she twisted herself erect in an attempt to relieve the steady, tiring pain. She wanted to lean back, but only the corner of a dresser was behind her, and when her back touched it, the edge cut into her skin each time the wagon jolted.

The wagon carried a jumble of furniture held in place with plowlines that kept pieces from falling out but could not keep them from rattling. Once-white metal bedsteads stood on each side of the wagon bed, with several pine chests packed between them. At the tailgate rode Penny's cedar chest, handmade by her father for her wedding and precious because it was the only gift he ever could afford to give her. A few straight chairs, handmade from oak saplings, were piled helter-skelter; Penny, Ellen, and their mother had twisted the corn-shuck bottoms when the older ones gave way; all the lower rungs had darkened from years of use as foot rests.

Mattresses gave off an odor of mildew and urine that hung over the entire wagon. Rather than clean the mattresses, summer showers had turned dust to stains that did not hide the years of human sweat that blackened the striped ticking.

Lanterns swung on both sides. Beside the cedar chest stood a barrel of water and a box containing cooking utensils.

Penny wanted to get somewhere, anywhere, just stop this infernal jolting and maybe the pain would get better. Last night had not helped, however, she reminded herself. Sleeping in the wagon eased her back a little if she kept her knees pulled up, but nighttime dew made her shiver so much in her sleep that every muscle in her body tensed up all over again. Every day the constant stink of the mules rose over the too sweet smell of the wild flowers that perfumed the road. When one of the mules dumped, the odor of manure rose up into her face and she wanted to throw up. Last summer she could wrestle a plow behind a farting mule and not be bothered by sun or smell, but today the afternoon heat beat her down and underlined the odors and the agonies. As sweat trickled down her back, she wondered if it were as frothy and salty as the patch of sweat seeping from under the mule's breeching. If the baby would just get born, she thought, surely she would feel better.

Penny's blue eyes and long, straight, brown hair highlighted by the sun were a sharp contrast to her husband's deep-set black eyes and dark, curly hair that fell over his forehead like a horse's forelock. Her face bore the exhaustion of years, belying her youth. At fifteen, she was not half the age of her husband but her gauntness and constant frowning added years to her face.

She sighed. Surely they'd get a place soon. Cropland stretched out on either side, row after row of corn, cotton, tomatoes, and okra. They had come through days and miles of untended land, but in the last three days had passed more than a dozen shanties where naked or half-naked Negro children played in yards shaded by mimosa and chinaberry trees. Penny figured the men were gone to the fields and some girl was inside cooking since smoke drifted from chimneys in back of the houses. The drifting smell of cooking—fatback, cornbread, and greens—kept her stomach churning.

"How come you ain't asking anybody about a place? We must-a passed a half-dozen places today," Penny asked Sam.

He said, "I ain't having no truck with no niggers. We gonna find us a white folks' place. I ain't never knowed there was so many damn niggers in the world."

At least, she thought, he and his brothers hadn't been too leery of niggers to slip into their fields after dark to help themselves to some of their vegetables. And a chicken when they could. She thought for a moment about how good that chicken would have tasted last night if they had just caught it, but she knew better than to think about food. It only made her hungrier.

Penny didn't care what color somebody was if she could just get out of the wagon and into the bed. Just for one night. But Sam didn't want to unload and set up the bedstead. He said it took too much time, but she figured he was as wo' out as she was and didn't have the strength after handling the mules all day, helping his brothers steal food, and getting up enough wood for cooking. It had been a week since they'd had any meat, and that was just a tough old hen. Everybody had yard dogs along this road, and the hounds set up barking from the time they heard the wagons till the dust had long been settled.

Her older sibling, Ellen, had never told her how hard it was to carry a baby. Ellen wasn't but twenty-three and already had four boys. Penny didn't want to ever be pregnant again, what with all the trouble she had even now. Seemed like she would never get over the up-chucks, even with all the snuff she'd dipped because Ma told her it'd keep her stomach settled. And just as bad, the carrying pain killed her back. But Sam wanted a passel of kids.

Just the other night, when she'd said, "I hope this-here is my onlyest baby," he said, "Takes a heap of boys to work a farm and make anything." And then he spat his tobacco into the fire and turned his back on her to go to sleep. Maybe if she was older and Sam was not so old she might be able to keep from having babies. But she wasn't old enough to tell her husband no—when they got married Ma told her she had to do whatever Sam told her to. She wished Ma and Pa had come with them, but Pa would never give up his whiskey-making to take a chance on going somewhere else, no matter how bad things got.

Ellen had overheard them talking and told her the same thing Ma had: "You kain't say no to your man." But look at all the babies Ellen had. Ever since she got married, Ellen had been swole up with carrying a baby and had to cook and wash and keep house for her husband. Penny knew about the birthing pain from hearing her own mother scream when her seven younger sisters and brothers got born. She already dreaded her time, and wanted it to be over.

"I know you're tired out, Penny. But there ain't nothing like having a baby. Once he's born, you'll fergit all about this-here heat and your hurting back. Babies are worth every bit of the pain, seeing as how much love you have for your children."

But Penny couldn't think of love, only pain and exhaustion. She said, "Maybe so. Jest right now, I don't want even this one, much less a passel."

Ellen and her husband, Jack, Sam's older brother, rode in the third wagon, carrying all the farm tools that banged constantly against the wagon sidings. A middle buster and a bottom plow rang together like a farm bell as they wobbled over all the other equipment. Ellen held her youngest baby in her lap or laid him on a croaker sack on the seat between her and Jack.

Ellen's other three boys rode in the middle wagon, where the stale hay provided Penny a bed the night before. The two older children wore jeans cut from their father's overalls; the youngest, only diapers that smelled and sagged. The sun had parched their skin a deep red-brown, and the dust added layers of red shades that seeped into their pores. When they scratched their mosquito and horsefly bites, their chewed fingernails left lines in the sweat-damp dust. Their backs bore welts from insect bites where they couldn't reach to shoo off the attacker.

All three resembled their father and uncles, with dark eyes, black hair that tumbled over their foreheads, thin mouths and sharp noses. None bore the lighter coloration or softness of their mother and aunt.

The oldest boy out-shoved the others to stay in the splash of shade cast by their uncle Gus. Mostly they lay in the hay and petted the four mixed-hound puppies that did not hesitate to defecate and urinate in the wagon bed.

The spotted hound mother and the redbone father trotted in the shade under Gus's wagon. Her teats, heavy with milk, hung low and swung from side to side, slapping her legs with every step. Their tongues lolled from the heat, slobber dripping. The mother carried the same exhaustion as the women in the wagons.

Penny placed a hand on her husband's arm as she pleaded, "Sam, we gotta git somewhere soon. This here baby's gonna git born right outchere in the road afore you know it. Right out here in front of Gawd and anybody else what comes along."

"Don't fret so, Penny. We gonna find a place soon." He shifted the wad of tobacco from his left jaw to the other side and spat into the dust.

Gripping reins in one hand, he wiped his mouth with the other, smeared the juice from his hand onto his overalls, took the reins back into both hands, and rested his elbows on his thighs.

"You been saying that all week. We gone by a heap of farms." She slid her palms down the side of her head, pushing her brown hair back, and lifted it off her neck to catch a breath of air to cool the sweat. She waved the bunched hair like a horse's tail to generate her own breeze. Although the sun had finally moved behind them, out of their eyes, it continued to feel like a hot stove to her back.

"I done toldcha. We gonna git a white folks' place." He slapped the reins lightly against the mule's back, his black eyes narrowed, his mouth a tight straight line.

She knew his impatience, had felt the back of his hand when he got riled up about something. Still, she persisted, sure he wouldn't slap up on her with the baby about to be born.

"Iffen it ain't soon, you gonna be setting up that-air bed right alongside the road."

"You keep on talking that way, you gonna make the baby git born. And iffen he gits born outchere, it'll be on the ground. I ain't unloading all that-air jest for you to lie on a bed."

They rode without speaking for a few minutes, and then she said, "I need to git out and walk awhile."

"You gonna start spitting up again?"

"No. I jest gotta git off-a the wagon. Maybe walking'll make me hurt less."

He lifted a hand to signal the others he was stopping and hauled back on the plow- linc reins. "Ho, there, Maude." Trace chains jangled louder, and Maude snorted as she halted, and then threw her nose forward to tell Sam to loosen up on the reins, that she wasn't going off anywhere. Sam let up a little and then glanced at Penny. "You make it by yerself?"

"I reckon," she answered as she rose and rested a hand on his shoulder. Maude stomped to shake a horsefly off her leg, and, afraid the mule was moving off, Penny clutched Sam's shoulder. He grabbed her hand until she settled herself and started off the wagon. Turning her back to the road, she leaned forward and lowered her left foot to the wheel hub. A pair of hands reached up to her hips, and she eased down.

"Thank-ee, Gus," she said to her brother-in-law.

He nodded and went back to his wagon as he wiped sweat off his neck with a piece of feed sack. The two older boys in his wagon tumbled out and ran to her.

"We wanna walk too," Virgil, the older said, grasping her hand while he rubbed a bare foot on his leg to chase away a bug.

She smiled at her nephew and turned back to the third wagon. Jack, Ellen's husband, called, "If they be trouble, they'll git right back in the wagon."

Penny waved to him and turned to the boys. "You tired of them puppies?"

"Naw," Virgil said. He wrapped both arms around her and spoke into her hip. "I love you, Aunt Penny. I jest wanna walk with you."

Their eyes met as he moved back. Although his round face smiled, his eyes carried the bleakness of hunger and hopelessness, so like Sam. So like all the men, she thought. *Sam's face has got all those lines wrinkled up around his eyes, just like Pa. Old with worry now, with the depression running us out of the mountains.* Virgil wasn't but eight, more than half her age, and he looked as tired and worn out as the men when they got to talking about making a living when there wasn't any work but bootlegging and nobody with money to buy the whiskey.

Small fingers wrapped around the thumb of her other hand.

"I kin keep up, Aunt Penny. I promise. I want to walk some too." Bobby's smile showed a gap between two crooked teeth, where he'd lost one last week. He snuffled up the snot that dribbled out of one nostril and then ran the back of his free hand under his nose and wiped it on his pants leg.

"Come on," she said. "We got to stay in front of the wagons or we'll be in all that dust."

As soon as she passed Maude, Sam slapped the reins, grunted a "git-up," and the wagons began to move again. The road felt hot to her feet, but at least she didn't have to smell the mules and breathe their dust. As they came up on a clump of blackberries, Virgil released her hand and ran to the ditch where he selected the largest berries and saved them in one hand curled to his chest. Penny kept moving, her brown hair hanging loose and her legs clearly outlined through the worn cotton dress. She squinted against the glare of the cumulus clouds that rose ahead of them and hoped they might at least have a shower. Maybe it would cool things off a little. It never got this hot back home in the mountains.

Behind her, the wagons did not slow up for the boy. Even Jack passed him. Ellen's mind turned to her nursing infant, and she sat with her dress open down the front and her teat pulled out. The baby's hands pressed against her like a kitten's paws pumping milk while it sucked.

"I gotta change him soon," she told her husband in a voice devoid of hope. She leaned over the baby for a moment, as if trying to pull energy from him. When she pulled herself upright, the baby gurgled and spit up milk over her for the second time. As he voided, the smell of urine and feces smothered the smell of stale milk that hovered around her.

"You best git back there and fix him," her husband said, his nose wrinkled at the odor.

The wagon bounced into a rut and then out again. Ellen gripped the baby with one hand while she stuffed her breast back into the dress. Swinging around on the board, she slid into the hay, careful to avoid both the puppies and the crockery jugs. She glanced over the tailgate to see Virgil running behind them, his small hands together as he clutched his blackberries.

"You better git on up here, boy," she called.

"I got some berries, Ma."

"Give 'em to your Aunt Penny. She needs 'em most."

As he trotted on by the wagon, the red bone hound left the shade to follow him as if he thought Virgil's hands held food for a dog. The hound poked his nose at the child's hands, and Virgil swung away to put his back to the dog.

"Git away," he yelled and kicked at the hound.

"Buster!" Ellen called, but the dog ignored her, his head turning forward, his attention diverted to something down the road, his ears half-raised, and his nose lifting for the scent.

"He be smelling something," Gus said. "Maybe a farmhouse with a dog up ahead. Hold up there, Sam. Lemme git a rope on them dogs afore they run off and git in another fight."

When the wagons stopped, Penny slowed her stride for Virgil to catch up. He held up his hands, offering her five blackberries, squashed until juice blackened his palm and his chest. "I picked 'em for you, Aunt Penny."

She let him place them in her hand and then carefully, one at a time, ate them, smiling and exclaiming over each one. If only her baby would be this good, she thought, have as much love for everybody as Virgil did.

Her back didn't ease up any, and after another hundred or so yards, she climbed back onto the wagon seat.

Half an hour later, they reached a one-room store hunkered beside the road, a glass-topped gas pump in front. Three chairs leaned against the wall to the left of the door, which gaped half open, showing only semidarkness. As they drove the wagons into the little shade offered by a pair of oaks, a boy about the size of Virgil slipped around the building, leaned on the corner, and studied them with almost yellow eyes.

Sunlight behind him made his unruly reddish hair seem on fire. Barefooted, he wore only overalls. One hand remained inside a pocket while the other clutched a piece of sugar cane on which he gnawed. His eyes settled on Penny's protruding belly.

"Whose store?" Gus asked

"My pa's."

"He inside?" Gus tied off the reins to the brake and stepped down.

"Naw. He's at the outhouse. Be in directly."

"Tell him we're inside. We'll wait," Jack said.

Ellen remained on her wagon seat, and with Sam's help, Penny climbed down and went to sit beside an oak. The tree draped its limbs so low that their tips had been shredded by children swinging their way across the grassless yard. The dust showed prints of children's bare feet as well as shod and unshod horse and mule hoofs. Manure piles had dried from the heat.

The two older boys tumbled from the wagon and immediately began to gallop around them. When the third child began to whimper, Ellen lifted him to the ground. With his diapers hampering his every step, he looked down to see where he was putting his feet and tumbled onto his face. He rose on all fours, threw his body upward, fought for balance, and waddled after his brothers, his belly thrust forward, rump thrust backward, and arms lifted outward and flapping like the broken wings of a bird. Bobby grabbed a stick and sailed it at a frightened squirrel. Their high-pitched voices lifted in a raucous melody of noise.

The redheaded boy watched from the corner of the building, still chewing on the now-juiceless fiber of the cane.

"You young-uns leave the squirrels be. We don't wanna git these heah folks thinking we don't know how to act," Ellen said.

The store owner's son walked toward them.

"I'm Charley," he said. He looked from Bobby to Virgil and

smiled, crinkling his freckled cheeks with his happiness. Freckles not only covered his face but also showed on his chest around his overalls' bib and on his shoulders and arms.

Virgil grinned back. "I'm Virgil. I'm the oldest. This-here's Bobby. He done lost a toof. Mine are mostly growed back in already. You lost your toofs, too?"

Charley jerked out the sugar cane and closed his mouth.

Virgil pulled his own lips back and stuck a finger in his mouth to show where one of his teeth was just coming in. "This here oughtta be about my last one. How old are you?"

"I'm seven. You like to fish?"

"Yep, I shore do. You got a good fishing creek hereabouts? We used-ta catch trout up in the mountains."

Charlie nodded. "Down yonderways," he pointed behind the store. "It's not far. It's got a lotta catfish and sunfish. Y'all going to settle around here?"

Virgil shrugged. "I dunno. Seems like we been traveling forever."

"She your momma?" Charley pointed toward Penny.

"Naw. She's my mama's sister. She married to my daddy's brother. My pa's the oldest one, the tallest one too." He pointed to where the three men were just entering the store.

They carried the rank smell of tobacco, old sweat, and manure into the store, the odors overpowering those of flour, leather and soap. They stood just inside, their eyes moving around the room to rest on the sacks of flour and the canned goods scattered on the shelves. Gus reached for a sack of flour but jerked his hand back as a middle-aged man came in from the back yard. Sunlight flamed his hair before he closed the door. Even in the half-light after the brightness, they could see the sleeves of his white shirt bore starched creases. In spite of the heat, he wore a tie.

"How can I help you?" He ran a hand through his hair, adjusted his rimless glasses, and looked directly at Sam.

Gus glanced at the man and then continued to inspect the shelved goods. His eyes rested on several bags of sugar pushed into a corner on a top shelf.

"We be hunting a place to work," Sam said. "A piece of land to grow some corn and maybe some place to work for real money."

"Nobody's got work for real money these days," the man said. "Lotsa folks growing corn around here. You might want another crop."

"We always grow corn. Need it to feed the mules and feed us too," Sam said.

"Nobody got money to buy sugar, neither, I see." Gus said.

The man jerked his head around to stare at Gus. "What do you mean by that?"

Gus smiled and shrugged. "Nothing much. I see you got a heap of sugar up there. Maybe y'all need a few more folks growing corn around here. To use up some-a that-air sugar." He walked over to the storekeeper and said, "I'm Gus Carter. These here be my brothers, Sam and Jack."

"I'm Lawrence Cunningham."

As they shook hands, Charley came to the door. "Pa, there's a woman out there about to have a baby."

Sam turned to the boy. "That be my wife, boy. You leave her be, you hear?"

"I ain't bothering her none. You going down to Dr. Jacobs' place?"

"We ain't needing no doctor. Never have needed one, not even when Jack there busted up his arm. I set it fer him," Sam said.

"Well, you might want to go see Dr. Jacobs, Sam. One of his tenants moved out last week, so he's got an empty house. You could probably work out a deal with him to share crop some land. Maybe work for him getting in the hay this summer." He grinned. "And get in a good crop of corn come spring."

"Where at's his place?"

He walked to the front door and pointed the direction the family had been headed.

"Down the road apiece. Maybe four, five miles."

"That be nothing fer us. We done come a heap farther'n that today. A little more ain't gonna hurt none. You reckon he be there?"

"He's there unless he got called away. You can't miss his house. He got a doctoring sign in front, by his mailbox." He jerked a thumb toward the southeast.

"We'll see to it," Sam said.

Charley whooped and ran over to where Virgil stood by a mule's rear and rattled a trace chain. "We're gonna be neighbors. I just know we gonna be neighbors. We can go fishing together."

"Where y'all coming from?" Cunningham asked.

"Up in the mountains. Two years our crops dried up. Only business left is whiskey, and nobody's got money to buy that," Sam said.

Cunningham smiled, showing even teeth, and said, "Oh, there's money here for moonshine. Just not enough people can make good whiskey."

"You got anybody who'll buy some?" Jack asked.

"Hold on there," Gus said. "We're looking for a place to live, not a place to run whiskey and git in trouble with the law."

Cunningham reached over the counter, pulled out a package of cigarettes, and offered the pack around. As it moved from hand to hand, he leaned his butt into the front of the counter, crossed his arms, and turned his eyes to the floor. Silence fell as the men lit their smokes from a match Jack scratched on the thigh of his overalls. Smoke hovered at eye level in the room, as if it were too lazy to move.

"You won't get in trouble with the law here if you've got whiskey. I saw your wagons out there. One of 'em's empty except for those puppies and a lot of hay. You want to swap a jug for some flour and sugar?"

"You bet we do," Jack said before the others could speak. "And iffen we git a place here, we kin make all you kin sell."

Cunningham's face turned into a smile. "Get a jug. I'll check it out myself and if it's good, we can deal." Jack strode out while Cunningham continued to talk. "I'm sick of the whiskey the niggers make. Some of 'em just don't do it right unless you stand over them."

"Don't nobody have to stand over us," Sam said. "We been bootlegging since my grandpa made it back home."

*   *   *

While Charley, Virgil, and Bobby whooped their way around the wagons, Penny leaned her tired back against an oak tree. She closed her eyes as she dug her fingers into her back and twisted herself to try to loosen the tight muscles. Legs stretched before her, the pattern of half-healed briar scratches like an unfinished quilt, she breathed deeply and dropped her hands into the unfilled portion of her lap. She felt the baby stir and hoped it would be a girl. Her husband would never forgive her if it were—he had no sisters and wanted no daughters—but as she listened to her nephews screech their way around her, she wanted no son. A boy was only noise, something to get dirty, and somebody to have to do for. She wanted a girl, someone to be hers, to stay home with her when the men followed the hounds after possums all night long.

She was so tired even her knees felt heavy while her legs lay flat on the ground. If only they would not have to keep on moving. She didn't think she could stand another night on the road, another day of bouncing and jerking in the wagon. She wouldn't even mind unloading the wagon while the men went out into the night to hunt for something to eat.

The red hound trotted over to her and licked her hand. She opened her eyes and scratched his ears as he laid his head on the shelf of her belly. "You ain't gonna be my onlyest baby afore long, Buster," she mumbled. "You ought to go on off and play with the boys."

He lifted his head, yawned, his tongue curling upward, and looked at her. She hugged him, pulled him over on his side until she could get both arms around him, and buried her face in his stubby hair.

When Virgil and Charley clambered onto a doubletree and tried to climb onto the mules by hauling themselves up the tails, Ellen got down from her wagon, pulled them away, and told them to sit.

"You ain't my ma," Charley said.

"No, I ain't," she said. "But iffen you gonna play with my boys, you gonna do what I say, you hear me?"

Charley's eyes widened, and then he slowly nodded. He stuck a hand into his pocket and pulled out three sections of sugar cane. "You want one of these?" he offered her.

"I'll let Penny have mine," she said as she took one section. "Thank-ee, Charley."

"I got another one she can have," he said and ran over to Penny. He extended his hand and she took a section and began to chew it, sucking out the sweet juice.

"Thank-ee," she said. "I ain't had nothing tastes this good in most a year."

"Your littlest baby is crawling under a mule," Charley said, pointing toward the diapered child whose small dirty hand reached for a steaming pile of fresh manure. Ellen ran to the boy and grabbed him up. She held him away from her body as the stench of his diapers reached her nose, and placed him in the wagon with the puppies. He set about hitting on his baby brother who had been sleeping under the wagon seat. The baby screamed.

She lifted the infant from the wagon and, unmindful of Charley watching her, unbuttoned her dress, pulled out a breast heavy with milk, and put the baby to it. The crying subsided as she walked back to the oak to sit beside Penny.

Just as she got settled, the men came outside and headed for the wagons. "Les go," Jack called.

Penny and Ellen pushed themselves up from under the tree and went to their wagons. As Penny reached hers, she placed a foot on the wheel hub, clutched at the side of the wagon, and began to pull herself forward and upward. Her foot slipped on the grease, her hands could not hold her weight, and she landed hard on her back.

Her breath swooshed out and she lay silent as she tried to breathe again and to swallow the scream that rose in her throat. Before Sam could step down, Charley ran to her and held out his hand as an offer of help. She took it, and this time as she stepped onto the wheel hub, she rested one hand on the boy's shoulder.

"I'm much obliged, boy," she said.

"You're welcome, m'am. I hope you ain't hurt." He smiled at her.

"She ain't hurt," her husband answered from the wagon seat. "And you ain't got no call to be putting your hands on my woman."

"He be jest a boy, Sam. He ain't causing me no harm."

Charley backed away as Sam called to his brothers, "Les go. We ain't got all day." To Penny, he said, "About five miles east, to where the man's got a doctoring sign at the end of the driveway. Should git us a house by tonight."

They left with five pounds of sugar, twenty pounds of corn meal, ten pounds of flour, a can of lard, a slab of bacon, and a confidence they were finally home.

Chapter 3

They saw no one on the road to the doctor's house. They passed four empty shanties, with doors sagging open and windows without glass. The abandoned land grew crops of Johnson grass, thistle and coffee weed. Quail called. Red-winged blackbirds rose ahead of them and settled behind. A hawk circled on the currents and plunged to earth where it stayed hidden in the undergrowth with his catch.

They had no trouble spotting the sign that announced Dr. Jacobs by name. The house sat back from the road, across a wide front lawn, and behind it stood several outbuildings, including a barn. They could see the garden, where a man in overalls and long-sleeved shirt, his head hidden by a large straw hat, followed a mule pulling a plow.

Sam halted his wagon on the road, handed the reins to Penny, and stepped down. Jack and Gus joined him by the driveway.

"I'll go talk to him," Sam offered. His brothers shrugged, and Jack said, "Go ahead."

As Sam approached the garden, the man spotted him, halted his mule, and waited. The smell of fresh dirt reached Sam, and he squeezed his hands as if gripping a plow handle. This red soil emitted a rich odor of moisture and manure that promised good crops.

"We be looking fer Doc Jacobs."

"You found him." He nodded toward the wagons. "Is it your woman's time?"

Sam shook his head, "No, I don't reckon so."

"How can I help?" The doctor was slim but not gaunt, one of his eyes deep hazel and the other brown. He pulled off his hat to wipe sweat from his forehead and revealed dull brown hair sweated to his head and in need of cutting.

Sam wondered at the man, a doctor who plowed instead of hiring it done, but maybe times were hard for doctors too.

"We hear tell you might have a place we could stay. There be two families and a single brother. We wanna sharecrop. Maybe work for cash too iffen you be needing some hep, like with that-air plowing."

Jacobs smiled as he wrapped the reins around the plow handle.

"Oh, I enjoy this. It gets me outside and away from sick folks. Yes, I do have an empty place just down there," he pointed, "less than a quarter mile. It's got five rooms and a kitchen with a wood stove. Ought to be big enough for all of you. At least for awhile."

"How much we gotta pay?"

"You got any cash to pay?"

Sam blushed and shook his head.

"I didn't reckon so. Nobody's got cash these days. I get paid with chickens and eggs, so don't fret. We'll work that out with time. I usually get part of the crops, and I don't cheat you. Family just moved out had a garden and some cotton and corn, but the drought about dried it all up. Let's see about getting your baby born and try to save the garden so you'll have some food. Meantime you take care of the crops those folks gave up on. You might be able to get something there."

Sam frowned. He'd never been offered so much for so little. "How much you want from them crops iffen we kin make something outta them?"

"Let's figure one bushel for every five." The doctor extended his hand.

"That ain't much," Sam said.

"It's a lot more'n nothing, which is what I'll get if nobody's there to work the fields."

Sam wiped his palm on his overalls and took the doctor's hand. He felt calluses on the doctor's palm, as well as physical strength in his handshake.

"You just follow the road the way you're headed. It'll be the next house on this side of the road. The well bucket's still there. And there's a barn, too, you can use to stall the mules. If you don't have any corn with you, just turn them into the pasture. There's plenty of grass and honeysuckle right now. You can be settled in before it gets dark."

"We thank you, Doc. We sure do." Sam nodded, turned, and headed for his new home, thankful they had found a place for his son to be born.

Chapter 4

The house squatted on a red bank like a gray-clad Indian squaw trying to hide her knobby legs. No sign of whitewash remained on the siding. Rocks supporting the floor joists at every corner had been supplemented by railroad ties as rain eroded the bare yard over the years. Assorted junk cluttered the red-dirt yard that the drought had cracked except under the shade of a patch of scrub plum bushes clustered around the well and fighting each other for the little nourishment offered by the clay. Empty peach crates crowded in the shadow near the door; corn cobs rotted among the rocks and sticks; tin cans rusted in an ageless heap behind the house; a tongue-less wagon crouched in the shade of the oaks near the unpainted barn, and a pile of ashes still smelled of burned cloth and tin cans.

Penny saw only beauty as the wagons rolled into the yard, for she was home—she would sleep in her own bed tonight, no matter how moldy the mattress had gotten.

She went into the house, into the back room, and waited for Sam and Jack to unload and set up her bed. She immediately lay down, closed her eyes, and tried to ignore the pain.

Ellen explored the house, pleased to find it spacious. A room for each of the couples, one for the children, and one for Gus. The once-large kitchen had been cut in two with a half-wall to create an alcove big enough for their eating table and the benches.

Sam and Jack unloaded furniture and toted the pieces inside while Gus tended to the mules. He left the jugs in the wagon, buried under the hay. After he inspected the well chain, he circled the house to locate the privy, which stood over a shallow ditch near the trees. He found a stack of stovewood near the back door and handed some up to Ellen to start supper.

Ellen made biscuits and fried up the bacon, figuring as hungry as they were, they might as well eat. Maybe tonight Jack would take Buster out for a possum or coon and tomorrow they could set out snares for rabbits. Life sure had gotten better.

Penny didn't get up when Ellen had supper ready.

"I ain't got the energy, El. I be hurting a heap worse. Could you close the door? That bacon smell's done got my belly all upset again."

"I'll save you some biscuits and bacon."

"Maybe later. You go on and eat." Penny grabbed her belly and moaned.

"You gitting pain sudden-like?"

"Yeah. I think I done broken my water. The bed seems awful wet and I know I ain't peed."

Ellen pulled up Penny's skirt and saw that birthing had begun. She hurried out to where the men waited to eat.

"Sam, yer baby's coming. You got the bed set up jest in time."

Sam nodded, smiled, and said, "I shore be glad it's her time. You take good care of her now, yer hear?"

"I will. Jack, see to supper for the chullen. It's in the kitchen and cooked. Sam, you git water on the stove right now. Don't know how long this'll take, it being her first one. Gus, you might better git some more stove wood. There ain't much in the kitchen. I'll holler when I need the water."

She picked up the lamp and went back into Penny's room. After she put the lamp on the floor, she opened up Penny's cedar chest at the foot of the bed and pulled out some of the feed sack cloths. Then all she could do was sit beside the bed and wait.

As the pain ravished her, Penny yelled. Ellen reached to hold her hand and flinched at the power in her sister's grip.

But the child refused to be born into the world of noise and violence. Wave after wave of pain rolled over Penny, and rolled over the baby from head to foot. The infant tried to shrink from the pressure of the spasms, the violence, and the screams that completely filled her world.

The men sat around the table and drank from the one jug Gus brought in from the wagon. Penny's screams reminded them of Ellen's deliveries and their own mother's, and they ignored the sounds. With time, however, the screams became ear-splitting even through the wall, and the men herded the three older boys outside and put them to bed in the wagon. After passing around a wad of tobacco, the men perched on the tailgate to chew, spit, and talk about the new boy coming into the family and their hopes for saving some of the abandoned crops.

Midnight came and even the hunting owls became silent. The chuck-will's-widow no longer called. Only a lone distant bullfrog harrumphed to the heat and the night. The men wandered into the house and left the three boys asleep in the wagon.

As Penny's screams weakened, Ellen began to fear for her. In spite of her pushing with the spasms, nothing seemed to happen. "I kain't push no more," Penny whispered.

"Let me take another look," Ellen said, pulling up Penny's skirt. "You done split open big enough, Penny." Holding the lamp so she could see better, she put her face closer, and when she saw the rear end of the baby trying to push out, Ellen felt bile rising in her throat.

"I'll git Sam in here for a minute. You try to relax."

"Thank-ee."

Ellen hurried to the front room and then to the kitchen alcove where she found the men sitting around the table and the infant, his diapers stinking, asleep on the floor. They were celebrating the pending arrival by passing another jug around the table.

"I'm scared." She clutched Sam's arm. "The baby be turned ass-backwards. We gotta git Dr. Jacobs up here." A tear trickled down her cheek and drew a stark line in the dirt.

"We ain't never had no doctor hep birth babies in our family."

"I know. But kain't no baby be born butt first. She's gonna die iffen you don't git the doctor. Might die anyhow, now. She kain't take no mo'. She done got too weak. And she's bleeding bad. Please, Sam. Go git the doctor." She gulped in a breath and tried to swallow a sob.

"I'll see her. Jack, run up there right quick and git him, will you?"

"I'm faster," Gus said, jumping up so quickly he knocked over the chair. "I'll git him."

"Hurry!" Ellen called to his back as Gus jumped out the front door and disappeared into the moonlight.

Sam went into the room, but Ellen wiped her face with her skirt tail before she followed him. With light from the one lamp he saw how Penny's face had paled since she came in to rest. She looked up at him and lifted her hand. When he took it in his, he felt coolness, weakness, and exhaustion, not the vibrancy and youth of his wife.

"You gonna be all right, honey," was all he could think to say. He felt wetness slip into his eyes and tried to will the tears back so she wouldn't see his worry, but her hand had gone limp in his. "She done passed out," he said, dropping to his knees beside the bed.

Ellen began to sob, and put a hand on Sam's shoulder, and then as suddenly turned away from him, going to the chair where she sat crossways, resting her head on the back while she cried. Sam watched Penny's chest rise and fall slower and slower. Neither spoke nor moved until Dr. Jacobs walked into the smells of childbirth, blood and death.

Ellen leaped to her feet and met the doctor beside the bed.

"You get out, mister," he said to Sam. "You," he pointed to Ellen, "how is she? How long's she been in labor?"

"Since a little before dark. I kin see the baby's butt. It won't git born. She done passed out. And seems like she just barely breathing."

He placed his bag beside Penny's head and reached for the lamp. Holding it near her face, he pulled up an eyelid, shook his head, and replaced the lamp.

Penny shuddered and her breathing stopped.

He ripped her skirt away and opened his bag, pulling out a scalpel.

"She's dead, but there's a chance that we can save the baby."

As the blade sliced into Penny's belly, Ellen felt the bile rush into her mouth, and she ran from the room, her hands pressed over her lips to hold back the vomit until she could get outside.

When he pulled the infant from her mother's uterus, the child screamed defiance at him, her face red with anger, her hands clenched into tiny fists. She had not wanted to come into this world of noise and smells.

Dr. Jacobs laughed softly. "You're a feisty one, young lady. Don't even need a spanking. Let's get you cleaned up."

He located lukewarm water in the pitcher and poured it into the basin. No towels, but some rags that looked clean. As he began to clean up the baby, Ellen returned, still wiping her mouth.

"You feel better now?" he asked.

She nodded. "I jest… Pen is my…. Was my sister."

"I'm sorry about her. But the baby's fine. Strong lungs. You need to finish cleaning her up and get a diaper on her."

As Ellen took the baby and left the room, he pulled the skirt back down over the lifeless form, gathered up his instruments, and went into the front room.

The men had returned to the table. At the sight of the doctor, Sam swung the jug onto the table and rose.

"She okay now, Doc? I kin see her?"

The doctor shook his head. "I'm sorry, Sam. She's dead."

In the silence, a gurgle rose from the bundle in Ellen's arms. Sam turned from the doctor to his child and back again, blinked, and shook his head.

"You saved my baby and I thank-ee for that. But how come you didn't save my wife?" His voice was cold.

"Nothing I could have done this late. It was a breech presentation. If I hadn't done a Caesarian —."

"Whatcha mean?" Sam asked.

"There wasn't a thing I could do. She was about dead when I got here. You want me to send someone out for the body first thing in the morning? And get you some help with the baby?"

Sam sank back down in the chair, wiping a tear with the back of his hand.

"I ain't got no money for a town burial. We kin bury her right outchere, kain't we?" His words quivered.

Ellen interrupted. "We don't need nothing fer the baby, Doc. We thank-ee fer ever-thing, but I done got a baby. This here one kin suck right alongside my Billy Jack. She'll be all right. Sides, I ain't got no girl baby." She turned to Sam and said, "We oughtta call her Penny after her ma."

"You can bury her out here. There's a small graveyard up the slope in back yonder. If you want to make her a coffin, get some wood off the back side of the barn across the road. Over at the end, where the old stall is. I'll show you the cemetery tomorrow."

"I'm beholden to yer," Sam said, and put his head down on the table.

"We all be beholden to yer," Jack said as he rose and held out his hand to the doctor. "We be beholden to you fer all time."

The doctor took his hand. "Let me know if you need help," he said and walked into the night.

PART II: LATE APRIL 1946

Chapter 1

After almost fifteen years, the Carter's home still squatted on the side of the road, in a barren yard of red clay that every rain turned to mud and every dry spell cracked into Rorschach patterns. The only visible difference in the house was the corn-shuck-bottom chairs that lined the porch and leaned against the gray clapboards.

The Carters had added to the assorted junk that decorated the yard when they arrived; empty boxes from the local bomb-fuse plant replaced the old cotton baskets. Corn cobs, empty wine bottles, and tin cans lay scattered behind the house. A fender-less car rusted in the shade of the oaks near the unpainted barn.

A prewar Ford pickup truck, its windows open for whatever breeze might blow through, sat in the shade of the mimosa tree near the well. From habit, not from hope, a lone chicken scratched in the dust. In the deep shade under the house a thin red hound sighed and shifted position, tired out from watching the efforts of the hen and too hot to bother about his fleas. Hearing rapid footsteps, he opened one eye to see a child's feet clad in dust instead of socks run behind a wobbling tire. He closed his eye again and let his tongue loll out in the dust of chicken shit and doodle bugs.

Penny leaned against the door jamb, one foot hiked up to form a chair for her buttocks. Her hands behind her supported her lower back. Her nipples poked against the front of her dress, their points kissed by the April sunlight that angled onto the porch as twilight approached. Although her eyes followed the child playing in the yard, her mind was on Charley. He was back from the war. Finally back. After two years of fighting that had followed three years of boarding school.

She stared straight ahead with the innocence of childhood and the un-comprehended demands of womanhood. Her face was delicate, the nostrils flaring like a newborn colt with mock anger, the lips full and in a perpetual pout until she became angry and then they became a thin line.

It was five years now since her uncle Jack caught them kissing, caught them with Charley's hand inside her skirt that he'd pulled up while kissing her. Nobody caught them the time she asked Charley if boys had the same long thing a stallion did; he had laughed and proudly dropped his overalls to show his. He had told her to touch it, had tugged it out of its sleep bed for her, and when she put her hand around it, it became a thing alive, leaping out from his body like a rigid snake and then spurting pee all over her skirt before it shrank back down to look like nothing.

She had felt it that time they were kissing, felt it when Charley pulled her close to his body, felt it erupt inside his pants and press hard against her belly, and felt her own belly try to reach out to take it in.

Shivering, she laid her head back against the door jamb and closed her eyes, to let her body remember and to feel the vacancy inside that she wanted him to fill. Charley would come back to see her. Maybe even today. He'd been home at least four days now.

A hen squawked and Penny turned to see her young cousin roll a tire as the hen fluttered away. The tire gained speed, began to wobble, outran the child, and rolled down the bank to settle in the ditch where it half-stood beside the footbridge from the road. She sighed and shifted against the door, hoping that if Charley drove by he would notice that she'd grown big breasts. One of the girls at school told her boys liked big breasts, and she wiggled again to make them poke her dress.

"Penny, don't you be standing like that. Everything you got shows up through that-air dress," Billy Jack called from inside the house.

She didn't bother to look over her shoulder at him, but instead poked her chin up a little higher. Let him look all he wants to. Billy Jack thinks he owns me anyhow. Jest let him look.

Although she turned her eyes to the boy in the yard, she did not register that he stared at the fallen tire, out of his reach in the ditch. He wore only belt-less jeans torn off at the knees. His dirty stomach hung over his pants as if it would fold downward from the inward push of his curved back. He scratched his hip under the edge of his pants and pulled them up, but they slid down again to hang on the protrusion of his rump. He grubbed in his nose and carefully examined his find before sticking the finger in his mouth and sucking it clean. He ran up the steps into the unmoving heat of the porch and crossed the floor on bare feet as silent as a kitten's.

Penny had to drop her foot to let him by. She tried to ignore Billy

Jack. He wasn't doing anything today but watching her and being no-account when he oughtta be out there helping his daddy.

Good thing there warn't any of the other men folks in the house, seeing as all they ever talked about was their likker still and cows. If Charley came by and heard them talking about stealing cows, he could get them all in trouble. If Mr. Cunningham ever learned her cousins stole his cows, he wouldn't care about their whiskey making. Charley never did care for Billy Jack or her other cousins cause they tried to tag along when he took Virgil and Bobby fishing. Virgil told her once the younger boys made too much noise, wouldn't bait their own hooks, and always threw rocks in the creek. Virgil never brought home fish when he took his brothers with him.

That was years ago. Now all she wanted was to see Charley. As she heard a car way off, she hoped that at last he was coming to see her.

Chapter 2

The Trailways bus pulled off the highway to stop crossways in the middle of the dirt road. The front door hissed open. Four rows back, Virgil stood up, his left uniform sleeve empty and pinned above the elbow.

"Hold on there, soljer. Let me git that-air valise down fer you," a black man called as he rose from a back seat. His hair white, his shoulders hunched, he was too old to have been in the war. He lifted Virgil's duffle bag down from the overhead rack.

Virgil nodded his thanks. Lots of people wanted to help him when they saw his left sleeve pinned up. At least for now, as long as they see the uniform, as long as the war is fresh in everybody's mind. Just give 'em time, he thought, remembering his father's stories about Grandpa, who lost an arm in the First War. Couldn't work the farm after that, and all the thanks he got was the sheriff always after him up in the mountains, always hunting his still and busting it up whenever he could. Virgil half-smiled. Pa said the sheriff never could catch Grandpa, though.

Already it was only the Negroes who offered help. None of the white men had risen to his aid. He stepped off the bus, and the old man stepped down behind him.

"Wants hit on yo' shoulder, suh?"

"No, thanks. I'll tote it by the strap. I don't have far to go." As the old man put the bag on the ground, Virgil reached into his pocket for some change, but the man backed away, both hands out palm first to him.

"Naw, suh. Naw suh. I's jest be glad to heps you, suh." He climbed back on the bus and the door hissed closed.

Virgil watched the bus pull off and disappear around the curve. As a slight breeze carried away the exhaust fumes, he smiled and closed his eyes. He took a deep breath of the hot dusty air, the air of home, the air of turned earth and manure, so different from the hospital air and from the smells of war, the smells of blood and gore. Even a stuck pig with its guts pulled out didn't stink as bad as a battlefield.

A bull bellowed the drawn-out call of a male to a cow in heat. A bluebird flashed across the road, perched on a cross-tie fence post, looked at him, and then dropped into a hole to feed its biddies. A crow called and then another, collecting the flock to harass a red-tailed hawk that circled near the ridge.

He was home. From the war. From the hospital. From the visit with his army buddy who helped him plan his years ahead.

Virgil removed his garrison cap, tucked it under the stump of his left arm, and wiped his face on his sleeve. At least he could feel at home, even if he still had on the uniform, he told himself. His black curls had been left on the floor beside the Army barber's chair three years ago, and he still kept the crew cut. His farmer's tan was gone, and the sun felt hot on his pale skin.

He ran his hand over his short hair, replaced the garrison cap, hefted his duffel bag by the strap, and slung it over his shoulder. The weight, so much less than a field pack, seemed light. On the left side of the road, he struck out with a marching pace on the three-mile walk to the house.

A few thunderheads in the southwest promised rain, but the white-hot sky told him the rain would be un-kept promise. The April afternoon felt too hot for rain, and the air smelled dry. Off to his left, the corn field looked barren, the earth turned up to a dry sky, waiting for rain.

The sweet smell that came with rain was not in the dust that rolled over him when a white 1940 Buick stopped beside him and a red head poked out the window.

"Hey there, soljer. How about a lift up the road a-ways?"

"Charley! When did you get home?" Virgil dropped the duffle bag as Charley scrambled out of the car.

"Last week," he said as they hugged each other. "Man, it's good to see you alive." He grabbed the duffel bag and threw it into the back seat. "Get in. What happened to your arm? When didcha get hurt?"

"Iwo Jima. You came through okay? I don't see anything missing."

Charley had not changed. Freckles covered his face and arms. His right eyebrow still gapped from the fight they'd had when they were 10 and 11, when Virgil pushed him down and he hit his head on a root. So much blood that afternoon, but not like the blood soldiers bleed, the rich bright red blood full of oxygen that leaves the body so fast—and so dead. His thatch of red hair was growing out from his military cut, too long to stand up and not long enough to comb down; he needed a hair cut. He wore a pair of jeans and a short-sleeved cotton shirt.

"I took some shrapnel in my leg," he patted the back side of his thigh. "Right here, but it wasn't bad. Just bad enough and late enough I was still in gauze when it ended. They sent word to Daddy, but I didn't come home. I got a job up north and would've stayed except Daddy telephoned—said he needed help. Can you believe it? Daddy spending money on a long-distance call? I got home four days ago. God, man, it's good to see you. We gotta go fishing real soon."

"You seen my folks?"

Charley shook his head. "No. I been meaning to stop by, speak to 'em. Daddy's had me really busy up at the store, but he sure is paying me good. I think he's trying to make up to me for sending me off to boarding school. I didn't do good enough up there to stay away from the draft, and he knows he could-a kept me out if I'd been here to register when I turned eighteen. He's running for county commissioner again, and he says he needs my help."

"He take on that job for life? Seems as far back as I remember he's held that office."

"Nobody's got the nerve to run against him. I don't even know why he politics, seeing as how nobody runs against him."

Virgil took a deep breath and sucked in the dust rolling behind them and into the windows with the heat. Sweat stood out on his face and dampened his clothes. "Somebody's bound to get up the nerve. Then what'll happen?"

"Oh, Daddy'll win, as usual."

"What if he doesn't, Charley?"

The red head shook and Charley smiled. The sun flashed into his eyes. "But he can't lose. Not in this county. You know that."

Virgil remained silent a moment, then arched his back, and stretched his right arm and what remained of his left over the back of the seat. "God, but it's good to breathe country air again, dust and all."

Charley stopped the Buick in front of the house where Penny was born.

"Come on in," Virgil said. "They'll be glad to see you. I know Penny will. She sure missed you when you got sent off to boarding school."

Charley saw her leaning against the door and his eyes latched onto her breasts. She looked his way and their eyes met. He swallowed and shook his head. "Better not right now. You go on in. I'm not quite family."

Virgil stepped out, reached in back, and lifted his duffle bag.

"See you," Charley said and spun dust as he drove away.

Penny ran toward the road, but as Charley's car roared off she suddenly stopped. Her face contorted into a frown as she realized he had only dumped somebody off and gone.

"Penny!" Virgil called.

Recognition flooded her face, and she yelled, "Virgil! Ellen, Virgil's home!"

He ran across the pine slabs laid lengthwise in the ditch to make a bridge, dropped the duffel bag, threw his cap into the air, grabbed his cousin, and swung her around with his one arm.

Tears streaming down her cheeks, Ellen ran to him.

"My boy. Oh, my boy. You done got home." She wrapped both arms around his neck and hugged him as she wept onto his shoulder.

Penny stood beside Ellen and tried to wipe her tears away before Virgil saw them.

Ellen stepped back, ran her apron tail across her eyes, and said, "You growed, son. You taller, but you skinny. We gotta get some meat on you. Oh, Virgil, what you gonna do with jest one arm?"

"Let me get my stuff and we'll talk." He got his duffle bag and started toward the house.

Billy Jack stuck his head out the door. "Hey, Virgil, you got back." He leaped off the porch and ran to his brother. His hair fell over his forehead and into his eyes.

At first, they stared at each other, as if not sure whether to hug or shake hands, and Virgil threw his arm around his brother and pulled him close.

"Hello, brother. I'm sure glad to see you. So glad you didn't have to go."

Billy Jack stepped back and reached over, almost touching the empty sleeve. "What was it like? Was it fun to kill all those Japs? What kind of gun did you have? How many did you kill? How is that—?"

"War isn't fun. My arm's okay. Lots-a boys didn't get home. I'm one of the lucky ones." He pushed his brother's hair out of his eyes. "You ought to get a hair cut. But then, I think you always needed to get a haircut." They laughed.

"Les sit and talk," Ellen said.

They went onto the porch, pulled the chairs from against the wall and sat. "Where's everybody else?" Virgil asked

"Sam's getting up hay down at Dr. Jacobs' front pasture. Jack's up to his still, and Hiram done gone fishing off to Rocky Creek."

"How's Doc Jacobs?"

"He's gitting along in years and don't git out like he used-ta, but he keeps on going. He done lost Jerome in the war. His widder moved in with the Doc last year."

"Oh, Gawd, I'm sorry to hear that, Ma. What about Bobby?"

She shook her head. "He didn't git home, son. He got kilt on a place called Bulge. They didn't send him home. He be buried there with the rest of the soljers what got kilt."

Virgil studied the floor while he tried to get a handle on his emotions. So many good men gone, so many of the friends he had made over the past three years. He would have been still in the Pacific, under the ground, if not for his sergeant. With his own leg injured, Sarge had tied a strap on Virgil's arm, and the two of them had helped each other get back to safety.

He closed his eyes and silently gave thanks that the war ended while Billy Jack was still too young to be drafted and he had not gone through that hell.

Penny pulled her chair close to Virgil. "How's Charley?"

"He got injured, he said, but not bad. He said he'll be by here as soon as he can. We ran up on each other down by the highway and he gave me a lift. I'd have rung his neck if he'd left me walking." He smiled at her.

"Oh, I do hope he'll come by. It's been a long time since I seen him. He's a lotta fun."

"You better not be having fun with him like you used-ta." Ellen's voice was stern. "I don't wanna catch him with his pants off or his hands on you. You ain't neither one chullen no more."

"Oh, Ellen, that was when we was kids. I ain't gitting in trouble with Charley."

"I don't wanna hafta whup up on him now, seeing as how I ain't got but jest one arm." Virgil realized he had slipped into the language of home, the language he had worked so hard to change since he'd been away.

Penny harrumphed and stalked off into the house. Virgil laughed.

He turned to Ellen.

"I'm going into politics. Sarge…"

"Who's Sarge?"

Penny walked back onto the porch and plunked down in her chair beside Virgil, crossed her arms, and pretended to ignore him by staring off into the yard.

"Sergeant Wilkes. He was in the Home Guard and in politics. Was mayor of his home town, down near Valdosta. He helped me when I got hurt, and we were in the hospital at the same time. He said the best job for a war veteran who got hurt is to go into politics. I can't do a regular job, can't do farm work except maybe feed chickens. And I don't want to do that forever."

Penny poked him on his good shoulder. "What kinda politics you gitting in, Virgil? You ain't planning on being mayor, is you? Who you think's gonna vote for a Carter around here, anyhow?"

"I don't reckon I'll run for mayor, Pen, seeing as how I don't live in town. I'm going to run for chairman of the county commission."

"You kain't mean you gonna run against Mr. Cunningham. He been chairman since forever." Penny's mind turned to Virgil and Mr. Cunningham fighting each other, with her and Charley in the middle.

"Times are changing, Pen. Times are changing. And I'm gonna change with the times. We have to if we figure on staying up. I want to do more than just stay up, I want to get ahead. Sarge said it won't be long now before everybody's got a car and every child goes to school real regular. The depression's over, and there's going to be jobs for everybody, even the women who want to keep on working. And there's gonna be a real need for farm products, so our family can do something besides work for wages or bootleg. The family can make a good living on garden crops. And when the boys get older, they can get work for wages. Real wages. Not farm wages."

Penny shook her head, and her long curls flashed across the frown that puckered her face. "I don't want you to run against Mr. Cunningham. You'll make him mad at us. And Charley ain't gonna like us anymore neither. Please, don't do this, Virgil."

"Oh, Penny, sweetheart, don't fret so. It's just gonna be politics, not personal. Nobody gets mad about politics. Besides, Charley's the best friend I ever had. He wouldn't be mad at me. He's not like that."

"Maybe he didn't stay mad before, like that time you cut his face all up fighting at the fishing hole. But he will now, iffen you go against his daddy." Penny's voice became a pout. "Please don't, Virgil."

Ellen shook her head. "I dunno, Virgil. You'll be crossing Mr. Cunningham. He could git mad and cost yer pa iffen he stops buying our likker."

"Oh, Ma, you know he won't do that. Nobody makes better whiskey. Let's talk about this tomorrow. I want to go see the rest of the family. Wanna walk down with me to the hay fields, Pen? I wanna see your pa."

"No, son," Ellen said. "I be needing her here. We gonna fix up a special supper for tonight. You run along. And stop by the doctor's house to say hello to him. But don't be long. It'll be gitting dark in about another hour."

"I will, Ma. I wanna talk to Doc about my plans. I may be a bit late getting home."

"Don'tcha be too late. Pen and me'll have supper fixed a little after dark. You hear?"

"I'll be back directly." He rose, touched a toe to his duffel bag. "I'll put this away when I get back."

Ellen rose and hugged him.

"It's good you be home."

He nodded. It was good to be home, to feel the acceptance, to hear the familiar voices and inflections, and most of all to know the safety every child feels, no matter the age, when his mama hugs him. Seemed all the boys over there cried for mama when they got hurt, their voices of pain calling in the night, calling in the midst of gunfire, the cries of pain louder than the M-16's and the hand grenades.

He strode down the road in his uniform pants, his shirt open halfway down his front to let the sun burn him to sweating and the air evaporate the sweat. The dust he stirred up settled on his pants legs and turned them a rusty hue.

The air tasted of distant rain and dust, and carried the smell of cow manure from the pasture beside the road. Sweat ran off his face, down his back, and darkened his shirt at the armpits. He stopped, turned his face up to the west, and closed his eyes. He let the sun burn its brilliance onto his eye lids for a moment, thought of being home, and tried to push the war from his mind and to erase the images of death that still haunted him.

Carolina jasmine perfumed the breeze that drifted from his right. He took a deep breath, as if to erase the odor of blood and death that he felt had imbedded itself in his skin.

When he set off again briskly, his legs automatically moved in rhythm to an unheard drill sergeant's cadence call. Down the hill, across the tracks, and half-way up the next hill before he heard the clatter of the hay rake and heard Sam's soft "git-up."

He smelled the new hay and saw the dust flowing before the wind. Nobody but Dr. Jacobs had hay this early in April, but Dr. Jacobs spent the fall sowing winter grass for an early spring cutting. Virgil crawled between the strands of wire and waited for his uncle to complete the next loop.

As their eyes met, Sam jerked the mules to a stop, twisted the reins over the rake handle, jumped down, and ran to his nephew. They hugged. Sam pounded Virgil's back, and then they stepped back to study each other.

"Gawd, Virgil, you sure do look good. How yer doing?"

"Not bad. I still need help tying my shoes, though."

"Boy, you're home. You don't need shoes here." They laughed. "Do it hurt anymore?"

"No, not really. Sometimes I think it's still there and try to do things with it. The doctors said it'll take a while to get over that. Where's Pa?"

"He's down to his still. Trying to git a run made tonight fer Charley to pick up afore day."

"I ran up on Charley, but he didn't say he was hauling bootleg for Mr. Cunningham these days."

"Yeah, he is. Every since he got back home. That old skeester what hauled for him got hisself kilt when he ran slap dang into a logging truck. He was loaded down with jugs. You could-a got drunk jest standing there and smelling it."

They laughed and Sam continued.

"We gonna be hauling the hay tomorrow. Sure would be like old times iffen you could be out here with us."

"Yeah. I sure wish I could handle a pitchfork still."

Virgil looked over the field and remembered his years of growing up on the Jacobs place: Pitching hay, trying to ride one of the unbroken horses without a bridle or saddle and getting dumped over yonder in the creek, shooting a good hound because it had gotten the taste of beef and pulled down calves. Memories seemed so tame and simple when compared with the war years. Especially when considering all the long months of pain and confusion in regard to his own future.

"Whatcha gonna do now? I mean, with jest one arm? You kain't do farm work no more."

"I know. I've got it planned out. I'm gonna run for office."

"You mean, like Mr. Cunningham?"

"Exactly. In fact, I'm gonna run for his job."

Sam threw back his head and laughed a deep belly laugh that shook its way up his body.

"What's so funny?"

"You and Charley. You ain't gonna have a friend when this here summer gits over."

"Oh, I'm not worried. It'll all come out in the wash."

"You shore kain't be airing out Cunningham's dirty laundry. You'll be airing out our'n iffen you do."

"I ain't about to tell folks he's the biggest bootlegger in the county." Virgil grinned. "Most everybody knows, anyhow. By the way, where's Pa's still?"

"Over yonder," he pointed to the north end of the hay fields. "On the back creek. The doctor doesn't git over thataway much anymore."

"I gotta go see the doctor, Sam. You know if he's home?"

Sam nodded, removed his straw hat to wipe sweat, and Virgil realized his uncle had gotten gray and old while he was gone off to war. "I saw him drive in about a half-hour ago and ain't seen him go off."

Virgil slapped his uncle lightly on the upper arm. "I'll see you at supper, Sam. You look mighty fine."

"You too, boy. You too. Shore is good to have you back home."

Virgil strode up the front driveway to the Jacobs' house. Nothing had changed here; the magnolias still swept their heavy limbs low; the azaleas still bloomed and threw perfume into his face; boxwoods gleamed with fresh, light-green leaves.

War hero or not, he was still a tenant and wasn't about to go to the front door. He went around to the back, where he had gone for his pay before being drafted. Jacobs' granddaughter watched him approach, her cotton dress flowing with the breeze and her blond pigtails flying as she pumped her swing roped to an oak limb.

Virgil remembered her as barely out of her mother's arms when he left home; he reckoned she was about five now. He waved to her and she let her feet drag the swing to a stop.

"You a soljer, mister?"

He knelt beside the swing and held out his hand. "That I am. My name's Virgil. What's yours?"

"I'm Sally Anne Jacobs. Mama and I live here with my grandpa. My daddy's dead. From the war. How come you aren't dead?"

"Because a real hero saved my life when I got shot in the arm or I'd be dead."

She got up from the swing and reached over to his empty sleeve. "You don't have an arm here."

"No, I don't have an arm there, Sally Anne. Is your grandpa home?"

She nodded.

"Reckon I could see him? Would you tell him Virgil is home and wants to say hello?"

"Yes." She turned and ran toward the back door, her voice raised, "Grandpa, Grandpa, Virgil's home. Grandpa, Virgil's home from the war."

Dr. Jacobs opened the screen door. His hair had gone white and his shoulders stooped. Sadness seemed to have settled into his eyes that once sparkled with excitement over every newborn foal, the hay crops, an extra large tomato, or even a vividly red sunset. Virgil felt his own insides stir, knowing the pain Dr. Jacobs felt at the loss of his son.

"Afternoon, sir," Virgil said, half-saluting.

"Virgil. It's good to see you, boy. How are you?" He came down the steps, letting the screen slap to behind him. Sally Anne dogged his steps, her small hand wrapped around his fingers.

The men shook hands and looked at each other. A tear crept into Jacob's eye and started down his cheek.

"I'm so sorry about Jerome, sir. So sorry. He was such a good man."

Jacobs shook his head. "He died trying to save a friend, but they both got killed. War is such a waste."

"Yes, sir, it is that. Sir, I wanted to talk to you about my plans."

"How's that?"

"Well, I was thinking. There's not much I can do to make a living with just one arm, except for politics. I was thinking of running for county commissioner this summer."

The old man frowned, and then a smile won the battle for his face. "You mean, against Cunningham?"

"Yes, sir. Being as I'm a war veteran, I think I have a chance. I sure do need to do something. I saved most of my war pay, so I've got money I can use."

"Oh, Virgil," he put a hand on the younger man's shoulder. "Save your money. I'll back you all the way on this. Jerome planned to do just that when the war was over. We needed Cunningham out of there a long time ago. We need somebody in office who'll at least not sell his moonshine at the courthouse." He paused. "You wouldn't be selling your daddy's whiskey there, would you?"

Virgil laughed aloud. "No, sir. But on the other hand, I wouldn't sick the sheriff on him or tell anybody where his still is. I couldn't do that to my family."

"Come on inside. Let's start planning for this election. July's not far off and we've got a lot to do." The doctor's eyes seemed to glow with new life, and as he walked up the steps, his shoulders rose and squared off.

Chapter 3

Twilight darkened the windows, but none of the men had returned for supper. In the kitchen, Penny peeled potatoes while her mind churned over Charley.

Billy Jack came to the kitchen door, leaned on the jamb, and watched them work.

"Ain't no need fer you to be hanging around like that, son. I ain't gonna finish fixing supper till everybody gits back. Besides, Hiram's likely to come in with some fish we kin fry up. Virgil shore would be happy to have some fresh fish outta Rocky Creek."

"Virgil's likely to be late gitting back if he gits to talking politics with Dr. Jacobs," Penny said.

Billy Jack grunted and went to the front porch where he sat down, tilted the chair onto its back legs, and began to whittle. When Charley drove up, he clunked the chair back down onto all four legs and leaned toward the front door.

"Oh, Penny. Charley's here."

She dropped her paring knife and ran to the front porch. Charley sat in the Buick and smiled at her. She ran across the slab bridge to the road and rested her elbows on the door top. She had to lean over to get her face on level with his and was aware that her position pushed her breasts out.

"I see you done got yourself back home, Charley. I'm shore glad you didn't git shot up and kilt."

"Me too." His dark eyes roamed down her frame and locked onto the view down the low neck. He could see her breasts, hanging free, inviting. He swallowed. "I thought Daddy was gonna send me to Siberia after our little fun. It took getting drafted for the war to get me out of that boarding school."

"Where's Siberia?"

"Oh, it's just a real cold place. Far away. And lonesome like me. I missed you."

He still wore freckles across his nose and all down his arms. The hair on his arms still flamed like that on his head. The scar from his fight with Virgil still cut across his eyebrow.

Susan Lindsley

"Yeah? Well, it's been a bit lonesome since you been gone. You staying to home now?"

"I reckon. At least for the summer. And hope Daddy doesn't decide to try to send me off to college again. At least I'm grown now, so he can't really boss me. How you like my car?"

"It sure is pretty. Ain't it your daddy's, though?" She slid a hand along the door top, her eyes alight.

"It's mine if I'm driving. Wanna go for a ride?"

She ran around the car, but as she opened the door, Ellen called from the porch. "Where you going, girl? I need hep with the cooking."

Charley waved. "Hey, Miss Ellen. I just wanna take her for a ride down the road. We'll be right back."

Penny grinned at him. "She ain't gonna argue with you."

He shifted into first and pushed the car faster than first gear allowed before he shifted through second and into third while the transmission screamed. He laughed. "We're not about to be right back. I got so much to tell you about."

"Well, ain't much happened here."

"Daddy tells me the whiskey business is growing and the cattle business is getting bad."

Penny felt her belly grab, a jolt like fire moved through her. Did he know about her daddy stealing his daddy's cattle? "I thought your daddy was doing real good with the cows."

"Rustlers been getting them. Started up about three years ago, during the war, when nobody could buy beef. Daddy thought it'd stop when the war ended, but it didn't. So, anyhow, he's hired a detective to put a stop to it."

"Oh?" She squirmed as she thought about the times they had meat to eat, meat to smoke and put aside for later—meat she knew had come from Cunningham's herd.

"Yeah. Fellow he met fishing down off Savannah. He used to be a sheriff down there. Name of Perry. Alexander Perry. I haven't met him, but Daddy says he really loves fishing. I reckon soon as Virgil gets settled back in, maybe we can go fishing. Take Perry with us over to the special fishing hole on Rocky Creek."

She didn't want to think of her family getting caught rustling, didn't want to think of Virgil taking Charley off fishing and away from her. She changed the subject. "I don't care about this Perry man or fishing, neither. Tell me whatcha been doing off in that cold place and in the war."

"Missing you. You know he sent me off because of you. Because of what he thought we were doing." He stretched his right arm across the back of the seat and let his fingers lightly touch her hair and brush it, smooth it, his hand as soft on her head as hers would be on a kitten's. She shivered, and his hand moved down to lie on her far shoulder.

"We ain't done nothing. Jest kissed." She didn't dare look at him, for if she did she would want to crawl into his lap.

"I know. But he didn't care. Made me go to that boarding school where I didn't do the studying I should've. That's why I got drafted. I didn't do my studying and let my grades go down. All I did in the war was march and march and march, just like in the song. And then I got shot in the backside."

"You got shot in the butt?" Both hands flew to her mouth and she bent over as she tried to hold her laughter inside but failed. Her light-brown hair fell around her face.

He laughed and pulled her across the car seat. She shook her head and, still giggling, pushed the hair out of her face with both hands.

"Not really. In the back of the thigh. But I couldn't sit for a long time. I've still got some of that metal in me, too. I reckon I'll be like those old soljers who can tell when it's gonna rain."

He turned on the headlights, and they rode in silence for about a mile as he eased his foot lighter on the gas pedal. "I'm glad to be home. It's been forever since I left here because of caring for you." His hand rose from her shoulder and pressured her head until she lowered it onto his chest.

His body felt hotter than the spring air, and she breathed deeply to inhale his scent, the smell she had dreamed about all the years he was gone. The emptiness inside seemed to grow and stir and demand in ways she didn't understand.

He slowed the car, stopped, and then backed into one of the driveways to his father's lands. He killed the motor and looked down on her. She turned her face upward, and he leaned over to kiss her. The position was awkward.

"We gotta move around a little, Pen. Turn around." He pushed her away and twirled his hand. "Sit with your back to the dashboard. That's it, and face me."

He wrapped his arms around her and pulled her against his chest. The bottom dropped out of her belly as his lips touched hers. His mouth opened, his tongue probed, and she opened her lips to let it in. She moaned, and a hand touched her breast. His fingers opened her dress front, and she knew she should tell him to stop, but she didn't want to stop. She wanted whatever he was doing, wanted him to keep on, and wanted the hand that was on her breast to stay there. It felt too good to stop.

A car approached, but they ignored it until the horn blared, bringing them apart. She sat up quickly, and felt giddy, out of herself. She glanced with half closed eyes toward the road. The car was gone, but the night was awash with color. "There's a fire!"

Red light flared across the northern sky.

"My God! I never knew they came this far south. I saw them once up north, but never here."

"What is it? Look. Some of it's turning green."

"The northern lights. They're somehow connected to the sun. I don't know exactly. Aren't they weird looking?"

The lights seemed to roll across the sky, dancing and twirling, changing color as fast as a kaleidoscope turned by a god's hands.

She turned to face him. "Yes. I ain't never seen nothing like it."

He whispered, "Forget about the lights. We got some making up to do." His lips eased onto hers as his hands pulled her toward him.

The strange lights dancing on his face gave him the appearance of a demented, decaying demon from the grave. She closed her eyes, relaxed to the wonder of his kisses, and yielded to the feelings stirring inside. His lips were hungry, eager, gaining appetite from the touch of hers, rousing a hungry need in her, his tongue inside her mouth where it pushed and probed and demanded.

Hands behind his neck, she opened her mouth wider, sucking at his tongue.

He pulled back to whisper, "Sweetheart, let's get in the back seat."

"Okay."

He opened his door, slid out, and opened the back door before she could get out. Then he reached for her, lifted her from the car, kissed her, and deposited her on the edge of the back seat. He slammed the front door and crawled in with her.

"Lie back," he said, and when she did his hands went to the top button on her dress and swiftly worked it. He laid her dress back as he opened the buttons, his eyes roving over her body as he revealed it.

His fingers moved from the buttons to her flesh, to touch and tease.

On finding her nipple, they tightened. She writhed and gasped with painful pleasure. She didn't care what he did to her as long as the pleasure continued.

The hand slid down from her breast to her belly, the fingers so light against her skin she wasn't sure he touched her. When they reached her thighs, they began to squeeze. She trembled against him when his finger slipped between her legs. Desire and anticipation overcame any fear she might have, and her legs parted.

*   *   *

"You're wonderful," he whispered.

"Oh, Charlie. I love you so much. I've loved you since I kin remember."

"And I've wanted you like this since you were a little girl. You are perfect, Penny. Perfect."

"Will you do that again?"

He kissed her, but this time his lips were closed and the kiss was no more than those Ellen gave her on the cheek on those mornings when she went to school. Maybe he was disappointed in her.

"What's wrong?" she asked.

"Nothing's wrong." He pulled himself up. "I can't do that again. My long thing that you like won't get long again for a long time."

"How long?"

"Too long."

"It's not too long."

They both suddenly burst into laughter. He wrapped her in his arms and pulled her into his lap. "You are the most delightful person in all the world." His lips brushed her neck.

"It oughtta wake up," she said as she slid a little back from him and reached down to touch his sleeping member. Her touch woke it, and it rose between them.

And collapsed as headlights flared across the car and a broken muffler roared down the hillside.

"Quick, fix your dress. It's Daddy." He jerked up his pants.

Penny looked down and discovered her dress gaped open and her entire body showed itself to his eyes. Her hands trembled with loss and fear as she tried to button herself up and at the same time to look out at the truck that had stopped in front of them.

She knew the Cunningham's pickup. Everybody this side of town knew it. She slid down in the seat, hoping to remain unseen.

Charley's hand reached for her. "Don't worry about him. I'm full grown now and he can't tell me what to do."

"Get yourself home, boy. Now." Cunningham's voice boomed through the evening.

"You can't tell me what to do any more, Daddy. I grew up in the war."

"I said now, son. Move. Don't make me come over there and whup you."

"You better do what he says," she whispered.

He shrugged. "Okay, Daddy. I'm going."

"You be at the house in five minutes or you don't get the car again, you hear me, Charley?"

"Yes, sir."

His father drove off so slow Penny wondered if he watched to see if Charley started up the car. They sat in silence until the truck's headlights passed around the bend and then they moved to the front seat.

"How in the hell did he know we were out here?" Charley asked the darkness as he cranked the car. "You'd think I was still only fifteen years old."

"It were about then you got him mad at us," Penny said.

He laughed. "Yeah, I remember. You wanted to know if all us boys had long things like the stallion Dr. Jacobs has, and Miss Ellen caught me with my pants down."

"And went straight to your pa."

"So he sent me off to boarding school. All boys. I saw enough male parts in those years to last me a lifetime, and then I got drafted and saw a heap more." His voice lost its humor. "Saw more than enough boys tore in pieces, too."

In the half darkness, she could see his hands grip the steering wheel as they rode in silence for about a mile, and then his right hand fisted and began to beat the wheel. "I'll be back to see you, Penny. Tomorrow." His hand reached over, touched hers as softly as a feather, and then squeezed her fingers. "That's a promise. He won't keep me away from you. Not any more."

He stopped in front of her home, leaned over, and brushed his lips over hers.

"You best be going." He reached across the seat to open her door.

A voice called from the darkness. "Hey, Charley, what's all them funny lights in the sky? I thought it were a fire off somewhere till it turned green."

"It's called northern lights. Nothing to be scared of." He laughed. "But I bet the voodoo woman is scared hexless over them." The men joined his laughter as Penny got out of the car.

She leaned back through the window. "You gonna come see me tomorrow, like you said?"

"Tomorrow. I promise." As he drove off, dust rose and floated on the light breeze.

Sam's voice carried his anger from the front porch.

"What in hell you doing riding around this late with that boy? You git yourself in trouble. You git yourself knocked up, you think his daddy's gonna let that boy marry you?"

"I ain't the one gonna git in trouble. All-a y'all will. You and Jack and Billy Jack. Mr. Cunningham done got him a man to jest catch the rustlers. And he'll git you. He'll git all-a-y'all iffen you keep on a-stealing his cows."

She flounced toward the porch, but had taken only three steps when a rope snaked out of the darkness to circle her. She threw it off before it pulled tight.

"Stop it, Hiram. I'm sick of your games," she snarled at her twelve-year-old cousin.

The boy giggled as he wrapped his lasso over his elbow.

Before she walked inside, she asked, "Any of you found that sow?"

"Buddy ain't found her yet," Billy Jack answered from the darkness.

"How come it's always Buddy got to do things around here? He ain't old enough to be out there hog hunting. Don't you never lift a finger at nothing cept stealing cows?"

"Who put a cockle burr under your saddle? You and Charley have a fight?"

Afraid her face might show what had gone on with Charley, Penny went inside and started toward her room. Ellen heard her and called her to come on into the kitchen.

"I thought you said you'd be right back. You done been off a long time with Charley. Don'tcha go letting him pull his pants down, you hear me? Reach me another couple of sticks of wood fer the stove. I want this here grease plenty hot when Virgil gits here."

"I see Hiram got some fish," Penny said as she glanced at a pan containing more than a dozen bream and two small cats.

"Ain't enough to feed everybody, so Virgil gits first choice tonight."

Her stomach reminded her it was supper time as the smell of turnips and fatback greeted her. Every meal included greens from the kitchen garden out by the barn. She bent over the woodbox, and as she reached down she saw a hoof extending from behind the stove.

"Ellen, had me that-air lamp."

"How come?"

"I think I done found that sow."

When she leaned far over, with the lamp over her head, she saw enough. "It's her."

Ellen walked toward the porch, her voice rising.

"Penny done found that sow you ain't been looking fer."

"Where at?" Sam rose to meet her.

"Back of the kitchen stove woodpile."

"She be daid," Penny shouted from the kitchen.

Nobody moved except Sam, whose shoulders slumped. "The last Gawd damn hog we had, and she had to go up and die on us. If we ain't got the damn-dest bad luck."

Ellen planted both fists on her hips. "Well, are y'all jest gonna sit there? Somebody's gotta git that thing outta the kitchen iffen you want me to finish fixing dunner. I ain't going back in there till you gits it out. And I don't want Virgil gitting back here and having to drag it off."

"Go git it out, boys." Sam waved his hand vaguely toward Billy Jack.

Hiram and Billy Jack looked at Sam and at each other, and Billy Jack shrugged his shoulders. "Reckon that means us." They both ambled toward the kitchen.

Penny watched them as they moved the stovewood and then struggled with the dead hog. They dumped it out the back door, wiped their hands on their overalls, and headed toward the front room.

"Don't leave it there. Drag it off somewhere," she said as Ellen entered. "It'll stink up the whole house."

"Git that thing drug off, boys," Ellen said.

"Okay, Ma," Billy Jack answered. He and Hiram dropped out of the door. Each grabbed a hold onto a back leg and pulled the sow off towards the outhouse.

"It already stinks in here," Penny said and wrinkled up her face in distaste.

"Kain't do nothing bout that now. In the mawning I'll git over to the doctor's and git us some Clorox and mop down back there. Les go sit until Virgil gits home."

Chapter 4

The moon stood above the trees when Virgil strode home to find the family sitting on the porch and supper getting cold on the stove as the fire faded into ashes. Silence and the smell of cold fried fish greeted him as he mounted the stairs. The lantern hanging from a roof beam gave enough light for Jack to see to work on one of his animal carvings for his youngest child.

Jack sat forward on his chair to carve. Shavings had already accumulated into a small pile between his feet.

"You been gone long enough, Virgil. How come you be this late fer supper?"

"I'm sorry, Ma. I got to talking to Dr. Jacobs and the time jest slipped by me."

"This here's yer family, son. We be glad to see you finally git home, but you acting like you ain't glad you's home."

Virgil sat in a chair with a corn-shuck bottom that he had helped his mother weave years before. "I shoulda come straight home, Ma. I'm sorry. Dr. Jacobs and I been talking politics."

"Politics? You ain't really gonna run against Mr. Cunningham, is you?" Jack asked.

"Why not, Pa?"

"Cause we git most all our money frum him. You think he'll buy our whiskey when you and him git into it?"

"Oh, shit, Pa—"

"You hush up that kinda talk, you hear me? I ain't gonna have that-air kinda talk in this here house," Ellen said. She rose and started inside. As she walked by him, he smelled the lye soap on her skin and in her dress and knew she had bathed and put on a clean dress for his homecoming.

"Yessum." His voice fell almost to a whisper as the shame of his absence overcame him. "I'm really sorry, Ma. I shoulda waited till tomorrow to see the Doc."

"Well, what's done's done. C'mon in and git yer supper. Rest of us done et."

She picked up the lamp in the front room and he followed her to the kitchen. The smell struck him harshly. "What's that smell? Smells like something dead."

"We been missing our last sow, and she up and died in here. BJ and Hiram done dragged her off. But we ain't gonna have no pig to butcher come winter. She would-a had a good litter."

He picked up a pink glass plate from the shelf, set it on the edge of the stove, and forked the two catfish onto it. As he added the hushpuppies, Ellen spoke.

"I wanted to put tomato in 'em, jest the way you likes 'em. But we ain't gonna have tomatoes fer another month er more. Wish they was still hot."

"It's not your fault, Ma. It shore do smell good."

He set his plate on the pie safe, dipped a Mason jar into the water bucket, and handed it to Ellen.

"Tote this out for me, Ma?"

He carried his supper back to the front porch, and Ellen followed with his water.

"Whatcha talking so long to Dr. Jacobs about?" Jack asked him before he even sat down.

He dropped into a chair and Ellen placed his water on the floor on his right side. He balanced his plate on his knees and popped a hush puppy into his mouth before he answered.

"About me getting elected this summer."

Sam chuckled. "It ain't likely."

"I don't know, Sam. The doctor thinks I got a chance. Lots-a people around here are tired of the way Mr. Cunningham runs the county. He got himself on the draft board and tried to keep Charley from getting drafted. And he did get every Jew over 17 sent off to war."

"Ain't but a dozen Jew families in town." Jack said. "They kain't elect you."

"No, but their money can. They own the newspaper and the dry goods store and the hardware store. They see everybody in the county, and most country folks run a bill with 'em. Hard to say no to somebody iffen you owe him. And every farmer in the county sits on the porch at the hardware store to sip moonshine and gossip on Saturdays. Doc says he kin git me a heap-a votes. All I gotta do is some talking."

"You got where you don't talk like us'ns now," Ellen said. "You talk more fancy-like than you did afore you went off."

"My sergeant helped me, Ma. Said I needed to learn how to talk like a politician. I fergits sometimes. But I don't wanna talk too fancy when I talk to country folk. I need to talk jest like 'em so they won't think I'm putting on airs."

"You ain't being honest iffen you change yer talk to suit who you're talking to," Jack said.

Virgil laughed, and the entire family joined in.

"Since when has this-here family been all that honest, Pa?"

"We don't cheat a man we work fer," Sam said.

"And we don't cheat a man what buys our likker. It's the best around," Jack said. "We don't cheat, son. Maybe we steal, but taking what you needs to live ain't the same as cheating somebody. You go telling lies, you same as cheating."

Virgil did not answer. He studied his plate as he wiped it with the last hush puppy. As soon as he finished the meal and emptied his water jar, Ellen jumped up and took the plate.

"I got us a apple pie iffen you wants some," she said. "I saved you a big slab."

Virgil patted his belly. "I'm about full, Ma. Maybe Buddy would help me eat some. How about it, fella? You eat another slab of pie?"

The child ran to Virgil and crawled into his lap. Virgil wrapped his arm around the child, rose, and followed his mother into the house to share his dessert with his brother. As Buddy consumed the pie, Virgil told his mother more of his plans.

"Dr. Jacobs wants me to stay down to his house. He's got an extra room, and he said iffen I'm there all the time, it'll be easier than him trying to find me when he wants me to meet somebody or to plan something. One thing I gotta do, Ma, that's gonna make the fancy white folks mad. I'm gonna help some of the Negroes get registered to vote."

"Niggers voting? We ain't never voted ourselves. How come you gonna help the niggers vote?"

"I need a heap-a votes to get elected. And I need to get you registered, too. You and Gus and Pa and everybody we know."

"You gotta take a test. I kain't but barely read my name. How kin I take a test?"

"I kin git a copy and show it to you. Show you what to do. You study it a little, and it won't be hard. I'm gonna show it to everybody who wants to vote. I'm gonna pay the poll tax too, with what I saved up in the war. Old Cunningham won't think to do that. It'll git me enough votes to win. Leastwise, I hope so."

"Iffen you don't win, you ain't likely gonna be staying home no longer. Whatcha gonna do?"

"I hafta win, Ma. I just hafta. I'll do whatever I have to. So will Dr. Jacobs. And I will win."

Buddy scrambled off his brother's lap and trotted through the house to the front porch. His voice flowed over his shoulder as he called, "Pa, Virgil's gonna win. Virgil's gonna win."

Ellen grinned. "That boy listens when you think all he sees is a piece-a pie. Wanna go back outside and watch them funny north lights?"

Chapter 5

Sunlight woke Virgil to the smell of coffee and the sound of sausage sizzling in the kitchen. He stretched until his feet pushed against the metal foot and his hand touched the wall over the head. He rolled onto his side, sat up, and picked up his army britches from the floor where he'd dropped them last night. After he pulled them on, he stuck his feet into his brogans and walked shirtless into the kitchen.

"Ma, you gonna git me too fat fer what overhauls I got," he said as he kissed her cheek. "I'll need them when I campaign out in the county and talk to farmers."

"Oh, go on, Virgil. You need some meat on them bones. That-air army ain't fed you worth shucks. You're a heap skinnier'n when you left home."

"I need some help with my shoes. Will you tie them for me?"

"Jest like you was a tyke." Ellen smiled as she knelt before her son and tied off his brogans. As she tied the loops into another knot, she said, "And I'll fix 'em so the briars kain't pull them loose."

He then went out the front door, circled to the outhouse, and when a buzzard flushed up from the dead sow, he jumped in surprise and then laughed at himself. The smell wasn't any worse than the outhouse, which wasn't as bad as some of the army latrines he'd had to clean. At least all they did with the outhouse was dump in some lye once in a while.

On his way back to the house, he stopped at the well and realized he couldn't draw up a bucket.

"Hey, Buddy. C'mere a minute."

The child left the hound and puppies under the mimosa tree and trotted to the well. With Buddy providing a hand, he drew a bucket. From more than seventy feet down the water felt almost icy as he sloshed it over his head and face. He used his fingers to comb his hair as he walked back to the house. Water still dripped off his hair and down his chest when he entered the kitchen.

"Where's everybody gone to?" he asked as he sat down to the table.

"Don't none of them tell me much about where they're off to. You going up to Doc's this morning?" Ellen said.

He nodded as he chewed sausage, and held up his hand to indicate he'd talk as soon as he swallowed.

"Yeah. I'm going to town to git some civvies and gonna start off right away getting into the running."

She reached into her pocket and pulled out a small booklet. "This-here's yer bank book where your money is. I ain't let nobody touch it, even when times was bad. I got Bobby's too, and we ain't touched it neither. It's your'n, Virgil, iffen you need it."

"No, Ma, I can't use Bobby's money. He'd-a wanted you to have it. You keep it for when times go bad." He slipped his bank book into his hip pocket as he rose from the table. "I'll be getting two suits and two ties. Only tie I ever wore was in uniform. It's gonna feel real funny to be dressed up like that all the time."

"You come back here and visit in your fancy clothes, now, you hear? I don't want you going off to live with Dr. Jacobs and us not seeing you. I don't keer how big and how mighty you gits, you gonna always be my boy."

Virgil wrapped his arm around her and spoke into her hair. "I ain't fergitting, Ma. I got a lot of love in me for you." He kissed her cheek and headed out. At the front door, he stopped, turned, and said, "I'll stop by real soon and show off my new suits. I promise."

With his uniform shirt hanging open and his duffle bag slung over his shoulder, he walked down the dusty road toward the Jacobs place.

*   *   *

At Dr. Jacobs' suggestion, his daughter-in-law, Janice, drove Virgil to Macon to help him select his politicking clothes.

"I'm glad to have you along," Virgil told her on the drive over. "I don't know anything about how to dress for this politicking."

The wind tossed her blond hair around her face and she constantly pushed it out of her eyes. He noticed they were green, and wanted to ask her why she'd married a Jew boy if she wasn't Jewish herself. He knew Dr. Jacobs wasn't one to practice all the religious doings like some people. His own family never bothered with all the church-goings-on the way some folks did.

She wore a store-bought dress, a lot fancier than his ma or Penny ever wore. And stockings. She'd checked her seams before they walked out of the house. How she was gonna walk in those fancy high heels all over the men's department at Davidson's he didn't know. The shoes must hurt her feet, they were so narrow.

But walk through the store she did, her stride strong and lengthy for a lady. She easily found what he needed, even to underdrawers. He felt his face redden when she picked them up and handed them to the clerk. Nobody but his ma had ever touched his underdrawers. She selected ties to go with his suits, and he let her decide.

"This tie is for when you talk to the town folks," she said as she held up a solid black one. "It's perfect for the black suit. And this one," she held up a striped one, "is perfect for the farmers."

"I'm gonna wear overalls when I talk to the farmers."

"No, no. Only when you go to the farms and talk to the people in the fields. You'll need a dress shirt and tie when you meet them in town. The overalls will remind them you're a farmer, but you need to show you're all business when you're in town. It'll do when you drive them in to the courthouse to get registered."

Three suits, underwear, socks, brown and black shoes, and a dozen dress shirts went into the shopping bags and boxes. As they walked to the car, he was glad they had found a nearby parking space; he didn't want to walk down a sidewalk with only a sack in his good hand while the lady beside him carried all those bundles.

He had spent more than he expected and worried on the way home about whether or not he would have enough left to do all he wanted to—pay the poll tax for a lot of the Negroes and pay his campaign costs. He reckoned he might have to borrow from Ma or from Doc Jacobs.

Chapter 6

Saturday morning Virgil donned a pair of his new pants and a shirt, and on Janice's advice, he wore a tie. He thought it was a good thing he was living here, seeing as nobody in his family could knot a tie and Janice made short work of it.

"Take the car," Dr. Jacobs had told him at breakfast. "Key stays in it, so use it when you need to. I don't go anywhere anymore."

Virgil decided the best place to begin was the hardware store, where every farmer stopped in during the day, some to just sit, some to buy rope, plow points, an axe or other tools.

Three older men sat on the front porch where they smoked, whittled, and watched the passers-by.

"Mind if I join yer?"

"Sit, Virgil. Good to see you back home safe."

Virgil sat and tilted his chair back to lean on the wall.

"How you gonna farm, boy?"

"Not gonna farm. I shore kain't wrestle a plow with one hand. Gonna git into politics."

One of the men laughed, one frowned, and the other shook his head and looked at his feet. At that moment, another customer walked out of the store.

"What'd I miss?"

"Virgil here's gonna git into politics."

The store owner heard the conversation through the open door and stepped outside.

"You boys gonna talk politics, you come inside where I got a fan going. It's too hot to sit outchere. 'Sides, I might miss something."

They carried their chairs inside and bunched them under the fan.

"Whatcha gonna run fer? Governor?

"Naw," someone answered. "He gonna run against Truman."

Virgil laughed with them. "No, I'm gonna run for county commission chairman."

"You gonna go up again ole Larry?"

Virgil shrugged. "Why not? Somebody's gonna put him out one day. May's well be me."

A farmer entered with a dozen eggs to swap for a hoe and joined the conversation. While they talked, they chewed tobacco or rolled their own cigarettes with Prince Albert or Bull Durham. The ring of tobacco juice in the spittoon punctuated the conversation, and smoke hovered in a thick layer above their heads.

"What kin you do fer us that ole Larry can't?" the store owner asked.

"I kin pave the roads he ain't bothered with so your customers kin git to town easier. Ain't that right, Mack? If yer road were to git paved, couldn't you git to town any time you wanted, not jest on Saturday?"

Mack nodded and walked to the door, spat across the sidewalk into the street, wiped his chin, looked up and down the street, and returned to where he had been leaning on one of the posts that supported the ceiling. "I reckon I could, Virgil. But whut fer would I be needing to git to town more'n oncest a week? The wife's still out there somewhere spending my money faster'n I kin make it."

"Well, Mack, soon as you git one of them tractors, you'll need to come to town for oil and gas. If the road's paved, the weather won't matter."

"I ain't needing no tractor."

"Well, maybe not. But think on it a bit. A tractor don't hafta be fed lessen it's working. You got to feed that mule every day, even when you got your crops laid by. And with electricity gitting all over the country now, next thing you know, your Miss Annie's gonna want to come to town jest to visit. All the ladies will have socials if I git elected and pave yer road."

"Ole Larry can pave the roads as well as you kin."

"Has he paved any? No. He's got that store out there with everything you can want. Hardware. Canned goods. Dry goods. Staples. He don't need to come to town like everybody else. He gits stuff delivered to him. All he comes to town fer is to walk around and smoke that cigar and look important. Iffen he paves the roads, then local folks'll come to town where they can buy cheaper. Iffen the roads stay dirt, folks can't git to town whenever it rains, and they'll buy from him."

"Why you want to run him off?"

"I'm not looking to run him off. I'm jest looking fer a job. I can't wrestle a plow no more or work a hoe. I ain't got a lotta education so I can't go be a teacher. But I can be your county commissioner and help all the country folk. I growed up country folk, so I know what country folk need. And I'll see you get what's needed."

"You gonna git everybody one of them tractors?" Mack grinned as he carved himself another chew and stuffed it into his cheek.

Everybody laughed, including Virgil.

"Wish I could. We'd be the richest county in Georgia if we all had a tractor. And every dairyman'd be rich too if I could buy all of them one of those new electric milking machines."

"I wouldn't use one of them things on my cows. It's likely to pull the tits off."

Laughter erupted again.

"What else you gonna do, besides pave the roads?"

"I got a couple of ideas. You know the fuse plant is closing down. We gonna have a lotta folks out of a job. I got a soldier buddy from the war whose daddy owns some factories up in Massachusetts. He wants one here in Georgia, and I'll get him to come here. We need something besides farming to keep the boys from moving up north to get jobs that pay real wages."

"That shore is true, Virgil. Already my oldest boy is talking about moving away. And my wife don't like the idea of not working for wages; she's been at the fuse plant ever since it opened."

"Mine too," another man said.

"Everett said one of his daddy's plants hires about a hundred folks. Men and women. That's enough jobs to keep everybody working."

Agreement spread around the group.

"What's the other idea you got, Virgil?"

"I'd like to see Sheriff Dixon have some help. We need a deputy, and I'd hire one."

"You gonna sick him on the bootleggers?" A snicker ran through the crowd.

"Well, fellas, you're gitting a bit close to home there."

"You mean you want to hire a deputy and you wouldn't want him to bust up your pa's still?"

Virgil laughed. "Would you put a deputy sheriff onto your own pa? Course not. Besides, what you got there in that-air Mason jar? It's likely my pa's."

Again laughter flowed through the room. The screen door opened and everyone looked up to see Ellen enter. The banter quieted. For a moment the only sounds were Ellen's footsteps as she approached the counter and the whump-whump of the overhead fan.

"You boys shore are smoking this-here place up," Ellen said, and smiled at Virgil. "You politicking, son?"

"He shore is, Miss Ellen. Next thing you know, he's gonna promise us a new truck."

"Oh, he got better sense'n that. The army ain't paid him enough to buy hisself a new truck. And the county ain't gonna pay him much neither. But he's truthful. He always do what he says." She stepped up to the counter. "Benny, you got airy shoe soles that'll fit these-here shoes?" She lifted one foot to reveal a hole worn through the sole.

"I think I do. C'mon." He led her to the other side of the store. All the men turned to watch the two as Ellen lifted her foot again to test the size of the patch. When she was satisfied, she followed him to the cash register, paid, and started to the door. Before she exited, she turned back to the men.

"You fellas git in line come July and vote fer Virgil, you hear?"

"Yes, m'am, Miss Ellen," floated out after her.

*   *   *

Monday morning Virgil dressed in his overalls and left the Jacobs' home to campaign among the country population. He drove the doctor's car and felt grateful for having his right hand so he could change gears. He stopped at each house or shanty, walked to the front door, and knocked. Only women greeted him since their men had gone into the fields.

He took time to talk to the women and then walked into the fields and down the rows of crops. He followed the plowing men to the end of the row, and they stood in the shade of an elm or an oak to talk. Virgil always praised the mule. He slid his hand over the haunches, often shifted the collar to relieve the pressure a little. Without fail, he would pick up a handful of dirt, work it in his fingers, and talk about the soil. He talked about the quality of the crops and asked what the men needed to increase profits.

No matter the need, he always worked the conversation to how much savings the farmer would have if he could get his crops to the grist mill or the canning plant or the cotton gin on a paved road. No more rutted roads or long delays in getting to market. He promised that his first act would be to pave roads.

Some farms hung on hillsides and lost soil to the bottomlands with each rain. He explained to these farmers how to plow along the line of the hill so the rows could catch the water as it ran downhill. He often knelt and used a stick to draw lines in the dirt as he talked.

Born to the land, he showed the farmers he was one of them.

"I kain't vote, Mr. Virgil," the Negroes often said.

But he would shake his head and say, "But you can. Everybody can vote."

"I ain't got no money to pay no poll tax."

"I'll pay it for you. That doesn't mean you got to vote for me. I hope you will, though. But you ought to vote."

The first time he drove a Negro to the courthouse to register, he was told, "Git that nigger outta here."

"I lost my arm to the war. And I saw a lotta Negroes fighting and dying. They've got as much right to vote as you. Let's not get trouble started. Not here. Not in my county. It's a mighty dry spring. Mighty dry. Everything's like light'erd out there."

At the implied threat of fire, Miss Birdie's eyebrows went up and she backed away from the counter and called her assistant.

"Daniel, come get this nigger registered. Get his poll tax and be sure he can read." She walked back to her office.

Day after day thereafter, he drove farmers and Negroes to town, and Daniel helped them register. Day after day the people who worked in the courthouse talked about his efforts and called him a "nigger-lover," but no one dared challenge him again.

Chapter 7

Jack drove Billy Jack and Hiram in his pickup down the moon-lit road to a narrow driveway and turned in. He followed the drive around an abandoned building about one hundred yards off the road and parked.

"You want we should oughtta pen 'em up in this-here corral?" Billy Jack asked.

"It be a good pen and ain't nobody never bothered us there. BJ, you and Hiram go git us two. I'll go over to Gus's place and see iffen he kin for sure git Murphey's truck tonight."

Although their pickup would take them into the woods, it would hold only one cow, which would have to be tied to prevent it from jumping over the side. They needed a high-sided hay truck. They always paid Murphey a dollar for the loan of his, same as Dr. Jacobs did when he used it for an extra truck to get the hay in before dark.

An hour later, a half-Jersey brindle bull began to shy away from the approaching boys.

"Throw it, damn it. Throw it."

Hiram had one rope looped over his head and under his arm; the other lay coiled in one hand except for the loop, which dangled from the other. He seemed to dance as his arm gilded forward to release the rope. The loop skimmed through the air, and when the running bull stepped into it, Hiram jerked the animal off his feet.

BJ ran forward, placed his knees on the bull's ribs to weigh him down, and reached over the body to grab a foreleg. He slipped one of the hobbles over it. Then he seized a thrashing hind leg, and in spite of the jerking, he looped the other end of the hobble around it and above the lasso. The bull couldn't get up until they let off on the hobble.

"Slack off," he said, and the rope went limp. Before the bull could roll onto his belly to rise, BJ slipped the lasso off the legs and thrust it over the shaking head.

Hiram trotted forward and looped the rope as he ran. He left only enough slack for BJ to fashion a halter on the bull's head.

"That's it," BJ said, rising. "Les git him up to the corral." He slacked off the hobble long enough for the bull to rise, and quickly re-tied it so the animal couldn't run.

Hiram pulled and BJ drove the bull from behind. When the animal stopped, BJ twisted his tail to persuade him to move forward again. The bull filled the air with loud bellows, and the other cattle crashed off through the underbrush.

Once the bull was tied in the pen hidden by undergrowth near the old tenant house, they walked back toward the meadow where they had caught him. But the cattle had gone off.

Five horses lifted their heads to stare as the brothers strode from a thicket into the deep grass beside the creek. The stallion whistled at them and trotted forward, ears alert, nostrils quivering, as if anticipating food.

"If that fool hoss comes close enough, rope him," BJ said.

"How come? We kain't sell him. Everybody knows that hoss."

"I'll use him to drive the cows close by you."

The stallion broke into a canter, head shaking, forefeet pawing the air, black mane flying. His hide rippled over heavy muscles, the glistening coat turning darker with sweat. He whistled again, and a colt charged after him, fuzzy tail lifted.

The boys stood and waited while the stallion veered to one side and began to circle them as if not sure he should approach. The circle became smaller when the colt skidded to a halt only a dozen feet from them and poked his nose forward. The stallion charged between the colt and the people, head low, ears back, to drive the foal away.

The rope moved, dropped, and the stallion reared to a halt as it tightened on his neck.

"I'll be damned," Hiram said.

"He kin be gentle as a baby when he's caught. He's got better sense'n to fight a rope." He extended his hand toward Hiram, who put the rope into it, and then BJ started toward the horse.

It backed away slowly, but BJ increased the pressure on the rope, extended one hand, and began to talk softly.

"You remember me, big fella. I'm the one what learnt you that you kain't fight a rope. Remember, fella?"

As if remembering, the stallion shook his head up and down.

"That ain't gonna hep you a-tall, big boy. You might's well quit trying to shake it off."

BJ's hand was only inches from the horse's nose. The stallion extended his head, sniffed, and snorted. Then he relaxed his ears, shot one hip, and succumbed.

"You ever ride him afore?" Hiram asked

"Yeah. Back a year ago. Jest hope he remembers he's been ridden. I don't think the doctor ever knowed." BJ used the free end of the rope to fashion a halter and made a chin strap from a hobble he took from his back pocket.

"You hold his head to give me time to git settled if he takes a mind to buck."

While Hiram kept a heavy hand onto the halter, BJ looped the free end of the rope over the horse's neck and tied it off for a rein. Then he moved to the horse's shoulder, pulled the reins up tight, and twisted his fingers into the mane. "Hold him now," he said.

The horse wheezed through his teeth as Hiram dug his fingers into the stallion's nostrils. BJ swung his full weight across its back and threw his right leg over.

When the stallion reared, BJ threw his weight forward and wrapped his legs tight around the horse's ribs. Hiram swung from the halter.

"Let 'im go."

Hiram did, landed on his feet and leaped aside as the stallion came down. BJ jerked the reins back and down, to force the horse's head into his chest and not allow him to drop his nose between his front legs.

The stallion made no other attempt to buck. He flattened himself out into a hard gallop, and the other horses ran off into the woods.

BJ let him run, knowing it was the stallion's last grasp for freedom, and in only minutes the horse gave way to the pressure of the reins and stopped. He pawed once, snorted, and relaxed. When BJ clucked, he stepped out.

Half an hour later, BJ found the cattle bunched in the woods on the side of the ridge away from their corral. Maybe he could drive them closer, but he figured it was better to rope one here. They could always drive down the old road that the woodcutters kept open.

He rode back to Hiram and helped his brother scramble up behind him. When he reached a field near the cattle, he dropped Hiram off.

"I'll push 'em up here where the moonlight be good. You be ready cause they may be a-running."

A few minutes later, BJ was again battling to stay on the now sweat-slick back as the horse cut behind and around the cattle to keep them on the sawmill road and headed back to the meadow. Only when he saw Hiram's rope snake out and a yearling fall to the ground did he pull the stallion to a halt.

Foam speckled the horse's chest, and salty lather whitened his head under the halter and on his back under BJ. When he slide off, BJ's feet tingled and his legs felt suddenly cool as the wind slapped his pants.

"Thanks for the hep, fella. You kin go back to your mares now," he said and pulled the halter off.

"Hey, quit talking to that-air hoss and come hep me."

BJ pulled another hobble from his pocket as he trotted across the meadow. The horse followed, his nose at BJ's back. A hard nudge threw BJ off balance, and he danced a few steps to keep from falling. He turned to glare at the horse.

It stood with eyes fixed on BJ, its chin tucked, ears forward, teeth crunching. BJ had to chuckle at the spoiled child begging for a bite to eat. He threw his arms around the horse's neck and slapped him affectionately. "You big bastard. I ain't got a damn thing to feed you. Now you git on back to your mares."

He pushed against the half-ton of bone and muscle.

The stallion backed away, nodded his head in agreement and shook it as if angry, and backed away.

"Go on!" BJ waved his hands in the horse's face, and it pranced back with a squeal. "Shooo. Go on," BJ snatched up the halter and waved it. The stallion reared, spun, and galloped into the trees; his forefeet pawed and kicked up clods of dirt, and his head twisted and shook as he squealed his anger.

"Hurry up, BJ. He's bout to git away." The younger Carter jerked the yearling's nose up and threw him down a second time as BJ ran to his side and then hobbled the bull.

"Ain't no way we kin lead him to that-air corral," Hiram said. "Kain't we pick him up on this-here road?"

BJ agreed. They pulled the bull up, led him into the underbrush, yanked him off his feet again, and tied his feet so he couldn't get back up.

They walked back to the wagon road, and BJ broke a limb on a pine so it fell over the road.

"This-here'll hep us find him. Les git to the house. Soon's Gus gits there tonight, we'll git both of these loaded up and haul 'em over to Macon."

"Kin I go with y'all this time?" Hiram asked.

"You better ask Pa. You know we git on the road about 4 o'clock so's we'll be there when the pens open."

"I wanna go. Jest one time. You always git to go."

"I'm older. Les git on home."

They set out for home, more than a mile away by road, but they cut across country on an old wagon road and were home in fifteen minutes.

Chapter 8: Later That Night

Gus took his foot off the gas pedal but did not brake so the truck would slow enough to let the car behind him pass before he reached the road to the old shack. He was early anyhow—it was only half-past three— and Jack would not be along for another half-hour. The vehicle behind him drew closer, honked, and pulled around. Gus glanced at it and swerved Murphey's truck almost into the ditch as the pangs of fear knifed in his stomach.

It was Cunningham's Ford pickup with a stranger driving. He had to be Perry, the private policeman. Cunningham never let anybody but Charley drive anymore, since his hired man got killed, and this man drove too slow to be going to Cunningham's house.

The pickup rattled into the woods, down the driveway toward their cattle pen. Had he been two minutes earlier, Detective Perry would have driven up on him while he waited for Jack and the boys.

Gus drove on down the road and around the curve. No sign of another vehicle. He turned off his lights, pulled into an abandoned wagon road and turned around. As he passed the lane a second time, he squinted through the shadows and saw a lone figure with a lantern ease away from the Ford. A tall, slim man. Lantern light glittered on a pistol strapped to his hip.

"Leastways he left it where we kin see it from the road," Gus told himself aloud. "But how'n hell do he know we got that-air bull tied up in there?"

He only shook his head, unable to answer. Maybe Jack would be able to figure it all out.

He spat his wad of tobacco out the window, turned around again at a driveway to one of Dr. Jacobs' hay barns, and sped toward Jack's home. He hoped to get there before the others left to meet him.

He was still afraid of what might have happened if he had turned into that lane in front of Perry. If he were face to face with the lawman, would he have used the .12 gauge, would he have shot the man? Gus knew he most likely would have.

When he careened into the yard, Jack stepped onto the porch, threw up his hand, and walked down the steps.

"What's wrong, Gus? You look sick," he said as he approached Murphey's truck.

Gus told him and added, "What we gonna do?"

"Ain't no need to git all in a lather," Jack said. "Lemme think." Thinking meant leaning against the hood of the truck while making up a cigarette. His heavy brows pulled into a black line, the only outward sign that he felt turmoil as he seemed to concentrate solely on the work of his fingers. He licked the cigarette paper to seal it, put it between his lips, struck a match on the back of his thigh, and lit it. He squinted as the smoke rose into his eyes.

"He kain't prove nothing even iffen he do find the bull. And he won't find nothing nohow, not the way we got it hid in that-air sticker pen. I'll ride down the road and see iffen he's left. You pull that truck back behind the barn so as he kain't see it iffen he comes by here."

Jack drove off in his rusting pickup, passed the lane in second gear, and looked for Cunningham's truck. He didn't see it. A few yards from the lane, he turned off the key with the truck in gear and let it choke itself down. If Perry were in the woods and heard the choking, he'd think somebody had car trouble. He got out, took the unlit lantern, and walked back to the lane.

As silent as the lights that danced in the night sky, Jack eased up the lane. No sign of a vehicle. He strode back to the main road, scratched a kitchen match on the base of the lantern, and lit the wick. The dew-wet grasses lay mashed in different directions from the vehicles that drove in and out, but the final trip had mashed the grass to point toward the main road. Perry had given up and gone.

The only other sign of traffic was wagon tracks where the neighborhood wood cutters, who had kept that lane open for years, had been in and out in their search for fuel.

Moments after he reached the house, he, BJ and Hiram were in Murphey's truck with Gus. They drove up behind the building that had stood for more than half a century; it had been abandoned more than a decade, since the voodoo woman became angry with its occupants and cast a spell on them. They had fled. Spanish bayonets lifted their spikes skyward, as if to pierce the moon and hold it unmoving in the sky. Weeds and blackberry runners, plum bushes and honey suckle had gone berserk since the house stood empty, and each plant vied with the others to dominate.

Jack and his sons got out of the truck, and at a nod from his father, Hiram threw a loop over what looked like a stob that poked up from the clump of Spanish bayonets. He pulled on the rope and opened a gate into a pen constructed of hog wire with the plants attached as camouflage. The frightened face of the mixed-breed bull glared at them in the lantern light.

While BJ waved his hands to give directions, Gus backed the truck close to the gate. Hiram scampered over the truck's hood and into the bed, and then slid a sheet of plywood off the truck to make a ramp.

As he walked down, he braced his feet sideways on the crossed one-by-twos to keep from slipping. He removed the hobbles and halter from the bull and then moved to its off side. The animal pushed his rear up and then pulled his front feet from under himself, to stand stiffly while he stared at Hiram.

Gus stood beside the front door, his face yellow in the moonlight. His .12 gauge double barrel shotgun rested loosely in the crook of his arm. BJ and Jack stood ready to shove the tailgate closed.

Hiram whooped and popped the rope toward the bull, which saw the ramp as a way to freedom and charged up it, his hoofs clattering and sliding on the plywood. Behind him, Hiram still whooped enough to sound like a charging company of Confederate soldiers.

A thin man came out of the shack's door and glided from tree to tree until he was only a few feet from the front of the truck. His faded denims, torn and ragged, blended with the gray shadows. In the quietness between two of Hiram's yells, his soft voice was explosive.

"Whatcha doing?"

Gus spun, jerked up his shotgun, and fired one barrel of No. 2 turkey shot into the man's chest.

Hiram tumbled down the ramp. The bull bellowed and tried to climb over the front of the truck. The little man turned and staggered toward the shack.

BJ grabbed the weapon from Gus and fired the other barrel. The man fell.

Jack grabbed the gun from BJ and turned his fury on both of the shooters. "What in hell y'all do that fer?" Jack's voice exploded with the same volume as the shotgun. "Stealing's one thing, but killing's another."

Pale-faced and shaking, his grin gone, Hiram stared at his father.

Gus spat off to the side, shifted his wad to the other cheek, and said, "We better close that-air tailgate while we got the critter in the truck. Else we'll be done wasted the night."

BJ glanced from Jack to the truck and back again.

"Go ahead," Jack said.

With a sigh of relief to be out from under the angry glare of his father, BJ leaped to the gate.

"Hiram, git up there and hep your brother," Jack ordered.

As the younger boys worked to close up the truck, Gus asked, "What we gonna do with that?" and nodded toward the dead man.

Jack didn't answer but walked over to the body and knelt. Gus followed.

"Looks like a tramp to me," Gus said.

"I hope like hell he is, so won't nobody be looking fer him," Jack answered as he reached into the man's pockets. He found only a worn wallet that contained a photograph of a little girl, a torn dollar bill, and a folded discharge form.

"He was in the army, but he warn't from nowhere close to here. Gus, see what you find inside. Could be he was sleeping there."

As Gus strode off, Jack replaced the paper and photograph, but stuffed the dollar bill into his own pocket.

"BJ. Hiram. Y'all hep me. We gotta git him on the truck. I'll dump him somewhere. Far off from here."

Gus walked back. "Nothing inside there. He musta been jest a tramp."

The boys pushed the body onto the truck's hood, and Gus climbed up to shove it over the cab and let it drop in the bed with the bull. The animal snorted at the smell of blood and backed away, head lowered.

As they stood a moment, in silence, Hiram turned his eyes toward the hillside where they had left the other yearling. "Look-a yonder. I see a lantern up there." He pointed toward the rise where they had hidden the yearling.

"Cut our lantern. It's gotta be Perry. He must be hunting fer that other bull. Somebody musta been in here after stovewood and heard 'em bellow. Quick. Les git outta here."

They piled into the truck. Jack took the wheel and Hiram sat on the cab roof with his feet dangling into the bed. Jack kept the headlights off as they eased down the narrow lane to the main road. He did not stop to close the gate but turned toward home. Headlights off, he kept to the middle of the dirt road.

They passed Cunningham's pickup parked on the driveway going to the other bull. Some 100 yards beyond the truck, Jack turned on the headlights. He drove directly to the house.

"All-a-y'all git out. You boys stay home, you hear me? Iffen anybody comes asking around, I done gone off somewhere, and you got no i-dee where. You remember that?"

"Yeah, Pa," they answered almost in unison.

"I'm gonna git rid of what's in the back of the truck. You do like I tell you to. And you ain't never seen what's in the back of that truck. You hear me?"

Hiram nodded.

"I kin hep, kain't I, Pa?" BJ's tone was almost a plea.

"No. Do like I done said. Gus, you take our truck home and wait. I'll tend to what's back there," he jerked a thumb toward the truck bed, "and then I'll bring the truck back to your house. Then I'll git my truck and come on home."

Jack didn't want Gus or his weapon anywhere near him tonight, and sending him home was the quickest way to get him far from the dead man. He drove off and headed across the county to an area where they never went for cows. He found it years ago, when another bootlegger told him it was a good place to fish for cats. It lay on the side of the county away from the Macon stockyards where Detective Perry would probably wait for them to deliver the bull.

When he reached the river swamps, Jack followed a narrow road under low-hanging branches. Limbs slapped at him through the window, and he worried about turning around, worried that maybe the old cow pasture might have grown up in brush. The headlights slashed white through the blackness beneath the tall trees.

The field opened before him and revealed the river, gleaming with reflected northern lights that rippled with the current through the blue shadows of the overhanging trees.

He dropped the plywood ramp and stepped aside as the bull charged to freedom. Then he climbed into the truck bed, lifted the body, and carried it to the riverbank. When he threw it in, the waters, orange-gold from the northern lights, reached up to swallow it, and for a moment Jack thought he was looking into hell.

PART III MAY

Chapter 1: May 1

Sam tilted the corn-shuck bottom chair on its back legs and hooked a naked foot on the rung on each side. He concentrated on the chunk of wood and his pocket knife as he whittled a rabbit for Buddy. BJ sat beside him and rolled a cigarette.

A pickup truck drove by, screeched to a stop, and backed up even with the porch. A tall, slim man dressed in overalls and a brown Sears-Roebuck work shirt stepped out.

"Morning boys," he greeted them as he strode across the bridge and into the yard.

"Well, John. Ain't seen you in a long time," Sam said and smiled. He folded his knife, shoved it into his overalls pocket, and put the wood chunk on the floor beside the chair.

"Has been a spell." John Hall removed his straw hat to run his fingers through his thick grey hair in an attempt to cool his head. "How's the family?"

Sam shrugged. "Oh, tolerable, tolerable. How's yourn?"

John spun his hat in his hand. "Fine, Sam, just fine." He grinned his pleasure. "The missus is gonna have another baby."

"That shore is grand. How many that-un make?"

John called them each by name as he ticked them off on his fingers. "Seven, counting the girl."

Billy Jack got to his feet grinning. "Here, you sit down a spell. You likely could use the rest."

"I don't really have the time, BJ. I just stopped by when I saw ya'll out here. I could use some help tomorrow with the fences. I had to fire my hired man. He warn't worth shucks and let my fences go. He knew better, but when the bottom rail rotted, he done swapped it with the top one. Too lazy to split another one. My daddy always said never let the bottom rail get on top. I wanna string some barbed wire. I'll need at least one of you, but I could use two or three. Pay you each a dollar a day. Probably take two or three days."

"We kain't tomorrow. Gotta put in some time with Dr. Jacobs. How bout day after?"

"That's fine. I already got wire and staples. I'll find our old broom handle for unrolling it. Pick you up right after good light?"

"Yep. That suits all-a us. You got airy posthole diggers and a stretcher?"

"I borrowed Doc's stretcher. I'm gonna nail to trees, so we don't have to dig any postholes. Trees don't rot off. I shore hope it don't rain. I know we need it, but not this week."

They all looked up at the cloudless, white-hot sky and Sam said, "It shore ain't likely to. Sit down, John. We gonna be eating in a few minutes and you oughtta stay. It ain't much but you be welcome to what we got."

"I should be going on home. The wife's expecting me for dinner and she'll be worried if I'm late. 'Sides, you know how nervous a woman gits when it's about her time."

"Jack'll be in directly, too. He'll be sorry to miss you if you go along. Did you know Virgil's home?"

"I shore didn't. How is he?"

"Got his arm shot off. Other'n that, he's good. He kain't farm no more, so he's gonna run fer county commission."

"Against old Larry Cunningham? He must be crazy."

Ellen walked onto the porch. "Heard voices," she said. "He ain't crazy, John. He's gonna win. Hey, Penny, come on out-chere. We got company."

"Well, you tell him he's got my vote."

In the kitchen, Penny had her mind on Charley, not on her cooking. She still felt him against her, still yearned for more of him, and wanted him to come back. Why hadn't he come back like he promised? He shoulda been here ages ago. His tomorrow had come and gone, and she had seen him drive by twice on his way to town. She didn't know how many times he'd gone by when she hadn't seen him. Why wouldn't he stop?

When Ellen called her, she was sure it was Charley. She dropped the spoon, jerked off her apron, ran her fingers through her hair and pushed it back from her face, and ran toward the front door, sure it was Charley. When she saw it wasn't, her shoulders slumped with disappointment.

If only Charley had been the one sitting on the porch, coming to see her the way he used to, maybe to talk with the boys or take them fishing on his daddy's big lake or down on Rocky Creek.

Ellen said, "Button up that dress right, Penny. You got no call to be leaving three buttons open like that. You show everything you got. Maybe your daddy don't notice, but I do."

Penny blushed, turned her back on Hall, and buttoned up the dress. "I'm sorry. It's so hot in the kitchen. I wasn't thinking."

Hall twisted his hat around his hand. "Miss Penny, my wife's expecting a baby soon. We might need some help tending to the other chullen if her ma can't git here. You wantta come sit with 'em if we be needing help? I'd pay you."

"Yeah. Sure." She shrugged and returned to the kitchen. The weight of emptiness sat on her spirits, pushed her down, lay so heavy on her that her shoulders sagged.

John's pale blue eyes followed her as she went inside. Her youthful hips swung easily, so different from the wide, tired hips of his wife. He forced his attention back to Sam.   Maybe he would stay to dinner—after all, if he didn't, the Carter men might think he was insulting the women's cooking. The Carter's reputation for avenging any slight was well-known. He didn't want his new fence cut or his barn burned or some cows to come up dead or missing. When he glanced at BJ, the youth bowed mockingly and offered his chair, his grin flashing the knowledge that he had seen John's eyes follow Penny.

"Penny sure has turned into a pretty woman, Sam," John said.

"She ain't but a kid," Sam said.

"Oh? How old is she?"

"Fifteen this summer."

"You gonna marry her off any time soon?"

"Billy Jack says he wants to marry her. I dunno. I ain't decided. She kinda likes that Charley, but he ain't gonna come calling here."

"Ain't she and BJ double cousins?"

"Yeah. But that don't matter none. Iffen he wants to marry her, I reckon I'll give it some thinking. That what you want, BJ?"

BJ grinned. "I shore do want to marry her, Uncle Sam."

"Well, boy, you best quit whoring with that nigger gal."

"Aw, c'mon, Sam. You know how it is. You do the same thing. Besides, when I look at Penny I git all itchy and I gotta do something about it. Better that nigger gal what'll let me than I go sniffing after some white gal and git myself in trouble."

Sam shook his head and eyed the ceiling.

Ellen walked back out. "Dunner's on the table. You might's well eat a bite, John."

John walked into the house with the men. The table was set with dishes like he had collected at the filling station when he bought five gallons of gas—all pink plates and cups and saucers. Even the pitcher for the tea was the same pattern, pink with irises on it.

Penny entered, a large bowl of turnip greens in one hand, a pan of cornbread in the other. The bread was thin, and she had piled several circles of the bread into the single pan. Ellen followed with a large platter of fried catfish.

Sam waved John toward one end of the table and scraped his chair up to the other. Hiram and Buddy came in and pulled up a bench on one side. They leaned their elbows on the table and revealed dirty hands. BJ sat across from them.

The women went back to the kitchen. In moments, Penny returned with the tall, tin coffee pot. She poured three cups full and left the room again.

"Kain't I have some coffee?" Hiram whined.

"Me, too, me, too," Buddy said and beat his spoon on the table with each word.

"No," Sam replied. "You ain't neither one old enough. You drink your tea."

John served himself as the plates came by, but was slack on taking much of the greens. He could see they were late pickings and tough, and oughtta be used to slop the hogs. He swallowed the greens after barely chewing them, and hoped the grease would help them slide down his throat.

The catfish, dusted with cornmeal and fried a light brown, were so good he wanted to empty the platter onto his own plate. Instead, he asked for a second pass.

Like the Carter men, he ate the fish with his hands, careful to nibble around the bones. Even filets couldn't be this good, he thought. When Penny came in again, he complimented her on the fish.

"I cotched 'em," Hiram said.

The cornbread dipped in the potlikker was the finest he'd ever tasted. Wished his wife could make it like this.

"Sure is good potlikker," he said. "Aren't Penny and Ellen going to eat?"

"Shore, but the women folks heah serves us and then they kin eat."

He forked the last of the greens into his mouth and reached for the coffee to wash them down. It was so strong and bitter he could barely swallow it, but he forced it down. He pushed his cup and plate back, relieved that he had been able to finish a decent plate and no one could be offended by how little of the greens he ate.

"More coffee?" Penny appeared at his shoulder, one hand folded into a fist and propped on her hip, which she shot to the side. Her stance pushed her breasts against the front of her dress.

Penny watched his eyes rove up her body, pause at her breasts, and then move up to her face. She half-smiled and lifted an eyebrow.

"No, no, thank you just the same." His eyes dropped to the table and to his cup. "No more. I've had plenty."

"Give him some coffee, Penny. He's jest being polite. I done seen him drink five cups running in winter at feeding time."

"Yeah, Sam, but that's in winter. I wonder, could I have some of that tea?"

She returned to the kitchen and brought out a tall, pink glass that matched the pitcher. The boys all drank from jelly glasses, same as his children. "Miss Penny, I'm honored to get to use one of your good glasses. I thank you."

Like the coffee the tea was strong, but it had a heavy load of sugar. He sipped it to make it last.

Ellen walked in. "Any of you seen my dish rag? I kain't find it nowhere in the kitchen."

"Me and Billy Jack put it on the mule's sore laig this mawning. She had to have something on it to keep off the screwworm flies, and that was all we could find." Hiram spoke around a mouth full of cornbread.

"Well, don't just sit there. Go git it. I gotta have something to clean up my kitchen with."

John's face paled and he felt a hard knot form in his stomach and try to rise. He swallowed it back down and hastily rose. As he backed toward the door, he said, "I hate to eat and run, folks, but I got to be going. My wife's gonna be mad as a wet hen. I do thank you for the good eatings, Miss Penny. Miss Ellen. You're both real fine cooks."

"Glad to oblige, John. Me and the boys'll see you bout daylight come day after tomorrow," Sam said.

"Well, good-bye." John tried to hold the smile until he was out the door. Moments later he pulled his truck over to the ditch, out of sight of the Carters, and quietly disgorged his meal.

Chapter 2: Four Days Later

Penny scrubbed the frying pan, her emotions welling up again. For the millionth time that day she wondered why Charley had not been back to see her. It'd been more'n forever since he came by that night. He loved her, he had to love her. He missed her. At least he said he missed her all the time he was away. How come he hadn't come by, at least to wave at her? He promised.

Tears came, and she hunched over with the pain inside. Maybe he didn't love her at all. Maybe he lied to her. Maybe he was like his daddy, who everybody said lied all the time just to get what he wanted. Maybe all Charley wanted was her naked in the back seat of his daddy's Buick.

She had to get her mind off Charley. She'd go sit with the men on the front porch. They always had plenty to talk about, even if it was mostly their likker stills and the niggers. Watching Jack whittle usually wiped all other thoughts from her mind. She stepped out onto the porch.

"Whatcha doing out there in the middle of the road, nigger?" Billy Jack said to the man walking by in front of the house.

"I's jest a-going home, Mista Billy Jack. I done been down to work for Doc, but he say atter yestiddy's rain hit's too wet to plow. So I's jest a-going home." Jefferson Sherman grinned and revealed nicotine-stained teeth and a gap where he had lost his right upper incisor in a fist fight. He wore a denim shirt outside the waist of his patched Army pants.

"Is y'all done heard about Noah?"

"Heard what?" Billy Jack laughed at his own thought before he said it. "He ain't got sick on his bootleg, is he?"

Jeff shook his head. "He done got cotched down to his still."

"Noah? You shore, Jeff?" Jack stopped whittling. "That damn old nigger's had a still since afore I got here, and ain't nobody never bothered him. Every sheriff we had knowed where it was and left him alone long's he give 'em a couple of jugs frum every run. How come we ain't heard nothing?"

"I don't know, suh. But Mr. Perry, he dun found hit and busted up all de barrels and such. He done even taked Noah off to jail."

"Well, goddamn him!" Jack smashed his knife forward, and it buried to the hilt into the red clay. "What in hell is he bothering Noah for?"

Jeff looked at his feet as if concentrating on the mixture of dried mud and manure caked on his GI boots.

"Doc say dat Mr. Perry done been hired by Mista Cunningham to figger where at all his cows done gone." His eyes narrowed as he studied Jack's face.

"Only about the cows? Not about the likker?" Jack asked.

"Dat's whut Doc say, yassuh."

"Then how come he's busting up stills?"

"I reckons cause he done found hit. He and dat GeeBee man be busting up de stills. Ain't nobody kin tell neither one of 'em nothing. Don't neither of 'em want no likker." He began to back away as his eyes shifted from Jack to BJ.

"Doc say what Judge Emerson done to Noah?"

"I axked him, and Doc say de jedge let him go seeing he gibe dem some money. Doc say iffen he been cotched dis week he be in jail till de July court. Dey done had court dis week and Doc got 'em to let Noah go free now stead-a waiting."

"Noah ain't got no money, Jeff. How he pay them?" Billy Jack asked.

"Noah got a heap of friends. Dey was deah to buy him free."

Billy Jack turned to his father and spoke too softly for Jeff to hear. "I hope this don't mean Noah's kid ain't gonna be at the still tonight. Reckon I better git down there and be sure he's stoking up the fire?"

"Wait'll dark."

"Lemme by," Penny said as she tried to walk between her uncle and cousin.

"Ain't you gonna fix supper, girl?"

"In a little bit. I ain't hongry, and Ellen's in the kitchen anyhow."

Sunken from lack of sleep over the past week, her eyes dominated her face. Her lips tucked into a thin line of anger, sadness, and lonesomeness.

Her thin cotton dress revealed that womanhood was no longer a promise. With the three top buttons of her dress left open, her breasts were visible, and she did not care if BJ or even the nigger in the yard stared at her.

Billy Jack ogled his cousin as she approached. Penny turned

sideways, her rear to BJ, to get between them. BJ reached out and squeezed her rump. When she jumped, he chuckled.

"Feels like you been gitting plenty to eat, honey."

"You keep your hands where they belong!" she screamed as she slapped at him, her eyes blazing.

"That exactly what I'm trying to do," he countered.

He wore only a pair of jeans. His lean chest was tanned a deep rusty-brown. Deep-set eyes danced with secret thoughts beneath long lashes that curled upward to meet thick brows. His nostrils flared slightly as he spoke, like a stallion snorting. His wide cheek bones tapered gently down to a firm chin that could have been chiseled from marble. He studied Penny with more sexual interest than she recognized.

"Oh, leave her alone, BJ. She be yer cousin." Jack threw the remains of his whittling stick toward the edge of the porch and shrugged when it clattered against the support post for the roof. "Where you off to?" he asked.

"I jest gotta git out a little bit. It's brinjin hot in the kitchen." She stopped on the stairs and turned to look at her uncle. Could he see she missed Charley? BJ probably did. But Jack probably stayed so busy with thinking about himself and his stills that he wouldn't notice. Her pa might, though, and she was glad he was off somewhere. It was bad enough with Ellen always after her about mooning over Charley.

As she reached the yard, she noticed Jeff hurrying off and wondered why he wasn't going toward his home but in the direction of the mule pasture. Maybe he's taking a shortcut.

Jeff had no intention of going home. His father would send him into the cotton field to chop out weeds for the rest of the day or his mother would nag him to split wood for the kitchen stove. It was just too hot to think about work that did not mean real money in his hand that he could spend on Saturday down at the juke joint. He wiped the sweat from his face with the back of his hand, glanced back to be sure that no one was looking, and cut into the undergrowth, headed for the barn. He had napped there before, in the hay piled in the middle stall. Three ageless oaks shaded the cedar shingle roof over the high loft. Heat lifted up and a breeze always drifted in. Moving air was cooler than stagnant air.

As he reached the barn door, he again looked toward the house, but he could not see the porch. He stepped inside, into the cooler air.

Last year's musty hay remained in the stall, the pile down to less than three feet. Motes hovered in the cracks of light and danced as the breeze slipped between the boards. Dirt daubers added mud to the patterns left last summer. A wasp nest clung to the corner under the loft.

He looked at the loft ladder, considered going up there, decided against the effort, and crawled onto the hay pile, where he lay flat on his back and tucked his hands behind his neck for a pillow.

*   *   *

Penny strode off across the pasture, her loneliness driving her. She ignored the tears running down her face. Why, oh why was Charley staying away? Was it like she overheard some of the girls talking at school, that if you ever let a boy have his way with you, he'll go find another girl?

The field was hot, and she had to dodge cow and mule piles. She halted in mid-field and pulled her skirt tail up to wipe the tears from her face. A young bull lifted his head, looked her way, and went back to pulling grass. A calf, unmindful of the heat, frolicked across the meadow, rear feet kicking as his head twisted. The mother lowed softly, but the calf romped on.

Penny stared at the cattle, but did not see them. Her mental eyes saw only Charley's face, the freckles that splashed all over his nose and cheeks, the lips that curled into a crooked smile and felt like heaven on hers.

She turned her back on the pasture and walked, head down, back toward the house. Laughter drifted from the porch. Sam was back, and somebody was telling stories. She did not want to go back to the house, seeing as how BJ would question her about her crying. He never missed anything about her.

The barn, shaded, offered a refuge. She went toward it and the shadowing oaks. Inside, she went to the stall with the hay still piled up for the mules. She could sit there until she got her mind settled a little.

A loud sneeze interrupted her sadness and she jumped.

"Who's there?" Penny's voice trembled, partly from surprise and partly from the lonesomeness that sat inside her.

"It's jest me, Miz Penny. Jefferson Sherman. I ain't doing nothing. I's going. I's going."

Penny sighed with relief and sank onto her heels. "You scared me most to death. I didn't know nobody was in here. I jest thought—" Her voice stumbled over a half-sob, half-laugh. "I don't know what I thought."

Jeff stood up, slid down the hay pile, and landed beside her. "I didn't go to scare you, Miz Penny. I's going."

Her hand snaked out and seized his arm as an idea began to form. "Wait!"

He looked at her hand clutching his arm, her fingers stark white against his darkness, and her gaze followed his. She released him and drew her hand to her lips. She could get back at Charley. If he was running around with another girl, she could—her mind seized the idea with the same determination she had known since before birth. She would do it. She would get back at Charley.

"Sit and talk to me awhile." She sat and patted the hay beside her.

Jeff hesitated, but under the force of her stare he moved slowly forward and sat. He did not speak but stared at the distance through the barn door.

Silence fell as thick as the heat, and in the silence came a low scraping sound. They both jumped. Jeff spun around and crouched, poised to attack or flee. The sound came again, and with it the heat shifted and the dust moved.

"Hit's jest the wind making de tree scratch up against de side of de barn."

"I shore didn't know what it was, Jeff. I'm glad you happened by or I'd-a been mighty scairt." Penny smiled. She paused, but he did not reply. "Hot, ain't it." It was more of a statement than a question. She pulled her hair back and up off her neck, and arched her head backward to catch the motion of the air on her shoulders and to show off her breasts.

She knew he looked at her, at the deep curves of her body. His gaze burned her and she wiggled to bulge even more against her dress.

"Yassum, hit shore is hot."

She sighed, dropped her arms, and looked at him as her hair cascaded down. Jeff's eyes widened as she sat up straight and unbuttoned her dress halfway down the front. His gaze seemed glued to her nakedness, and he swallowed. His hand trembled as he turned away and picked up a strand of hay to break into small pieces.

"Yassum, hit shore is hot. Dat's how come I's done come in heah for a nap. Dem oaks keeps hit cool in heah. But I gotta git on down the road, Miz Penny."

She shifted position, wiggled down until she was almost reclining, and propped on one elbow. She wanted him to think she didn't know her dress had crawled up her thighs.

"I seen you go by the house jest about every day since you come home. We always knowed it was time to start fixing supper when we seen you going home in the evenings."

Jeff turned his head halfway away and rolled his eyes back to look at her legs. His voice almost faltered. "Dat's Doc's doings. He say five o'clock is quitting time, lessen we's gitting in de hay. Time fer the marrieds to git on home to dey wifes."

At his reference to marriage, Penny cut her eyes away and fumbled nervously with the buttons down the front of her dress. Jeff watched every move of her hand.

"I ain't married neither, but I has to work like I is." Her voice trailed off only to suddenly leap back at him. "Billy Jack talks about going whoring. You ever go whoring?" Penny's stomach tightened. She was close to the point that she couldn't back out of this plan. She shivered, partly in anticipation and partly in fear.

Jeff only stared at her.

"Well, Jeff? You ever have a white girl? BJ says he goes whoring with the nigger girls. Do you go whoring with a white girl?"

"I bestis git on de road, Miz Penny." He did not move. But his eyes could not stay still and shifted from breasts to thighs.

"Did you?" she asked again.

"Miz Penny, I best git outta here." He leaned forward as if to rise.

She seized his arm, and they both looked down at her hand.

Hay motes floated in the sunbeams that shone between the siding planks. A carpenter bee hummed as he sawed a hole in a beam. A crow cawed as it flew by. In the distance, a bull bellowed. The oak scraped against the barn again as a breeze moved through and set the motes dancing.

Her grip on his arm tightened and she pulled him toward her. Her other hand went to work on the last few buttons of her dress. She would get back at Charley now. This would teach him. The determination rising in her was as strong and fierce as that which almost prevented her birth.

She placed his hand on her breast and clutched it to her.

"Look at me," she said.

He cut his gaze to the side, away from her. His hand on her breast trembled.

"Look at me, Jeff. In the face. Look at me in the eyes."

His face turned up, and his dark eyes settled on hers. Fear and desire mixed in his face, and his hand began to tighten on her breast.

"You got another hand. You shuck off them coverhauls."

His hand went to the straps and slid the clips free. As he pushed them off, he lifted his lower body to free his feet, and she saw he didn't wear any underdrawers. She lay back and held her arms up to him.

His lovemaking was slow and gentle and exciting, but when it was over, she cried.

"What's de matter, Miz Penny?" he whispered into her ear. "I ain't hurtcha, is I?"

"No. I jest—I don't know—. "

He rolled off, propped on an elbow, and looked at her. His palm lay on her belly. She covered her face with her hands to suppress the sobs that shook her entire body. He touched her, and her body responded by stiffening.

Jeff circled her with his arms and pulled her head onto his shoulder as he lay back against the hay. Through her tears she saw her hair tumbled over his ebony chest and quickly closed her eyes against the sight. Her crying intensified. She wanted Charley to hold her same as Jeff was doing.

His arms tightened around her until she could feel his muscles flex. His large rough hands patting her back were as soft and reassuring as his voice.

"I ain't meant ta hurt you none, Miz Penny. Hit's awright now. You jest stop crying, honey." The words were all the same, as lulling as Ellen's crooning to quiet her when she was a baby.

"You awright?" he asked, his eyes widening as his brows lifted.

Wordlessly, she nodded and almost choked as she swallowed.

"Hey, Penny! Where you at?" Billy Jack's voice came between them.

"I gotta go, Miz Penny. Kin I see you again?"

Before she could answer, Billy Jack called again. "Hey, Penny!"

"I best git," Jeff said. He scrambled up, grabbed his overalls and shoes, and ran across the pasture, barefooted and naked. He reached the trees before Billy Jack reached the barn.

Chapter 3

On the hillside above a swamp on Cunningham's land, his Buick eased down a long-abandoned road, stopped in the clearing beside a crumbling chimney, and closed its eyes to the night. Moonlight shadows moved with the night wind to show a house as half decay, half more-recent but abandoned construction.

Crickets chirped; a fox trotted across the meadow, his red coat almost orange in the light. As a rabbit darted from the underbrush the fox leaped after him.

"Oh, Charley, look!" Karen Emerson said and clutched his arm with one hand while she pointed the other after the disappearing animals.

"He won't be able to catch the little critter," he said and slid his arm around her shoulder. "Why don't you show me some of that concern?" He kissed her lightly on the cheek and kept his lips only inches from her face as he lifted his free hand to turn her chin toward him.

She relaxed and turned her body toward his, let herself be pulled almost into his lap so that she lay in his arms and leaned her back against the steering wheel. She kicked off her shoes and propped her feet against the door. Hands behind his neck, she watched Charley lean forward to brush her lips with his. She lay against his left arm while his right hand roamed over her body, found her waist and pulled her blouse free from her skirt. His hand teased up inside her clothing to her breast. She trembled against him as his hand touched bare flesh. His sudden erection throbbed against her belly.

The hand moved down, down to her skirt, pulled it up, and moved between her legs. His tongue probed, pushed, insisted. She became aware only of his hand as it moved up her thighs to her underpants, and then up and over the elastic and down, down and then up and into her.

Headlights slashed through the night, cut by the trunks of trees, and flashed across their faces. As his hand pulled out, she gasped disappointment.

"Better button your blouse," Charley whispered and pulled her up. His voice scratched with anger. He reached into his pocked for his handkerchief and began to wipe his hand.

Two cars pulled up and stopped. One set of headlights cut off, but the front one stayed on. When footsteps crunched alongside the car and a flashlight blinded them, they were fully dressed and sitting quietly, holding hands and sharing a cigarette. Neither of the young people spoke.

"Oh, it's you, Miss Emerson. Don't you know you young people shouldn't be out here like this? It's not safe."

She cocked her head, smiled sweetly, and asked, "And why isn't it safe, Sheriff? Don't our law officers keep the county safe any more?"

"Clear them out!" a gruff voice said impatiently from the direction of the other car.

"Okay, Charley, take her home," the sheriff ordered.

"Why?" Karen demanded, and as Charley's hand reached for the ignition, she snatched the keys away. "Why should we let you tell us we can't stay on his daddy's land? Besides, you can't even be here legally yourself unless you're enforcing the law or some such."

"Why the hell do you think I'm out here at this time of night? Not just to run some brats like you home for my health. We're running you home for your own sake."

"Oh, hush. We can get that kind of lecture at home. We're big enough to know what we're doing." She glared at him a moment but turned her smile on again and asked, "Do you know what you're doing out here?"

"We're after moonshiners. Now give Charley the keys and y'all go on home."

Charley held out his hand for the keys but, still smiling, Karen dropped them down the front of her blouse and patted herself to show they were secure inside her bra.

"We're going with you," she said to the sheriff. To Charley she said, "Come on," and slipped her hand into his again. She tugged him after her as she slid across to the door. If she let Charley drive to another isolated road tonight she would become shamelessly aggressive.

"Now just a minute, young lady!" The impatient voice halted her as the other man appeared beside her. "Just where do you think you're going?"

"With you," she said. Her tone implied he must be simple-minded to believe otherwise. She stepped out of the car.

"You think you can wander through that swamp and come out in one piece?" He laughed as his eyes roved slowly down to her two-inch heels and back to her tight blouse. His face showed frank appreciation. "Someone like you has got no business running around a swamp." He looked at Charley. "Unless—"

"That's enough, Jake!" the sheriff said. "This here is Judge Emerson's kid. And he's Cunningham's boy."

"That so?" Jake mused soberly. "Then they better hightail it back to town. We got work to do."

"You also have company," she said.

Jake turned, hands on hips, disgust on his face. "Look here, Miss. You're both society kids out on the edge of a swamp in the middle of the night. Don't make things worse for yourselves. Anybody can look at you two and know what's going on. Just get in your car and go. Go to another swamp if that's what you want, but go, and be quiet and quick about it."

"You're going after a still, aren't you? And since you're not a local man, who are you? State or Federal?"

"GBI. And yes, we're going after a still and are not about to wet nurse you two. It took me long enough to locate this one, and I don't want any trouble from either of you." He wagged a finger at them.

"We won't be any trouble, mister. Will we, Charley?"

"No, because we're leaving," Charley said.

"Go ahead if you want to. I'm going with them."

Charley's tone showed his frustration at being interrupted when he was getting what he wanted from Karen, and anger at Karen's not wanting to leave with him.   "Then go ahead, act like a fool. Just give me back those keys and you can walk home!"

She laughed, the sound floating like dry leaves through a windless air. "If you want them, take them!"

Glowering, he reached for her, but she danced lightly away, and the sheriff stepped between them.

"None of this squabbling, kids." He spoke harshly as he gripped Charley's arm. "And keep your voices down. They're less'n a half-mile from here, and we don't want to scare them off."

"Nobody's going to scare them away." Karen tossed her head. "Unless, of course, we have to get back in the car. I think it would be most fun to sound your battle cry for you. Which would you prefer, a steady blast or a lot of short ones? We can always play 'shave and a haircut, two bits'. Can't we, Charley?"

Jake spun her around roughly by the arm. "Just what do you mean by that crack?"

"That unless we go with you, I'll make enough noise to raise the dead—and scare off your precious bootleggers."

"If your dad was here—"

" 'Were here.' 'If my dad were here,' not 'was.' But he's not, so let's go." She smirked.

"Looks like they've got us over a barrel," the sheriff said.

"They'll never make it through the swamp. Not in those clothes. She'll start to whimper as soon as she gets a good snag from a briar." Jake smirked back.

"We'll see. Let's go." Karen grinned.

"What about it, Charley?" the sheriff asked. "You gonna talk her out of this? Your dad won't like it at all."

"If she wants to go, hell and high water—" Charley shook his head.

"Who's that coming?" Jake interrupted as headlights moved shadows rapidly across them.

As the lights went out, their absence left the group night-blinded. When their eyes adjusted they saw Alexander Perry striding forward.

"Hello, Dixon," Perry greeted the sheriff. "Looks like you've got yourself a handful."

"Alex! How did you find out about this? We thought we'd kept this still raid pretty quiet. Jake didn't even tell me until he was ready to come out here."

"I've been chasing my rustling friends all day. When I saw your tracks coming in, I thought I'd finally caught up with them. Instead, I get to help raid a still."

"Looks like we've already got plenty of help," Jake jerked his thumb toward the couple.

"You mean something you've got to help." Perry's grin broadened into laughter.

The lawmen laughed. Sheriff Dixon's smile faded.

"Maybe we oughtta forget it tonight. They're going to be nothing but trouble."

"Forget it, hell!" Jake was adamant. "I found this thing today, and the mash was ready. They're bound to be running it tonight—and this is the biggest still I've found in the county. We're going in, and if these young fools want trouble, they can have it."

"You sound pretty determined," Perry said.

"I sure as hell am," Jake replied. He lowered his voice so that the young people could not hear him. "And no politician's brat is going to change my mind. Her father's going to hear about this."

They squatted beside the drive while Jake sketched a crude map of the swamp. "There're two ways in, this road, and a cow path—"

Minutes later, their plans made, the three men drew straws to decide who would escort the young people through the swamp, and Perry won their company.

"Lucky for us you came along," Jake grinned.

"You two stay with him," Sheriff Dixon told Karen.

"What do you mean, 'stay with him'?" Karen demanded.

"I mean that two of us are going around the swamp to come in on the other side. If the bootleggers are down there we'll flush them out. Just you remember, if there is any shooting, keep low. I won't take responsibility for either of you. You get hurt, remember you asked for it. Far as I care, you're just two civilians in the woods in the middle of the night. I'll tell everybody we didn't even know you were here. You got that?"

The two men left and the shadows swallowed them soundlessly.

"Is this just a trick to keep us from going?" Karen glared at Perry, her hands on her hips, her eyes squinted.

He shook his head and explained. "No. We're to give them half an hour to get around the swamp. We'll start in then, seeing as it'll take us all another half-hour to get close to the still. Chances are the moonshiners will head out along either this path or the one the sheriff is on, depending on who gets there first. And we'll catch them between us."

"Why won't they just run off through the swamp?" Karen asked.

"You'll see when we start down that path," Perry replied. He lay flat on his back and watched the stars.

They stood by the car to wait. The moon splashed white through the trees. Crickets chirped to the night, and nearby a chuck-will's-widow sang its mournful love song to the un-answering night. Something moved through the brush so softly it barely rustled hardwood leaves.

"What's that noise?" Karen asked, stepping closer to Charley.

"Probably a fox or a coon. Be glad it's not rabid or it'd be coming for you," Perry answered without moving his hands from beneath his neck.

Karen tugged Charley toward the car.

"Let's wait inside," she said.

*   *   *

Karen saw Perry rise and start to walk away. She quickly opened the door and scampered out.

"Not going off without us, are you?" she asked.

Perry stopped, turned, and waited.

"Coming?" Karen turned to Charley.

Defeated, Charley shrugged and got out of the car.

Moonlight penetrated enough through the thick branches overhead to deepen shadows and show the vague outlines of a path. Karen immediately saw why the bootleggers wouldn't run off through the swamp. The path ran a low ridge, but water spread on both sides. Hummocks of saplings and tall trees, with vines running up and briars beneath, interrupted the water. Karen imagined moccasins slithering through the darkness and moved closer to Perry and his flashlight.

Perry led them for almost half an hour before he ordered them to silence. "It's not far now, so for God's sake, be quiet. One sound of people and they'll run like rabbits. See that light?" He pointed to a scarcely visible flicker. "They're probably in the middle of a run. You two should stay here. It could be dangerous."

"That's exactly why we came!" Karen whispered. "Let's go. I've never seen a real still. I don't want to have to fall down and yell or something." She wasn't about to tell him her feet hurt and her legs throbbed from the long rough walk.

Perry shook his head. Either the judge had been too busy with other people's children to bother about his own or had worried too much over her.

"Okay, let's go." He blew out a deep breath. "Walk slow, and keep it quiet."

When they reached the edge of the man-made clearing, Perry pointed to a depression and whispered, "Gulley. Get down there and stay low. You can see everything from there." Perry watched them for a moment and then turned his full attention to the still.

He counted four one-hundred-gallon barrels of mash and could not suppress a soft whistle of surprise. Two men sat against the stump of one of the trees that they had cut down for firewood. Perry knew that this was more than a two-man still. It had to have backing and a lot of it. No wonder Jake had been so determined.

A spotted hound dozed beside the men, and Perry recognized it as the same dog that he had seen at Noah's still. One of the men rose, and as he moved into the firelight Perry recognized Amos, Noah's son—no wonder the dog was there. The Negro boy ambled to the creek, removed a five-gallon jug from under the end of the tubing and replaced it, his movements so quick he lost only a few drops of the precious white gold.

"Dat makes fourteen, Mista Billy Jack," the boy told his companion as he placed the filled jug with others.

Perry grinned and had to suppress a whoop. This was the Carter still, and if he couldn't catch them rustling cattle, the still would sure do for now. But where did the money come from? And the sugar? In his attempts to pinpoint the still owners, he had checked every source of sugar in three counties, but the Carters never bought enough for anything more than home use.

The dog suddenly leaped up and, barking, ran toward the path where Sheriff Dixon and Jake should be. Perry groaned, but the sound went unheard as the two boys ran directly toward him. Pistol in hand, Perry stepped into the clearing.

Without breaking stride the Negro swerved to his left, toward the gulley. "Stop or I'll shoot!" Perry warned.

Billy Jack skidded to a halt but the Negro never hesitated. Perry fired a warning shot, and the youth leaped into the air with legs pumping as he tried to jump the gulley.

An arm shot up, grabbed the leg, and pulled him down. The sounds of a scuffle ended with a dull thud and the white couple climbed the low bank. Charley dragged the limp form of the Negro into the meadow as Jake and Sheriff Dixon trotted forward.

The dog had quit barking and now tried to sniff everyone as he pushed his nose into each man's crotch. Dixon kicked it in the side and it yelped and ran off into the darkness.

"You shouldn't have hit the nigger so hard," Charley said.

"I had to," Karen said. "When he pulled that razor, I just had to—" Her voice drifted off. She trembled, and her face showed stark white in the shadows.

Jake knelt beside the limp form and said, "He'll be okay. What happened?"

"He pulled a razor and Karen let him have it with her shoe."

The sheriff nudged the boy with his toe. "Oh, leave him be!" Billy Jack blurted out. "It ain't the nigger's fault if some big shot boy tried to act like a hero. Any goddamned nigger in Georgia would-a done the same thing."

"You shut up, Carter. Save your talking for the judge. And you better be glad nobody was hurt or you'd be tried for the same thing—attempted murder!" The sheriff's face was red with hate and embarrassment. Cunningham paid him not to raid the Carter still.

Karen freed herself from Charley's arms and dashed to Perry. "Please, you can't let Dad know about this! He'll kill me!"

Perry's eyes smiled but his face remained stern. "You'll have to testify. After all, you're the only witness that the nigger tried to slash Charley. The judge will have to know."

Charley said, "I don't think you can blame the nigger. After all, he was weaned on a razor and when he saw danger, he reached for it without thinking. They all do. You men know that."

Perry asked, "Do you think we can forget it, Jake? This is your baby."

"Oh, stop it!" Billy Jack spat at the sheriff's feet. "You men make me sick. You'd fergit it iffen Charley had kilt the nigger. You'd even fergit they been down heah and call me a liar iffen I said they were."

Dixon's fist flashed into his face.

"Another word out of you—" Dixon did not finish; he did not need to.

The boy groaned, and Perry turned to Charley.

"If you two want to see a still, better go look now. It won't be here much longer."

Karen grabbed Charley's arm and led him toward the creek to explore the layout of the still, to taste the gushing stream of liquid, and to poke her fingers into the barrels of mash.

The youth sat up, his eyes pools of white in a black face. Blood oozed down the side of his head.

"I's sorry, boss," he muttered. "I didn't go to do no harm."

"The young man has decided not to prosecute you for attempted murder if you help us out here," Jake said. There was a long pause before the full impact of the words hit the youth. He began to tremble and tears rolled down his face unchecked.

"Who's behind this?" Jake demanded. "Who's been keeping you supplied and selling the liquor?"

The black face turned from man to man and finally came to rest on Billy Jack. The Carter boy shook his head.

"You ain't gotta tell 'em nothing. They ain't gonna do nothing to us cause that gal is heah and she's the judge's kid. They don't want him to know they let her come down heah. Jest you keep your—." The blow was expected, but it sent Billy Jack reeling to his knees and drew blood. He remained silent.

"I asked you, boy, who's in charge of this still?" Jake repeated.

"Ain't nobody but us been heah," he answered; his eyes shifted from Jake to Billy Jack, who was scrambling to his feet.

"I didn't ask you who had been here. I want to know who's been helping you. Where do you take the liquor? You'd never sell that much to a few friends," Jake said.

"We jest sells it to some folks us knows and dranks the rest."

"Not that much, you don't, boy." Perry stepped forward. "It'll be a lot easier for you if you tell us."

The white eyes rolled from Jake to Billy Jack to Charley and back again. "Deah ain't nothing to tell."

Jake Wilson continued to probe. "I'd hate to see a boy your age go to jail for trying to kill a white boy."

"Please, suh, don't. I kain't tell you nothing." The boy began to cry again. "I kain't tell you nothing, suh."

"Either you talk or you go to jail. You understand that, don't you?" Jake asked.

"Yassuh, I knows hit. But I kain't tell you, suh. Iffen I do, Mista Cu—."

"Shut up, boy!" Billy Jack shouted and ducked the sheriff's next swing. "Y'all trying to get that boy kilt?"

"That's enough!" Perry cut in, his hand on the sheriff's arm. "He's right. We could get him into a lot of trouble."

He jerked his head toward the forms bent over a mash barrel. Jake and Dixon followed his gaze, and both nodded.

"Let's finish up and get out of here," Jake said. "You two can help us out by chopping up everything. You do have axes don't you?"

"Yassuh, we's got some."

"Then get one and start chopping. Every barrel and that pot too."

The prisoners obeyed. They overturned the mash barrels and hacked the slatted wood until the mash ran across the clearing. By the time they left, mash, barrel staves, fresh whiskey, broken jugs, and smashed metal covered the ground.

In single file, the prisoners alternated between them and the young couple bringing up the rear, the group walked out of the swamp along the road used to carry supplies in and the whiskey out.

Chapter 4: The Next Day

Virgil pulled open the screen door and walked into the county jail office. He had to squint to see in the unlit semidarkness of the closed-up room after leaving the bright summer sunlight. The brick building was no cooler than the outside, and sweat trickled down his back and saturated his shirt at his armpits.

Sheriff Dixon slept in a straight chair leaned back against the wall, with his feet on the desk and hands folded across his slightly protruding belly. He snored.

Virgil reopened the screen door and it slammed it to. Dixon jerked awake and dropped his feet to the floor.

"Whatcha want?" Dixon asked as he began to focus.

Virgil wrinkled his nose at the smell of the slop jar which floated in the air from the hallway behind the office. With the heat closed up in the brick building, the stench started him coughing. He took off his hat and placed it on the desk.

"Virgil. You're mighty dressed up today," Dixon greeted him.

"I've had a visit with the judge. I came to get BJ out."

"You done put up his bail?"

"Yep. You ever empty that slop jar? Smells like it's been full a week."

"I was gonna let BJ tote it out this afternoon. Now you going to get him out and I'll have to do it." Dixon shook his head. "You got the papers?"

Virgil took the papers from inside his coat pocket and handed them to Dixon. His entire body felt damp. He shucked out of his coat, looked for a coat rack, and then hung it over the back of a chair. With the handkerchief he pulled from his back pocket, he swabbed the sweat from his face. The handkerchief was already soaked. It was too hot to do anything but sit in the shade and fish. Too hot to politic, but he had to get BJ out of here and then go talk to people. And never mind the heat if he wanted to beat Cunningham.

After studying the papers a moment, Dixon rose and picked up his keys. "C'mon."

"I need to talk to him a minute before you turn him out."

"He's not taking this seriously a-tall. To him it's all a big game."

"I gotta make him realize it's serious."

They entered the cell block, which consisted of three cells. BJ rose from the bunk in the middle one as they approached.

"Hey, little brother," Virgil said. He gripped one of the cell bars, the steel as smooth to his palm as the handle of a plow that had been smoothed by months of wobbling in human hands. The warmth of the steel flashed across his mind as not what he had expected a jail cell to feel like.

"You sure got yourself a peck of trouble. I thought you knew better than to try to make whiskey." He winked at his brother.

The smell of the slop jar almost overpowered him. He glanced at Sheriff Dixon, who leaned against the wall nearby, his attention on his fingernails as he cleaned them with the small blade of his pocket knife. But, like Virgil, he wrinkled his nose at the odor.

"Hey, Virgil. I didn't figger you'd be coming by, seeing as how you're gitting to be a big mucky-de-muck." BJ looked over at Dixon. "Hey, Sheriff, you gonna let me talk to my brother or you gonna stand there and listen?"

Dixon shrugged and walked out, but left the door open between his office and the hall. When a strong breeze puffed between the window bars, it pushed aside the slop jar odors to bring in the smell of coffee and frying pork from the diner across the street.

"Wish you could-a brought me some of that-air bacon I smell from Libby's Diner," BJ said. "It shore do make me hungry, smelling most as good as Ma's cooking."

"I'm getting you out, BJ. And you gotta stay away from the still, you hear me? Everybody's gotta stay away till we find a way to handle Perry and that Jake Wilson. Ma put up all she's got to bail you out."

"Ma? Where'd Ma git any money?"

"It's Bobby's. Money he sent home from the war. She held onto it. Judge Emerson set your bail at five-hundred dollars. Didn't cost Noah's boy but fifty dollars for his bail. You promise me you ain't gonna do nothing stupid, like try to run off outta town? You run off and cost Ma her money, I'll find you and whup you good. This here's all the money Ma's got that hers. I might have only one arm, but I mean it, BJ."

Virgil's voice was flat and firm, unlike the happy brother BJ remembered following to the fishing holes. He's changed a lot what with the war and now getting into politics.

"I ain't about to run off. I promise. You really gitting me outta-here?"

"Yes. Hey, Sheriff. You come open the door now?"

Dixon sauntered back, a toothpick between his lips, his eyes focused on the ring of keys in one hand that he was sorting through with the other. He poked one key into the lock on the cell door and turned it, but held the door to while he spoke.

"I reckon Virgil told you if you try to run off, it'll cost all the money your ma put up to git you out. You understand? Her money says you'll be here when your trial comes up."

BJ nodded. "I ain't running off nowhere, Sheriff. Where'd I go to anyhow? This here's home."

As Dixon pulled the cell door open, BJ grabbed up his shoes and shoved by Dixon. He grinned at Virgil.

"You got me a ride home?"

"Let's go, brother," Virgil said, and BJ followed him to Dr. Jacobs' car.

Chapter 5: Two Days Later

Jack drove the pickup slowly down the twisting rutted road. Pine limbs screeched against the faded paint and lashed into the windows. The three Carters jostled against each other, and the truck groaned in dismay at the bumps. Jack skillfully dodged the larger rocks and straddled the wheels over the deeper ruts cut by years of wagon wheels. When they reached a meadow, he drove across it, passed the abandoned church, and parked behind a thicket of young pines so the truck would be hidden from anyone chancing into the meadow.

"We're early," Jack said. He opened his door, turned sideways, rested his feet on the running board, and leaned his elbows on his knees while he rolled a cigarette.

"Reckon whatever happened to the voodoo woman who scared off the preacher from here?" BJ asked to his father's back.

"I dunno. She's gone from around here. Maybe dead. Ain't heard tell of her in a spell."

Hiram climbed out. BJ came after him, reached behind the seat and pulled a brown-and-white crockery jug from a pile of croaker sacks. He pulled the stopper with a loud "thunck."

"Go easy on that, son," Jack said.

The only answer was a loud chuckle from Hiram as his lasso fell cleanly over a headstone in the graveyard.

"Hiram, you put that rope in the truck," Jack said.

"Aw, Pa."

"Go on. Put it away. We ain't outchere to play."

"Okay, Pa." Hiram rolled up the lasso and shoved it behind the seat.

Half an hour passed. The sun dropped behind the rim of trees and threw scarlet under the edge of the western clouds. From the swamp below them a chuck-will's-widow called to darkness as the sun dragged its colors down and left only purple clouds that darkened to black. The moon whispered light across the woods as it rose.

Even Hiram fell under the spell of twilight and sat on the tailgate to listen intently to the aching call of the chuck-will's-widow and the chirp of crickets. The deep-throated bellow of frogs drifted from the stream flowing from the spring on the west side of the church.

A quiet rustle of the underbrush pulled their attention to the woods beyond the cemetery. A white man carrying a shotgun stepped into view; a Negro stood behind him.

"'Lo, Gus, Frank." Jack nodded to them. His boys joined them, and Billy Jack began the ritual with the jug. It passed from man to man as they talked. No one passed it to Frank.

Gus wiped the back of his hand across the thick growth of beard in an attempt to clean off the dripping alcohol. But days of drippings from food, tobacco, and alcohol had stained it a motley brown.

"You oughtta set up your own still, like I done told you afore. Get shed of Cunningham. He gits all the money and you-uns takes all the chances."

Jack held up his hand and shook his head. "We done been through that, Gus. Reckon as long as Cunningham'll keep the sheriff offer our tail, we'll keep on running it for him."

"Well, he ain't keeping that GBI man off-a you, nor that Perry man neither."

"I ain't gonna have to pay nothing. Old Mr. Cunningham'll come through and pay my fine." BJ's tone implied he already had the promise.

In the pause that followed, Gus only shrugged at the foolishness of his kin.

"Frank, we gonna butcher." Jack said. "They's too many folks watching the sale yards nowadays for us to try to sell them bulls in Macon. I got a butcher shop set to buy all the hindquarters, loin and straps we kin bring in."

Frank's teeth flashed white as he smiled, "Yore cows, Mista Jack? Or is we gonna git us some cows?"

Billy Jack answered the smile. "We is gonna us some cows. All we got to do is catch 'em and cut 'em up."

"You shore nuff got yoself de right man. I kin butcher any cow hereabouts."

"Even Doc's?" Jack asked, his voice soft.

"I done butchered my share of his cows, Mista Jack. I de one what pulled down de shed dat time, and he don't know to dis day who done it. Got myself a nice fat yearling, but had to leave half of it right deah cause I didn't have no way to tote hit all home."

In the silence that followed the jug passed around again. This time,

Jack handed it to Frank. He had committed himself to them. Dusty sleeves wiped across the mouth of the jar before white or black lips closed over it.

"Somebody's coming," Jack whispered before the jug completed its circuit. "Put out that cigarette, BJ."

They listened. Leaves rustled. The sound confused the men, who at one moment thought they heard a human and then thought they heard a slow-moving four-footed animal.

Jack thumbed everybody off the driveway and they followed their shadows into the darkness.

Two figures came into view down the old road. A sparking couple, Jack saw, probably headed for the privacy of the abandoned church. Jack looked from them to the truck, tucked his lips in, grateful that long habit forced him to hide it.

Shadows dancing around the couple hid their faces, but the man's long, easy, swinging stride was the strut of a man who knew he had a willing woman on his arm. They stepped into a patch of moonlight; light hair showed beside an ebony face, and they were in shadows again.

"A goddamn nigger with a white girl!" Billy Jack said, his hand a vice on Jack's arm.

"Quiet!" Jack's whisper was as violent as the oath.

"But she's with a nigger!"

"We ain't got no truck with jest any ole nigger what kin git himself some white trash girl," Jack replied.

"I'll kill 'em!" Hiram rose, only to be snatched back by his father.

"You ain't gonna do no such thing boy. Now you jest—"

Crackling underbrush jerked the Carter's attention and they turned, to see Frank running for the thickets. Billy Jack laughed harshly.

"That's one nigger that ain't gonna give us no trouble."

"Ain't that Penny with the nigger, Jack?" Gus whispered, but his words fell like a shout.

Jack glared at his brother before he turned back toward the couple, but they had disappeared into the church. He shook his head.

"Naw, that couldn't be Penny. Sure looked like it might be, with that light hair and all, but she don't know no niggers."

"You always tell me I fergits things," Hiram said. "Has you done fergot she knows Jeff?"

Jack smiled. "That boy? He don't even know he's a man yet."

"Come off it, Pa!" Billy Jack's laugh was without humor. "Liza's been putting me off a long time, and she's done been with him. She's having his baby a-fore too long now. 'Sides that, he done been in the war."

"Yeah. They say them foreign women folks like our soljers, even iffen they is black. And sump-em else. I hear tell Jeff been going round bragging bout having a white gal. My old woman may be a nigger, but she ain't no liar," Gus said.

* * *

Penny clutched Jeff's hand, her eyes wide with curiosity and fear, as they neared the church. She pulled him to a stop and leaned against an oak for a moment, as she remembered the times she had tagged behind Virgil and Charley when they came over to explore the church.

They had always come here in daylight. Even then, it seemed haunted, with the graveyard all around the building, the tall pines shading every side, the massive oak out front that Charley said was a hanging oak that the white folks had once used to hang uppity niggers. Limbs had raked the sides of the building with the breeze. Squirrels had scampered over the tin roof where their nails scratched like somebody trying to get out of a coffin.

Years ago, Virgil and Charley had climbed up to the open beams overhead and hung down a plowline to make her a swing. Charley had taken a board off the outside wall, notched each end, and fitted it into the rope.

Charley had pushed her in that swing until she had risen almost to the rafters, and their laughter had filled the building and floated outside on the summer wind. She remembered the smells of dust, bitterweed, and crepe myrtle, remembered the spider webs that hung like lace in the corners and from the ends of the rafters, remembered the smell of the bat droppings on the floor near the west window that now was closed up with boards.

Charley had told ghost stories that made her shiver and brought laughter from Virgil. From the old church, they had gone down the hill to the stream where the boys fished and she lay on the mossy bank to listen to them chatter.

She could almost smell the fish they had cooked in clay packs that afternoon beside the creek, could almost see the crayfish flip their tails and dart under the banks when, at Charley's insistence, she leaned over to look.

She had not been back here since that afternoon they had played until dusk. A barn owl had perched on the peak of the roof and screamed like a woman being killed. Charley told her painters did that, screamed like a dying woman, to get the man of the family to come rescue her. When the man came out of his house, the wildcat would kill him.

She wondered if the swing were still inside.

"Les go," she said. "It ain't got no haints."

Hand in hand, they went inside. Moonlight filtered between the boards across the windows just enough to show heavy cobwebs and thick dust and to create a haunted atmosphere. Seven pews remained. The altar lay on its side. The swing still dangled from an overhead beam.

Jeff pulled his shoulders back. "I hear tell hit do got haints."

"Ain't you scared?" Penny asked. She moved closer to him.

Scattered clouds scuttled across the moon, and a light wind dancing through the cobwebs threw shadows as heavy as the dust.

Jeff lifted his chin. "Naw, course I ain't scared. I don't believe in haints or conjures."

"I hear tell this-here church got conjured." Penny shivered involuntarily.

"Dey say de preacher what come from Detroit hexed hit cause his wife died right-chere in the middle of his sermon. Some folks say de voodoo woman hexed hit. Niggers don't come here no moah. Don't nobody come heah no moah. When de preacher cussed it is when we stopped having our meetings heah and built us de new church over to de river."

Jeff smiled down at her. No hex could bother them tonight. This would be better than in the barn when they had to listen out for her cousins.

Penny shuddered as if to shake off the cold clammy hand of a ghost, but her mind could not escape the memories.

"Me and my cousins used-ta come up here and play some, it being so close to the house. I was always scairt to walk on a grave out there, scairt the ghosts'd come up outta the ground and git me."

"You think haints be in here?"

"No. We used-ta play like it, but that was a long time ago. Iffen there was haints here, we'd of seen something of 'em back then. I remember when old Ida Bell conjured your Lucy Bee. Gawd, but that was awful scary!"

She remembered the spring night shattered by the unending beat of a stick on an oil drum. She had gone with Virgil and Charley when they heard the voodoo drum, gone with them across the woods to the old Richardson place where Ida Bell lived. All the white folks said she was crazy, but the niggers said she was voodoo and were scared of her.

The three of them had come up on Ida Bell's house and hid in the bushes to watch. Her front yard was like everybody's, bare dirt that she had raked with her yard broom. Only she raked hers into a pattern, into circles, two matching circles. A big oil drum, taller than Penny, sat in the middle of one circle; a low fire burned in the middle of the other. Half-way between the two lay an oak log about two feet across, its bark stained brown. While they watched, Ida Bell laid out a chicken, chopped off its head, and chanted, sang, and danced around the fire, all the while shaking the chicken's blood into the fire.

Stronger than the smell of the fresh chicken blood, an odor she was used to from all the ones she'd cleaned for supper, was the chokingly sweet smell of a gardenia bush that bloomed beside the house. That smell rose in her memories.

As did the words the voodoo woman had spoken in a rhythm that seemed to pulse with her heartbeat, not only in the past but now also. Only two words made sense, the name Lucy Bee, who lived down the road on the other side of the Jacobs place. Later Charley told her it was all African words and the conjure woman hexed Lucy Bee that night.

When the chicken had quit bleeding, she had laid it out on the oak log, used the thin long-bladed knife to open its hind end, and drew out its entrails, which she carefully spread out on the log.

The conjure woman sat down on the ground, crossed her legs Indian fashion, and began to poke and shove at the chicken parts. She would lift up both hands, shake them quickly and chant, and then bend over the entrails again.

When Virgil sneezed, the voodoo woman leaped to her feet and ran in their direction. The three of them fled.

The childhood fear swept over her and pushed her into the warmth of Jeff's arms, which he wrapped around her. Only the night sounds of crickets came into the building.

"You scairt?" Penny asked. "You wanna leave here?"

"Ain't nowhere I wanna be cept-in with you. Dat's nuff talk bout haints, honey. You come heah to me."

He grinned down at her, twined his fingers into her hair, and pulled her head back. Her lips parted eagerly under the pressure of his, and she pulled herself closer to his hard frame.

His fingers found her dress, unbuttoned it, and closed over her breast. She moaned her pleasure and unsnapped his overalls straps as her dress fell to the floor. She jerked the straps back and down with such force that she pulled him off balance. He fell, and Penny went down with him and sprawled over him. Laughter filled the night.

"Guess that's one way to lay down," she giggled, wiggled herself firmly atop him, and propped her forearms on his shoulders.

"But I's supposed to be on top," Jeff grinned and slid his hands up her legs to grip her buttocks. He turned her onto her back and eased his legs between hers. His tongue probed her mouth and they made love.

Love and time stopped as a bellow rang against the church, echoed from the rafters, shook the cobwebs, and separated the lovers.

"Haints!" Jeff leaped up, stumbled and fell flat as his feet tangled in his overalls.

"That's Hiram!" Penny rolled into a crouch as Jeff struggled to untangle himself.

"Oh, Gawd, Penny. We got troubles."

Naked, she ran to the door, threw her weight against it, and slipped the crude locking bar into place. She felt the door tremble beneath the force of one of her cousins.

"They done locked it!" Billy Jack shouted.

"Billy Jack? You heah me?" Penny yelled.

"I heah you."

"Y'all go on off. This-here ain't none-a your affair!"

Jack answered her. "It's any man's affair if a white gal ain't got no better sense than to fool around with a nigger! Ain't no white man living'd let you do it. Now you open this heah door!" Although he was shouting, his voice carried no anger, only firmness and determination.

"No! I mean it, Uncle Jack. Y'all go on off, all-a-y'all!"

"You going to open this heah door?"

Jeff's arms tightened around Penny in the second before she answered. "No!"

"Git this door down." Jack's voice had dropped, but she could hear him ordering the others.

The building trembled as the Carters' combined weight lunged against the door.

"Git out a winder," Penny hissed at Jeff and pointed to one.

Jeff ran, but as he pulled at the boards covering a window, the door collapsed. The four Carter men plunged into the thick shadows, half-falling, half-running into the room. Gus fired his shotgun toward Jeff, and Jeff collapsed onto the floor, blood running from his leg.

He tried to crawl, but Gus ran to him and poked the shotgun barrel into his face. He rolled onto his side, clutched his injured leg, and then lay still except to rock with the pain.

"Don't move, nigger," Gus said.

"Git outta heah!" Still naked, Penny screamed, her fists clenched at her sides, her eyes narrowed with fury. "You ain't my pa. You got no say so over me."

Jack glared back, his eyes flicking over her nakedness before his palm slapped against her face. "You bitch!" He shoved her towards Billy Jack and ordered, "Keep her out of the way!"

Billy Jack grinned at Penny as she fought him. With a hand wrapped around each of her wrists, he had no trouble holding her. His eyes feasted on the ripeness of her body. Her breasts swung back and forth as she struggled.

"You might's well git still cause you ain't going nowhere," he told her.

Gus stood quietly beside the fallen Jeff, his shotgun in both hands still pointed down, his eyes, however, turned toward Billy Jack and Penny.

Jack reached down, rolled Jeff onto his back, and kicked him between the legs.

Jeff screamed as the pain racked through him. "Oh Lawd, Jesus."

"Gawddamn bastard. You best pray you die fast."

Jeff rocked with the pain and clutched his bruised genitals; he squeezed his eyes shut, as if Jack would disappear if he couldn't be seen; tears coursed down the creases of grief. He would die. Slowly.

Jack swung his booted foot hard into his groin again. "Jesus ain't gonna save no nigger, nigger. Jesus was a white man!"

Hiram hollered, "We gonna do the saving. We's gonna save Penny." His foot followed Jack's, to strike Jeff's clutched hands.

Penny wrenched both arms downward, into BJ's thumbs, and broke his hold. She ran toward Jeff.

"Save me? You gonna save me from what? You too late. You're all too late."

Jack grabbed her shoulders and shook her hard.

"What do you mean? You ain't saying—?" He pointed at Jeff. "You ain't saying you let him—? Did he rape you? Did he?" Jack shouted.

Tears streaming down her face spattered him as he shook her. Her words were almost choked from her.

"No. Oh no, Jack, no! He didn't have to!"

"You goddamn slut!" Jack's fist slammed into her face. Without waiting to see her crumple to the floor he spun toward Jeff and kicked him again. "Git up, goddamn you!"

Jeff crawled to his knees and backed away on all fours, but did not try to get to his feet. He continued to look at the floor.

"Please, Mista Jack, lemme go! I ain't done nothing you ain't done did." Lids closed over reddened eyes.

"Drag that-air black bastard outta here!" Jack spat on Jeff. The spittle hit him on his cheek and ran down his face.

"Hiram, skinny up there and git down that-air swing rope."

Hiram climbed the rope, straddled the beam, cut both rope ends free, draped it over the beam, and slid down the rope. He then pulled one end, and when the rope fell, he handed it to his father.

"You stay heah with Penny," Jack said.

"Aww, Pa, I wanna go with you," the boy pleaded. "It ain't fair to make me miss the fun all-a the time."

"You heard me!" Jack's finger shook under Hiram's startled eyes. "You stay heah and you keep her heah. You hear me, boy?"

Slowly, Hiram nodded.

"It ain't gonna be pretty out there, so don't you let her come atter us. You hear me, Hiram?" His voice turned gentle. "No matter what she says or does, you keep her heah till I come back. You let her leave, and I'll beat hell outta you."

"But how come Billy Jack always—?"

Jack slashed the rope across his son's face, raising welts.

"I said you stay heah!" In the same motion he turned to Billy Jack, nodded to Gus, and said, "Grab aholt-a his laigs and les go."

Hiram moved a few steps after them as they dragged Jeff toward the door, then stopped, turned, and went to sit beside Penny, who still lay on her side, unconscious.

A few minutes later Penny opened her eyes, turned over, and tried to sit up. The side of her head hurt, and when she raised her hand to her cheek, she felt the swelling. When her eyes focused on Hiram, she seized his arm.

"Where are they?" Her voice was hoarse with fear. She struggled upward, winced as pain coursed through her head, and stood up. She leaned on Hiram's shoulder.

"Now, Penny," Hiram rose with her, "ain't no need for you to worry about nothing. Pa said for you to stay heah. He's gonna do what he gotta do."

She shook her head slowly and then dashed for the door, but Hiram was faster and grabbed her arm.

"I be sorry, Penny. I kain't letcha go out there. Pa said he'd beat me." His grip was soft, gentle, a boy holding onto someone he loved, someone he wanted to save from whatever was going on outside.

But Penny plunged toward the door again. There was no gentleness in Hiram's large hands this time. He spun her against the wall, a hand on each shoulder, and shook his head.

"I said I be sorry, Pen. I ain't gonna hurt you none, but you gotta stay heah. Pa done said so."

She struggled in his grip, used both her hands to pull against one of his, but his hands were like vices.

"It ain't no use. You ain't going nowhere." He shook his head. "I ain't wanting to hurt you none."

"But they'll kill him!"

"Shore. They gotta kill him." His voice was calm, disappointment the only emotion. "I'd kill 'im too, but Pa made me stay heah with you. I'd kill any goddamn nigger what laid a hand on a white girl."

She lunged forward again. "But you'd crawl in the hay with any nigger yourself!"

"I ain't never! 'Sides, it ain't the same," he replied.

"Why?" She stopped struggling and squinted into his eyes.

Hiram's face began to furrow as he tried to remember what Billy Jack said when he asked to go whoring with him. His words came slow and he stumbled as he spoke.

"The nigger women's fer anybody, cause the chullen is black. But if a white gal gits caught by a nigger, the bastard is black and not white like the ma, and that's why." His lips curled upward and he nodded his head once, emphatically, proud of remembering. They always said he wouldn't remember his own name if they didn't call him to eat.

The night shattered and crumbled around her feet as the knife edge of screamed terror slashed down her back and into her belly. The scream rose in pitch until her ears hurt, and finally it choked into a gurgle and died.

In the loud silence, Penny fainted.

Chapter 6: Later That Night

"Come on, scaredy cat," Karen Emerson called over her shoulder as she ran toward the old church. It was good to be free again, away from the eyes of grownups who treated her like a prisoner. Ever since her father had found out about her going on that still raid, he had tried to keep her at home. The few times he'd let her see Charley, he had demanded she be home before dark. She lied tonight to get away—told her father she was going to a picture show over in Macon with a girl friend. He'd never know that she was with Charley tonight. Not even Sara knew why she'd called Judge Emerson's home and asked if Karen could go to the show with her in Macon. Sara knew only that she'd lied to The Judge.

Karen threw back her head to let the wind lift her hair and she flung her arms wide in the ecstasy of freedom. She watched the sheep-like clouds sail between the stars. Like white ghosts in a dark sea they seemed to chase the moon. When she stood still, she could imagine the clouds were still and the moon rushed across the sky.

The wind whispered to the leaves as if singing a courting song that wrapped her into its embrace and made her want to dance. A barred owl hooted far off and another answered. She smiled to herself—they were like her and Charley the way they talked love to each other.

With a soft laugh she pulled herself back to the present and skipped through the deep shadows toward the dark hulk of the church.

"They say it's haunted," she called over her shoulder.

"You believe in haints?" Charley asked.

"Of course! Don't you?" She waited for his long stride to overtake her. The wind tossed her hair into her face, and she brushed it from her eyes, and then dropped her hand to his. He squeezed her small fingers.

"Sure you want to explore this place? Probably full of bats and snakes and spiders." He cut the arc of the flashlight upward to the church and then across the weeds to the scattered graves and back to the sagging door of the church.

Night sounds added spookiness to the darkness. Dogs barked from three different directions; somebody whooped his hound on a summer run; the night wind picked up and rattled two naked limbs together like a skeleton shaking its bones.

"They say the niggers left here when someone conjured the place. Looks like the haints used the door for a chair and it wouldn't hold them up," he said.

The night shattered as a barn owl screamed.

Karen shivered. "What's that?" She stepped closer and took his hand.

"It's a barn owl. They sound like painters."

"Painters?"

"You know. Wildcats."

"Oh!" Her laughter floated as easily and lightly over the night air as the clouds overhead. "Let's see what's inside." She leaned backwards, toward the church, arm outstretched, and pulled him gently by the hand.

Charley did not move as a cloud slipped away from the moon. He hadn't been here since he came home from the war. So long ago he came here with Virgil and they learned about sex, masturbated together, pissed together over by the pine tree to see who could piss the farthest. And from here one evening, he had gone with Virgil and Penny to watch the conjure woman. He erased the sight of her holding up the chicken with blood dripping from its headless neck. He wasn't here to remember the conjure woman, Virgil, or Penny.

He turned his mind and his eyes onto Karen. Maybe going inside the church wasn't such a good idea. Brought his memories back. And might scare her. Maybe he ought to spread out his jacket under the pine, on the soft needles. His thoughts brought a reaction from his groin. He didn't want to wait for her to play games.

"Hey!" Her voice and playful punch in the chest aroused him from his thoughts. "You waiting for some angel to fly down here, or you scared to go in there? Or you wishing I was somebody else?" She giggled through her pout.

He smacked her rump. "You're too much devil for any angel to try to come around. Probably scared off all the haints too. Come here."

She snuggled against him and brought her arms up and around his neck. The flashlight cut a wide swath through the night as his arms circled her. She pressed her body against his erection, wiggled as if promising, but only kissed him lightly and slipped away before he could stop her.

"Come on," she urged, "before midnight comes and the haints leave."

He followed her up the narrow steps. A board creaked, and they froze in mid-step like two puppets suspended in the air. A second passed before they realized the source of the sound and giggled.

"It's the conjure woman's bones squeaking a warning," he whispered. And with a chuckle, "Ladies first," he pushed her forward, into the blue moon-shadows of the door, and turned off the flashlight.

"Coward!" She growled at him. He laughed again as she reached for his hand. "Turn that light on!" Karen demanded, her voice a little angry, a little afraid.

He flashed the light around the room. "I was about to offer to go gallantly ahead and sweep away the devil's lacy cobwebs," he offered, "but I don't see any."

"Well, come on," she tugged at him. Having seen the entire room, she no longer felt the anticipation and fun of fear of the unknown.

"Hey, wait a minute!" He pulled her back. "Look at all those footprints! No wonder there're no spider webs in here."

He moved the circle of light across the floor and the footprints. Dust that rose in little puffs as they had walked across the floor whispered mustiness into their nostrils. He shined the light over the disturbed dust and spotted handprints. When the light hit a darker spot, he jerked it away. Maybe somebody had a pissing contest here. Maybe not. Maybe whoever had been here had slipped away as they approached. He felt his erection shrink.

"Guess one of the ghosts must have fallen when it tried to fly." Karen's voice was chilly.

She wasn't sure if it was his or her own heart that she heard, but she was sure it wasn't his eyes that she felt on the back of her neck or his fingers ruffling her hair. She spun to him, grabbed his hand with the flashlight, and ran the beam in a quick arc around the entire room.

Wooden pews stood like soldiers on parade under command of the fallen and equally dusty altar. The beam of light danced weirdly through the broken spider webs that dangled from the naked beams overhead.

Charley noticed the swing was gone. No, just the rope. The board lay over near the altar. No one else in the room, though. He breathed deeply, and Karen found her own courage in a long-drawn sigh.

"Guess we scared ourselves. And scared the ghosts off," he whispered. "Come on." He guided her toward the rectangle of lighter darkness that was the door, and she made no comment of resistance.

As if to shake off a clammy hand she shivered once, violently, as she went through the door.

With her hand in his, she let him lead her away from the church and away from the car. At the edge of graveyard Charley turned off the flashlight and dropped it into his jacket pocket. The moon shed enough light that the flash wasn't needed. He led her to the pissing pine, now much larger than when he and Virgil had used it for a target. The bed of needles might have redbugs, but who cared?

"Want to sit and watch the clouds chase the stars?"

"Uh-huh," she replied, knowing he was thinking the same thoughts that had occupied her mind more and more in the days and nights they had been forced apart.

He spread his jacket for her and they both sat. He took her hand lightly. "I love you," he whispered. Maybe this time will be better. Not in the back seat of a car like the other two times, but out here in the open, with the dew chilling the night and the moon getting high. Just say the right things.

Karen leaned into his kiss, and he felt her passion rising. She unbuttoned his shirt and slid her hand against his chest and downward to unbuckle his trousers. They fell onto their sides and almost tore at each other's clothes.

A steady, slow squeak overhead interrupted Karen and she pushed against him. "Somebody's out there," she whispered.

"Nobody's there."

A pair of feet dangled against the sky from the oak a few yards away.

Her scream erupted from her throat and spread in waves across Charley's startled face. Her fingers bit into his arms, her body heaved as she drew breath for another scream. Her face drained to pallid. He followed the frozen glare of horror in her eyes, over his shoulder, upward into the oak.

A black form moved slowly with the wind, back and forth, like the steady movement of a pendulum.

He swallowed a scream and reached for the flashlight to dispel his fear.

"It's all right, honey," he tried to reassure her with a laugh that only echoed her fear. "Somebody's trying to be funny and scare off anybody that comes out here." He tried to believe his own words as he pulled her to her feet.

Her hands on his arms were like five-pointed ice cubes clutching him. "Oh, Charley, let's get out of here," she sobbed against his chest. Her voice was hoarse from her screams.

"Let me show you it's nothing—" he began, but she backed away, hands over her face, fingers curled over her lips as if to hold in another scream.

"Wait a minute!" he called and leaped forward to grab her, to pull her back into his arms.

Tears came as her fear released itself in deep racking sobs. He patted her back gently with one hand and clicked on the flashlight with the other. He cut the beam upward, to a pair of black, blood-coated legs.

The light stopped, the arm frozen until the horror itself seemed to drag the light slowly upward, past the matted cut on the thigh, over the remains of the crude castration, across the slashed torso, to the pain-ridden agonized face and the wide, bulging, white eyes. The light clattered to the ground as he pushed Karen aside and vomited.

Chapter 7

Lights illuminated the trees and turned weeds to white shadows. Tires spit rocks and dust into the air as the car stopped at the church door.

Sheriff Dixon stepped out from behind the wheel. Slumped over and white-faced, Charley remained in the passenger seat.

"Where is it?" Dixon asked, not waiting for the second car to squeal to a halt behind his. Charley pointed toward the oak, a black ghost in the moonlight, and the sheriff strode forward. He dropped his cigarette, paused to crunch it, and then strode briskly with his flashlight illuminating the path.

As he neared the tree, Jake ran up to join him. They both pointed their lights up the tree, and as the lights hit the corpse they cut off simultaneously.

"How could anyone do that to a man?" Jake's voice almost trembled, and he swallowed the bitter taste rising in his throat. He had seen many things, bodies rotted from the river, headless soldiers in battle, a child smashed by an angry father, but never before had he wanted to empty his stomach. He reached into his shirt pocket, discovered he'd left his cigarettes in his car, and muttered, "Got a smoke?"

The sheriff didn't answer; he fumbled in his pocket. He pulled a Camel from the pack, stuck one between his lips, passed one to Jake and struck a Lucifer on his pants' leg with trembling fingers. The wind snuffed the match before Jake's cigarette touched the flame, and with a whispered "Damn," the sheriff yanked another from his shirt pocket. He willed his hands to be still as he cupped flame from the breeze. Neither man spoke until the bitter-sweet smoke had scorched their lungs.

The sheriff spat a tobacco leaf, could not get it free of his lip, and pulled it off with a finger.

"He must have been with a white woman and got found out. No other reason for anyone to do that."

Jake dragged deeply on his cigarette. "That's probably true." He exhaled smoke with his words, the heat searing his throat to rid his mind of the sight of the corpse.

"But who? It'd have taken at least three men, maybe more. His hands weren't even tied. And Jeff is—was a mighty strong man," Dixon said.

"You know anything much about him, Charley?" Jake asked. Charley did not answer. "Charley? Where'd you go to, boy?"

Charley answered from near the car. "All I know is he sometimes worked for Daddy and sometimes for Dr. Jacobs."

The wind pushed a cloud from the moon and swung the corpse. The rope squeaked against the bark like the wail of a banshee in protest. Far off thunder rumbled. Both men shuddered.

A flashing light brought their attention back to their cars. Charley stood off to the side, one hand resting against a tree, his body bent over as if he'd vomited. Headlights swept through the trees and the other car stopped behind Dixon's. The lights blinded the men and stayed on bright after a door slammed.

As he approached, Perry called, "Hello! Am I too late for the fun?"

"Afraid not," Dixon replied. "But how did you know?"

"Judge Emerson called me. Something about his girl and young Cunningham finding a body out here. What happened?"

"An old-fashioned lynch job. Looks like the reply to a rape to me," Dixon answered.

"What makes you think he raped somebody? I haven't heard about one," Perry said.

"There's no other reason to castrate a man before hanging him," Jake shook his head. "Too bad the Emerson's girl saw that."

"The Cunningham boy's over by the car," Dixon said as he jerked a thumb in that general direction. "He said that the girl saw the corpse first and then he turned the flashlight on it. He thought it was some sort of trick until he saw it. He thinks Karen didn't see much, just the shadow, but Lord only knows why not, when she's got her nose stuck into everything else."

"What with this and his almost getting cut up in that still raid, you'd think he'd know enough to keep his girls out of the woods," Jake said.

"What were they doing here to start with?" Perry asked.

"I gather it was their idea of fun to chase ghosts or something in the church. I've heard all sorts of stories about it being conjured," Dixon said.

Perry took a deep breath. "Well, the main reason I'm here is that Emerson wants this whole thing kept quiet."

"Oh, Gawd, Alex! This is murder, even if it is a nigger. What does he mean, he wants it hushed up?" Jake almost shouted.

"Perry's got a good point, Jake. Think what'll happen to this town if the news gets out about this, with Emerson's girl in the middle of it. They'll figure she was out here boffing the—." He looked over at Charley and then lowered his voice to a whisper. "They'll say she was boffing the nigger. It'll ruin Emerson, and we'll be out of jobs so fast we won't know what hit us. We ain't gonna find out who did this—it could have been most anybody. And won't nobody really care he's dead, except his mama."

"I hear tell he used to run one of the Carter's stills for them," Jake said. "Back before he got drafted. That so?"

"Every nigger boy in this end of the county's worked at one-a their stills some time or another," Dixon said.

Jake waved his forefinger at nothing in particular and at his thoughts in general. "You don't suppose—?" he mumbled. "It's not probable, but it might could be. I saw them talking—never would-a thought about it if you hadn't mentioned them." He quit thinking aloud and looked toward Charley, who strode back and forth alongside the cars, well out of hearing. Still, he continued in a whisper. "It must have been the Carters. I'm willing to bet money that Penny was messing around with him."

"Nawww," Dixon waved a hand at him. "White trash hate niggers cause each one thinks he's better'n the other. Never would-a happened."

"Well, I don't know," Perry said. "It could be. That girl's not a child anymore. She's all woman looking for a man, and I don't think she'd care where she found one."

"I'm going by to see them and—" Jake began.

"Hold on, now, Jake," Dixon cut in. "You go messing things up, and I wouldn't stop to guess how Emerson would take it. He's got a lot of power."

"This is murder you playing around with!"

"He rutted a white girl," Perry said. "And even if it were the Carters, I say more power to them! I'd have done the same. Now drop it, Jake, before you get fired. Emerson's got a lotta pull up in Atlanta."

Dixon nodded his head toward Charley. "And don't mention what we think to Charley yonder. Less anybody else knows, the better. You hear me?"

"I hear you," Jake said.

"Wouldn't any twelve men in this state convict even a Carter if what we think is true," Dixon added.

Jake reached into Dixon's shirt pocket for another cigarette, struck a match on his thigh, and cupped his hands against the wind. His face showed despair and frustration; he knew he could not change their minds or the minds of others. Maybe if he could trap the Carters in something else they would admit to this. Maybe. And if he investigated this killing and botched it, if word got out about Karen's being here—. Perry was right, he decided. Emerson had enough power to cost him his job, his mortgaged home, and his reputation. Jake puffed out the match.

"Okay, have it your way, but cut me out of it. You get the coroner to fix the papers, to lie to the newspapers, and to his family. Tell them you found him half-eaten by turtles in the river for all I care. Just let me read about it."

He strode back to his car and drove away. By dawn the murder would show as an accident on all records and by tomorrow night even Charley would have convinced Karen it was some sort of freak accident.

Chapter 8: Two Days Later

Penny leaned against the jamb of the kitchen door and looked down at the ground almost three feet below her. How many hours had she stood here, how many days, and wondered if Charley would come by again. Seemed like all she heard about him now was about how he took the judge's daughter off into the woods. He likely never would come back by.

Jeff never would. And now Charley might not either, if he ever learned she had been at the church with Jeff. At least Ellen believed her story about falling when she lied about how she got the bruises on her face.

She closed her eyes and shook her head. If only she could erase the sounds of his screams, but they seemed to echo in her head. She folded her arms across her belly and hugged herself. Thank goodness Jack didn't let her watch. Even the sounds were enough to make her want to up-chuck.

Emptiness filled her.

Silence filled the house, but the world outside stirred with noise and activity. Buddy yelled as he ran and played with the hound and her puppies. A crow busied himself in the yard where it pecked through some of the trash BJ had thrown out down by the outhouse. Far off over the trees, a buzzard circled, black against the white-hot sky until he tilted and sunlight turned the underside of its wings from black to white. The air smelled of drought, the outhouse, and the pile of trash that smoldered in the side yard.

What little wind could find the energy to move only pushed hot air around and did not bring coolness. She sighed and turned back to the stack of dirty breakfast dishes that now would have to be scrubbed. She'd left them for hours while she stared out the door, and the grease had hardened.

She poured warm water from the pot on the stove into the dishpan and began to wash the dishes with a chunk of homemade lye soap and a rag from one of her worn-out dresses. She then stacked them in a second pan of cold water to rinse. Sweat accumulated on her forehead and ran down her face into her eyes. She frequently swiped it away with the back of her hand. Once she slung water from her hands and used her skirt tail to wipe the sweat off her face. The back of her dress and the armpits were soaked. She wished Ellen would get home from helping out down at the Jacobs place.

Seemed like every since Virgil got home and moved in down there, Ellen had to go help out. Seemed like Janice didn't know how to do diddly-squat.

When she heard a vehicle stop out front she hurried to the door as she wiped her wet hands on her skirt tail. Maybe, just maybe, it would be Charley. Oh, please be Charley. Her lips tucked in and she sighed her disappointment when she saw it was only John Hall.

He walked up the steps and stopped at the front door, where he smiled at her and removed his Sunday hat. He had a different look about him as he stood with his feet wide apart, his shoulders slightly slouched, his left thumb hooked in his pants pockets. He wore his town suit with a white shirt.

"May I come in?" He bowed slightly to her.

She shrugged. "Shore. Uncle Jack and Pa done gone off with Virgil to—." She paused, hesitant, and then decided he would know soon enough. "To see about a lawyer fer BJ's trial when it come up."

John nodded. "I heard about the raid."

"Heard what?" Buddy trotted in the front door. His cut-off jeans hung over his rump. Dust coated his legs and hands. Dog smell floated around him.

Penny squatted so that Buddy would not have to crane his neck to see her face.

"Honey, you know Billy Jack got put in jail." She ran her fingers through his hair to comb it. "They caught him down at the likker still. But don't you go fretting none. Uh-ohh. You got a tick here. Hold still." She pulled the parasite from his head, walked to the fireplace, put the tick on the brick hearth, lit a match, and put it to the tick.

"That's best way to kill one of them," John said.

"They gonna make him stay in jail?" The small dirty face puckered into a frown and the near-black eyes begged for reassurance.

"Course not. He gone with yer pa. You seen him rightchere this mawning."

John Hall put a hand on the boy's shoulder. "They'll decide sometime this summer, Buddy. You don't go fretting, you hear? They'll just make him pay some money is all. Now you run along outside and play and don't worry. Billy Jack's a big boy and can take care of himself. Don't you go fretting."

"Sure, Mr. John," the boy grinned and ran toward the door.

"Don't you go running in the house," Penny said, but Buddy had already leaped the steps and churned up dust as he landed. He disappeared, and John stepped outside to watch him crawl into a clump of plum bushes to join the puppies in the shade.

"Well, what I really stopped by for was to tell you I got another boy." His face creased into a pleased grin.

"Why that sure is grand! I be mighty glad fer you. When was he born?" She wished she had a baby of her own, a baby of hers and Charley's.

"Just this morning. I've been over to the hospital with my wife. Look, I got a nigger to stay with the chullen today, but I wondered if you could come stay when I'm gone to work tonight. Like we talked about before. I'd come for you this afternoon, about three, and drive you back soon's I get in from work. I'm not going to work late. I'd come home by midnight."

With a shrug, Penny replied, "I don't know." She didn't want to go. Suppose Charley came by to see her and she was gone up the road. But it'd mean some money all her own, money she wouldn't have to ask her pa for. She'd never had money of her own.

"I gotta ask Pa."

"I'll come by for you later, then. Sam didn't mind when we talked about it awhile back. I'll pay you two dollars. My wife's ma'll be here tomorrow, so I won't need you then. And would you tell Sam I'll be needing some help down to my place in about a week?"

"Two dollars? That's more'n you pay Pa for a day of heping out." She broke a straw off the broom by the fireplace and began to chew it. "Sure, I'll be glad to tell Pa." She could buy a new dress to wear if—no, when—Charley comes back by.

With a slight frown that hovered above his too-short nose, he stared at her for a long moment and she realized that she had never really looked at him before, in all the times he had been to the house to see her father.

His face had burned dark from the sun except for a white band across his forehead where his hat sat a little crooked. Bristles speckled his face. As he turned to look at her she followed the angular planes of his face up from his hard chin to his pale blue eyes that bored at her from under an unbroken ridge of black brows. Something about the look in his eyes made her think of Charley.

"Hey, why so thoughtful? Tell me, what's going on in that pretty head of yours?"

She shook her head. "Nothing. I'll be ready this afternoon." She walked to the door, and he followed.

"You'll remember to tell your pa I'll be needing some help along in about a week or so? Depending on if we get rain or not?"

"I'll tell 'im," she replied.

"Well, I better be getting on home." As he stepped onto the porch, he pulled his hat low over his left ear.

She stood in the doorway until his truck's roar had faded into the distance and the dust had settled. Buddy came up on the porch to stand beside her and watch the truck.

"I'm gitting hongry," he said.

"Okay. I think there's a biscuit or two left from breakfast. Les go see."

While Buddy ate his biscuits, Penny dried dishes. She sighed. It was gonna be a long morning with this heat if Buddy stayed inside. Maybe after he ate, he'd go back out and play with the puppies or roll that tire around the yard or pitch rocks at the outhouse. Even though he'd been spanked for pitching rocks, he'd do it when Jack and Ellen were gone off.

She heard another car, but knew it wouldn't be Charley. Even when it stopped out front, she kept on with the dishes. No need to hope.

"Hey, anybody home?" Charley called from the front door.

Penny dropped the pink glass dish she was drying and it smashed across the floor as she ran to the door.

"Charley! You came back."

He held his arms out and hugged her as she rushed into them.

"Course I came back. I hadn't been gone anywhere." He pushed her back to arm's length and looked down at her. "How you doing?"

"Hey, Charley," Buddy said.

"Hey, Buddy. Whatcha doing inside? It's a perfect day to be out in the sun and playing with your tire."

The child grinned and pushed his way between them to return to the plum bushes and his dogs.

"Oh, Charley, I have missed you."

"Me too. Where is everybody else?"

"They done all gone off. You here to see me or one-a them?"

"Well, it's for sure I'm not here to see Virgil."

"You mad at me cause of Virgil?"

"I'm not even mad at Virgil. He can't beat Daddy. Come July, we'll be going fishing again. Come here."

He pulled her into his embrace, but she pushed away and backed up a step.

"What you wanting, Charley? You jest want me to lie down for you? That all you want from me?"

He rolled his eyes and shook his head.

"Of course not, Penny. You're special. Real special."

"Yeah? Then how come you was down in the woods with that Karen Emerson? Everybody in town knows about it."

"Oh, that." He turned his back to her for a moment, ran both hands up the side of his face and through his hair, and turned around as his hands dropped. "My pa wanted me to take her out, and she asked me to take her off to the woods. Didn't anything happen, thank goodness. The law came through there to raid BJ's still, and I insisted we go along. That way, I could get away from her. I don't want anybody coming between us, Penny. Don't you know how much I care about you?"

"You ain't caring enough to be here like you promised."

"Daddy's got me running his whiskey. I got no time for anything else."

"You got time for Miss Priss Karen."

"You think Sam'd let you and me go riding again after dark? I got some time at dark, just before I make my runs. That's all the time I got. I sure missed you. I've wanted to be here. I've missed the fun times we always have."

He stepped forward and caressed her cheek.

She turned her face into his hand and closed her eyes. His lips touched hers, gently, almost a question, and her answer was to open her mouth for his tongue. She raised her arms to circle his neck and then sagged into his embrace as he pulled her closer.

"Ooooh. I got to come up for breath, Penny." He looked down at her, and she looked up into his eyes as he eased her back a little.

"Do you want to do it?" she whispered.

"I don't want anything more."

"Then lemme close the door. I don't want Buddy walking in."

She went to the porch for a chair and then pushed the door to. She studied the chair and door a moment and then pushed the back of the chair under the door knob.

"You done this before?"

"No. I ain't never."

She walked over to the double bed where BJ slept and began to unbutton her dress. She wore nothing under it.

Charley quickly removed his shirt and pants, and then sat on the bed to remove his shoes.

"Take 'em off," she said, touching his shorts.

He stood and let them fall, and her eyes focused on his penis.

"You gonna make it git long?"

"No. You are. Just touch it like you did before and it'll get as long as you want it to."

Two hours later, Buddy banged on the door and yelled, "Penny. Penny. Lemme in. The door won't open."

Charley grabbed his clothes, ran into the room where Penny was born, and closed the door. Penny slipped into her dress and let the boy in.

Chapter 9: That Evening

Sam was walking home when he got a lift with John, on his way to pick up Penny. Once at the house, he told her of course she could go tend to John's chullen.

"You go on, Pen. You done promised the man to hep out. He got chullen at home and he be needing to git to work. He gonna pay you jest to sit at his house and put the chullen to bed."

She went, sure that her pa would take her two dollars when she got home.

Wordlessly, she rode the four miles to the Hall home.

When he stopped the truck in the yard, John leaned over her to open the door. As his arm brushed against her breast, he jerked back.

"I'm sorry. Can you get the door?"

She nodded and pushed it open.

"You tell old Bess she can go as soon as she shows you around the house. She's already cooked supper, so all you have to do is just be here if something happens. Feed 'em if they get hungry. Sleep if you want to. I can wake you when I come back. I won't work overtime. I'll be back about midnight."

She slipped out of the truck and watched him back around the yard and drive off in a cloud of dust. As she started toward the house a fat, aging Negro woman lumbered out to meet her.

"Is you Miss Penny?" Her arms crossed under her bosoms as if to support their size, she studied Penny from head to bare feet.

The woman frowned, curled her lips out, and nodded her approval; the ends of her knotted kerchief bobbled on her head like two loose-fitting horns. Bess padded inside, and Penny followed her into a dim house and the warm smell of beef stew.

The woman led her from room to room.

The four older boys played marbles in a room that held two double beds. They had drawn a chalk circle on the floor, and the two oldest were competing; the other two watched. The oldest looked about twelve, the youngest maybe five. Their faces were all alike—round, chubby, and dirty. The humidity and heat plastered their dull brown hair over their foreheads. They wore only their undershorts, their torsos bare to the mosquitoes; welts covered their bodies from insect bites.

They looked up at her. The oldest grinned, with his pa's smile, and then they ignored her as they returned to their game.

Penny asked their names, and each looked up as his name was called.

A girl and a child not much more than a year old napped in another room, where a cradle awaited the new child. The girl wore only homemade cotton panties; the baby, only diapers. Like the older boys, they were covered with red welts from mosquitoes, horseflies, and redbugs.

Penny then followed Bess across the hall to a large room with thick curtains pulled across the windows. A wide bed dominated the room, its red spread a violent glare in the soft light from the afternoon sun that filtered through the drapes.

"Mista John say you is to stay here iffen you wants to sleep." Her eyes rolled over Penny and to the bed as she measured Penny's youthful, lithe form against the wide, aging body of John's wife.

"De kitchen's dis-away." She led Penny toward the kitchen and the source of the smell of beef stew. A large, covered black pot sat on the wood-burning stove. Penny took the handle, opened the door to the firebox, and saw hot coals with one fresh log.

"Don'tcha think that'll keep it hot enough fer the chullen another hour or so?" Penny asked.

Bess nodded. "I reckons. De cornbread be here." She pointed to a cloth-covered pan sitting on the pie safe. Then she went over to the wall and picked up a canvas bag that Penny knew was what she was toting her share of food home in.

"I's going," Bess said and stalked toward the back door.

Penny stood on the porch and watched her heavy hips sway as she lumbered down the narrow lane toward the train tracks, her carrying bag in hand. When she disappeared around the bend, Penny went inside.

She walked directly to the room with the sleeping children and bent over the toddler's bed. She had forgotten how little a child was. This'n wasn't more'n a year and a half. It was hard to remember Buddy's being this little, but she dug into her memories until she found the child who had jerked his arms and legs and gurgled at her. Remembering, she smiled.

She wanted to pick the little one up and hold him, to feel his warm softness in her arms and to protect him from the unpleasant stickiness that hovered in the air as a warning of a coming storm. She wondered if he was afraid of thunder like she used to be when she was little. He looked so hot. Sweat covered his face with tiny droplets that built up and ran through the dust on his cheek. A large thick scab marred his forehead as it peeked from beneath his hair, and she wondered how he'd managed to injure himself. He seemed too little to be walking.

She brushed his thick curls back from the wound. When she tugged at his arm to remove his thumb from his mouth, he immediately shoved it back, sucked vigorously, then returned to a deep sleep. Penny smiled.

Restlessness overtook her within an hour, and she wandered around the house. The older boys came into the kitchen to ask for food, and she scooped the stew into bowls and laid out slices of corn bread. She joined them. None of them spoke to her after asking for food.

She wondered what to do about feeding the two littlest ones, but since they were sleeping, she left them alone.

As the boys started out of the kitchen, she noticed a welt on the oldest boy's back, near his waist, with a dark spot in the middle.

"Wait a minute, John Jr. You got a tick on your back. C'meer."

He walked over and turned his back so she could remove it. After she dropped it on the stove top to sizzle, he walked up beside her at the stove.

"I got another one, Miz. Can you git it off-a me?"

"Sure. Where is it?"

"Rightchere." He pulled down his shorts and pointed to his penis. "Under this-here."

They all began to giggle.

She rolled her eyes. "You gonna hafta git that one off yerself. Put your britches back on. And all-a-y'all git to bed."

He shrugged and pulled up his pants. As they left the room, their giggles floated back to her.

She washed dishes and cleaned up the mess where they'd spilled stew and crumbs on the table. Then she had nothing else to do. Darkness was falling, and she lit one of the lamps, walked through the house to check on the children again, and placed the lamp on a table by the front door.

She went outside and sat on a porch rocker, laid her head back, closed her eyes, and thought about the morning with Charley.

He loved her. He'd said so. She wrapped her arms across her chest, hugged herself, and smiled.

The rocker squeaked with her movements. Behind the house, the stream gurgled and bullfrogs croaked. Two chuck-will's-widows called to each other. The odor of mud and the stench of the outhouse drifted onto the front porch. A barred owl called his constant query of "Who cooks for you" from the dead hickory beside the stream. Clouds scudding overhead blocked off the moon and stars and then moved away to open up the night again. Distant thunder grumbled, and heat lightning flashed on the southwest horizon. Rain would be here before day.

Her mind, however, smelled only Charley's body and heard only his voice whispering love.

She rocked and dreamed as the clouds thickened and thunder rumbled closer. The air became more humid, and sweat clung to her in spite of the night breeze building up. Near ten o'clock, when the moon faded completely behind the cloud cover, she got up, went inside, and took the lamp to the bedroom.

Before she sprawled across the bed, she lifted the globe, turned the wick down to a low flame, and blew it out. In a few minutes she was asleep.

*   *   *

She awoke. Her eyes flashed open and then closed quickly against the sudden, bright light. A black shadow hovered over her, and she sucked her breath in to scream, but a hand clamped over her face and held her down.

Someone chuckled and whispered loudly.

"It's me, Penny. John Hall. I didn't go to scare you. Now don't you go scream and wake up the children."

Penny went limp with relief. Hours must have passed; the night air was whipping its way through the open windows. The rain hadn't come yet, but she could smell it in the air. Dampness had cooled the night. The chuck-will's-widows had quieted as if they had sought safety from the coming storm. Even frogs and crickets had gone silent.

She squinted in the light.

John stood beside the bed, the lit lamp in one hand. She sat up, swung her feet onto the floor, and shoved her skirt down as John's eyes turned to her exposed thighs.

His blue work shirt gapped open at the neck and hung half out of his wrinkled blue trousers.

"Here's the two dollars," he said and handed her two folded bills. "I sure appreciate your staying. There wasn't any trouble, was there?" He did not meet her gaze but kept his eyes focused on her breasts, which pushed hard against the twisted dress.

"No, didn't nothing go wrong," she said as she shook her head. She took the money and stuffed it into her pocket. "Thanks." She tried to swallow a yawn but it forced itself up and out. She was tired, and her back ached from sleeping in an unfamiliar bed. She seemed to hurt all over. She would be glad to get on home to her own bed. To relieve some of the stiffness, she twisted her body and stretched her arms high before she got up.

As they headed for the front door, a cloud spat lightning with a loud crashing cough and rain rattled on the tin roof in a loud melody that increased in intensity. Penny stopped at the front door and looked out. It wasn't rain, but hail making so much noise. She backed up.

"I can't let you go out in this storm. The hail's big enough to hurt. We'll have to wait." His arm reached out to encircle her shoulder. "You come on back to bed. Get some sleep. I'll wake you up when the storm's over."

Penny did not resist, partly because she was still almost asleep and partly because she had no reason to think she should. She stretched out on her side across the wrinkled spread and listened to the storm pound the tin roof. Like a lullaby, it sang her to sleep in a few minutes.

She awoke to a pressure against her back, an arm across her body with a hand inside the front of her dress. The smell of whiskey reeked stronger than that of grease and tobacco smoke.

As she sucked in her breath to scream, the hand rose to her mouth. She grabbed at the wrist, but it held her like a vice.

"Don't you make a sound, you hear me?" John spoke against her ear.

She tried to think about what to do. Thunder shook the house; lightning brightened the room more than the single lamp burning near the bed. She pulled against his arm again, but the hand only pressed tighter against her mouth.

"I won't hurt you. But you gotta keep quiet. You hear me? You're not gonna wake up the boys. You can let my arm go if you gonna be quiet."

She released his arm, and the pressure on her mouth relaxed.

"You unbutton your dress all the way down."

She did not move, but gritted her teeth. She wasn't going to give in to fear.

"Unbutton that dress and slide out of it, or I'll tear it off and you'll go home naked. Do it. Now."

The hand gripped her shoulder until she knew she would carry his hand print tomorrow as a black bruise. She'd get away from him and get home. Go alongside the edge of the road. He wouldn't run after her, not and leave his babies by themselves.

He turned her onto her back, and she covered herself with her arms although she had not opened her dress. A flash of lightning showed he was naked. A calm violence and determination filled his face. His lips were pressed into a tight line; his eyes seemed to glow even when the lightning faded. She quit struggling as fear consumed her and her resistance shattered. She unbuttoned her dress.

"Take it off."

When she shucked it off, he pulled it from under her and dropped it on the floor. He dropped his body on top of her.

Seeking hers, his lips brushed her cheek then closed over hers. His teeth crushed her lips, and she tasted whiskey. He's gotta be drunk or he'd never dare, she thought. His hands gripped her shoulders and pinned her to the bed. She twisted her head back and forth as she tried to free her lips from his.

He rose up on his hands, all his weight on her shoulders.

"You know you want this. I saw it in your eyes today. You want me, and you can quit pretending not to."

"I don't want you. I never wanted you. You're an old man. You've been an old man since I kin remember. Why would I ever want you?" Her eyes half-closed in fury.

She spit in his face.

He slapped her.

"Well, pretty lady, you gonna get me, want me or not."

"My pa'll kill you."

"Everybody knows you sleep around with that Cunningham boy. Nobody'll believe you."

He rose, shifted position, put a knee between her legs, and again dropped his weight onto her. His hands twisted into her hair and forced her head still. He rubbed his unshaven face against hers and then pushed his tongue into her mouth.

She grabbed at his hair, but he released her shoulders, grabbed both wrists, and pinned her down with her hands at shoulder level.

"You can quitcha fighting and enjoy it or else I'll do it anyway and it'll hurt. What's it gonna be?"

She narrowed her eyes as her gaze shifted from one pale eye to the other. She knew what to do.

"Okay, John. Turn me loose. I ain't gonna fight you no more. I kinda likes the feel of your thing down there." She forced a smile and hoped it looked real.

"Well, it's about time." He pulled her hands over his neck.

"No, I don't wanna hold you like this. Let me touch you. I wanna feel it and touch it and make it bigger. Please, John." She moved her hands from his neck to his back, and then slipped her right hand down between them. "Turn on your side a little bit so's I kin reach you good."

He did, and she caressed his chest and his belly, and slowly reached for his erect penis. Her fingers touched it lightly and wrapped around it. He moaned his pleasure.

With a quick movement she tightened her fist around it and twisted.

He screamed and clutched himself as she released him and he rolled away.

She scrambled off the bed, grabbed her dress, and ran to the door. He lunged after her and one hand snaked out to grab her. He seized a handful of hair, but she jerked her head forward and left him only a few strands of hair.

Dress in hand, she ran naked through the house, out the front door, and into the pelting rain and darkness, grateful that the hail had ended. Less frightened by the storm before her than the shadowy figure behind her, unmindful of direction, her nakedness, the coolness of the rain, or the violence of the lightning, she ran.

Across the yard, down the driveway and up the road she ran. Mud clung to her bare feet, its weight increasing with each step. She heard him behind her, heard his heavy panting, heard his feet splash in puddles.

Nowhere to go but into the woods, where maybe she could hide. He'd catch her if she stayed on the road. She jumped the ditch and plunged through blackberry bushes that clawed at her legs and gashed her until she left a trail of blood. She ran on into the deeper blackness of the woods, every branch a thousand-fingered hand that reached to her. Every rock and bush bruised and slashed at her feet, her legs, or her body.

Lightning snatched a tree and split it.

Screaming, Penny spun and changed directions, and the woods opened into a meadow. She stood panting, looked around, and wondered where she was. Her fear turned to anger as she thought about John. She would get back at him.

If only she had insisted he drive her home in spite of the hail. If only she had not gone back to sleep.

"Nothing looks so good as a sweet, sleeping girl." BJ's words came to her. As she crossed the meadow, the grass slapped her and the wind echoed the words over and over. "Sweet, sleeping girl."

Penny shivered with loneliness.

Suddenly frantic, she began to run again, a tired unsteady gait that threw her to her knees time and time again as she crossed the meadow. She plunged into the woods again and as she reached a fence she saw it barely in time to keep from crashing into its barbs. She crawled under the wire and scooted down the briar-covered bank to the road, only to stand uncertain. Which way was home? Had she gone in a circle or crossed the Hall farm and come out on the other road?

She finally began to trot to her right, and kept to the outside edge of the road so she would not stumble in a rut. Five minutes of running left her exhausted. She stopped, wiped the rain from her face with her dress, and put it on.

The storm had moved away, the rain now only a sprinkle, the lightning more distant. Only the gurgle of water running the ditches and far off thunder sounded.

She kept a constant watch on the side of the road with hopes of seeing something familiar. If she went the wrong way, she would wind up at the Cunningham place instead of home. She didn't want to see Charley now. Another quarter-hour and she saw the sassafras tree at the end of Dr. Jacobs' driveway. She was almost home.

She went to the well and drew water to slosh some of the mud off her feet and legs. Even two buckets left her feet stained with the clay's red hue.

When she walked into the house, only a lit lamp welcomed her. BJ and Hiram snored in the front room, but did not awaken as she walked through. She went to her room, lay down, and sobbed with relief. She would have to tell Pa in the morning.

Chapter 10: The Next Day

"It's almost noon. What's the matter with you?" Ellen asked as she shook Penny awake. "You ain't never slept this late."

Somewhere outside a hen cackled as she came off a nest. Without even thinking in terms of time, Penny knew morning was almost gone. Sunlight streamed in the window, but Penny felt cold as she awoke and her feet hurt. Then she realized she still had on her wet dress. She shivered as she remembered. The sound of a car's struggling in the slick road outside her window drew her gaze, and fear swept over her as she thought John might be on his way to the house right now, in that car outside.

Her face throbbed where he'd hit her, and she didn't want to turn over for Ellen to see the bruises.

"What's wrong?" Ellen sat on the bed, put her hand on Penny's shoulder, and turned her over.

Penny threw her arms around Ellen and buried her face in her shoulder.
"I thought he was gonna—he tried to—. Oh, Ellen, I was so scairt."

Ellen smelled of sunshine, lye soap, and bacon. She hugged Penny, who erupted in sobs against her shoulder.

"You talking about John Hall? He try to do something to you? He tried to git inside your britches?"

She nodded into the comfort of Ellen's shoulder. She did not want to look at her aunt, did not want to see the questions. All she wanted was comfort.

"You let him?"

"No! I never! I got away. I ran home in the rain."

"You shoulda got me up. Jack and Sam would-a gone down there and whupped him."

Penny jerked upright as a rock thunked against the side of the house.

"That-air's Buddy throwing them rocks again. I'll hafta whup 'im this time."

Penny's sobs quieted into hiccups, and as she pulled away from Ellen, she kept her gaze down.

"He hit you in the face?"

Penny nodded. "What kin I tell Pa? He be needing the work.

What's he and Sam gonna do iffen John don't give them no work? Onlyest thing we'll have is whiskey money and what they git for them cows. And a little work fer Doc Jacobs."

Ellen looked her niece over and said, "First off, we'll tell 'im you took a bad spill going outta the door in the rain and smashed up yer face. Tell 'im you stove up bad so's you don't hafta do nothing today. Lemme think on what we gotta do about Mista Big Britches John Hall." She stood and paced across the room and back.

"I'll figger something out. He ain't gonna git away with this. I promise you. C'mon. Go git a bucket of water in here, clean up, and put on something fresh. I be in the kitchen frying you some bacon. We got biscuits left over."

Penny nodded and set about the assigned tasks. Her face still stung where he'd slapped her. When she took off her dress, she saw the imprint of his hand on her shoulder. The skin on both wrists was sore where his grip twisted it.

As the hate and anger welled up in her, she determined to get back at him. Why, that boy of his wasn't even twelve and he wanted her to play with his thing. Probably seen his pa play with his ma, the way they had all those babies. They had more chullen'n Jack and Ellen.

By the time she got to the kitchen, Buddy sat at the table, lured in from the yard by the smell of fresh bacon that filled the house and drifted out the windows. Two slabs still sizzled in the hot grease.

"It's ready in a minute," Ellen said. "Set yerself down and put yer feet into that-air wash tub. I put some of Doc Jacobs' carbolic acid in there and it'll take out some-a the hurt."

Penny did so and looked over at the grocery bag where Ellen laid out the bacon to drain. Six slices already lay out, and Ellen took up four more slices and spread them out beside the others.

"You want a egg? Buddy brung in four jest now."

"That would be good, Ellen. But ain't you needing to save 'em for Pa and Jack?

Ellen looked over her shoulder at Penny, met her eyes, and shook her head.
"You had a bad time. You need sump-em sides a biscuit or slab of corn pone."

"Me too," Buddy said. "I want a aig."

Ellen smiled at her youngest and ruffled his hair. "Awright. I'll fry one up for you too, seeing as you found them."

As soon as they finished eating, Buddy ran back outside. Her stomach warm with the heavy food, Penny felt better, less tense, and less afraid.

"Awright. Tell me whut happened last night."

"It started to hail real bad afore we got outta the door, and he said for me to go back to sleep till it got better. I'd been sleeping when he got there and was plum wo' out. So I did. He smelt like whiskey when he woke me up by crawling all over me. Said if I didn't let him do what he wanted, he'd tear up my dress and throw me out in the rain. Naked. I was too scairt to do anything."

"But you got away. How?"

Penny grinned for the first time. "I told him I wanted to touch his thing. He let me, and I grabbed aholt of it and twisted real hard."

Ellen threw back her head and laughed. "Bet he squealed like a stuck pig."

They fell silent. Ellen put her chin in her palm, her elbow on the table, and pondered. Her face squeezed into a frown, her eyes narrowed. Penny waited for the decision.

"We gonna let the men go on and work for him. You don't say nothing. Not to your pa and not to Jack neither. Not to no one a-tall. Iffen they know, they'll do sump-em. Like whup him. That'd git them in the jail, and we ain't having that. Soon's it gits dry, they'll git in his hay. Atter they git paid, you and me, we'll git him back. We'll light a Lucifer to his hay barn. That'll learn him."

Penny smiled and nodded.

"Yer feet feeling any better?"

"Yeah. That acid stuff of Doc Jacobs' shore is good."

"You go on and set yerself on the porch and take it easy the rest of today. You still got his two dollars?"

"I dunno. I'll go see."

She went back to her room, picked up her dress from the floor, and checked the pocket. The two one-dollar bills, soaked, had stuck inside the pocket. She went to the kitchen to show Ellen.

"You put that somewhere special. It's your'n. And don't you go giving it to your pa."

Back in her room, Penny studied what few things she had as she sought a hiding place where no one else would look. She had only the bed, a chest of drawers, and a chair in her room. Under the mattress she thought, but then discarded the idea since she knew BJ kept his pictures of girls under his mattress. That's the first place one of them would look.

The walls were plastered from waist up, but below the chair rail, narrow boards ran up and down. One was loose over by the head of her bed, and when she remembered, she pulled the bottom end out a little and stuck her folded bills behind it. Unless they knew about the loose board, none of the men would look there for it.

Ellen came to the door just as she straightened up.

"I'm gonna tell your Pa I got the money from you," she said. "He don't know I keeps back a few cents every week and got some spare coins hid in the kitchen. Iffen I didn't, Jack and your pa would lose it all playing poker upstairs over at the drug store."

"Thank you, Ellen." Penny went to her aunt and hugged her.

PART IV: JUNE 1946

Chapter 1: Three Weeks Later

As Penny dried and stacked the last plate, Ellen put them on the shelf above the pie safe. Penny carried the dishpan to the back door. The soapy water had gone cold and a thin film of grease floated on top. She dumped it out the door, returned to the table for the rinsing water, and poured it out.

"I ain't gonna fret about water fer tomorrow till tomorrow. Les us git on up the road." Ellen reached for the box of kitchen matches and removed two.

"We jest taking two Lucifer's?" Penny asked.

"Ain't but two of us. Kain't figure no reason fer taking more'n two. Kin you?" Ellen smiled.

Penny returned the smile and shook her head.

"Les git a move on, then. We got a fur piece to walk afore it gits plum dark."

They walked through the front room and out onto the porch. Jack and Sam had tilted their chairs onto the back legs. Each was busy with a knife and a block of wood.

"That-air oak's kinda hard to carve, ain't it?" Ellen asked her husband.

"Yeah, I reckon. But it'll hold up fer the boy. This-here's gonna be a train engine. Sam's making a caboose. Buddy's always wanting to go down to the rails and see the train go by, so I figure he'll like these."

"Me and Penny's going fer a walk."

"You what?" Sam's hands stopped moving as he looked up to Ellen and then Penny.

"We gonna go fer a walk. We got thangs to talk about. Women things. We'll be back directly. Don'tcha go fretting none."

"It'll be plum slap dark in a bit."

"Don't matter. Look fer us when we walks in."

Jack shrugged and returned his attention to the block of wood that had begun to resemble a train engine with a smokestack that flared out at the top.

The two women walked down the steps, crossed the ditch, and strode off into the twilight.

The wind had fallen asleep early and waited for complete darkness before it would rouse again. Dusk wrapped its silence around them until the crickets began their evening songs. A chuck-will's-widow called from a cedar off in the pasture. Night creatures began to prowl in search of another meal.

"That ole owl sure has caught himself something," Ellen said.

"Sounds like it's courting," Penny said.

One tightened its talons on its prey so that it screamed. Then the owl called. Down the swamp, the female answered. With relief, Penny heard the swoosh of wings as the one nearby carried the prize to his mate.

"That screaming was gitting to me," she said.

"Iffen I'd-a thought it were a rat, I wouldn't of cared."

"Me neither."

They walked in the silence. Twilight deepened and the yellowness faded. Dampness drifted as a mist rose and wrapped around them as if trying to bring a chill to the hot night.

A bullfrog harrumphed and splashed into Persimmon Creek as they crossed the bridge. Far off, a voice hollered at a hound as it took up a trail. Venus began to twinkle at them.

"It shore is a nice time-a-day," Ellen said. "When we-uns come down here the year you was born, I thought there wasn't any such evening to be had after them mountains. Up yonder we had cool all-a-time. Like it's here in October."

They walked in silence for a quarter mile, and then Ellen began to question Penny.

"How come I seen you up-chucking the last couple of days? You done got yourself in trouble, ain't you?"

Penny stopped walking. How could Ellen know? She'd been so careful to get outside when it started. To get to the outhouse before her stomach lurched and emptied. Maybe Ellen smelled her yesterday, when the vomit got all over her front before she reached the outhouse. She thought she'd gotten back inside without anyone knowing. But Ellen had been real watchful ever since Jack had killed Jeff.

What iffen it's Jeff's baby, Penny thought. She wanted it to be

Charley's, but supposing it weren't.

"What makes you think I'm in trouble? I got a upset stomach, that's all."

"You ain't been on the rag, Penny. I know you been up and down the road with Charley. And I don't know what all you done did with that nigger boy. Or when. And jest how fer did John go? Did he git it in you? You any idea when you got caught? When was you on the rag last time?"

Penny tried to think back and remembered the day Virgil got home, when Charley had come by after Virgil walked down the road to see her pa and Dr. Jacobs.

"I ain't sure, Aunt Ellen. I think, right about when Virgil come home."

"Afore you run around with Charley?"

Penny nodded. " I think so. I ain't sure. You know I ain't no good on time."

"It oughtta be his'n then. Unless you messed around with that nigger boy."

Penny sighed, but did not reply. She didn't want to remember Jeff. Every time she thought about him, all she remembered was the screams that night. His terror. Her horror at what her kin had done to Jeff.

"Well, Penny? Didcha?"

She nodded.

"You mess with him more'n once?"

Penny nodded again.

"Awright. Les hope it be Charley's. We-uns tend to that-air later on. You best be glad Jack ain't said nothing to your pa bout that nigger. What was you doing, messing round with him anyhow?"

"I'm lonesome, Ellen. I'm so lonesome I hurt on the inside."

"That ain't no reason to open up your laigs for a boy, much less to whatever man come along." Ellen stopped.

"Don't nobody love me."

"You kain't believe that. Why, your pa loves you so much he'd kill any man what laid a hand on you."

"That ain't the same."

"Spreading out your laigs don't make a fella love you. All a fella wants from a girl is for her to lay out on her back and let him use her like a whore. You gonna lay out for him, he better love you first. And you better love him too. Else, you gonna be having a bastard baby."

"I love Charley."

"Well, I love your pa, but he ain't my man, and you ain't seeing me spreading out for him, now is you?"

Penny, her face turned down so she watched her feet in the deepening night, shook her head.

"And look-a-here at me and you. I love you. I hepped bring you in this world the night your mama died. I'd not be walking up this-here road to burn that-air barn iffen I didn't love you."

"It ain't what I mean. It's Charley. I want Charley to love me."

"Well, gitting mixed up with some nigger boy ain't gonna make Charley love you."

"That ain't why I did it."

"Then howcome?"

"Because." Penny couldn't explain the emptiness she felt, the fierceness within that yearned to fill that emptiness. "I don't know. I'm jest so, so empty. So lonesome."

"You shore you didn't spread out for John, for him to fill up that empty? We ain't going on up the road lessen you swear to me you never did."

"I never! He be an old man, Ellen. Old and smelly and drunk on whiskey. I never!"

"Les git a move on, then. We got a fire to git going. We already be at the lane."

"I kin see the lights from the house," Penny said after they walked less than thirty yards.

Two squares of lamplight flickered through the darkness. They had to pass the house to reach the barn, which sat some fifty yards beyond it, straight down the lane.

"He got two hounds," Penny said.

"They come out barking, we jest call em over. I got us some cow bone from yesterday's stew to keep 'em busy."

"We gonna hafta move fast to git by the house afterwards."

"I been here enough times when their first two babies got born. I hepped brang 'em both. I know a shortcut down to the train tracks. We kin be there in two shakes of a cows' tail. C'mon."

As they neared the house, one of the dogs began to bark and ran out to meet them. Both women moved closer to the trees flanking the lane. The front door opened, and John stood there, a black shadow against the light as he tried to see into the darkness.

"Whatza matter, Red?" he called.

By then, Red had reached the women and he fell silent as he recognized their smell. Ellen handed him the bone, and he trotted off to gnaw it. The other hound did not appear.

"He's just barking, I reckon," John called over his shoulder. "I'd thought he'd gone running off with Diamond." The door closed.

"Shut yer eyes a minutes, Penny. Let 'em git used-ta the dark again. I kain't see nothing right now after looking at that-air light."

"Me neither."

They stood a moment, eyes closed, and then Ellen opened hers. "Keep yer eyes turned to the ground or you'll go night blind again," she said. "Kin you see now?"

"Yeah."

"Les go."

They reached the barn, where fresh hay scented the air. As they walked around to the back, to enter on the side away from Hall's house, a cow lowed a soft welcome and began to drop splats onto the ground.

Once inside, Ellen felt around with her bare feet.

"Ain't enough hay on the ground here. He musta let them cows come inside to clean up what spilt offa the hay truck. You skinny up the ladder and shove down some more."

Penny could barely make out the ladder, but as she reached it, her foot clunked into metal. The sound of the tool hitting the floor was muted by twenty years of manure that had never been mucked out and had dried to a soft powder.

"It's the pitchfork," Ellen said. "Take it up there and shove off a big pile."

Penny wrapped her hands around a rung, moved up five steps, and reached down for the pitchfork. Climbing was more difficult with one hand holding the tool, but she reached the loft, shoved the pitchfork ahead of herself, and climbed into the hay.

With the pitchfork she soon had a mound of hay on the ground that reached right up to the loft. Dust coated her arms and hair. She sneezed as she tossed the pitchfork across the loft. She itched down her back from the straw that slid beneath her collar.

"C'mon down," Ellen called. "You got enough hay down heah to do ten barns. This-un's gonna go quick."

"He ain't gonna be putting it out, is he?" Penny asked as she climbed down the ladder.

"Uh–uh. It gonna go fast. Here. You set the first Lucifer." Ellen extended one of the kitchen matches to Penny.

She struck it on the ladder, cupped her hand around it, picked up a handful of hay, and held it over the flame. As soon as it caught, she tossed the flames to the bottom of the stack.

"Ain't you gonna light yourn?" Penny asked as she stared at the flames.

Ellen's smile showed in the dancing fire. "Course I am." She struck hers on a side board and bent down to light the base of the hay stack on the side away from Penny's.

"We gotta git," Ellen said and grabbed Penny's hand. "C'mon."

Ellen led her from the barn and away from the house down the driveway. They had not reached the train tracks when they heard John yell about the fire. Ellen grinned at Penny.

"He ain't gonna come sniffing round you no more."

"He ain't never gonna know, is he?"

"He know right now. Ain't nobody messing with us less they wants their barn burnt. He knowed that ever since we come down here frum the mountains."

They came out of the woods, and the tracks stretched before them. They side-stepped down the bank, crossed the narrow ditch, and scrambled up the gravel bed. Starlight was bright enough to turn the tracks into white bands that called them home across the darkness.

To their left, the flames turned the night sky orange and the rising smoke sat heavy in the air. Ellen reached over to her niece and hugged her.

"Les git on home. We got to tend to Charley."

"I itch something fierce, all up my back. I mused-ta got hay down my dress."

"Slip outta the dress and let me rub down yer back and git some of it off-a you."

As Ellen rubbed her back, Penny rolled her shoulders and laughed. "That shore do feel good. I ain't had my back rubbed before."

"You ain't never been in a hay barn like that afore, neither."

Penny's laughter died as she remembered her time in the barn, in the hay, with Jeff. She probably itched then but was too involved to remember.

"That's good. Lemme git my dress on and we kin git home."

* * *

"You see that fire up the road yonder?" Ellen asked Jack and Sam as she and Penny walked up the steps onto the porch.

Both men had quit whittling and now stood, each leaning against one of the porch posts, to look across the fields and pastures to the north. The entire sky flared red.

"It's worsen them north lights what went red and green. That-air got to be up to the Hall place," Jack said.

"Hot as that is, must be his barn," Sam said.

"Now how you reckon his barn cotched fire?" Ellen asked.

Penny remained silent, and while everyone else stared off into the distance, she slipped silently into the house. Let Ellen tell them whatever she wanted to. She didn't want to hear it. She had her satisfaction, and she hoped John Hall was up there in a real tizzy and knew it was her.

He'd think she had told her pa and that her pa had done it. Then he'd wonder how come her pa hadn't whupped him instead of helping gather in the hay. He sure would have a puzzle to figure out. Leastways, wasn't no way anybody could say they'd done it.

She went into the kitchen, remembered they had not drawn water for the morning, and took the water bucket back to the porch.

"Pa, we fergot to git water fer breakfast. You mind drawing up a bucket?"

Sam's silent reply was to take the kitchen bucket and walk off toward the well. In a moment, the pulley squeaked as he lowered the well bucket. In the silence of night, she thought she heard the bucket as it splashed into the water. Then the pulley squealed again, and moments later Sam returned.

"Here ya be, baby," he said and set the bucket on the porch before he mounted the steps.

"Thanks, Pa."

Sam sat and tilted his chair.

"The fire looks bout to burn itself down." They all looked. The glow no longer flared and flickered but seemed steady and smaller.

"I reckon if it's John's, he might-a made somebody really mad," Ellen said.

As Penny went inside, she heard Ellen say, "I gotta tell you, Sam. Penny's gonna have Charley's baby. We gotta do sump-em."

"I'll kill the bastard," Sam got up so fast he kicked over the chair and it spun off the porch.

Penny set the bucket down in the front room and eased back to the door, where she stood just inside and listened.

"You shore it's Charley's baby?" Jack asked.

"What're you talking about, Jack? It couldn't be nobody else's," Sam said. He pounded a fist onto a post. "He the only boy ever been hanging around her. And he ain't been around much. You shore she's got a baby coming?"

"I know it," Ellen said.

Ellen narrowed her eyes and turned her gaze on Jack. He nodded. He wasn't about to say a word to Sam about Jeff. Let that dead nigger lie dead and hope to God she didn't have a nigger baby. Sam'd beat her half dead if she did.

"Whatcha looking at Jack thataway fer?" Sam asked. "He know sump-em I don't?"

"No, no," Ellen said. "I jest got to thinking bout what you said. Charley ain't been around here much. He been running around with the judge's girl. Iffen he gits her pregnant too, she'll marry him afore you know it. We gotta git aholt of him first."

"I'll git on up the road right now," Sam said. "Keys in the truck?"

"Yeah, like always," Jack said. "But holt on a minute, Sam. We gotta git this-here all figgered out. We need to talk to Virgil. Him and Charley been best friends forever. He needing to know."

"They ain't best friends no mo'. What with Virgil running up against Mr. Cunningham."

"Still, wait till tomorrow. I'll git down to Dr. Jacobs and talk to him and Virgil."

"Best we wait, like she says, Sam. Virgil's got a good head. Better'n our'n. He kin git things done we kain't."

Sam sighed. His breath rose from deep inside and poured his agony out into the night. Back home a girl in the family way got married, and the boy knew better'n to say no. Charley would be different.

"Awright. We'll git Virgil to hep us with this." He pointed off to the northwest. "Looks like that-air fire done burned itself out. Next time John comes by, we needs to ask him iffen it was his barn."

Chapter 2: The Next Day

"You mean to tell me Penny's pregnant? She ain't but fourteen." Virgil's voice rose into a shout. "I oughtta kill that son of a bitch."

"We ain't wanting him dead, son. Jest married to her," Ellen said.

"It's all over town he's going to marry Karen Emerson in August," Dr. Jacobs said.

"Well, that-air's in August. This here be June. He kain't marry her in August iffen he be married to Penny. And my girl ain't having no bastard," Sam said.

"You sure she's pregnant?" Dr. Jacobs asked.

"I'm shore. She ain't been on the rag for more'n two months now. Not since Charley come sniffing round. She was out real late with him the very night you got home, Virgil. And took off with him again about three weeks later. She says she ain't had no period since that last time with him."

Dr. Jacobs smiled.

"I've never been in on a shotgun wedding before. It ought to be easy, though. I can get a preacher I know in Macon to come over. He can have the papers you need. We won't have to do a syphilis test seeing as she's pregnant. I can swear to that. I'll get Charley here. Sam and Jack, you'll have to be here with the shotgun. Can't let that boy try to run off, can we? That okay with you folks?"

Ellen nodded. Virgil looked at his father and uncle, and they nodded.

"How about, let's see. How about Friday? This is Tuesday. I'll go over to Macon now and get it all lined up. We'll keep it secret till Thursday evening and tell Penny then. That night, I'll send Jupiter up to Lawrence's to tell him I need to see Charley alone down here. I'll make up something about the election. That I'm trying to get Virgil out of the house or something. That'll get him here."

Virgil walked over to Sam.

"I'm sorry, Uncle Sam. I though better of Charley. If you'd rather, we can have him locked up, seeing she's not but fourteen"

"That ain't it, boy. I married her ma when she warn't but fourteen. And Ellen and Jack got married when she warn't but fourteen too. She gotta marry that boy. Or I'll kill 'im."

Sam no longer sounded angry, simply sure of the coming events. Marriage or death.

Chapter 3: Friday

The Carter family walked to Dr. Jacobs' house to ensure that Charley wouldn't see their truck when he arrived. Penny wore a flowered summer dress made from a swatch of store-bought cloth, her only dress not made from feed sacks. She gripped a handful of flowers that Ellen picked from beside the road as they walked over.

Sweat beaded on Penny's face. Her hands trembled. She wanted this wedding so bad, and feared Charley's reaction when he walked in and saw her there. For the first time in her life, she was afraid of him.

Suppose he said no. Suppose Pa took him outside and beat up on him. Or Pa and Jack shot him, like Pa said he'd do. Penny swallowed the bile that kept rising in her throat. She hoped she wouldn't throw up again today. Four trips to the outhouse this morning to upchuck. Most days it wasn't but once, maybe twice. Today she was too scared to keep anything down.

And Dr. Jacobs' daughter-in-law had baked her a cake, a white cake with white icing and two little pink hearts overlapped. Dr. Jacobs had cooled some of his homemade scuppernong wine in his icebox. The two of them had planned a big party for the wedding.

The Right Reverend John Williamson of the Holiness Church of the Christ Risen had come over from Macon. He had all the papers they needed, including the license that Charley was going to have to sign. A bottle of ink and a pen sat on the table beside the papers.

Sam and Jack waited in the kitchen with their shotguns. Every time one of them coughed, Penny shivered. She could see her pa from where she sat, and every time he snuffed out a cigarette on the bottom of his boot, he started to roll up another one. He'd be plumb outta Prince Albert long before Charley got there.

Virgil sprawled in an armchair, his face leaned over for his chin to rest on his one hand. Today he wore a pair of gray pants and a white shirt. Even a tie. She had never seen Virgil in a tie before.

The door knocker fell, once, twice, and Dr. Jacobs hurried off to the front door. She heard Charley's voice.

"Morning, Doc. Daddy said you needed to see me. Something about Virgil getting on your nerves? What can I do about it?"

"Come on in, Charley. Let's talk in the parlor."

Footsteps moved down the hallway and into the room across the way. Those windows had been shuttered and locked earlier. Jack and Sam came out of the kitchen. Virgil raised his hand and his relatives followed him to the parlor door. Janice came next, and The Right Reverend came in last.

"Hello? What's this? Looks like a Carter party," Charley said as they entered and spread across the wall on either side of the door. "Whoa, Virgil. What's with your folks and those shotguns? You think I did something to you in this election campaign?"

Virgil shook his head.

"No, that's not it. We're here for a wedding."

"Wedding? Who's getting married?"

"You. You and Pen."

"Hold on now. You gotta be joking. I'm not marrying Penny. I'm set to marry Karen Emerson in August. We've set the date and she's ordered invitations."

"Penny's gonna have your baby. And us Carter's don't have bastards. This-here be yer wedding day, boy." Sam's voice was flat and cold as a slice of watermelon out of a deep spring.

Charley looked from person to person. His face began to turn red; the freckles faded into the blush. He raised a hand to point to Sam.

"She's just saying it's mine. She's likely been messing around with other fellows, too."

"That's a lie and you know it, Charley!" Penny screamed, ran across the room and slammed the flowers over and over into his face. "That's a lie. That's a lie."

Charley raised his arms to fend off the attack.

"I ain't marrying up with this hellcat!"

Ellen grabbed Penny and pulled her back.

"He deserve more'n that, honey child, only we'll let the men whup him some iffen he be a-needing it. You git on back here a minute."

Jack and Sam stepped forward, and Charley backed up until he hit the wall.

"You got nowhere to run to, Charley," Virgil said. "You may's well give it up. You gonna marry Penny either before or after you take a beating. Marry before, and the only beating you'll get will be a slap on the back from your in-laws." Virgil looked at his friend, saw the fear, and shook his head.

"I wish it didn't have to be this way. But like Sam said, us Carter's don't have bastards." Virgil turned around. "Preacher, you come on up here and let's get this wedding over and done with."

"I won't really be married, Virgil. I'll tell everybody you folks forced me to."

"Won't work, Charley," Dr. Jacobs said. "A shotgun wedding is just as legal as any. You'll be signing off on the license and everything will be perfectly legal."

"Not without the blood test."

Dr. Jacobs smiled and shook his head. "She's pregnant, son. The law allows the marriage without a test when the girl is pregnant. Another thing. You know she's not but fourteen. If you decide not to marry her, you could go to jail for rape. If you survive what her pa and uncle do to you."

Charley gulped. One hand came up and rubbed over his face. His eyes flicked from person to person and finally settled on Penny.

He shrugged his surrender.

"My pa's gonna kill me. Kill me plumb dead. But I reckon I got a better chance with him than with your folks, Virgil. Awright. But I don't have a ring."

"I do," Janice said. "If it's okay with you?" She looked to Jacobs.

He nodded, and Janice pulled off the gold band given to her by Dr. Jacobs' son when they married in the same parlor before her husband went off to die for his country.

She handed the ring to Virgil, who stepped up and stood beside Charley.

"I'm your best friend, and I'll be your best man."

"I don't like this one bit, Virgil," Charley said.

"Maybe not. But you been messing around with Penny since ya'll were children. Everybody knows your pa shipped you off cause you got caught messing with her long time ago."

"That was kid stuff."

"But getting her pregnant isn't, Charley."

The Right Reverend opened his Bible and began to read. His voice carried the sing-song so common to revival preachers who were more concerned with their own importance than with the congregation.

"Let's get the wedding over and done, Preacher," Charley said. "I'm not in any kind of mood for a lot of preaching."

The Right Reverend went directly to the marriage pages. When he asked who gave the bride, Ellen nudged Sam toward his daughter, and he pushed her over to stand by Charley.

"Me," was all he said.

The wedding over, the Reverend said, "You may kiss your bride."

Penny looked up into his eyes and saw anger recede as he lowered his lips to hers. She parted hers and probed with her tongue. He pulled it into his mouth and began to suck on it. Everything fell from her life except Charley. The nausea left, the fear left, and all energy left as she melted into him.

"Hey, that's enough," Sam grumbled. "He said kiss, not make love to. You come up offer her."

The couple separated for a moment. Penny glowed. Charley wore caution and fear like a blanket. He would have to face his father.

"Let's go sign the papers," Virgil said. "then we can have cake and wine that Miss Janice has so graciously provided." He smiled at her and bowed slightly.

Jack and Sam carried the shotguns into the dining room and held them until the papers were signed by the couple, the Right Reverend, and both Dr. Jacobs and Janice as witnesses.

"I'll take these right in and get them registered in the courthouse this afternoon," Dr. Jacobs said. He stuffed them into his medical bag. Janice immediately picked it up and carried it off to another room as he poured two goblets of his scuppernong wine. He handed one to Penny and one to Charley.

Everyone else crowded around, hands out, ready for a glass full. Sam and Jack gulped theirs down, and the doctor refilled their glasses and told them to hold off on drinking. As soon as everyone had a glass, he raised his and said, "To the happy couple."

Charley's wine lasted two quick swallows. Penny tasted it, found it sweet, and drank it right down, unmindful of the slight burning in her throat. Warmth spread inside and she shivered. She smiled up at Charley.

"That's real good, Doc. Kin I have some more?" she asked.

"It's your wedding day. Why not?" He poured her another glass.

Afraid the party would turn rowdy after everyone had two glasses, Jacobs put the decanter aside and suggested they have some cake.

"Come on, Penny. You get to cut the cake. Both of you." Janice took Penny by the hand and led her around the table to the two-tier cake. A silver cake server lay beside it, and a stack of plates waited to be filled. Linen napkins and silver dessert forks awaited use.

Penny looked at the server and at the cake, and then turned to Janice. "Kin you cut it? I ain't never cut a cake like that."

"Sure." Janice smiled and began to serve the cake. She passed a fork and white linen napkin with each plate.

An hour later, as the couple prepared to leave, Sam hugged Penny.

"You make him a good wife, sweetheart."

"I will, Pa."

"You come see us, now, you hear?" Ellen said as she hugged Penny.

As the newlyweds started to the door, Janice called to Charley to take Penny's bag, a paper grocery sack that held her few clothes. Jack and Sam picked up their shotguns and headed for the door behind them.

Ellen followed, her mind on the evening Penny was born. That stubbornness had only gotten stronger, and Penny had held out for what she wanted. Now pray Gawd they figured right and the baby really is Charley's and not Jeff's. Iffen it be Jeff's, she thought, and Charley don't kill her, it's fer sure her Pa will half-kill her and plain out kill the nigger baby.

Chapter 4

The couple walked to the Buick, its tail high in the air. A whiskey hauler with an empty trunk, its heavy shocks lifted the rear end an extra two feet. Charley walked directly to the driver's door. Unaware that he should have opened the door for her, Penny let herself in the other side.

He had not bothered to pull the car into the shade, and an hour in the summer sun had turned it brinjin hot inside. The seat was so hot she immediately got out, reached into the paper sack of her clothes, where Charley had put it in the back seat. She took out her second dress and laid it on the seat.

The inside of the car smelled of cigars and whiskey. A quart Mason jar half-full of moonshine sat on the front seat. As she slid across toward Charley's side, she bumped it and it started to fall. She grabbed it as Charley yelled, "Watch out!" and grabbed for it.

"I weren't gonna let it spill," she said. She held it up and smiled, her eyes alight with laughter.

"I'll put it in back. "

She didn't see any signs of laughter in his face as she handed it to him. He wedged it against her sack of clothes and slid under the wheel. She snuggled up against him.

"Oh, Charley, I'm so happy."

"I gotta change gears, Penny. Sit up till I get us on the road." His voice dripped anger.

She sat away from him and watched as his hands and feet worked the gears and clutch. She wanted to touch his hand that wrapped around the gear shift knob beside her knee. The hair tufted on each knuckle and growing up his arms had bleached almost white from the sun. His skin was tanned and bore a reddish tint from recent outdoor work. His childhood freckles still smattered across his nose and cheeks and down his arms.

"Whatcha do to your hand?" she asked as she touched a scuffed place on his knuckle.

He slowed at the end of the drive and shifted into first to pull onto the road. "I scraped it stuffing whiskey jugs in the trunk. Bumped up on the spare tire. You'd think I'd know where it is after all this time."

As soon as he shifted into third, she reached for his right hand, pulled it away from the gear shift, and lifted it over her head and around her shoulder. She laid her head sideways on his shoulder so she could look up into his face.

He hadn't shaved. Funny, she hadn't noticed his bristles earlier. But she was too excited at the wedding to notice. The whiskers showed as red as his hair.

"I'll remember today forever. I ain't never been so happy, Charley."

The air blowing in the windows swept her hair back from her face. A smile hovered on her lips as her mind looked into her tomorrows and saw half-formed dreams of days and nights of only herself and Charley. And the baby.

Oh, Gawd, she thought. Suppose it ain't redheaded. Suppose it's got black kinky hair like Jeff. I can't let myself think about it. Not today. Not today. Not on my wedding day. Even Janice is happy for me. And gave us her own ring from where she got married during the war.

She held her hand out, looked at the ring, and smiled.

"I'm so glad to be married to you. It's my dream come true. And it was a pretty wedding, warn't it? And that cake Janice made fer us. It shore was tasty. Bestest thing I ever put in my mouth. Iffen you like it, I'll git her to learn me how to make one."

"I liked it fine." He didn't sound anywhere near as happy as she felt.

"You mad at me about the wedding?"

He shrugged. "I got no right to be mad if I put that baby inside you."

"Well, you did. You know you did." She sat up straight. "How come you said it like that, like 'iffen' you did?"

"You didn't mess around with anybody else, did you, Penny?"

"Who else I got to mess around with? You all I ever wanted. Every since I kin remember. Every since you showed me—you know." She kept her eyes down, her gaze locked on the road in front of them. If she looked at him, he'd know she was lying, and he couldn't ever know about Jeff. He'd kill her and throw her in the river like a croaker sack of unwanted puppies. When he did not speak, she glanced back up at him.

His attention seemed to be only on the road ahead, a road he could drive down with his eyes closed. She settled against him in shared silence.

Hay fields and pastures scented the air with the smells of fresh cut hay and manure. A meadow lark lifted its song to the day and showed its yellow belly on a fence post. A bluebird lit on another post and ducked into a hole with food for its young.

The farming odors fell under the strong putrid half-decay smell of a skunk that ran in front of the Buick too fast for Charley to miss it.

"Oh, shit," Charley said. "That's all I need now. Daddy's gonna kill me without that."

"The stink'll go away, honey. Pa got skunk on him one time when he thought the dog'd treed a possum in the ground. Only it was a skunk. The smell came off atter awhile."

"It's not the same with a car. This one'll stink for weeks. I hope I killed it. It's gotta have rabies to be running around in the daylight. Oh damn, damn, damn." He pounded his fist on the steering wheel.

"Don't cuss so, Charley. It ain't nice."

"Don't you start in telling me what to do, you hear? I got enough to worry over without you getting on my back."

Tears welled up but did not wash away her pain. He was mad at her. He never wanted to marry her, just make a baby with her. And then try to say it warn't his'n. She warn't about to let him talk to her that-away. Jack never raised his voice to Ellen, and even when Sam learnt she was gonna have Charley's baby, he hushed up his mad real fast. She'd have to figure out what to do.

"I don't mean to make you mad, Charley. It's jest Ellen wouldn't never let her boys cuss, and you ain't never cussed around me afore." She pulled away from him. If he was gonna be mad, she could too. He wasn't going to get by with telling her what to do or yelling at her like that.

His arm tightened and pulled her back. He slowed the car, turned her face up to his, and quickly kissed her.

"I'm sorry, Penny. If we're going to be married, we don't need to be fussing at each other. I'm a little scared of seeing my daddy."

"He ain't gonna be mad. You haul all his likker for him in this here car. He kain't git mad at you. He ain't got nobody else to haul for him, is he?"

"No. Fella hauled while I was gone got killed by a logging truck.

That's why Daddy asked me to come home. Maybe you're right. Maybe he needs me enough he won't yell at us."

As they approached the driveway to the Cunningham house, they fell silent. The drive circled through a woodlot of oaks and hickories and ended in the front yard of a farmhouse with a porch going all the way around. Rockers lined the porch as if awaiting an influx of visitors. Screens held up windows to let the breeze in and keep the insects out, and curtains drifted with the breeze in every window.

An oak towering on the south side threw a summer-long patch of shade on the house. Beneath the oak sat an old pickup and a new blue Packard, its white-walls gleaming.

He parked beside the Packard to catch some shade.

"Your daddy's got a new car."

"Yeah. Hadn't had it more'n a week. He's had me wash it for him twice already."

The white-painted clapboards contrasted sharply with Penny's knowledge of country houses. Hers had never seen paint. Dr. Jacobs had not painted his since she could remember, and the paint on his had gone gray. She'd never been to the Cunningham house before, and was surprised at the sharpness with which it stood against the trees.

"It's pretty," she whispered. "So white my eyes hurt from jest looking at it in the sunlight."

"Daddy's painted it every couple of years all my life, except during the war when he couldn't get paint. He had a couple of niggers out here painting for two months back in the spring. Well, let's go."

As she got out of the car behind him, she noticed a lone cloud off to the east. For once in her life, she didn't feel alone; she took his hand as they started toward the house.

"You not gonna take my bag?"

"Not now. I'll get it later, after I get you settled in."

Birds flitted in the magnolias and crepe myrtles. A young mockingbird tried his music, and a jay screamed at them as they headed for the porch. Side-by-side, they walked up the steps. She paused beside one of the rockers a moment, pushed against the high back, and watched it rock. A black-and-tan hound beside the front door raised his head, thumped his tail, and went back to sleep.

"I wanna sit out here and rock and jest look at everythang."

As he pulled open the screen door, he called, "Daddy, I'm home."

"I'm in the kitchen. Come tell me what Jacobs wanted."

The hallway seemed dark after the bright sunlight. A parasol stood in the base of a hall-tree to the left. A straw hat and a felt hat hung on the highest hooks. As they passed along the hall, she noticed several paintings in heavy gold frames, each frame with what looked like a gold oak leaf folded over each corner.

"Who're all these people?"

"Family. Mostly Mama's family. I'll tell you about them all later."

They entered the dining room, where the table was set for two. Penny gawked at the richness around her. Plates sat behind glass doors. Silver goblets lined the shelves of a cabinet. More paintings hung along one wall. As she passed the sideboard she was struck with the glitter of silver candle sticks and silver trays. She didn't have time to take it all in before they entered the kitchen.

Silence for about five seconds. A Negro maid stood in front of the stove and stirred a pot of something that smelled like butterbeans and fatback. She turned slightly to see who had entered, and Penny saw she carried a baby in her belly. A lot further along than Penny. A pork roast sat cooling on a glass platter. An apple pie still steamed from the top of the pie safe.

Cunningham sat by the window on the far side of the kitchen, in an armchair beside a small table. An ashtray and a tumbler of his whiskey sat on the table.

"What's she doing here?" Cunningham jabbed his cigar toward Penny, his face contorted into an angry snarl.

"Daddy, I got married this morning."

"You what? You mean you married this bitch?"

"Don't call her that, daddy. She's my wife. She's gonna give you a grandson."

"I don't need any bastards in this house!"

The Negro girl dropped the spoon, but only Penny noticed.

"And what about Karen Emerson? What about your wedding plans with her? You got anybody else pregnant, too? You're throwing your life away."

"Daddy!"

"Git her outta my house. I won't have any slut here, you hear me? Those Carters aren't fit for anything but breeding babies and making whiskey. Git her outta my house."

"It's my house too, Daddy. Mama left it to both of us."

The two men glared at each other until Penny pulled on Charley's hand. He turned to her. Tears streamed down her face, and she released her grip on his hand.

"I'll go, Charley," she whispered and turned away. This would never be her home. All her hope gone. She could not stop her tears but tried to keep from crying aloud as she walked back into the dining room. She pushed her shoulders up. That old man would never see her crying. Never know she knew about him, either. Talk about bastards, will he? Well, that nigger gal's got his bastard in her belly. He's got no call to damn Charley, seeing as how he's doing the same thing.

A hand touched hers, wrapped its fingers into hers.

"You come back here, Charley!"

"No, Daddy. She's my wife now. You taught me yourself that a wife comes first. She goes, I go. You can stay in the damn house alone for all I care." To Penny he said, "Come on. We'll find us a place to stay."

"He got no call to be mad at you fer giving me a baby. Look-it that nigger gal he got."

"That's different. He'd never think about marrying her and she knows it. Never help with the baby, neither. She's jest a nigger."

They walked out. Charley let the screen door slam as they left.

The shade of the oak had not moved away from the car. The cloud off to the east seemed to be exactly where it was when they went inside. The hound lifted his head again, whacked his tail twice, and flopped his head back down. The mockingbird still sang over in the magnolia. The same jay squawked at them as they crossed the yard to the car.

Her dreams had collapsed, but the world took no notice. Nothing had changed but her future.

They reached the car and stood on each side, and talked across the roof.

"Ellen'll let us stay back at the house," she said.

"I think we need a place of our own."

"You got any money?"

"Not much. A little left from the army. I spend what Daddy pays me. I got to get a job, too."

"Was you really gonna marry Karen?"

He shrugged and looked away, his eyes focused on a distant buzzard that caught a wind current and rose as it circled. He did not look at her as she continued to question him.

"Well, was you?"

"Daddy wanted me to. He figured he'd get more respect if I married the judge's daughter."

"Was you gonna git another place with her or stay at your pa's? How was you gonna pay fer living with her iffen you ain't got no money now?"

"We'd have lived at Daddy's, I reckon."

"You got her caught, too?"

"I'm married to you, Penny. I won't be messing around. I swore to God I'd be faithful, and I will. So quitcha worrying about something from yesterday. It ain't gonna happen again with her. Okay?"

Penny nodded, and they got in the Buick and left.

"Your daddy's gonna be mad at you, taking his car."

Charley laughed and bounced a fist onto the steering wheel.

"Let him. I got to pick up a lot of whiskey this evening. And deliver it. And collect the cash for it. Daddy won't need the car if he's got no whiskey to deliver."

"You mean you gonna keep on selling Jack's? Not let your pa have it like always?"

"Yep. And Gus's. And Noah's. I know everybody who buys it and everybody who sells to Daddy. I'll keep on picking up and hauling and collecting. Only I'll be keeping the money now, not taking it to Daddy. Then he'll be really mad."

"He might be coming after you to git the money."

"He can't do a thing. What's he gonna do? Tell the sheriff? Can't you see him going to Dixon and saying something like, 'My boy is stealing my whiskey, and he won't bring me any money.' " Charley began to laugh so hard he had to pull off to the side of the road. She caught his laughter and joined him.

* * *

Charley drove into town instead of going to the Carter home and went directly to Libby's Diner, where he pulled into the shade of an elm tree. Four other vehicles had been parked in the shade of the elm earlier in the day, but the sun had moved over to touch its heat on two of them. He pulled beside the one on the end, to where the shade was moving, so his car would be bearable when they came out.

"They buy from you?"

"No. I know it's not fancy, and we ate all that cake, but maybe—. Well, I thought before we go to your Aunt Ellen's, I'd take you out for something to eat. They fix a good hamburger here."

"I ain't never et at the diner. Thank you." She scrambled out, trotted around the car, and reached for his hand. "You gonna tell 'em we's married?"

She could almost see his mind working as his eyes darted down the street toward the courthouse and back to the diner. His eyes seemed focused way off, as if he were seeing Karen. Penny knew he wasn't about to tell anybody anything. He'd drop her hand before they went in and act like he didn't care about her. He still had his mind on that Karen girl.

He looked down to her and shrugged. "Why not, seeing as how we are." His expression changed from distance to decision. He grinned, slipped his arm around her shoulder, and pulled her close. "Sure, I'm gonna tell 'em. Let's go."

He opened the door and the smell of bacon, toast, biscuits, coffee and tobacco floated out to meet them. As she moved ahead of him, he released her hand, and as he entered behind her he took it again. She glanced up and smiled at him.

"Let's sit here," he indicated a booth half-way back. She sat down, and he indicated she should move over. He sat beside her.

Cracked leatherette covered the seats. Although the wooden table bore scars and initials that had blackened over time, the top felt smooth from years of plates, cups and utensils sliding across it.

The waitress, with an apron over a summer house dress and her brown hair pulled back into a severe bun, came over, plunked down two napkins and forks, and asked, "Whatcha want, Charley?"

"Hamburger all the way for each of us. And a Coke."

"Who's your lady friend?"

"She's not my lady friend. She's my wife. This is Penny Carter Cunningham."

"Wal, I'll be. The randiest boy in town is married. Ain't nobody gonna believe it. What happened? They hold a shotgun on you?"

Penny and Charley glanced at each other. Penny blushed. Charley guffawed.

"The judge know?"

"Not yet. Reckon I oughtta stroll over to the courthouse and tell him?"

"Not if you don't want to get whupped up on. Let him jest hear about it if you're smart." She turned to the cook and called, "Two cows all the way." To them she said, I'll git y'all's Cokes." She walked away.

"Who's she?" Penny asked. "I don't know her and she knows all about you."

"Nita. She's Libby's daughter and's worked here since I can remember. She keeps up with everybody in town and out in the country too. Worst gossip in town."

"Who's worst gossip in town?" the waitress said as she put two sweaty, cold Coke bottles on the table.

Charley grinned at her. "You are."

Nita shrugged and said, "That's why you told me, a-course. I'll see to it the judge knows before you git back to your daddy's house."

"Cows up!" the cook called.

*   *   *

An hour later, Charley stopped the Buick outside the Carter home. For the first time he did not stop on the road but drove into the yard from the upper side of the well, along the same wagon trail the Carter's used. He parked in the shade where the Carter's parked their trucks.

Ellen had reached the porch by the time they got out, and she called, "You in trouble already?"

Charley reached for Penny's hand.

"No, Miss Ellen. My daddy threw us outta the house. Might my bride and I rent a room from you until I can find a home for her?" He grinned at her and bowed slightly.

"Well, I never. That-air man's a fool, throwing you out. How's he gonna git his likker toted all over town?" She sat down in one of the porch chairs.

"Oh, Ellen, Charley's got it all figured out. He's gonna sell the likker and keep the money hisself instead of taking it to his daddy. He'll git as rich as Mr. Cunningham afore you know it."

Ellen slapped her knee. "By gumption, that'll learn the old man, Charley. Y'all pull up a chair and set a spell."

"I need to do some getting around. First stop is Jack's still. He's supposed to have a run ready today."

"Naw, boy, you sit. You got no need to be running around right now. But first, you need to put that car over across behind the barn.

Your pa come along and see it, he might try to drive it off. We ain't telling him you're staying here. Let 'im go looking when he's over his mad."

"I don't care about him getting over his mad. I won't be getting over mine." He reached over and touched Penny's hair. "He treated Penny worse'n he treats his nigger. I won't get over that for a long spell, Miss Ellen. And I'm gonna take all his whiskey business. Let 'im go on to town and talk to the buyers. He won't have anything to sell them, but I will. He doesn't pay much of anything for the whiskey. I reckon y'all know that. I'm gonna double what he pays, and sell it a little cheaper than he always has. That way, everybody'll sell to me and buy from me. I won't be cheating the men taking the risks.

"I really need to get around the county this afternoon and let everybody know that although I'll still pick up from them on schedule I'll have to be a day later paying them."

"Some of them ain't gonna wait fer their money. Jack wouldn't, ceptin he be knowing you good. Them what's always done business with your pa, they'll want they money when you pick up, like always. They ain't knowing iffen you'll be good fer it."

Charley nodded and sat down. "I thought I had it all figured out." He slumped forward, his hands between his knees, dejection sitting on him like a sack of cottonseed hulls.

Penny reached over and took his hand. "We'll figger something."

"You quit ya fretting," Ellen said. "I got me some money tucked back. I kin let you use to git started. Jest you kain't go telling nobody where it come from. Not even Jack. You hear?"

"I hear you real good," Charley said as he sat erect. He pulled out his cigarettes, and as he lit one Penny took a deep breath; the smoke smelled so different from that of the cigarettes her family men rolled from Prince Albert. She enjoyed the smell of Charley's, the same smell she associated with Charley since he used to steal his daddy's cigarettes.

"Miss Ellen, I can't believe you're keeping money secrets from Jack. I've always thought of you as the most honest woman around."

"He know I got Bobby's money," she said. "He jest ain't knowing how much. I done used some to git BJ outta jail, and I'll git it back soon as his trial's over. That-air's gonna be a heap more'n enough to pay his fine. And what I got left now'll be enough to git you started good, and then we'll put it all back for another hard time."

Chapter 5

That night when Jack and Sam came home they found Penny and Charley sitting with Ellen on the front porch. Jack picked up the carving he had worked on the night before, sat down, pulled out his pocket knife, and whittled while they talked.

"Thought you and yer lover'd be off somewhere," Sam said to Penny. "Whatcha doing back home?"

"Daddy threw us out," Charley said. "Miss Ellen's taking us in until I can get us fixed up somewhere."

"You ain't got no money of your'n, is you?" Sam asked. He sat in one of the chairs, tilted it back, and leaned forward to prop his elbows on his thighs.

Charley shook his head. "Not now. But give me a few days. I'm taking over Daddy's whiskey trade. I've run it since I got home and know everybody he deals with. I'll buy from y'all and from Gus. And I'll keep on selling it to the drug store and county hotel and the whore house—"

"Whore house?" Ellen interrupted. "We got a whore house here?"

Charley laughed. "Afraid so, Miss Ellen."

"Whereabouts?"

"What's a whore house?" Penny asked.

Charley's eyes rolled as he turned to his bride. Sam and Jack laughed. Ellen spoke. "It's where the men go for a woman. Like they's married to her but instead they pay her."

"Like BJ's always talking about going to?"

"Yeah," Ellen said and turned to glare at Jack. "Where I been hoping his pa ain't taking him."

"Whereat is it?"

"Downtown. On the second floor of the drug store. It's one of our best customers."

Jack looked up from his carving.

"What you gonna do when your pa comes fer his car and his customers?"

"I'll have it all worked out in about two days. He can't find anybody around here to face me down over this."

"Supposing he hires somebody to do his hauling?"

"That ain't likely. Old Plute used to haul, but he's too old. By the time Daddy could find somebody, I'll have the business in my pocket. Daddy won't be a problem. Will you all sell to me?"

Jack nodded. "Shore."

"Sam?"

"Course I will, son. You family now. Mr. Larry ain't family, not after how he treated my girl. Anybody bother you and yer business, you tell me. Ain't that right, Jack?"

"Yep."

Charley rose, bent down to kiss Penny on the cheek, stepped inside for his hat, and announced, "I gotta go see some of my sellers."

Penny rose.

"Take me with you."

"Not tonight, sweetheart," Charley said as he shook his head. "I got to pick up from two stills. I can't have you in the car tonight. I'll be back afore long."

He walked off into the darkness and a moment later the Buick roared off as it spewed a cloud of dust onto the porch.

PART V: JULY 1946

Chapter 1: Sunday Before Election

"Don't you even think of being seen in nigra-town today," Dr. Jacobs said. "I've got five men passing out these flyers at the Negro churches this morning." He handed a copy to Virgil, who began to read.

County Commissioner Chairman Cunningham will be at Carver High School tonight at 8:00 o'clock to talk to the good colored people about the election. Come by for a Co- Cola and a Hershey bar.

"Where'd you get this?" Virgil asked.

Jacobs grinned. The lines in his face softened and his eyes caught sunlight that streamed in the window. Virgil thought that sparkle belonged more to a courting man than to one helping win a political race.

"I printed them up."

"You what?" Virgil began to chuckle.

"Well, I actually went over to Macon and had somebody there print them. We've got 200 copies out to the Negro churches today. Cunningham has no idea."

Virgil shook his head. "You lost me somewhere, Doc. If Cunningham doesn't know about this, how can he be there?"

"That's the point, Virgil. He won't be there. I've planned it all out. You show up at eight o'clock and speak. I've arranged for a pickup truck to come over a little after eight, loaded with tubs of co-colas and boxes of Hershey bars. You'll get their vote, not from the co-colas and Hershey bars but because you showed up and he didn't. With them and the white farmers who're also tired of Cunningham's lying, you'll win."

"I ain't so sure. Soon as people find out we set it all up, I'll be run outta town."

"Nobody'll find out. I've written you out a talk, so all you have to do is wear your suit pants and a tie. Not your work clothes. Show respect. They'll all be in their good clothes too. I'll tend to the rest of it."

He handed Virgil several pieces of notebook paper, covered with the doctor's elaborate handwriting. Virgil began to read to himself. After a moment, he looked up and smiled.

"I like it. It'll work."

Jacobs nodded. "It will. Now let's go get some dinner."

They walked from the doctor's office through the house to the dining room. Sally Anne had almost finished setting the table, and when she saw the men, she ran over to Virgil and wrapped her arms around his waist.

"Hey, Uncle Virgil."

"Hello, sweetheart."

"Hi, Virgil," Janice said as she came in with a large tureen of stew that scented the air with warmth and hominess. "Hope you're not tired of beef stew and potatoes."

"I'll never get tired of your cooking. Best thing that's happened to me since I got home is eating your cooking."

Virgil pulled out a chair for her, and they sat down.

"Sweetheart, will you say grace for Granddad?"

Sally Anne recited the same short prayer she said at every meal. Janice served stew into bowls and passed them down the table, and they ate as a family.

* * *

A few minutes before eight that evening, Jacobs drove him to Carver High and parked in the deep shadows under the oaks across the street. They sat in the car, arms resting on the open windows.

"He'll be along directly," Jacobs said.

Perhaps seventy-five Negro men and women roamed around the yard, many dressed in their Saturday town clothes, some dressed in their Sunday best. All the women wore hats, carried black purses, and held gloves. The society of the black community had come, as well as many of the poorer farmers and working families.

At precisely eight, a blue Packard drove into the schoolyard, its white-walls gleaming, the driver obviously Lawrence Cunningham with a felt hat pulled slantwise over his left eye. As always, his arm rested in the open window. The car slowed, cut sharply away from the building, gained speed, and fled the dirt parking lot.

While dust still floated over the crowd, Virgil stepped from Jacobs' car, his speech in his hand, and strode toward the front porch. Sweat ran steams down his face. As he walked he stuffed the paper into his shirt pocket and pulled out his handkerchief to wipe sweat off his face. Even at sundown, the day was still brinjin hot.

"Hey, it's Mr. Virgil," somebody called.

"You gonna talk to us, Mr. Virgil?" another called.

"You bet I am," he called back. "Just let me get up on the steps here."

The crowd backed away, giving him walking room, and he mounted the four steps to the concrete porch under a 3' x 3' roof. When he turned to face them, they quieted.

He looked from side to side. "Did you see that blue Packard?"

At least fifty "Yessuhs" floated to him.

"You reckon old Larry Cunningham is scared to get outta his car here? Reckon he's scared to talk to you good colored people?"

"He oughtta be mo'n jest scared. He done lied. He said he gonna gib us a co-cola if we be's here."

"Well, folks, I'll tell you the truth. I figured he wasn't gonna be here. I've known that man all my life, and I figured he was gonna run away from you good people. So I went to see the man down at the A & P, and got three tubs of co-colas and some candy bars on the way."

Cheers rose from the crowd.

"Until the truck gits here, I wanna talk to you. Come Tuesday, it'll be time to vote. This-here is the first time a lot of you are gonna vote. I'm counting on your help. Counting on you to help me be your county commissioner. We got to take the county away from Larry Cunningham. He didn't keep his promise to you today. He got scared and he ran away. Ain't that right?"

The crowd roared.

"And you gonna vote for me, for Virgil Carter, come Tuesday? Ain't that right?"

"Yessuh," roared like a thunderstorm from the parking lot.

"Who you gonna vote for on Tuesday?"

"You, Mr. Virgil," overpowered the other responses of "You, suh."

"And who's gonna pave this here parking lot for your chullen?"

"You, Mr. Virgil."

"Who cares most about the poor folks in this county?"

"You, suh."

"Who can the colored folks count on to help them?"

"You, suh."

"Here come those co-colas now," Virgil said and pointed toward the entrance to the parking lot. A pickup truck kicked dust as it roared up, and the crowd surged toward it as if afraid there would not be enough treats for everyone.

Someone dropped the tailgate, hopped into the truck bed, and pushed the No. 10 foot tubs toward the back where hands reached into the ice and pulled out the bottles, passing them back until the tubs were almost empty. Everyone had a Coke. The driver, meantime, had stepped out of the cab and began passing out candy bars.

Laughter filled the evening air as Virgil mingled, passing around his church key, the only one available, so everybody had to come to him to open the Coke bottles. He held out his hand to shake with the men and gave a slight bow to the women.

The town's lone black physician came up to Virgil. "Mr. Carter, I'm Dr. Watson, and this is my wife, Lucy."

Virgil extended his hand, shook with the doctor, and then turned to the wife. "My pleasure, Mrs. Watson."

He noticed her eyes widen slightly at his show of respect, and then she smiled.

"I was going to ask you if you thought a co-cola and a candy bar were enough to buy votes."

"Never, m'am. I don't think a vote oughtta be for sale. I hope my show of respect will help me get elected."

"I've never seen Cunningham defeated in anything he wanted. But you might manage this. Who was in the car?" Dr. Watson asked.

"What?" Virgil pulled his head back, his face contorted as if in confusion.

"That Packard. You know Mr. Larry isn't going to run off from a bunch of niggers."

"Truthfully, Doctor, I have no idea who was in that car. It looked like Mr. Cunningham. I knowed him all my life, and that sure looked like him to me."

"You wouldn't be—?" Dr. Watson began.

"Willie, you hush up!" His wife jabbed her elbow into his side so hard he flinched. "You show some respect for your next county commissioner."

"I was about to ask if you're being truthful, but I reckon the missus means I can't ask you." The doctor laughed.

"Dr. Watson, I honest to God have no idea who was in that car."

"Looked like Larry to me," Dr. Jacobs said as he walked up to them.

"Looked like him to me too," said Lucy Watson. "You really going to pave our parking lot here?"

"Yes," Virgil said. "And fix up the playgrounds. I know it's usually the school board, but they ain't gonna do nothing for you colored people. So when I'm elected, I'll make them fix it all up, just like they fix up things for the white chullen. Fair is fair. If a colored man can fight in the army, he should have the same chance at learning that a white boy has."

"Hey, Mr. Virgil," someone called. "Kin we take them extra co-colas home to the chullen?"

"Shore can. Y'all figure out how to split them up fair. I ain't gonna tell you how to divvy 'em."

Another whoop rose up, and the crowd collected around the pickup bed. No one pushed as the people talked about how many children they had at home and who ought to have what. Some settled for the candy and others took the drinks.

"You got yourself a lotta votes, Virgil," Dr. Watson said.

Virgil noticed the absence of the "mista" and smiled. He had a friend in Dr. Watson now.

"I sure hope so, sir. And hope you'll spread the word tomorrow if you're offering me your support."

"I certainly will," Mrs. Watson said. "My sewing circle meets in the morning, and instead of sewing we'll spread out over the colored part of town. We'll roust out the votes for you. Everybody who got registered will be there."

"That's mighty kind of you, m'am."

The crowd thinned quickly. A few came over to say goodnight to Virgil when they saw him talking with their doctor. But Virgil noticed that everyone smiled at him and raised a hand as they left. These people would stand for him on Tuesday.

Dr. Watson held out his hand again. "I'm proud to meet you, Virgil. Best of luck on Tuesday. I'll pray for you."

"And I for you, sir," Virgil said as he clasped the doctor's hand. He then bowed slightly to Mrs. Watson.

"It's been my pleasure, m'am. I hope to see you again soon. And I'm much obliged for all your support."

The couple strolled toward a black Buick parked beside the porch.

Virgil began to feel secure about the election as he rode home with Dr. Jacobs except he wondered who else knew the secret of the handbill and the driver of the Packard. He had to ask.

"Where did you find a car like Cunningham's?"

Jacobs laughed. "I didn't. It was his."

"It couldn't be. He didn't know about this."

"He didn't, but Charley did. That boy has turned into a Carter since he married Penny. He hotwired the car, stole it from his daddy's yard, and then took it back. But don't let on I told you."

Virgil laughed the rest of the way home.

Chapter 2: Election Eve

After midnight, Virgil walked to the back door of the courthouse. It was unlocked. He swallowed. If he were caught inside tonight, he would be in real trouble. While his stomach churned more than it had since he went into battle, he stood inside the door and listened. Sweat ran down his back. He wiped moisture from his face and rubbed his hand on his pants.

Only silence and darkness. He faced a long dark tunnel of hallway, with moonlight filtering in at each end through the windows of the heavy oak doors. He tried to soften his footsteps.

Even in the darkness, he knew where he was going. He'd spent hours in the courthouse since he decided to run for commission chairman and knew every office and every individual who worked here.

When he reached the fourth office on his left, he tried the door and found it unlocked, just as the cleaner had promised. He went in.

Enough moonlight filtered through the window for him to see the stack of ballots on the counter that separated visitors from the employees. The top one would be numbered with zeroes and a one. He would not remove the top one or the next few.

He lifted some of the ballots and put them off to his right. Then he removed some from the remaining stack, placed them down the counter to his left. He replaced those that were on top of the stack and tidied them up by patting one edge while he propped the stub of his other arm against them.

He'd have to be sure to tear off all the number stubs, just as he'd told all the Negroes and his supporters to do. If Cunningham made a fuss over how many ballots were used, there'd be no way to tell which were really voted.

He picked up his stack of ballots, stuffed them under the stub of his arm, and opened the door. Silence greeted him. No lights anywhere. He walked out of the office and down the empty hall. His shoes echoed in the empty building.

At the back door he let himself out into the shadows of the oaks. No one was around. The town slept. A small dog yipped down the street. The dampness of night wrapped around him and held his sweat in his clothes. He shivered and hurried through the shadows. No one had seen him. No one would ever suspect he had been into the building except the cleaner who had come to him with the suggestion and left the door unlocked.

A match flared under an oak as he walked back toward the car, and Virgil halted, a knot in his stomach. The match went up a little until it revealed a familiar black face that erupted into a smile. As relief flooded him, Virgil raised his good arm in salute. The door would be locked in minutes.

Now all he had to do was vote these ballots. Tomorrow the trick would be to get them into the courthouse and into the ballot box. The briefcase he'd carried everywhere for the last month would be so familiar to the courthouse workers that no one would even notice he had it.

Chapter 3: Election Day

Cigarette in hand and briefcase at his feet, Virgil waited at the courthouse. Seven o'clock, the time for voting, had come. He wanted to be seen around the courthouse all day as people came in. He might not be supposed to push for votes, but he could say good morning.

The election committee hadn't shown up. Virgil dropped the cigarette and stepped on it when he saw Betty, secretary in the county commissioner's office, stride up the walkway from her car, her high heels clicking on the concrete.

"Morning, Miss Betty."

"Morning. You here to vote for yourself?"

"I wouldn't vote for anybody else. Look's like you're the first person here. I thought we could vote right at seven." He grinned. "You sure look pretty today. That a new dress?"

She returned his smile and looked down at herself.

"No, but thank you." She unlocked the front door, and as she started to push it open, Virgil's arm came over her shoulder and took the weight. He pushed it open, and the movement of air lifted her perfume to his nose. She smelled of gardenias.

"There you are, m'am."

"Why, thank you, Virgil. You can get a lot of votes with kind words about a lady's dress and helping her with the door. That what you're angling for?"

He smiled and shook his head.

"No. Just trying to mind my manners. And impress a beautiful lady."

"Aw, go on, Virgil." She blushed. "I reckon I better get on up to the office. Mr. Larry'll be along directly, and I got a lot to do today."

"You get to work this early every day? I thought usual hours started at half-past eight."

"That's right. But Mr. Larry gets picky and makes me do things over a lot."

Virgil shook his head and looked down at his toes. His black shoes shone with a GI shine he had worked on himself the night before, after he voted the eighty-seven ballots.

"The county pay you overtime?"

"No. Just the same every week. I've worked for Mr. Larry for seven years and still get the same pay."

"I get elected today, I'll change that. I promise."

"You sure got my vote. I got to get to the office before he shows up. See ya later."

She strode down the hall and entered her office.

Virgil decided to wait on the front steps rather than be found inside. He leaned his butt against one of the columns and pulled out his cigarettes. He was lighting one when Judge Emerson walked up and nodded to him.

"Morning, Judge," Virgil said.

The judge nodded again, opened the front door, and walked in.

Nothing like being ignored, Virgil thought. Well, that'll change after today. These stuck-up big shots'll give me some respect when they have to come to me to get their roads paved. Everybody wants their roads paved now.

"Morning, Virgil. You here to vote already?" Daniel, one of the election officials, stopped, held out his hand, and said, "Reckon you'll run ole Cunningham out?"

"I hope." Virgil smiled, put his cigarette between his lips, and took the official's hand. "You gonna be here all day?"

"No. There's three of us. Counting Miss Birdie. We'll all work awhile. It might get busy, what with all the politicking you been doing."

"The more voters come in, the better my chances. I 'spect a lotta Negroes are gonna vote, now that Truman's got things changing."

"Well, you sure worked hard to get 'em down here and registered. Surprised you didn't get the Klu Klux on your tail."

"They know if they get on my tail, they got my whole family to deal with. But I'm keeping you from your work. You go on along. I saw yesterday you got the booth already set up in the hall."

"See ya," he said and went in.

Moments later, Dr. Jacobs hurried up the walkway. His coat was rumpled and his tie askew. "Sorry I'm late, Vigil. That baby took a lot longer coming than I expected. Everything going along alright?"

"Yes. I'll stay outside and greet people awhile like we planned if you can sit inside and watch that box. And feed Daniel a lotta co-colas. Be sure Mr. Cunningham don't do anything like I'm gonna do." Virgil grinned.

"I won't leave unless you're in there. I'm going to make Daniel turn that box over to be sure it's got no extra ballots in it from last night, too."

Virgil stayed in front of the courthouse to greet both the county employees coming in to work and the public coming in to vote. He had prepared a greeting that let him campaign while not campaigning.

"Good morning. I'm glad to see you. I just want to say hello." If he had not met the voter, he gave his name.

When Lawrence Cunningham waddled up the sidewalk toward the front door, Virgil stepped down the stairs to greet him.

"Good morning, Mr. Cunningham. How are you today?"

Cunningham glared at him and looked at the outstretched hand. More than a dozen people watched. His right hand was empty, his left held a briefcase. He reached his right hand up, removed his cigar from his mouth, and shook it at Virgil.

"I'm not about to shake hands with you, you scallywag. Here I help out your folks all these years, and you dare to do this. Git outta my way, boy." He slammed the cigar down at Virgil's feet.

Virgil stepped aside. He knew word of the episode would spread among the voters.

Soon after eight o'clock, the town people had gone to their jobs, and only a farmer or two showed up to vote. Virgil went inside.

As he approached the table where Daniel passed out ballots, he smiled; two empty Coke bottles sat on the floor by the wall, behind Daniel. A half-full bottle sat on the table at his elbow.

Some ballot box, Virgil thought. A cardboard, toilet-paper shipping box turned upside down. The bottom had become the top, with a 2 X 6-inch slit for shoving ballots through. If anyone kicked the box, ballots might fall out from under the side.

Dr. Jacobs had pulled up a chair and sat across the table from the official. Virgil perched on the second step of the stairs going up to the courtroom and the three of them chatted about the heat, about crops drying up, about watermelons finally coming in good, and about Gene Talmadge probably getting too old to be governor again but probably going to win anyway.

By ten, Daniel no longer sat still. He squirmed. Virgil knew he had to go pee.

Virgil pulled his briefcase up onto the step beside him and unhooked the clasps. When Daniel went down the hall he would have to move fast. But Daniel turned his eyes to the briefcase.

"Whatcha got there?" he asked.

"Cigarettes," Virgil answered and reached inside to pull out a fresh pack. He flipped the pack to Daniel. "Would you open it for me, Daniel?"

"Sure." He opened it and tapped the pack on the side of his hand until some of the cigarettes moved out. "Here ya' go."

Virgil pulled one out, stuck it between his lips, and took the pack. As he pushed it into his shirt pocket, Daniel got to his feet.

"Doc, you watch out here, for me? I gotta go pee. I know I ain't supposed to leave but I gotta. Jest tell anybody to wait, will ya?"

"Sure. I'll stay here. Glad to watch for you."

Before the men's room door closed, Virgil reached into his briefcase. When he heard the door click shut, he pulled out a handful of folded ballots. He shoved them under his other arm and reached back for the rest. He took three strides, pushed them all into the box, backed up to the stairs, and sat down.

"You move pretty good for a shot-up soldier." Jacobs smiled.

"Yeah. Now all we gotta do is be sure Cunningham don't do the same. I'm gonna be out on the front steps to talk to folks. You want me to get you a grilled cheese down at the diner?"

"Later maybe. I'm not going anywhere either. Let's eat after Daniel leaves and the next official gets here. I'll walk over to the diner for a sandwich while you sit here. "

*   *   *

The day passed with the two of them taking turn about in the hallway. Several times, Cunningham came from his office with briefcase in hand, walked up and down, seemed to snarl at them, and chomped his teeth on his cigar.

"What you doing here, Carter? You're not supposed to be asking for votes in here. I saw you shaking hands with people all day."

"He's not asked for a vote, Mr. Larry," Curtis, the afternoon official said. "I've been watching him."

"See you do," Cunningham said and left for his office.

When the voting ended at seven o'clock, both Virgil and Dr. Jacobs leaned against the wall only a few feet from the ballot box. No one had inserted more than one piece of paper.

Curtis turned the ballot box over. It had no bottom, so the slotted top became its bottom. He scooped up ballots, shoved them into the box, and pushed it toward the office door.

Cunningham came out of his office, briefcase in hand, and started to enter the office behind Curtis.

"I think you should leave that briefcase in the hall, Larry," Jacobs said. "Shouldn't anything come in here except that ballot box. I'm like you. I want to watch the counting to be sure it's correct."

"None of you're supposed to be in here," Curtis said.

"Well, we're gonna be sure nothing goes wrong," Jacobs said. "We'll not be in the way. We're going to be sure the only ballots on the table come out of that box from the hall. Nobody put in any extras all day. I'm going to be sure nobody puts extras in tonight while you count."

"I wouldn't do such," Curtis stated. "You calling me a crook?"

"Of course not, Curtis. Somebody might come in with a briefcase and push on the table. When the ballots fell, he could add a few." The doctor smiled. "I never have doubted you. I delivered you, saw you grow up, and know your mama would still whup you if she thought you did wrong."

"All-a-y'all wanna stand over by the door?" Curtis smiled. "I don't mean no offence to any-a-y'all."

Dr. Jacobs and Virgil leaned against the wall on one side of the door. Cunningham stood near the table, briefcase still in his hand.

"He means you too, Lawrence," Dr. Jacobs said. "Come on over here. And why not put your briefcase out in the hall? Virgil's is out there."

Cunningham turned, walked out the door, put down his briefcase and returned to stand, arms crossed, in the doorway.

"Excuse me, Mr. Larry," Daniel said from the hall. "I need to get in to help count."

Cunningham stepped aside and said. "You boys count 'em right, you hear?"

"Yes, sir," Curtis said. Then he and Daniel lifted the box and dumped the ballots onto the table.

"We can't start counting until Miss Birdie gits here," Daniel said.

"She's not likely to care, long's both the candidates are here," Jacobs said.

"You gonna argue about anything, Mr. Larry? You want we should start counting? You can watch close. Or you wanna wait?"

"Start counting," Cunningham said.

"Let's separate 'em first. Forget all the rest of the elections. Put those for Virgil over here," Curtis pointed to one end of the table, "and for the chairman down here."

They had separated more than half the ballots when Miss Birdie walked in. Her square-heeled black shoes sounded in the hallway long before she entered the room. She wore her white hair twisted into a bun on her neck. Her face showed miles of roads where the years had walked and sorrows had rampaged. She had become a widow two days before her wedding when her betrothed had been killed in a farm accident. Her mouth set into a tight line as she saw ballots spread across the table.

"You were supposed to wait for me," she said.

"It's my fault," Jacobs said. "I told them you wouldn't mind, seeing as both Lawrence and Virgil are here to be sure neither side's doing anything. They're only counting for commission chairman. Nothing else." He smiled at her.

She smiled back. He was a widower now and her age.

"You boys go on and separate them, then. Afterwards, we'll tally up everything else."

*   *   *

The stack on Virgil's end was obviously higher. Miss Birdie sat down and began to count by moving the ballots one by one into another stack. Her voice was soft, but everyone heard her.

Total for Virgil, 586.

Total for Cunningham, 542.

"Didn't more'n a thousand people vote! He stuffed the ballot box!" Cunningham yelled his anger.

"No way he could-a," Daniel said. "I was there until Curtis came along. I checked the box this morning. You saw me, Dr. Jacobs. There wasn't a ballot in it. How could he stuff it with one of us there all the time?"

Virgil turned to Cunningham.

"I'd appreciate your help as I get to know the job, sir."

"Bastard. You go to hell. You think you're so damn smart. You just try to do the job." He slammed his cigar to the floor, reached into his pocket, and took out his key ring. Everyone watched as he removed a key. He threw it at Virgil's feet.

"Let's see how good you are, boy. You got the job starting tomorrow. Miss Birdie, I resign."

Jacobs raised a hand.

"Larry, I know you've got personal things in your office. Let me go with you and help you get them out. You don't want Virgil packing them up for you." He stooped, picked up the key, and then headed for the door. "Come on, Larry."

They walked out.

"Congratulations, Virgil. You're our new county commission chairman." Miss Birdie smiled. From the pleasure in her smile, Virgil knew he had at least one supporter in the courthouse.

Daniel and Curtis looked at each other, and then stood up to vie with each other to congratulate him. But their voices rang hollow. As he realized they were Cunningham people, he knew they would have been adding ballots themselves if he and Dr. Jacobs had not hovered over that box.

"I'm gonna just sit over there out of the way, if you don't mind, and wait for Dr. Jacobs to come back by."

He listened to the votes being counted for Gene Talmadge, who took almost every vote for governor that was cast in the county. Virgil smiled to himself. He had voted those extra ballots for ole Gene too. And Truman. A half-hour later, as Virgil put out his second cigarette, Dr. Jacobs walked in.

"Here's the key to your new office, Virgil. Congratulations. Want to see your desk?"

"Sure. Let's have a look-see." Virgil grinned, and they walked down the hall together.

Chapter 4: The Next Week

Since the Carters moved to the county the only major change at the courthouse square was that cars and pickups now parked among the horses, mules, and wagons.

The Monday after the election when court opened, the courtyard and the street filled with wagons and pickups that usually came to town only on Saturday. Some curious, some concerned, some sympathetic, some delighted, the country people, black and white, had come to see one of their own on trial. Like them, the defendants struggled to scratch a living from soil, whiskey and hope.

Men milled around in the yard, and segregated groups gathered under the oaks. The sun had already burned the air, and they all knew the courtroom would be brinjin hot. Although many waved their hats before their faces in an attempt to generate coolness, they only moved hot air, for the July humidity refused to let sweat evaporate. The morning breeze had retreated from the heat.

Sweat beaded on every face; every man's armpits darkened. Tobacco plugs passed hand to hand as the men gossiped. White and black alike seemed to know that the Carter trial would be more than the average "Guilty. Fifty dollars or six months" affair that all other bootlegging cases had been. Anticipation ate at the people like hunger gnawed at the starving.

The story of the Judge Emerson's daughter going on a still raid ran around the crowd. When the Baptist preacher arrived and told one of his neighbors that he had married Karen Emerson to Lawyer Andrews, the word spread quickly through the crowd, and the question "was she pregnant with Charley's baby?" followed. If so, some of the men asked, how was the judge gonna pay off Andrews for making an honest woman out of her?

The courthouse clock bonged nine and the crowd pushed inside and up the narrow stairs. Those who thought they would be first in the courtroom discovered the Carter men already there, lined up on the front bench. Virgil stood by the barrier and talked with a young attorney who was new in town.

Fans turned slowly overhead. Anyone who had a cardboard fan from the funeral parlor used it. Others used their hats. No breeze drifted in the windows to carry out the thick odor of human sweat. The rancid-sweet smell of fresh manure on someone's brogans drifted through the room as people stirred. A few noses wrinkled at the smell; most ignored it as familiar.

The room buzzed with voices, loud, raucous, and half-whispered, and with laughter. Except for the Carter men, the front row was filled with the same local loafers who sat in the same seats season after season to absorb other people's business and spread it across the countryside.

Potential jurors sat on one side of the room, the same men who session after session were the only ones considered fit to determine guilt or innocence.

Negroes filled the balcony. Shuffling feet periodically struck a lunch-filled lard can with a loud clatter. A white-haired old Negro sat at the railing, looking down at the suited men scattered around in small groups in the railed area near the judge's bench. Noah clenched his hands together to halt their trembling. His son would go on trial today as he himself had last court session. His pocket held a handkerchief knotted around what he hoped would be enough money for the fine.

Jack and Sam wore stiff clean shirts. Their necks showed a white, un-tanned ring from last night's hair cuts. Virgil sat at the aisle, with Jack next to him. He was concerned about his brother, worried that Judge Emerson might have heard about his daughter's adventure the night BJ was caught.

Hiram, clad in a new shirt and overalls, sat between Jack and Sam. He too had had a haircut. Ellen had told him he must look good for his brother. He wanted BJ home, home to help catch the yearlings and to help get another still going. Hiram enjoyed lassoing the cattle, but Pa had him working too hard down at the new site for the still. It was work he didn't like. BJ had to come home today.

When Jack pulled out his cigarette makings, Virgil reached over, put his hand on his father's, and said, "Not here, Pa. Judge Emerson don't like smoking."

Jack nodded and stuffed his papers and tobacco bag into his shirt pocket. The string dangled out. "He care iffen I chaw?"

"Spittoon's all up yonder, for the lawyers. Kin ya wait?"

"I reckon."

Virgil looked back at the crowd and realized that the room had filled up. The bailiff, who stood inside the door under the balcony, began to turn people away.

"Sorry, boys, but there ain't nowhere left to sit. Y'all will just have to wait until somebody leaves."

A group of lawyers huddled in low-voiced conversation off to the side of the judge's bench. Virgil watched them; one was Jenkins, the prosecutor. Local lawyers, with cases expected to be heard today or here to see what happened to the new commissioner's brother, chatted with one another. Matthew Rogers, BJ's attorney, who moved to town less than a month ago, sat against the wall, alone.

The two men who had helped the sheriff catch Billy Jack, the gaunt-faced Alexander Perry and the smiling GBI agent whose face was new to Virgil, stood in front of the rail where they chatted and chuckled at each other's stories. Virgil wondered if they were discussing his brother.

As he looked for Dixon he thought back to the time he had first seen the sheriff; he had been only a boy then, that night his father had first taken him to the still and the sheriff had found them. Dixon had appeared from the darkness and simply stood a few yards away, shotgun held across his chest, and asked if they were the Carters. He told them to finish the run, bottle the liquor, and carry it to his car, three miles away.

The sheriff had not arrested Jack then, or even admonished him, but every time they moved the still to a new location, Dixon was able to find them, to force the liquor from them. Then, after Pa agreed to sell all he made to Cunningham, as Gus and Sam did, Dixon had left them alone.

The agreement had been that as long as all three Carters made whiskey and sold only to Cunningham, the sheriff would never raid a Carter still.

Now with everybody selling to Charley, Cunningham might have told the judge to be harsh on BJ. It'd be like old Larry to avenge himself on any Carter now, since Penny married his son and Virgil put him out of office. Revenge always tasted sweet, even with smell of rotting mash in the background.

The bailiff began his sing-song chant, the crowd shuffled onto its feet, and the chatter and laughter died out as Judge Emerson entered in his black robes. He had gone bald except for a ring of gray that circled his head like a wreath. He looked over the room for an instant, mounted hidden steps, and sat behind the bench. He picked up his gavel and banged once, and the chanting bailiff hollered for everyone to sit.

Silence settled over everyone. The judge's gaze wandered over the room and then came back to the front to settle on the Carters. He locked eyes with Virgil for an instant.

Virgil saw a hardness settle on Emerson's face and knew that trouble was on the way.

In voices too low to be heard, the bailiff, judge, and Prosecutor Jenkins talked. Lawyer Andrews, who represented Amos, caught with BJ at the still, walked up to the bench, and the talk stopped.

"Call the case," the judge said.

The bailiff opened a side door, and Dixon came in with Noah's boy.

Dixon led Amos to face the judge. Andrews stood on one side of him and the frail, solemn-faced prosecutor on the other. The two white men talked back and forth for a few minutes and then the prosecutor said something to the defendant.

The single word, "Guilty," seemed to be shouted in the stillness of the waiting room.

"Fifty dollars or six months," the judge stated and smashed the hammer briskly.

Virgil shuddered at the coldness of the voice and the finality of the hammer.

Feet shuffled around overhead in the balcony, and a moment later Noah scurried down the aisle, handkerchief in hand, to buy his boy back. The bailiff waited patiently as the old man's rheumatic fingers struggled with the knots and counted out five dirty, wadded bills.

Dixon told Amos he was free to go, and as the two Negroes hurried back up the aisle, the bailiff opened the side door for the sheriff. Dixon vanished, but the door remained open.

Virgil felt confident now. That fine was standard for the judge; surely he would fine BJ the same. He had more than two hundred dollars in his pocket, and knew his pa also had money. Probably from selling some of Cunningham's cattle.

"That jedge ain't gonna be as hard on Billy Jack as on that nigger, is he?" Jack asked.

"I dunno, Pa." Virgil shook his head and shrugged. "We'll hafta see. If he's fair, he won't charge BJ any more than he did Noah's boy."

The crowd stirred as Dixon returned with Billy Jack at his side. This was what they had waited for, and people edged forward in their seats as the young attorney went to meet Billy Jack. Hiram rose, crawled over his father and Virgil, and sat by the aisle.

"Be still," Jack whispered. "You got no call to be moving around. Sit and stay sat."

Virgil's hand begin to sweat and shake, and he jammed it into his pocket so Hiram would not notice. But he could not stop the churning in his stomach.

Hiram kept wiggling and almost bouncing in his excitement. The boy had clenched his hands into fists that he held almost at chest height and shook as if ready to do battle. His lips were pressed into a thin line, and he squinted as if daring the judge.

Gawd, Virgil thought. I sure hope Hiram doesn't get riled up if they send BJ to jail. He almost tore the door off the school bus every time he saw BJ get on. Addled as he is, we shoulda made him stay home.

BJ looked so young now. Virgil caught his eye, nodded encouragement, and smiled. He sighed his relief when his brother grinned at him almost cockily. The boy would be all right.

The attorney met him and guided him to the defense table. But the judge spoke before they sat.

Voices carried suddenly, as if everyone had agreed beforehand that the crowd should be allowed to hear what it had come to hear.

"Step forward," the judge ordered and waved BJ to the foot of the bench. The youth had to tilt his head back to look at the judge. His lawyer stood on his left; Jenkins, on the other side.

"You represent him?" Judge Emerson asked, and he pulled down his glasses to look at the attorney.

"Yes, Your Honor."

"New in town?"

"Yes, Your Honor."

"You ready for this case?"

"Yes, Your Honor."

"You got a name?"

"Yes, Your Honor." The attorney paused, and someone snickered. Even Virgil smiled at the repetition. "It's Matthew Rogers."

"How you gonna plead him?"

Virgil held his breath. If BJ made the wrong decision—

"Guilty, your honor."

Virgil exhaled.

BJ had made the right decision. Attorney Rogers thought they had a chance if they insisted on a jury trial, but Virgil had disagreed. Jack didn't care what they did, as long as BJ got to come home.

A trial would mean everybody would know about Karen and Charley being out in the woods in the middle of the night. Then, if BJ were found guilty, Emerson would be rough on him no matter what promises the lawmen had made.

"Is that how you plead?"

BJ dug into his ear and looked at his finger as he rolled the wax into a ball and thumbed it off.

"I was there when they come up on us at the still, iffen that's what you mean."

"You do understand what you're on trial for, do you not?" the judge asked.

"Sure. For being stupid enough to git caught making likker."

A titter ran through the room and faded among the steady swish-swish of fans. BJ turned away from the judge and grinned at the audience.

"Is this the boy's first offence?" Judge Emerson asked Henry Jenkins.

"First time we've been able to catch him at something, Your Honor."

The titter rose again, lived longer, and died quickly as the judge slammed the gavel down.

"You could have phrased that better, Henry. That's not a proper answer, and you know it."

BJ interrupted. "Nothing wrong with what he done said, Jedge. This heah is the first time they been able to cotch me." Pride dripped from his voice.

Judge Emerson, his attempt to remain solemn obvious, nodded slowly. "Is there anything else that I should know about the case?" he asked Jenkins.

"Just one thing, Your Honor. The still was a rather large operation, and in the opinion of the arresting officers it was financially supported by someone other than this boy or his family. We are interested in learning the identity of the man or group of men who supplied the still."

Looking down at BJ, who returned the gaze steadily, Emerson asked, "Who financed the still, Carter? This man knows who it is."

"Is there a law what says I got to answer that?" he asked.

Jenkins gasped; Rogers looked at Emerson before answering.

"No, Billy Jack, there is no law that you have to answer unless you take the witness stand under oath, which you haven't done."

He grinned, nodded his head once at the judge, and turned to wave at his family.

Emerson pursed his lips thoughtfully and asked, "How old are you, Carter?"

"I don't know," he shrugged. "Old enough."

"Old enough to know better than operate a still?" Emerson asked.

"Oh, there ain't nothing wrong with running a still, Jedge. What's wrong is gitting caught at it. I'm old enough to go whoring is what."

An audible gasp rose from the audience. Virgil squeezed his eyes shut and covered his face with his hand. While despair and laughter fought for control, he kept his face down.

"One thousand dollars and two years." The gavel crashed down.

No one moved. Silence descended, so thick that the overhead fans seemed explosive.

Hiram leaped up, jumped over the railing between the public and the lawyers, and ran toward the bench.

"You let the nigger go for jest fifty dollars! What you got against my brother? He ain't said a damn thing about that gal of yourn being out there whoring in the woods!"

Perry and Dixon grabbed him and pinned his arms back.

"Get this man out of here!" Emerson rose, his face burning red, and pointed to Hiram. "Lock him up. Lock him up. I don't care how old he is." He walked from the courtroom and let his private door slam behind him.

"Go home, Pa," Virgil said. "Go home and stay there. I'll see what I can do here. Don't you try anything, Pa. Please? I'll do what I can for Hiram."

Jack nodded. He and Sam pushed their way through the crowd. Hands reached out, touched him; voices called, "can't believe," "I'm sorry," "it's too much," "no one ever."

Virgil heard the same voices. They were right. And he couldn't believe the sentence and he couldn't believe Hiram. Only twelve years old, but he stood taller than BJ and looked a lot older. And in jail for sassing the judge.

He fought to reach his brothers, but Perry had already shoved the handcuffed Hiram to the side door. Virgil managed to push through the attorneys to reach BJ.

"You ain't got a-nuff money, is you?" BJ asked.

"No, we haven't. Even so, he said two years besides the money. I'll do all I can, BJ."

"You ain't getting him out, Virgil. He's mine for two years. You shouldn't-a gone against Mr. Larry like you done," Dixon said and smiled.

"You telling me he paid the judge for that sentence?"

"I ain't telling you any such thing." But Dixon winked.

"Yeah? I think you are. Well, Emerson's time will come too. He's got to run for office himself one of these days. Nobody likes to see a child jailed. How long you gonna keep Hiram locked up?"

"Till the judge says to let 'em go. C'mon, boy," Dixon said as he pushed BJ out the door. "You git on home, Virgil. You can't do nothing about any-a this."

Virgil turned back into the courtroom. Lawyer Rogers stood by the defense table, his fingers idly moving a few sheets of notebook paper around.

"I can't believe what the judge did," he told Virgil. "It's the kind of sentence he'd get for killing a nigger. You want me to talk to him about Hiram?"

"Kin we do anything?"

"For Hiram, yes. I can probably get him out tomorrow. But BJ? No. Only thing I know is to appeal. That'll take months. And cost a lot. As it is, you've got to come up with the thousand, and he's got to do the time."

"I'll figure something. Jail could ruin him. Thank you for helping. How much do I owe you?"

"Just the twenty-five. No more. I really feel bad about charging you that, seeing as what happened. I'll let it cover getting Hiram out."

Chapter 5: Two Nights Later

Billy Jack paced the cell, his mind storming with fury. The judge's words, "Two years, two years," matched his steps and twisted inside his head. All cause Penny had to go get caught with Charley's baby, Judge Emerson went and took it out on him. Warn't his fault Penny couldn't keep her legs together and Charley couldn't keep it inside his britches. Probably got that Karen Emerson knocked up too. That's probably why the judge got so mad at all his family.

Leastways they got Hiram out yesterday, and he was gone off home with Virgil. And Pa had come by. Dixon had stood right by the cell almost the whole time, except for the minute he'd gone to the office when somebody came in, long enough for Pa to tell him to be ready. Pa would come back tonight, come get him outta this here jail house afore they sent him out on the chain gang.

"Not even the niggers gotta spend two years in jail fer moonshining. Jest me. They think they're gonna make me swing a pick with niggers and call me a white nigger. They'll have to kill me first," he whispered to the darkness.

He stood at the barred window and looked into the night. Moonlight brightened the outside world enough that he could see the empty street stretch toward home. He slammed his fist against one of the bars and then jerked it back, wrapped his other hand around the bruise, and cursed again.

Five steps and turn, he moved with precision and exerted as little effort as possible. His body a fatless machine, lithe and durable, seemed cut with the exactness of an Apollo. His face had lost its cockiness and hardened in the past two days. Thick black hair tumbled over his eyes and shaded them to deeper blackness until he pushed it back with his fingers. When his teeth were not digging into the quick of his nails, his lips pressed into a tight line. His nose flared with each breath, like a stallion's as he approaches another to fight.

Night sounds drifted into the cell. A far-off horn, a low whine as an auto hurried to outrun dawn, the ever-present chirrup of tree frogs and crickets, the distant whoop of a coon hunter as he called his hounds home from another summer practice run.

The soft, low whisper of a whip-poor-will drifted from below. Pa's call. He had finally come.

BJ stopped pacing, reached under the mattress, and pulled out the rope he had made from ripping up his sheet. It wasn't but maybe ten feet to the ground out his window. In whispers, Pa had promised him a pistol and escape.

His hands steady with the sureness of freedom, he unrolled the rope and dropped one end through the bars. The rope tightened and jerked for a moment while Pa tied on the pistol, and then two quick tugs and a steady weight told him to pull the rope up. Each time the gun clattered into the bricks, the sound seemed to explode into the pre-dawn silence. Light glittered on metal as he reached through the bars to seize the pistol.

He tugged it through and, with a smile, cradled it in his hand. He moved it up and down slightly as if weighing it. Satisfaction curled around his lips.

In the light of the window, he turned it over in his hands, found the release, and pulled the S&H .22 revolver apart. He glanced over the cylinder, counted the nine cartridges, and reassembled it.

He whip-poor-willed and listened for the echo to come from below, an echo followed by the faint sound of feet moving lightly through the darkness.

Waiting for sunrise became easier. Morning meant breakfast and freedom. Freedom. Maybe out of the state; into Florida maybe, or west to Texas.

"No," he whispered to himself. "No, I gotta git aholt-a that damn judge first. I swear, yer honor, I oughtta kill ya fer what you done to me. Only I ain't. I ain't shore what I'll do, but you ain't never gonna fergit Billy Jack Carter. I swear you ain't."

The day was full born when lights coming on inside the cell and hallway pulled him from the window. He stretched out on his back, twisted his arm under his head and kept his fingers wrapped around the gun.

"Morning, Billy Jack. You awake?" asked Mrs. Dixon as she neared the cell with his breakfast.

He went through the motions of awakening—stretched and yawned—before he replied.

"Morning." He wished Dixon had come up himself.

Ain't right to put a gun on a woman, but I reckon iffen I hafta I hafta.

Motionless, he waited while she balanced the tray on her knee, opened the cell door, pushed her way inside, and placed it on the small table.

"I fixed you some fried eggs and some ham and—."

"Don't you say no more," he interrupted. He sat up, showed her the gun, and rose in one even motion that carried him to her side.

Mrs. Dixon turned around, looked into the small black hole of the pistol turned up to her face, only an inch from her chin. Her mouth opened, her breath sucked in, her eyes pushed out.

"I wouldn't scream iffen I was you, cause iffen you make your old man come a-running, I'd hafta shoot him."

Her thin pale hand trembled as it rose to cover her whitening lips. She backed away. He followed her until she bumped into the cell wall near the window.

"Guess that-air's far as you going," he said. As she sucked in another breath, his voice hardened. "Don'tcha scream." She trembled against the wall. "You done been too good to me for me to have to mess you up, m'am. Now you turn around and face that-air wall. And jest remember iffen your old man comes up here I kin shoot him afore he kin set eyes on me."

She hovered against the wall like a hen desperately trying to protect her biddies from a fox while sure of approaching death.

He stuffed the pistol into his belt and ordered her to put her hands behind her. He wished Hiram were here. Hiram might be damned addled, but he could tie a knot that would hold, and the old woman shook so much it was hard for him to tie her wrists with his sheet strips.

"I ain't liking to do this-here to you, m'am, but iffen I don't, you'd holler no sooner I git outta that door. And I jest ain't gonna go on no nigger chain gang—not for you nor your husband nor nobody."

"Don't do this." Her voice was a hoarse whisper, raw with terror, thick with suppressed tears. "Don't, Billy Jack. You'll just get in more trouble. You can't get away. You don't have a chance to, not now, with all the ways there is to track somebody. You turn me loose and I won't tell on you."

"I ain't a-going on that chain gang with a bunch of damn niggers. I'd rather be daid." He yanked the handmade rope through the window bars so fiercely he pulled her off balance. He caught her before she fell and then worked quickly. Gentleness left his hand as he stuffed a piece of sheeting into her mouth. Her eyes bulged like balloons floating in a murky sea beneath the unbroken ridge of arched gray eyebrows.

He snatched his shoes from under the bed and crept towards the open door and liberty, stopped, looked hungrily at the food. His hunger won. Holding the shoes under his arm, he shoved ham and biscuits inside his shirt, gulped the milk, and with a final glance at the woman, padded noiselessly along the hallway and down the stairs. Once in the alley, he shoved his feet into his shoes and trotted toward the street.

Pa dozed in the truck a block from the jail. When BJ saw his father huddled against the passenger door, he scrambled under the wheel. Grinning, the youth jabbed his father and laughed.

"Hey, you ain't aiming to sleep all day?"

He cranked the engine and the motor roared in the still-sleeping neighborhood. Jack grunted and sat up.

"Whatcha doing driving?"

"You was sleeping, and I done driven in the hay fields. I'm gitting outta here fast as I kin, Pa. How come you parked this side-a the jail? Now we gotta go past it."

"Don't matter, son. We'll be outta heah in a minute and then you kin catch the Trailways and git away."

He didn't plan to go away at all. Not until he came back to town tonight to visit that judge.

The truck sputtered and coughed along the street as BJ struggled with the stick shift. When they passed the jail, he heard Mrs. Dixon scream.

The sound ripped into him, pulled his eyes from the street to the jail where he saw her, mouth wide and full of sound. His foot jammed down on the gas pedal and the truck lurched forward.

"Toldcha I oughtta be driving," Jack said.

They were two miles out of town when they heard the first faint squall of a siren behind them.

"That was too damn fast!" he muttered, shaking his head. He tightened his grasp on the wheel until his veins bulged along his arms and red and white splotches appeared on his fingers.

Distance became meaningless; the countryside, trees, fields, and livestock did not exist. Only the sound behind him, the thin white line stretching ahead, rising and dipping over the hills to freedom, composed his world. His eyes flickered from the road to the mirror, from the straight line ahead to the flashing lights behind him. The sheriff's car was faster and moved closer with every mile.

He pressed the accelerator, but the truck had already reached maximum speed. He straddled the tires over the dashed line and leaned forward like a jockey to coax more speed from the machine. The black car crept closer, and BJ could see Dixon's features when he turned to look over his shoulder.

Pa spoke softly. "It ain't nobody but Dixon and he ain't fixing to stop us. He ain't even bout to try."

"Shoot him." Billy Jack thrust the pistol at his pa.

"That there's Dixon, boy!"

"I don't give a damn! Shoot him! I ain't fixing to go back to jail. You hear? I done heard all about them chain gangs, and I ain't gonna go on one."

"I heard you, boy." Pa leaned far out the window and shot easily, quickly, as if the pistol were simply an extension of his hand.

"Hit him?" Billy Jack asked, his face alive with fear, as Pa slipped back inside.

"I don't never miss," Pa said as a car came over the hill in front of them. "Look out!"

Tires screeched as Billy Jack jerked aside and then back into his lane. Pa clutched for balance and his left hand seized the wheel. The truck lurched to the right, ran off the shoulder, bounced over rocks, listed, roared through the soft earth, and crashed onto its side.

BJ fell onto his father as the truck continued to slide along the ditch and glass broke and metal crashed. He vaguely heard another pistol shot as the truck slammed into a tree and stopped.

"C'mon," he said to the inert form of his father. He ignored the searing pain in his leg as he frantically sought the pistol, found it, lunged upward through the window, and dropped into the ditch. His right leg buckled and refused his weight. He fell flat onto his stomach, dropped the pistol, and began to scrabble for it.

The stranger's vehicle slowed, but as the sheriff scrambled out of his car, the driver roared off.

BJ's right hand closed over the pistol butt.

Steam rose from the sheriff's car, and the breeze moved it toward BJ. The smell of antifreeze on the hot motor reached him before the sheriff spoke.

"You all right, Billy Jack?" The sheriff ran through the steam cloud toward him. "You damned idiot. Why'd you have to go and—?"

Billy Jack fired once. Dixon halted in mid-stride and looked down at himself, apparently surprised as the blood spread over his chest. He then looked up at BJ and tried to speak. Blood erupted from his mouth, and he sank to his knees, fell forward onto his face, and lay still.

When he was sure that Dixon was motionless, BJ turned his attention to his leg. He ripped open his britches to expose a deep gash, the flesh turned back like half-sliced beef. He tore off part of the pants leg, ripped it into pieces and bound the flesh back together. The cloth soaked through before he jerked the final knot.

He stuck the pistol in his belt, grabbed the truck to pull himself to his feet, and tested the strength of his leg. It would hold his weight if he could hold the pain.

Silence answered his call to Pa. Limping and leaning on the truck, he worked his way to the front to look through the opening that had been the windshield. Pa looked busted up. BJ leaned into the opening.

"Pa? Pa?" He put his hand on his father's shoulder and pushed slightly. "Pa?"

The rusty smell of blood rose into his face. Blood and urine. His pa had wet himself. A gash on his forehead had spread blood across his face, and it dripped off his forehead onto his shoulder. BJ saw one arm twisted almost backwards.

"Don't push on me, son. It hurts like I been kicked all over by a brace-a mules." He opened his eyes, looked at BJ, closed them again. He took a deep breath, grimaced, and asked. "You shoot Dixon?

"Yeah."

"He dead?"

"Yeah."

"You gotta git me outta here."

"I'm scairt I'll kill you iffen I pull on you."

"I be about dead, BJ. My laig's bleeding worse'n my head. You git me outta here and put that pistol in my hand. You hear me?"

"But Pa."

Jack closed his eyes and clamped his teeth together. "Now."

BJ leaned in as far as he could, grabbed his father under the shoulders, and pulled. Jack moaned. BJ pulled. Jack screamed.

He lay his father on the bank. One leg was badly smashed, and BJ used his and his father's handkerchiefs to tie a make-shift bandage to stop the bleeding.

Jack groaned and reached out with his left hand, his unbroken arm. "Gimme the gun."

"I need it, Pa. I gotta run. I gotta git outta here."

"Gimme the pistol and you git." He shuddered. "Now, boy. I'm dying. Let 'em say I shot Dixon. I ain't having them blaming you. Gimme here."

BJ reached to his belt and pulled out the pistol.

"Heah, Pa."

Jack took it in his left hand, lay it on his chest, and began to rub it all over.

"Whatcha doing, Pa?"

"Fixing it so yer fingerprints ain't on it. That-a-way, they'll think I done shot Dixon. Hurry up, boy. Git going. Head fer the swamp off to the south. That'll gitcha toward home. Sam and Gus'll be looking fer you, come dark. Go-on, now."

"I don't wanna leave you, Pa."

Jack trembled with the pain and did not answer.

"Pa? Pa?"

BJ, unsure whether or not his father had died, turned away to consider himself. He put all his weight on his good leg and leaned against the truck as he glanced around.

The sun had crawled over the ridge east of town and turned the dew-wet grass into a dazzle of light. A few cattle stared at him from the meadow on his right. Oaks rose up the hill across the road. Somewhere a crow cawed and a jay answered in anger. Then silence. The road stretched away, empty, as if taunting him, inviting him while refusing him.

BJ turned to his father. He was so still. Was he breathing? BJ leaned over and put his hand on his father's chest. It was still. His father looked unseeing at the summer sky. BJ shuddered.

He limped toward Dixon's car, but even before he reached it he knew Pa's shot had smashed the radiator. The rank odor of a burned motor came to meet him with the steam. In angry, desperate fear, Billy Jack smashed his fist against the fender.

He had to get away from here, had to get home, home to Sam. He'd help now. Every lawman around would be after him. Even with Pa trying to take the blame, they'd figure he killed Dixon. Leastways at first. They'd follow him no matter where he got to as long as they thought so. If Pa was right and they figured Pa shot the sheriff, they'd still be after him. He had to run.

He looked at Dixon and the back of his shirt now red-brown with blood that already drew flies.

He got what he asked for, BJ thought.

Hatred fled before fear as the sun flicked at him from a car window over the hill. He hurried toward the sanctuary of the trees to the south; he had to force his stiffening leg to support him.

Chapter 6

When the driver saw the wrecked vehicles, he pulled up beside the truck and stopped. As he stepped out of his car, he was struck by the rusty smell of blood and the buzzing of what seemed like a million flies already congregating. One look at Jack assured him the man was dead, his eyes staring at nothing. The man swallowed bile and longed for a Mason jar of the whiskey he knew Jack perked alongside a creek somewhere.

The other body lay face down in front of the sheriff's car. The man squatted, rolled the body over, and gasped.

"OhmyGawd, it's Sheriff Dixon."

His trembling hand rose to his mouth, he shuddered, and his weight carried him so far backwards he sat down hard on the dirt beside the body. Flies lit on the upturned face and gathered around the eyes. The man leaned off to the side and vomited.

He crawled away from Dixon's body and continued to heave even after nothing came up. When the spasms quieted, he rose, dug out a handkerchief, and wiped his mouth. He spat several times, but couldn't produce enough spittle to get rid of the taste of vomit, and reached into his pocket for his cigarette makings. While leaning his butt on his car door, he rolled a cigarette, licked it to seal it, and lit it with a kitchen match he struck on the back of his leg. He pulled the smoke deep, the cigarette tip so hot that on his second and third drag the smoke almost burned as he sucked it down. He dropped the stub, ground it out on the road with his brogan, got in his car, and headed off to town.

He pushed his 1932 Plymouth until the steering wheel shimmied and he feared the car would break down. He slowed before he entered town when steam rising from the hood told him a hose had ruptured. He stopped in front of the diner.

The jail would be empty, and he wasn't about to go to the house in back, where Sheriff Dixon lived, and tell his wife the sheriff was dead. He ran to the diner door and burst inside, into the steam, heat and smell of breakfast. Four men looked up from one booth, and two men who sat at the counter turned to stare when he slammed the door open. Nita stood by the back booth that was occupied by a passing-through couple.

"What's-a matter with you, Carl?" one of the men asked. "You awright? You look like you done seen a ghost."

"Dixon," he stammered as he tried to catch his breath. "He's laid out dead on the road. About five miles outta town. There's a busted up truck there, and Jack Carter's dead too."

All six local men rose. The couple stared. Napkins fell to the floor. A coffee cup knocked over on the table went unnoticed, and coffee ran to the edge and dribbled onto the floor. Nita ran up to Carl. The cook left the stove untended. Everyone talked at once.

"You sure it's Jack Carter?"

"Billy Jack's in jail."

"Maybe Jack busted him out."

"Where's Miz Dixon at? She takes in the food."

"Something's on fire."

"Oh Lawd," the cook said and ran back to the stove where three eggs had started to burn. Smoke rode along the ceiling from the kitchen.

"Where-at kin I find that Mr. Perry what Larry Cunningham hired?

"He's the only law here now."

"I know where he lives. I'll go git him." Silas ran out the door.

"He comes in here to breakfast every day, long about nine," Nita said. "It's likely he ain't even up. Y'all may's well sit."

They did. She gave Carl a full mug, swabbed up the spilled coffee, tended to the waiting stranger couple, and distributed more napkins to the other booth before Perry strode in and pulled off his hat. His uncombed hair stood up at all angles. Gray stubble covered his face. His tie dangled over his shoulder and his top shirt buttons were open. His pants showed dirt from yesterday's wear.

"Who found 'em?"

"I did. They're out about 5 miles. Both dead. Looks like they shot each other. They both got a pistol." Carl's hands trembled so much his coffee sloshed and splashed onto the floor.

"You men stay here. I may need you later. I'll look into it all."

*   *   *

Perry headed for the jail, walked through the empty building, and then went to the house behind the jail. A rap on the door brought Mrs. Dixon from her kitchen.

"M'am," Perry greeted her and removed his hat. "Is the sheriff hereabouts?"

She shook her head.

"He's gone after Billy Jack. That boy got a pistol from somewhere and he actually tied me up and got away. I've never been so scared in my life." Tears began to slip from her eyes and down her face. She pulled a handkerchief from the pocket of her house dress and wiped her eyes. Her hand shook. The smell of fear surrounded her. "I tried so hard to be good to that boy. He's just a boy. Just a boy. And Judge Emerson was so hard on him I felt sorry for him. Only he's gone bad, Alex. He's gone bad." She shook her head as she stuffed her handkerchief back into her pocket.

"I'll go see what I can find out. You be alright here?"

"Oh, sure, Alex. Why wouldn't I be fine? I'll be over these here shakes in a little while. The sheriff might need some help, you think?"

He didn't want to tell her he thought her husband was dead. He'd better be sure before he said anything.

"I'll drive out and see what I can see. Be back soon as I learn something."

He put on his hat and tugged it lower over his right eye as he walked away. The poor woman, he thought. No way to make a decent living on her own. She'll have to take up housekeeping or slinging hash over to the diner just to get by. And she'll have to move, seeing as the county owns that house. He shook his head. Death is as final for so many left living.

He stopped at the diner long enough to ask Carl to ride out with him, and then drove out to the wrecks. Dixon lay dead a few yards in front of his official car and still gripped his pistol. Jack Carter had died near his truck, and his pistol lay in his open hand, his finger in the trigger guard.

"You stay back here by my car," he told Carl. "I'll look things over."

Perry walked from one to the other as he studied the layout of vehicles and bodies. He knelt beside each body to study the injuries. Flies rose from both men, and eggs clustered in white patches by their eyes, their mouths, and on the raw flesh.

A lot of damage to Jack for him to be able to shoot straight. But the Carter's were known for their skills with firearms, he thought.

Other footprints showed that someone else had moved around the area. Some he knew belonged to Carl. Another set showed him that the other person suffered an injured leg. And had left, headed south across country. Billy Jack.

He'd get the tracking hounds from Macon and find that boy. Somebody had to replace Dixon, and Sheriff Perry sounded good. One sure way to get that job was to bring in the Carter boy. It sure would help him get to be sheriff if Billy Jack had done the killing, but it looked like Jack himself killed the sheriff.

"Hey, Carl, c'mon over here."

"I ain't wanting to get close up again," he said.

Perry shrugged and explained what he had deducted.

"Looks like Jack and the sheriff killed each other, and Billy Jack ran off and left his father to die if he wasn't already dead." He sighed. "Well, I need somebody else to see what I'm figuring on. We better go get the undertaker and get him to tell Mrs. Dixon. I shore don't want that job."

Chapter 7

Perry drove to the Jacobs place, parked near the front door in the shade of a magnolia, and strode to the porch steps. The door opened before he reached the porch, and Janice smiled.

"Welcome, Alex. What brings you out here today?"

Her smile faded as she realized he did not smile back, had not shaved, and looked as if he had on yesterday's clothes. He removed his hat and shook his head.

"It's not good news, Mrs. Jacobs. Not good. Is Virgil here?"

She glanced over her shoulder at the sound of footsteps. Dr. Jacobs stepped out right behind her and smiled at Perry.

The officer shook his head. "Sorry, Doc. I got bad news. I need to see Virgil."

"Somebody call me?" Virgil spoke from the hallway.

"C'mon in." Janice pulled the door wider, and she and the doctor backed up into the hallway.

Virgil extended his hand to Perry, who moved his hat to his left hand and shook with Virgil.

"I'm sorry about what's happened. It's your daddy. He's dead."

"Dead?" Virgil backed up two steps and sat down in the hall straight chair. "How? What happened?"

"Best I can tell, after he broke BJ outta jail—"

"Broke BJ out? He wouldn't have."

"Well, he did. Slipped him a pistol. Had to've been your daddy. BJ stuck a pistol into Mrs. Dixon's face, tied her up, and walked out. Dixon chased after Jack's truck, and it wrecked. Dixon's car's shot up, Jack's dead with a pistol in his hand, and BJ's gone. I've sent to Macon for the bloodhounds. Looks like BJ's hurt and bled some. He left a good trail. We'll find him."

Virgil shook his head and pressed his palm against his forehead. It couldn't be. Not now. Not when everything was getting better. What got into that boy's head? An appeal would-a gotten him out.

"I didn't stop by your mama's, Virgil. I figured you oughtta be the one to tell her."

Virgil nodded without looking up.

"Thank you for coming by, Alex," Dr. Jacobs said. He led the officer to the porch.

Perry left. He would meet the dogs at the jail and find that boy. Then Judge Emerson would appoint him the next sheriff. He'd no longer be just a temporary law officer that Virgil would not keep on the county's payroll.

* * *

"Take my car," Dr. Jacobs said as Janice knotted Virgil's tie.

"Seems I'm always taking your car. I'll have to get one soon so you can keep yours. Thank you, Doc."

"I'll go with you," Janice offered.

"I gotta tell Ma and then go to the undertaker's. It ain't something you wanna do, Janice. You oughtta stay home. You had enough dying."

She shook her head and placed a hand on his arm.

"I'm going with you. To town and to see Ellen. We'll get though this together. Okay?"

Virgil nodded. "Thanks."

When they reached his childhood home, Ellen heard the car and came out. Her face lit up with a smile as soon as she saw them both.

"You coming to give me some news?" she asked as she wiped her hands on the apron Janice had bought for her a week ago.

Virgil did not answer, but hurried to the porch, where he pulled his mother tight against his chest.

"Oh, Ma." His body shook as he tried to hold back his own tears. He couldn't let his mother see him fall apart. He was the oldest now and had to be the strongest for Ma.

"What's wrong, son?"

"Pa's dead."

Ellen pushed him back and peered into his eyes, where she saw only sadness and truth.

"How?"

"I ain't fully shore, but I hear he busted BJ out, and they ran off with Dixon chasing after them. Dixon's dead, too. And BJ's disappeared off in the woods."

Both of Ellen's hands rose to hide her face and to try to hold back the gasp that erupted from her. Tears slipped out, and she quickly tried to wipe them away. Virgil pulled her close again.

A long minute passed, and then Ellen pushed herself away.

"Bring him home, Virgil. We'll bury him over by Penny. Keep him close. Long's we remember him, we'll keep him close. You do that, you hear?"

"Yes, Ma. You want Janice to stay with you while I'm in town? Where's Penny?"

"She done gone off with Charley." She noticed Janice standing only a foot behind Virgil. Janice. She'd thought they were coming to tell her they were getting married. Instead, she'd lost Jack. Married him way back in the mountains, so far away she barely remembered the mist that rose every morning like a ghost chasing the sun. They used to run over the mountains to their special little cave, where he'd taken a quilt, and he got her pregnant with Virgil when she wasn't more'n fourteen. She closed her eyes and sighed.

"Yes, Janice. Please. Stay here with me." She reached for the younger woman. "I need to talk to somebody, and only a woman who done lost her man can know how it be. Much as I love Penny, she kain't understand losing yer man."

As the two of them went inside, Hiram walked around from the outhouse. "Hey, Virgil. Whatcha doing home?"

"Sit down." Virgil sat and nodded to another chair.

He explained what had happened and ended with, "We gotta be strong for Ma. We can't go off crying or cussing or such. You understand?"

Hiram nodded, but his eyes seemed to watch another place or thing that wasn't Virgil and wasn't home.

"Do you understand me?" Virgil asked again.

Hiram's eyes returned from somewhere and focused on Virgil; he nodded, but still Virgil noticed his hands, those huge hands clenched into hammer-like fists so tight the knuckles whitened beneath the tan.

Hiram had turned his mind to something, and Virgil wondered what could so enrapture that simple mind.

Chapter 8

With the rising sun on his right, BJ twisted and fought his way around vines and briars, stumbled across gullies, and pushed aside the low thick limbs whose needles reached constantly toward his eyes.

He was two miles into the woods when the dogs' bellows of delight told him they were on his trail. He did not know these woods and had already crossed a dry hollow and had to climb another ridge. He worked his way down the other side in hopes of finding a creek, but the hillside was rough, and he had to follow a cow path he had found. He tried to hurry, but taking only a hopping step on his right leg was not speedy walking. He needed to find the swamp, get into a creek, lose his scent in the water, escape the dogs, and only then look for the way home.

His leg ached. When his stomach growled with hunger, he remembered the food inside his shirt. He ate as he moved, hastily, careful not to spill precious crumbs.

The woods became silent ahead of him as birds halted their song, lizards peered from beneath cover, and animals froze until he passed. The silence lingered behind him.   Crashing in the underbrush halted him as fear rose inside and turned the food into a greasy lump of terror. He crouched beside a tree, ready to leap aside. A hog charged toward him, skidded, and turned back into the thickets. He swallowed and shivered his relief. The food rose, and he vomited.

Fear sank into his insides like teeth. Brinjin hot even beneath the trees, the sun-soaked air dried him before he could sweat, tickled his throat, and turned his lips into patterns of dry cracks like a baked river bed. Blood oozed down his leg and collected inside his shoe.

The pines began to thin out, to stretch higher toward the sun-bleached sky, and to become scattered with oaks. As the downward slope steepened, he felt the warm dampness of the swamp rise and whisper promises of safety. He tried to jog, crouched over to ease the pain by gripping his thigh, but after a few steps he fell into his half-walk, half-hop.

His eyes showed his relief as he found the spring, a moss-covered terra cotta pipe sunk deep into the black bog of earth. He lay flat on his belly to plunge his face into the water. Crayfish raised small clouds of sand as they backed to the edge with their pincers raised toward him, and spring lizards scampered into the moss when his reflection touched them. He drank deeply and savored the mossy taste as the coolness spread in his belly and helped untie it.

He pushed himself erect and followed the trickle of overflow to the creek where water tumbled in a thin fall over the red-clay bank. As he neared the edge, frogs croaked and splashed to safety. The bank seemed to groan beneath his weight as it sagged and threatened to sink into the hollow undercut by floods.

He backed away and peered into the shadows upstream. A smile curled his lips. He had a choice of directions. The dogs would have to go upstream and find the other spring that fed the creek before they would start downstream. He'd go downstream after he left a trail to lure the dogs upstream. Then he would head for the river.

Sitting on the bank, he slipped off his shoes, tied the strings together to hang them over his shoulder, and pushed himself downward. Once he found a footing, he walked upstream a few steps in the mud to leave a visible trail, and then he stepped into midstream, onto the hard clay that curled and jutted from the water's movement. Water lapped against his legs and danced sand about his ankles as he splashed downstream. Each step had to be tested before he could trust his feet not to slip on the clay. He could not touch the bank, could not touch anything now, or the dogs would find his scent.

His leg began to throb with his pulse, a dull pain that growled in his throat each time he forced the muscles to take his weight.

The men and dogs must be close since they moved faster than he could. If only he could bypass another creek, they would have to follow it up-stream and give him more time.

Underbrush thickened on the banks until only a rabbit could fight his way through, but the concave sides of the creek, washed clean and undermined by flood after flood, offered only trailing ends of briars and insecurely footed willows to impede him. Twice he had to stop, to wait motionless while a snake slithered away into a hollow somewhere in the bank.

The hounds' bellows changed tone behind him. He stopped, listened, and smiled as he recognized the disappointment of a lost trail. He could forget the dogs now; two creeks were behind him. Somewhere ahead lay home. Home and safety.

If he could jest come up on somebody's still, he'd know what creek he was in.

By afternoon, his leg burned with fever. His left shoulder began to ache from the constant bumping of the shoes still tied together and draped over it. The backs of his thighs tightened up with each step from the unaccustomed action of his rolling, hopping walk. His eyes, staring constantly at the ever-changing light and dark of the water, had become red-rimmed.

Hatred for Emerson drove him on through the heat of the afternoon and beyond his exhaustion.

Chapter 9

Virgil followed the undertaker home with his father's body and helped carry the simple pine casket into the house. Ellen and Janice had already pulled the dining table into the front room, and they placed the casket on it.

Ellen put her hand on the wood and rubbed it, felt its roughness and the hard knots of the pine boards. A lot better than what they had for Penny so long ago. And better than what she had for her third son when he died of the whooping cough two years later. She never thought she'd bury somebody else here, never thought she'd outlive Jack. Every time she had a baby, she'd thought it would kill her same as birthing Penny had killed her sister.

Her mind raced over what she might have to do to live, with Jack gone and BJ gone. No more beef, no more whiskey money.

"I gotta figure a way to make it, son," she looked over at Virgil.

"We'll figure together, Ma. It'll work out."

Janice put an arm around Ellen. "I was frightened, too, when I lost Jerome. But Dr. Jacobs has been a lot of help. We'll all pitch in and help you."

Ellen patted the hand on her shoulder. "Thank-ee, Janice." After less than another minute of silence, Ellen turned around to Virgil. "Didcha find out what happened?"

He nodded. "Looks like Pa shot the sheriff when they wrecked. Pa was hurt real bad when the truck turned over and he killed Dixon and BJ ran. They're looking for BJ for running away, but not for killing Dixon."

Ellen nodded. "He'd do that fer his boy. Whereat you reckon he's gone to?"

"I dunno. Perry's out with some dogs to track him. But you know BJ. He's like a haint in the woods. They may never find him, even with the dogs. Has Sam been home?"

"I ain't seen him since he left out early to go down to John Hall's to hep build his new barn. Could you go git him to come home? "

"Right away, Ma. You stay here, Janice?"

She nodded, and Virgil left for Hall's.

The new barn was taking shape. All three brothers had regular work every morning, before Hall went to his job at the Air Corps Base. On days that Hall took off work, they stayed on the job from day to dark. When Virgil drove up, Hall called a stop to see what he wanted.

"How ya doing?" Hall called.

"Not good," Virgil answered, removed his hat, dropped it onto the seat, pulled out a handkerchief, and wiped his forehead. "Sam. Gus," he called as he put the handkerchief back into his pocket, "I need you to come to the house."

"What be the matter?" Sam asked as he walked toward the car. Gus followed.

"Pa's dead. C'mon with me."

They got into the car as Hall began asking questions, but Virgil waved him off. He explained the events of the day to his uncles as he drove home.

When they entered the house, the men stopped to stare at the coffin before they acknowledged Ellen. Virgil felt their helplessness as they turned to their sister-in-law without words.

She rose, walked the few steps to Sam, and he dropped his hat as he grabbed her, bent down and buried his face in her hair. "Oh, Ellen, Ellen."

His body shook as sobs erupted. Ellen had to try to comfort him, and, unable to watch their pain, Virgil stepped out onto the porch. Janice followed.

They sat in silence for a moment, and then Janice reached for his hand. He smiled at her and murmured, "Thanks."

A moment later, he stood up, frowned, and turned quickly from side to side.

"Where's Hiram?"

"I dunno. He sat out here for a long time, just sat." She looked away, hesitated, and continued. "When I came back from the outhouse, maybe a little before noon, he was gone. Ellen said he left with the shotgun and a bunch of shells. She couldn't stop him."

"Oh, God, he's in trouble. I gotta go look for him."

"You want me to stay here or go with you?"

"I dunno. I don't even know where to start looking."

"He didn't tell Ellen anything more than he had to do something."

"I gotta find him. Maybe you stay here. I dunno what to do other than to go to town and see if he's there. Have you seen Charley and

Penny? Any idea where they've gone?"

"No. Ellen said when they left this morning, he said they'd be late coming back. I reckon they still don't know."

In town he went straight to the diner. Only one customer hunched over a coffee cup, and Nita leaned on the counter in front of him. Neither had seen Hiram. He rode around town, up each street, but saw no sign of his brother. He finally returned to the diner. Mid-afternoon, and now no customers. The waitress sat on a stool and sipped a milk shake as she listened to the radio station WMAZ from Macon.

He glanced down the row of booths. Each one still housed a full-to-overflowing ashtray that added their scent to the smell of strong coffee. He sat in the second booth, and when she rotated the stool and started to rise, he said, "Summa that coffee I smell. Black."

She nodded, circled the end of the counter, and picked up the coffee pot. She paused to pick up a spoon and an off-white mug with a blue band around the top, and set both on the table.

"You look a mite worried, Virgil," she said as she poured his coffee. Before he answered, she continued, "This here is strong and bitter. It's been sitting since dinner time. Well? Whatcha so worried over? They find BJ yet?" She sat down across the table from him, reached into her apron pocket and pulled out a pack of ready-made cigarettes with a few Lucifer's stuck down inside the cellophane. She lit it while he spoke, and turned her head to blow the smoke away from his face.

"Not yet. Perry's a good lawman and he's got dogs. I hope they don't shoot him when they catch up. I'm still looking for Hiram. Been all over town and all up and down the road from here to Ma's place and Dr. Jacobs. I jest kain't figger what-all he's up to."

"How's he taking what's happened with BJ? If he's riled up bout that, no telling what the boy'll do, addled as he is."

"How much trouble can a twelve-year old get into?"

"He looks twenty." She turned to the front of the diner as the screen door opened, glanced back at Virgil, and said, "Gotta go." She rose and said, "What kin I get for you, Jake?"

The GBI agent shook his head and strode toward Virgil. Virgil rose.

"You look mighty serious, Jake." Virgil extended is hand, which the agent gripped firmly.

"I'm truly sorry about your pa. He was a fine man. Hard to believe he'd-a shot the sheriff, but I know how a man tends to look after his young."

"Sit," Virgil offered and pointed to the opposite side of the booth as he sat. "How about another cup here, Nita?"

Jake sat, and both men remained silent until the second cup arrived and Nita poured coffee. When he declined sugar and cream, she returned to her stool at the counter.

The agent took a deep breath. "This seems to be a day for bad happenings. Judge Emerson's dead."

Nita spun around on her stool. Virgil looked up from the coffee cup he had been studying.

"He have a heart attack?"

"If you call a load of buckshot in the chest a heart attack. Somebody unloaded on him, right inside his front door. He let in whover killed him."

Virgil closed his eyes. Not Hiram. Please, God, don't let it be Hiram. "Who?"

"We don't know who or when. Bill Roberts had an appointment and when the judge didn't answer the door, he tried the screen and walked right on in. Found him dead in the front hall and called me over in Macon. First I knew about Dixon getting killed, too."

"Karen been told?"

"Yeah. I told her husband. He looked like he was gonna die, seeing as he was depending on the judge to help him with his practice. He'd-a gotten a lot of cases assigned. Not now, though." He continued to talk about Karen and her future and her husband's lack of legal acuity and whether or not the judge from Macon would be coming over to hold court.

Virgil heard only a drone as his mind wandered to Hiram. He mentally kicked himself for not being more alert. Every since the trial, Hiram had smoldered about how Emerson hadn't been fair to BJ. Was the boy somewhere in the woods looking for Perry? Was he gonna come after Jake next because they made the arrest? He shook his head to rid himself of the thoughts.

"What's the matter?" Jake asked.

"What? Oh, nothing. I'm worried about Ma is all. I reckon I better get on home." He dropped a quarter on the table, shook hands with Jake, nodded to Nita, and headed for the car.

Where was Hiram now? If he'd killed Emerson, who would he

look for next? "I've gotta find him before he shoots somebody else. But where in hell do I go looking?" Virgil muttered.

A car pulled in beside him as he started to back out, and he turned off the switch. Laughing, Charley and Penny got out of their car.

Virgil dropped his forehead on the steering wheel and bounced it lightly. Gotta stop looking for Hiram long enough to tell them what happened and to send them home.

Chapter 10

The shrill laughter of children floated into the bottom and reached BJ in the creek. A dog barked far off, too far away to have smelled him. Frustrated calves, separated for a night from their mothers, bawled their loneliness. Twilight was coming and would leave the stream without shadow or sunlight.

The odor of muck rising from the creek bed as his feet stirred the bottom never ended. He passed cattle crossings where manure still steamed on the pathways. Once a bull raised his head from the stream, water dripping from his mouth, and stared at the approaching man. BJ waved an arm at him, and the bull turned and ran up the bank. It stopped on the edge of the creek bank and watched BJ splash his way along the creek.

With darkness would come the dew. Cold dew. No matter how hot the July afternoon, if you got still after sundown and the dew damped your clothes, you would shiver away the night.

He longed for the coolness to come. He wiped his sleeve across his face, but it was too soaked to remove his sweat. He wanted to be home, to sleep on his own mattress, not on the cold ground. Even the heat inside the house, with no wind and so much humidity the sweat would not evaporate, would be welcome. Even Hiram's snoring would be welcome.

At the next cattle crossing he limped up the bank. Maybe he could find a barn for the night. No way to sleep in the middle of the creek. He reached a meadow and started to cross it when he heard a plane circling overhead. Squinting against the glare, he saw an Air Corps plane so low he could see the co-pilot's face and the binoculars. Perry musta called the Air Corps from over at Warner Robins to help find him.

Pain forgotten, he ran back into the creek and the shelter of entwined limbs. His body screamed in protest at his demands as he hurried downstream. Every step created a silver spray of water that flew back onto him. When his feet slipped on algae-covered rocks and clay, he grabbed at the roots and branches along the bank to keep from falling.

When he heard the dogs, panic seized him and pushed him onward.

He fell, but fear lifted him again and turned his mind from the pain in his leg and from the bruises and briar scratches that came every few yards. Panic shouted at him to hurry, hurry, hurry.

A fallen tree, its trunk studded with jagged remains of limbs, blocked him. He placed both hands on the trunk as if it were the back of a horse, and flung himself up so that his belly lay along the trunk. As he flung his legs over, a stob dragged through the crude bandage into the fester of his wounded thigh.

He screamed his agony, clutched himself to hold away pain, and dropped into the stream. Water flooded into his open mouth. Blood, like the red soil he had plowed and worked, flowed downstream in a harsh streak.

Convulsed and coughing, he sat up to grip himself above the fester and rock his torso. "Oh Gawd! Oh Gawd! Oh Gawd!"

Eagerly, voices rose upstream. Dogs yelped their delight. Billy Jack rose out of his pain and onto his feet. But his leg refused his weight. He began to crawl downstream, goaded by the excited baying of the hounds.

A stick dug into his belly. The creek bed narrowed, and as the banks rose higher on each side, they curved away at water level like long caves burrowed by some ancient animal. He crawled into the deeper blackness under the bank and squeezed his body against the cool dampness of the soil. Propped on his elbow, he seized a small bush, broke it, swept away his trail of retreat, and stuffed the bush under the bank at his head. He waited, his head tilted, listened to the approaching dogs, and pressed his face against the coolness of the bank. He closed his eyes to the pain in his leg.

"Don't let them see me. Gawd, please don't let them see me."

As if in answer, Billy Jack felt the bank tremble as the men stomped by overhead, their voices lifted and shrill in anticipation.

"He can't be far now," a voice said. "Turn them dogs lose. They'll stop him."

Another voice said, "Finish him, you mean. No, we ain't turning these dogs lose to kill him like them other dogs chewed up that nigger. I want to see Billy Jack burn for what he done."

He recognized Alexander Perry's voice and shivered.

The voices faded into the crackling underbrush, a sound like fire moving overhead. Pain in his leg penetrated almost to his brain with its intensity and heat. The creek's gurgling magnified his thirst, but he didn't dare move with his hunters so close.

He waited for the silence of empty woods, for the earth to still, for the wind to sleep, and for only the upper branches to catch sunlight.

A shotgun broke the twilight. Once, and then as rapidly as BJ could have pumped it. A .12 gauge. Five shots. Not plugged. Perry and his friends had found something, but not him. Maybe a half-mile away.

They'd not come back his way, at least not tonight.

But Gus and Sam would look for him soon. Once they learned that Pa was dead, one or the other would come to find him. And old Spot would find him. Soon as they put Spot on a coon trail and hollered, all he'd have to do was holler back to Spot, and they'd find him. He had to wait, wait and keep that leg cool.

He muttered, "Oh, Gawd! Don't let them come back," and clamped his hand over his mouth, his eyes widening at the loudness of his own whisper in the close confines of the creek banks. It seemed to echo and re-echo from the banks and inside his head, a shout to the men that they had passed him by.

He listened, his body stiff, steam rising from him as the fever dried his creek-soaked clothing. The evening wind rattled leaves. A hunting owl swooshed nearby and its victim squealed. A cow lowed. Crickets called to the night. Then another shot, farther away than the others. Whoever it was must have reloaded; he was moving away, far enough away for BJ to get out from under the bank and get a drink.

As BJ stuck his face into the creek and began to slurp water, a thick-bodied snake undulated up stream, its tongue flicking at the man-smell, its flat head lifted, the elliptical eyes staring ahead as if into eternity.

BJ drank. The snake watched.

When BJ lifted his head, the snake slithered under the opposite bank and lost it self in the darkness.

"Gawd, but that tastes good."

Far off, a dog barked "trail" and a man whooped the hound on. Gus. Gus was coming.

He stood, grasped the root of an oak that twisted along the bank, and raised his voice to Spot. Gus answered. BJ laid his head against the root and cried.

*   *   *

Atop the next ridge, Gus sicked Spot onward, and the hound responded with a yelp that he was on a trail. His barking intensified as the raccoon treed, and BJ knew Gus would have to pull the hound off the coon to get him headed down to the creek.

He dragged himself up the bank by pulling on tree roots that dripped with moisture and felt almost rotten-slick to his touch. When he could reach bushes farther up the bank, he used them to pull himself on up to dry land, where he lay flat on his belly to catch his breath.

He breathed in the moistness of the bottomland, the rich soil washed from the hillside together with the fertilizer and the topsoil plowed for more than a century. Vines pressed into his face; dampness soaked upward to cool his body. He turned onto his side to relieve the pressure against his injured leg.

Gus whooped the hound again. BJ sat up and yelled, his whoop a cross between a bull's bellow to a cow in heat, a soldier's scream as he charged, and a panther's yowl at his own loneliness.

BJ's call to Spot echoed through the night. A passing owl dropped his mouse and swerved away with a sudden flapping of wings. A fox yipped and scooted through the brush away from the stream. A boar hog grunted as he crashed away from the sound. The night went silent. He waited for what seemed forever for Gus to whoop again. Slowly the nocturnal creatures around him began to talk to each other again—the tree frogs, the crickets, and a night hawk. A pair of owls hooted to each other down the creek.

The night smelled of fresh dew and loam, rotting oak leaves, and a skunk somewhere upwind.

Spot yelped that he was seeking another trail. Gus whooped him on.

In the shadows cast by the moon, BJ pulled on his shoes. He was through wading in creeks tonight. The shoes felt tight on his feet, but at least he wouldn't step barefooted on rocks, sticks and briars now, and the shoes were nearly dry.

A half-hour later, he saw the lantern through the tree. Its movement in Gus's handmade the tree trunks dance and the low leaves shimmer with gold.

"Hey, Gus. Over here."

"You awright, BJ?" Gus stepped into sight. Clad in his overalls, he carried the shotgun in one hand and the lantern in the other.

BJ thought he looked old. His face seemed more lined tonight.

Maybe it's the lantern light. Maybe it's cause Pa's dead.

Before he could answer his uncle, Spot trotted up to him and licked his face. BJ wrapped his arms around the dog and buried his face in its neck. The dog smelled rank with something he'd wallowed in, but BJ didn't care. The hound whipped him with its tail.

"Good boy, Spot." He looked up at Gus. "I'm shot. It's my leg. I kain't walk good."

When Gus set the lantern down, the light turned the rotting leaves golden. He knelt beside BJ's bad leg, untied the rag, and looked at the injury.

"You shore got a mess. I gotta git you to Doc Jacobs." The slash seeped a red-tinged fluid but no longer bled freely.

"They'll be looking fer me there. I gotta git somewheres else."

"Naw. You be better there'n anywhere else. 'Sides, there be some talk you didn't shoot Dixon, that your pa did."

BJ and Gus stared at each other for a few seconds. BJ turned his head as a tear pushed out of his eye. He wiped at it with his wrist and shook his head, but said nothing. How could he tell his uncle that Pa had taken the blame?

"Awright. We'll talk later. Lemme see you stand up on it."

He held up one hand, which Gus took and held, and he rose. "I kain't put my weight on it much." He hobbled a couple of steps and turned to look at Gus.

"You lean on that-air tree a minute. I'll fix you a leaning stick." Gus pulled out his pocket knife and began to work on an oak sapling. In a few minutes, he had cut it down and trimmed the fork into an arm rest. After checking the length, he trimmed off another two inches. "That'll hep ya git up to my truck. It's not more'n a mile, and I kin drive ya from there. I kain't tote ya no more. You done got too big."

BJ tried the makeshift crutch and after a half-dozen steps was able to negotiate his way behind Gus. But after less than a half-hour, he stopped. They had not covered a hundred yards.

"I gotta rest. I'm plum slap wo' out." He collapsed onto the ground and lay on his back. He pulled his legs up so his feet were flat on the ground and his back at ease. "Jest gimme a few minutes."

"You want me to go git Sam? Both-a us could tote you outta here."

"What I need is Dr. Jacobs' horse."

"Kain't nobody ride him, not since his boy got kilt."

BJ laughed. "How do you think I pushed that-air last yearling to

Hiram? I been riding that stallion since before Jerome went off to war."

"Well, we ain't got that stallion. You think you kin make it some more?"

He nodded, reached for a hand up, and they moved along through the night. The lantern threw shadows of bodiless legs that swung back and forth in the darkness. The crutch bit into the leaves and stirred up the musty smell of rot as well as the clean smell of moist soil. To BJ it was the smell of spring plowing without the hot, sweet smell of the mule's manure and sweat.

As they crossed a meadow, fireflies danced. A nighthawk fluttered from a cedar on the edge, and Spot growled.

"Whatzit, boy?" Gus whispered.

Spot nosed the air, turned his head slightly, and then, snarling, he dashed toward the other side of the meadow.

"Sump-em's wrong." Gus said.

Spot slammed into something and the fight began. The dog and something rolled into the meadow, both animals growling as their bodies tumbled over each other. They could see Spot's white and a light-colored body that showed some white.

"Damn! It's a fox," Gus said. He clicked the safety off the shotgun and moved across the meadow. "You stay back, you hear?" he told BJ.

"That-air fox's gotta be mad, Gus. You be careful."

"Hey, gimme that stick," Gus returned and took BJ's crutch. "I'll whack him. He'll run and then I kin shoot 'im." He held the lantern and shotgun in one hand and with the other he gripped the stick, over his shoulder and ready to strike.

BJ leaned forward, put both hands onto the ground, and lowered himself. He couldn't run if the fox came after him, and his balance was too poor to keep on standing.

As the two animals rolled closer to him, Gus brought the stick down hard and hit both the fox and Spot. The dog howled and ran. The fox rose, staggered, saw Gus, and started toward him. Gus dropped both the lantern and the shotgun, gripped the stick with both hands and slammed it onto the fox's head. The animal fell and did not move.

Behind him the broken lantern spilled kerosene and flames.

"Gus. The lantern!"

Gus grabbed the shotgun from the edge of the fire and began to stomp the flames, but they roared across the meadow of broomsedge. The night wind was up enough to push it beyond Gus's control. In seconds, the fire rose as high as his head and raced across the meadow toward the trees

"Git up, git up," Gus called as he picked up the crutch. Clutching it, he ran back to BJ.

"It's going away from us." BJ began to rise like a cow; he pushed his rump up first and then, holding onto the stick, he pushed his front end up

"Yeah, right towards our truck. It's up over the hill yonder."

"The fire's gonna die out in them oaks. Them leaves ain't gonna burn, not with the dew on 'em."

"Maybe. But it's gotten mighty hot in that broomsedge. And we kain't git up the pine hill with that-air fire going. It'll git through them oaks and run up the hill faster'n you kin move."

"I kin give it a try. That fire slow up enough, you kin whup it out with a limb."

After feeding on the broomsedge, the flames slowed dramatically when they reached the hardwood leaves, but the heat they created had already generated a rising wind that sucked the fire onward. It had widened, and when it reached the hill, it fed upward and dried its fuel with its own rising heat.

"I kain't do nothing against that-air fire by myself, but Gawd-damn if I ain't gotta try."

The fire crawled through the leaves, grew another foot wider with every yard it moved uphill, and increased in intensity as it climbed higher. Pines needles waited silently to provide better, faster-burning fuel.

Gus broke a pine limb and began to beat on the flames, but the fire had too big a start for him to be effective.

The hillside lit up. Tree trunks stood like black soldiers at attention against the red as the fire climbed honeysuckle and saw briar to reach the crowns of the seedling pines. The wind increased with the fire, and the fire intensified with the wind as they fed each other.

BJ sank to the ground, helpless and hopeless, as the moon lifted itself out of the pines on the eastern ridge and the fire backlit the western ridge.

Chapter 11

"I smell smoke," Ellen called from the front porch. Off to her left, the sky brightened as the fire neared the top of the ridge. Ashes danced in the air around her as the wind thickened with smoke.

"Fire!" She dropped the water bucket and turned to run back inside.

Sam almost collided with her as he raced to the front door; they juked back and forth before he grabbed her shoulders, held her still, and stepped around her. He jumped from the porch and dashed around the house. Flames on the ridge brightened the rising smoke, and sparks mingled with stars as they rose.

Charley joined him in the yard.

"We gotta set a backfire. Charley, git some Lucifer's off-a the mantle piece. Ellen, git down to Dr. Jacobs and send him for help. It's bad. It looks like it gonna git up in the tree tops. Hurry!"

"I'll git Dr. Jacobs," Penny called. "Ellen, you go with them."

"No," Charley yelled. "You stay here, Penny. You in no shape to go running up and down the road."

The wind pushed the smoke directly toward the house.

"He's right," Ellen said and ran off into the darkness, her feet sure of the way. Moonlight brightened as she ran, and it showed her the lighter roadway in the band of darkness thrown by the trees. Fear gripped her belly, fear that the house would burn, fear that Jack's body, laid out in the house, would burn and she wouldn't be able to bury him. She smelled her own fear in her sweat. The fear kept up with her as she ran and hovered over her as she pounded on Dr. Jacobs' door.

"Dr. Jacobs! Dr. Jacobs! Fire!"

Virgil shoved the screen open and stepped into the smell of his mother's fear and the odor of burning pine. The western sky glowed.

"I'll git some help, Ma. C'mon." Virgil ran down the steps and into the yard, his mother right behind him. "I'll get Plute's boys. They'll help out." He got into the driver's seat of Dr. Jacobs car while Ellen scrambled into the passenger seat. He sped down the driveway and away from the fire, to a tenant house less than a half-mile down the road.

Depressing the horn with his stump, Virgil yelled, "Fire!" out of the window as he drove into the yard. Three Negro men ran from the house.

"Git in, quick," Virgil said. As soon as they were in the back seat, Virgil turned around in the yard and headed toward the fire.

"Sam and Charley done gone down to the creek to set a backfire. Y'all git on down the hill quick as you kin. You got any Lucifer's?"

"No, m'am. But iffen they do, us-ens kin light up off-a their-un's."

Before Virgil cut the engine off, the three men jumped from the car and ran toward the fire.

"I'm going down there, Ma."

"No, Virgil. Please. Stay here. It's yer pa. Iffen the fire gits up here, I don't want he should burn up. Please, son. Stay with me. Penny kain't hep me move him into the road iffen we has to."

"Awright, Ma. Let me take the doc's car back. He don't even know I done took it." Virgil slipped back into his family's language without thinking.

"You git back here quick as you kin, you hear?"

"Awright, Ma." Virgil cut off the switch and got out, walked around the car, and took his mother's arm. She didn't need to be helped or guided across the yard, but tonight she seemed frail.

"I'll be right back," he said as Ellen reached for Penny.

                              *   *   *

Sam and Charley ran down a path behind the house, passed the outhouse, crossed another ditch and a woodcutter's drive. The creek lay ahead. Sam thought the fire might jump it, seeing as it wasn't real wide and vines growing from one bank leaned over to grab a-holt on trees on the other side. The fire had an easy route across.

They scrambled through underbrush to reach the creek and plunged down the bank without bothering to go upstream the hundred yards to a cattle crossing. Charley dug out the matches, scraped one across the back of his thigh, and cursed when it broke.

"Slow down, Charley. Slow down. This here ain't the first fire you fought."

Both men gasped for breath from their run. Charley's hands shook, but the next match caught, and with it he set a backfire in four places a few feet from the creek.

"Gimme a couple of them Lucifers," Sam said, his hand palm up to

Charley. "I kin work off one way and you t'other." He dropped some matches into his overalls pocket and pulled out his pocket knife.

"Here's you a limb fer pushing the fire," he said as he cut a pine branch for Charley. "You got ya knife?"

"I got my britches on, hadn't I?" Charley answered.

They worked their way along the backfire and swept the flames away from the creek to move them toward the oncoming fire. The flames rose enough to help them see as the smoke thickened and hid the moon.

Sweat ran over Sam, sweat from his exertions and sweat from the heat of the fire. I'm gitting too old fer this, he told himself. Last time was when Jack's still fire got out. Must-a been ten year ago but we had us a heap of hep then.

He looked back toward Charley. The younger man worked steadily as he pushed the backfire into the low pines that covered the ridge. Sam realized he had not moved half the distance Charley had.

"Mista Carter! Mista Carter!"

"Down heah," Sam called back.

"We's cummin, suh."

Three Negro men ran up.

"We gotta keep the backfire moving away from here." Sam gave quick instructions and passed out matches. The men spread out and continued to build the backfire.

They forced their flames into the wind and created an ever-widening burn to halt the approaching fire.

Sweat dripped down Sam's face, ran down his back, and drew lines of cleanness in the soot on his face. His feet got hotter as he stomped on the smallest flames. His hands began to ache from gripping the pine limb.

The backfire roared up the hill and into the pine crowns; at it reached the ridge top, it met the approaching wildfire. Sparks continued to fly in the wind, to sprinkle the night with firefly-like specks before they died. Ashes drifted in the wind like snow.

The two white and three black men joined up and watched as the fires swallowed each other. A few flickers came along the ends, and the men hurried up the hill to flail them out with pine limbs.

"Yooo," Sam called.

The others answered and came to him. One of the black men grinned and said, "Mista Carter, suh, you's as black as us-ens. You is too, Mista Charley. You look jest like us niggers."

"Yeah? Well, we done it. We done stopped that-air fire."

"Yassuh, we sho did."

"Les go home," Sam said. "See about the women folks."

When they reached the house, Sam went directly to the well and drew up a bucket.

"Dipper," he said to Charley, and as the younger man held it out, Sam filled it. One of the Negro men had already picked up the Mason jar kept by the well for any passing Negro to help himself to water. Sam filled it and then emptied the rest of the bucket over his head. He put the bucket on the well ledge and rubbed his hands over his hair and face. The fire smell stayed with him and the soot streaked, but the coolness revived him. He drew another bucket up and drank directly from it.

Mason jar and dipper appeared before him, and he filled them both again. They stood around the well while they drank and tried to cool down, until the Negroes said goodnight and left with Sam's promise of a jug of whiskey apiece tomorrow and "Much obliged."

As Sam and Charley crossed the yard toward the house, a pickup rattled by, stopped a little distance down the road, and they heard the doors open and close.

"Sound like the niggers got a ride," Charley said.

"Iffen the truck'd a-been here, I'd taken 'em home myself. We couldn't of done it without them hepping."

Virgil spoke from the porch. "We need to go find BJ. He's down there somewhere."

"You reckon BJ started that-air fire?" Ellen asked as she came up behind Virgil.

Sam answered. "He wouldn't a-purpose. And Gus oughtta done found him by now."

"You heard Gus whooping at Spot while you were out there?"

"Not a sound since right after he left. Nothing with that-air fire going."

"Let's go, Sam, Charley. We better help find 'em both."

Sam's legs ached. He wasn't sure he would be able to keep up with the younger men, but they had to find BJ before Perry did.

*   *   *

Scattered stumps continued to burn after the flames passed, the light'erd knots supplying hours of resin for the flames.

"Them-there stumps'll give us enough light to git to the truck," Gus said.

"Iffen it's still there."

"We gotta git up there and see. Leastways, we ain't heard it blow up."

With BJ leaning and hopping, they rested often. In about a half-hour, they heard voices on the hill. The fire had burned out any place to hide, and with nothing better, they each stepped up against a tree trunk and waited.

On the hill, a lantern swung shadows into the night

"Yooo, Gus! You hear me?"

"It's Virgil," BJ said. "Yoooo, Virgil. Down here!"

Silence moved with the shadows through the ashes as Virgil, Sam, and Charley ran down the hill. Virgil's empty sleeve whipped like a dropped leash behind him.

"You awright?" Virgil asked as he reached them.

"He done got himself shot in the laig," Gus said. "I couldn't tote him and my shotgun. And Spot got in a fight with a mad fox. He gonna die with the rabies."

"He already be half-dead," Sam said. "We seen him up to yer truck. Looked like he were in a bad scrap. Virgil, you tote the shotgun." He looked around. "Where-at's your lantern?"

"I kicked it over when Spot and the fox got into that fight. It's what started the fire. Y'all set a backfire?"

"Yeah," Sam said. "It's too rough fer making a cat saddle to tote him out. We'll hafta take turns toting him piggy back."

"Anything left-a the truck?" asked Gus.

"Yeah. It's a bit scorched up some, but mostly the fire done jumped over it."

"How'd you find us?"

"I knowed you'd gone looking fer him. When we seen the fire, Virgil got Plute's boys to come hep. We set a backfire down to the gulley and it ran right on up the hill. I done promised all-a them niggers a jug tomorrow."

Charley interrupted the discussions.

"Gus, you tote the lantern. I can tote BJ piggy back. We'll stop when I get tired."

With his uncles' help, BJ crawled onto Charley's bent-over back, wrapped his arms over the man's shoulders, and hung on. Charley hooked his arms under BJ's knees, straightened up, and started up the hill.

Before they reached the truck, another half-hour passed and they stopped four times for Charley to rest. Spot greeted them from the truck bed with a low whine as if in apology for whatever he did that got the stick laid over his back.

"He got tore up bad, Gus."

"Yeah. He gonna git the rabies," BJ said.

"Maybe not," Charley said. "The dog doctor might can give him some shots. Can you make it in if I back you up to the seat?"

"I thinks so."

Virgil opened the door and Charley leaned back a little until BJ's butt hit the edge of the seat.

"I got it," BJ said.

The strong odor of Ellen's bread and sausage rose from a paper sack on the seat. His mouth watered and his stomach growled. He turned around to face the windshield, pulled his legs into the truck, and closed the door, his mind on nothing but food.

"I made it."

"Yer ma sent me off with some biscuits," Gus said as he opened the driver's side door. "Here they be." Gus opened up the paper sack on the front seat and removed four biscuits, each with a slab of sausage inside. BJ wolfed one down in two bites. Cold and greasy tasted good.

"Hold up there, afore you make yourself sick," Gus said. "Here. You need some water." He handed over a Mason jar.

"I had plenty of water down to the creek. But this-here is from home. It shore do taste good, especially with Ma's biscuits. Ain't we behind the old nigger church?"

"Yeah. Not that far from home, neither. I reckon it done burned down, howsomever."

Different images of the old church came to Charley, BJ, and Gus, but no one mentioned it again.

"I reckon I didn't know where I was, seeing as I was in the creek bed. Iffen I'd come up on a still, I'd-a figured my whereabouts. Pa told me to go south and I did. He shore was right. He shore took keer of me."

The image of his father, empty eyes staring at the sky, overwhelmed BJ, and he laid his head on the dashboard and began to sob, the deep racking sobs of sorrow, loss, guilt, and emptiness.

The others backed off and let him cry.

Virgil walked away from the truck, down the blackened road, so the others would not see his struggle to control himself. They'd have to bury his pa in the morning. And he had to find Hiram.

But where in the hell had he gone off to?

* * *

The truck cranked without any problems, and with Sam, Charley, and Virgil in the back, Gus drove down the blackened woods lane, out to the dirt road, and to Dr. Jacobs' house.

"I'll roust him out," Virgil said as he jumped off the tailgate.

He entered the back door without giving thought to the smell that floated from him. Ashes flaked his hair, and where he had wiped sweat off his face, he had smeared soot across his forehead and down his cheek.

"By God, you look like you've been in the fire," Dr. Jacobs greeted him.

"Yeah. We found BJ. He's out in the truck. Shot in the leg."

"Let's get him inside," he said. "To the exam room."

They hurried to the truck, where Sam and Gus had already helped BJ onto Charley's back. They went inside.

Janice walked out of a door into the hall as they entered.

"Is he all right?" she asked.

"Miss Janice," BJ answered for himself, "I reckon I am now's I see your pretty face." He grinned at her.

"Posh, Billy Jack. You're nothing but a flirt. Here, let me get that door." She stepped ahead of them down the hall and opened the door to the examining room.

It looked more like a hospital room than a room in a home. A table sat in the middle, and cabinets filled with various instruments and equipment stood like ranked soldiers along the walls. A stethoscope hung on a coat rack in the corner. The odor of camphor filled the room.

"Put him on the table," Janice said.

They did. The smell of wood smoke and dirty men overpowered the camphor odor.

"Everybody out," Jacobs said as he entered. "Except you, Janice. I'll need your help here."

They left, and Dr. Jacobs cut away what was left of the pants leg over the injury. "Looks like you been wallowing in the mud, son. This is not going to feel too good. Janice, get me the turpentine."

When he poured the liquid on the raw cut, BJ howled.

"Hold on, son. It could be worse. This'll keep it from hurting so much tomorrow."

With Janice providing instruments as he asked for them, Jacobs cleaned the wound, stitched it up, and added more turpentine.

"I'm not going to put on a bandage. That needs the air, and now you need a real bath. I'll send in Gus to help you. Come on, Janice."

They walked out and found the three Carter men and Charley standing in the hall, each with a cigarette. Sam held an ash tray that already contained several butts.

"What'd he holler so about?" Sam asked.

"Turpentine," Jacobs said and smiled.

"I'd-a-hollered too," Virgil said. "You got any sulfa here?"

"No. I'll go to the hospital and get some. Gus, you need to get him cleaned up." He jerked a thumb over his shoulder. "There's a bathroom on t'other side of the room."

Gus entered the exam room, and Jacobs continued, "Virgil, you got something he can wear? You know we got to take him back to jail at some point."

"Let 'em stay here for awhile. I'll trust him not to run off, seeing as how he can't, anyhow. And I got to appoint a new sheriff."

"You not going to wait on Judge Emerson?"

"Emerson's dead and—"

"The judge? Dead? How? When?"

"Took a load of buckshot in the chest. I'm scared it was Hiram. He's gone off somewhere. God only knows where."

"You better get yourself to the jail early tomorrow, then. Perry might think he's next in line. Who you going to appoint?"

"Gus."

"Gus?" Sam laughed.

"Gus?" Jacobs smiled. "That's going to upset the applecart around here."

"Virgil." Janice placed a hand on his shoulder and smiled. "You need to get some rest. You look exhausted."

"I've got a funeral to plan, and I gotta go see about Ma. Are you coming with me, Sam?"

"Take my car," Jacobs offered. "I know Ellen's in a fret. Maybe you go up with him, Janice. She could use a woman's support."

"Lemme get some clothes for BJ," Virgil said and mounted the stairs two steps at a time. He was back in minutes with underwear, a shirt and a pair of jeans. "These ought to fit. I'm taller, but he can roll up the pants legs." He handed the clothes to Sam and turned to Janice. "You really want to go with me?"

She nodded.

"Then let's go to the house."

A lone lamp burned inside the kitchen, and through the open door he saw Ellen standing at the stove as she poured up a cup of coffee. Virgil sighed and leaned his head for a moment on his hand gripping the steering wheel.

"Let's go on in." He stepped out and started around the car to Janice's side, but she had already opened the door and gotten out. He took her by the arm and helped her cross the bridge over the ditch.

"Ma," he called as they walked up the steps onto the porch.

"Oh, Virgil," Ellen's words were echoed by the crash of a coffee cup on the floor. Ellen ran through the house toward him.

She gripped him with a fierceness he did not know she possessed and sobbed without control; her tears soaked his shirt. All he could do was hold her with his one arm and the stump of the other as tears rose in him and began to flow.

Chapter 12: The Next Day

Long before the sun began to lighten the horizon, Sam was up. He stoked the stove fire and drew three buckets of water for the wash basins that sat on a shelf beside the well. He scrubbed his face, rubbed the stubble of his whiskers, and decided not to bother with shaving. He took the third bucket into the house and started a pot of coffee. When it began to perk, he woke Ellen.

She almost walked in on the newlywed's room when she went to wake Penny, but remembered Charley lived here now and removed her hand from the knob. She knocked and called, "Time to git up."

Penny answered, and in a few minutes the two women had begun to mix biscuits and fry sausage. The men wanted to begin digging the grave as soon as it was light enough to see and before it got brinjin hot.

They filled their plates and coffee cups and then went onto the front porch to eat. Charley and Penny sat off to themselves but remained silent. While they ate, Virgil arrived.

"You et?" Ellen asked.

"No."

"There's plenty. Let me fix ya a plate."

"I'll git it, Ma.

"I'll hep him, Ellen. You finish your breakfast." Penny rose and headed for the kitchen.

"Thanks, Penny," Virgil said as he walked into the kitchen. She smiled at him. He noticed her face was pale in the lamplight. "You feeling alright?"

She shook her head. "No. I got the vomits some. Ain't hungry a-tall."

She sliced three biscuits in half, lathered them with butter, poured on some homemade cane syrup, piled on three sausage patties, and put the plate on the pie safe.

"Whatcha want to drink? Coffee?"

"Yeah. Any milk in the icebox?"

"Plenty."

He opened the oak box and pulled out the pitcher. Cream sat thick on top. Penny handed him a knife, which he used like a spatula to lift off some cream. Just enough, he thought as he used the knife blade to stir his coffee.

By sunup, the men were on the slope behind the house, mattock and shovel in hand, to dig the grave. They would lay Jack to rest beside his third son, dead for almost ten years. His sister-in-law lay on the other side of the boy.

They dug for more than two hours. The red clay had turned brick-hard during the summer dry spell, and they took fifteen-minute turns swinging the mattock. While that man rested, another shoveled out the loose dirt and clods. Virgil could only watch.

That afternoon, he and BJ watched as Sam, Gus, Charley and Dr. Jacobs lifted Jack's coffin and carried it to the grave, where they set it down on the ropes they would use to lower it into the ground.

Since his uncles and BJ had nothing to wear but clean overalls, Virgil too wore his work clothes. Charley dressed in a pair of slacks and cotton shirt. Without their hats, the un-tanned band across their foreheads gleamed in the sun. Penny, Ellen and Janice had on the same dresses they had worn to Penny's wedding.

The slight breeze dried sweat as rapidly as the thirsty sun sucked it out of them. A shadow passed over, and then another. Virgil glanced into the white-hot sky and saw two low-flying buzzards. He shuddered. They couldn't be after Jack. They drifted off in the direction of the fire.

Dr. Jacobs led the service, which he limited to reading the 23 psalm and saying a short prayer. He ended with, "and may God rest his soul."

"Amen" echoed his concluding words.

The pallbearers took up the four ends of ropes, swung the coffin over the open grave, and lowered it into the ground. One by one, the family members took up a clod of dirt and dropped it onto the coffin. While BJ balanced on his crutches, Virgil reached down to hand him a clump of dirt. Then Charley, Sam and Gus set about filling the grave.

The buzzards circled again, and this time as the shadows floated across the crowd, everyone looked up. Not only the two that Virgil saw earlier, but a dozen or more. Searching; seeking; smelling food.

Chapter 13

After they ate the dinner that Janice had brought, Virgil turned to his brother. "BJ, you got to go back to jail. I'm sorry, but you got to."

"I ain't going back, Virgil. Perry'll kill me. And I ain't gonna go on no nigger chain gang."

"No. We gonna appeal. Nobody's gotten that kinda sentence for making whiskey. And you're not but fifteen. That oughtta count for something. I'm going to town to talk to your lawyer. And you're going with me. Dr. Jacobs'll take care of you over there at the jail."

"I sure will."

"Gus, I'm gonna appoint you sheriff. You'll be the one to take him in. I got that power with Emerson dead."

"You mean, me? Sheriff?" Gus laughed. "You teasing me? Everybody in town knows I make whiskey."

"When you take BJ to jail, they'll know you'll be a good lawman. It'll work. Nobody'll say you show favorites if you take your own kin to jail."

Gus nodded.

"He be right," Sam said.

"I agree," Dr. Jacobs said.

"Then it's settled. By the way, Cunningham's been paying Dixon some $3,000 a year. We'll keep you on the same salary. Let's get on to town. I'll see the lawyer and be sure he's gotten the appeal started. BJ, you'll be out by the time your leg's well."

"You gonna pay me that kinda money?" Gus asked, his eyebrows raised and shock stamped on his face.

"Dixon got it. I know it was for protecting Cunningham's whiskey business, but it was tax money. So why shouldn't you get the same pay?"

Gus shook his head in disbelief.

"What about Hiram?" Jacobs asked. "Any idea yet on where he's gone?"

"I don't know," Virgil said. "Unless he's gone off and died somewhere."

"Them buzzards look to be about where I was last night. You don't reckon they be after Hiram, do ya? Come to think on it, I heard a shotgun last night, not long afore you come up on me, Gus."

"I heard it too, but I figured it were somebody hunting and not shooting too good."

Virgil frowned with worry. Had the boy gone out shooting up the night? If he wasn't out there dead somewhere, where was he?

"We gotta find Hiram," he said. "Gus, soon's we get BJ here locked away and you git your badge on, we gotta go see what them buzzards are after. Hiram shoulda been home last evening, no matter where he's gone off to."

*　*　*

The jail stood empty and silent. No deputy. No sign of Perry. They walked into the back, where BJ went into his old cell and sat down on the bunk.

"Ain't no call to go locking up the door, Gus. I ain't gonna run off again."

Gus grinned at his nephew. No way for him to run off again, either.

"Lock the door, Gus. You got to treat him like any other man you jail. Only way to keep the town happy right now," Virgil said.

BJ shrugged and nodded, and Gus pushed the door to. But he had to search for the keys, and could not find them.

"They must be at the undertaker's. Dixon must've had them in his pocket. I'll go get them." Virgil walked out the door and down the two blocks to the undertaker's, where he collected the keys.

"I appointed Gus Carter sheriff until the next election. You can spread the word. He's brought BJ in and locked him up. He'll finish up his sentence until his appeal is done. I figure any man who'll go out and find his own kin and bring him back to jail deserves the trust and the job."

The undertaker agreed, and handed him Dixon's badge.

With BJ locked up and the sheriff's badge pinned on Gus's shirt, Virgil and Gus went to the diner across the street.

Nita looked up as they entered.

"Howdy, Virgil, Gus," she greeted them.

Every head turned their way.

"Folks, Gus here is the new sheriff. He found BJ last night and has brought him back to jail. We've learned it was my pa and not BJ who killed Dixon. I want you to show Gus here the same respect you gave Dixon. Not many men would be honest enough to bring in his own kin."

Someone snickered. "Ain't many men running a still honest enough to be sheriff."

Laughter rang out. Someone raised up a coffee mug. "Here's to the new sheriff."

Virgil remained standing with Gus beside him.

"Anyone know anything about Alex?"

"He left here yestiddy with them Macon deputies and them tracking dogs. Ain't seen 'em since," Nita replied.

"Anybody?" Virgil asked.

Heads shook and a few people spoke up with, "I ain't seen him since yesterday."

"Anybody seen my brother Hiram?"

Again heads shook.

"You ain't found him yet?" Nita asked.

"Not yet. We hadn't seen him since about lunch time yesterday."

"Anybody know about them buzzards over to the south?" Gus asked.

One man spoke up. "They's a heap of 'em. I seen 'em when I stopped off over to the grist mill. They're about a mile or so off in the swamp from there. Hey, I jest remembered. I seen them hounds from Macon running loose down the road apiece. How come you reckon they got away from them deputies? They was dragging their ropes."

Virgil and Gus looked quickly at each other.

"We best be taking a look," Virgil said.

"Ain't no cows over that-air way," Gus said and turned toward the door.

"You want some coffee afore you set out?" the waitress offered.

They shook their heads.

"We just ate dunner," Virgil answered. "Thanks, though."

They walked out and eased the screen door closed.

"You don't reckon it's Hiram out there?" Gus asked as they got into Dr. Jacobs' car.

"I dunno. It's either Hiram or them deputies. No way they'd turn them dogs loose."

He drove two miles to the grist mill and then another mile closer to the circling buzzards before he stopped. They set out on foot.

The going was easy through the corn field, but when they reached the thickets Gus stopped and pulled out his knife. "We needs us a stout stick." He began to make snake-licking sticks from two sweetgum saplings.

"It's sure sticky," Virgil said as he gripped the end of his.

"Shore it is. It's sweetgum. It's gonna run juice. Take a-holt of it away from the end stead of putting yer hand right on the end that-away. You done been away from home too long."

Virgil smiled and did as he was told. Never too old to learn what he should already know, he reminded himself.

They bee-lined toward the buzzards and slapped their way through thickets and brambles. In a half-hour the vultures circled over them. The wind blew into their faces, and Gus stopped, lifted his nose to the wind like a hound, and sniffed.

"Whatever it is, it's close by."

In minutes they both began to choke on the stench as the feeding buzzards rose in a cloud. Three human bodies lay bloated in a tiny meadow. Without discussion, they circled the bodies to get upwind, but the smell of decaying flesh filled the area. Buzzards circled overhead and some lit on nearby trees to watch the intruders.

"Looks like Alex and the two Macon deputies who run the dogs," Virgil said.

"How kin you tell with them et up so much?"

"Perry had on a blue shirt like that when he came out to tell me about Pa. And you can see the other two are in deputy shirts. They must've been with the dogs. Looks like they got shot in the chest with buckshot.

"Hiram took Sam's shotgun yesterday, Gus. I think he shot Emerson and then came outchere and shot them."

"Where-at's the boy, then, Virgil? Where'd he go to? He ain't got nowhere to take hisself 'cept home."

"I dunno. Nobody's seen him. Can you track him from here?"

Gus began to scout, bent over, his eyes half closed to concentrate more intently. As he came to an overgrown path, he spotted crunched grasses, bent away from the meadow.

"He went this-away. You stay there, Virgil. Keep them buzzards off-a them bodies. I'll find Hiram."

A few minutes later, Gus yelled. "Virgil! C-mere quick!"

Virgil ran down the path and found Gus sitting on the ground beside Hiram. The boy lay curled up on his left side and his right hand clutched his right leg. A dead timber rattler lay a few feet away.

"Oh, God," Virgil dropped onto his knees.

"I'm gonna be awright, Virgil. I kilt the snake and I fixed my laig where it bit me. I jest hurt a heap and ain't feeling like walking none."

"Let me see your leg."

Hiram sat up, waved at the flies on his overalls, and pulled up his pants leg to show the injury.

"That ain't no snake bite," Gus said. "Looks like you blew your laig up."

Hiram smiled. "I shore did. It's too far fer me to git home 'thout fixing up that-air bite, so I fixed it. Took one of my hobbles and tied it around my laig, and cut me two cuts and got the powder outta one of them shells and packed it in the cut. And lit me a Lucifer to it. Plum blew out the pizzen. It hurts too much fer me to walk on though. And it's all swole up now."

The hobble had sunk into his flesh as his leg swelled. Below it, his leg had turned blue. Virgil had seen enough battle field injuries to know his leg was lost. If not his life.

"Gus, we gotta git that line off his leg."

"Yeah. I know." Gus pulled out his pocketknife, lit a match, and scorched the blade.

"Hold on, Hiram. It's gonna hurt some." He pushed the blackened point of the knife flat against flesh until he could wiggle it under the cord. When he pulled the knife up, it sliced the cord in two.

"Stay here with them dead 'uns and keep them buzzards off 'em. I'll tote him outta here and to Dr. Jacobs. I'll git hep quick as I can."

"Key's in the car like always. Gus, you be careful, you hear."

Gus helped Hiram up onto his good leg, and then Hiram crawled onto his back. Stooped over and carrying Hiram piggy-back, Gus headed toward the car while Virgil went back to keep the buzzards flying instead of eating. It would be a long afternoon.

Chapter 14

Gus toted Hiram piggy-back until his legs throbbed and his back ached. He thought the fire had worn him to a frazzle, but that wasn't nothing like toting his nephew. Hiram might be just a boy, but he must-a weighted in at more'n a hundred-fifty pounds, and he was as dead weight as three bags of cottonseed meal.

At least with a sack of feed, he thought, ya kin put it across your shoulder and not have it hanging off yer back the way Hiram was. Ya gotta bend over all the time iffen you tote somebody who's got a-holt of yer neck. And ya kain't git under limbs easy, neither.

Low branches had to be dodged; briar patches circled; a creek crossed. They finally reached the edge of the pines.

"I kain't go no more, Hiram. Ya gotta git down awhile and let me git a rest."

The boy grunted and began to release his hold around Gus's neck. Gus let go Hiram's good leg and eased him down.

They both stretched out on the pine straw. Gus thought about all the red bugs he was getting, laid out like that, and figured he'd have to scratch all night. No way he could rest if he stood up and leaned on a tree. And sitting on that-air downed tree trunk would be jest as bad fer the red bugs.

"Muh laig shore do hurt," Hiram said.

Gus rolled up on his elbow and reached for the overall leg. When he pulled it up, he was again struck by the mess Hiram had made and the blueness of the flesh. The doctor was for sure gonna have to cut that leg off.

"I'll git us going in a minute. Try to rest."

Gus knew if he closed his eyes he would immediately go to sleep. He pulled his hat over his face to keep the sun out of his eyes.

A yellow bird flew overhead, lit on a limb about head-high, and threw music at them. A squirrel saw him and began to bark, its tail flashing faster than a mad cat's. Alerted, a jay began to scream.

"Kin we go on?"

Gus heaved himself up.

"Gimme yo hand." He reached down.

Hiram placed his hand in Gus's, and Gus helped him to his feet, turned his back on Hiram and waited for him to clamber on.

"Pull that bad leg up first."

With Hiram finally settled, they moved on. Gus wasted no energy on talking.

*   *   *

When they reached the car, he placed Hiram in the back seat and drove directly to Dr. Jacobs.

"Wait here," he said as he honked the horn. He got out and half-trotted to the back door.

Janice stepped onto the porch before he reached it, and he saw Sally Anne peek around her skirt.

"I got Hiram with his leg about shot off. The doctor home?"

"Papa!" she called over her shoulder.

"I'll get him," Sally Anne shouted and ran for her grandfather.

"What's the matter?" he asked as he reached the door.

Gus told him as they hastened to the car. Janice followed, with Sally Anne only a step behind her.

When he saw Hiram's leg, Dr. Jacobs turned to Gus, nodded for him to step aside, and spoke too softly for Hiram to hear.

"The leg's gotta come off. I can't do it here. He'll have to go to the hospital."

"I gotta see to Virgil, too."

"Oh, no," Janice said. "Virgil's not hurt too?"

"No, m'am. He's off in the woods and I gotta git some hep. Doctor, kin you drive Hiram to the town doctor and drop me off at Libby's?"

"Sure. Let's go."

"I want to go to Virgil," Janice said.

"No, m'am. There—" he looked at Sally Anne, who had tried to slip away from her mother to go to the car. "There ain't no need. Virgil's fine. He be tending to something I gotta see to. That's all. Ya oughtta stay here. This here ain't hardly fit fer men to tend to, and for sure not fer women."

"I'll be back with whatever news there is," Dr. Jacobs said. "Okay?"

Janice nodded and led her child back into the house.

*   *   *

As they drove to town, Gus told Dr. Jacobs about the bodies they had found and asked who would help carry them out. Jacobs suggested that Jake might still be in town and that Gus should have another law officer present since Hiram had done the shooting.

Jacobs dropped Gus off at Libby's and headed to the clinic. At the diner, Gus found Jake at the counter with a co-cola and a slice of apple pie, which he ignored while he flirted with Nita.

"Jake, I need some hep."

"Well, well. I see you got Dixon's badge."

"I ain't so sure I want it right now. We done found Alex Perry and them deputies from Macon what run their dogs. They be dead off in the swamp. Them buzzards took us right to 'em. I need hep gitting 'em outta there afore them buzzards eat 'em up."

Jake rose, left his pie, and grabbed up the co-cola bottle to take with him. At the door, he turned, set it on a stool, pulled out his wallet, and left a dollar on the counter.

"Let's go."

*   *   *

Four hours later, they had moved the bodies to the undertaker's with the help of deputies from the next county. All of the officers had vomited, as if taking turn about, before they had the bodies on the stretchers.

Gus wanted to get out of his clothes. They would stink of rotting flesh forever. But he didn't have time. He and Jake went from the undertaker's to the clinic, where they began the long wait, while Virgil took Dr. Jacobs home and to get Ellen.

"I dun lost my man to a gun, one-a my boys to the whooping cough, one to war and one to jail. Now I got one-a my boys a-dying from snake bite." She turned to Sam. "Go with me. I kain't stand nothing more."

Sam wrapped an arm around her shoulder and walked beside her to the car.

Charley and Penny followed them to the clinic. The family men paced the floor, rolled and smoked cigarettes, or sat with their chairs tilted against the wall while they stared at their hands. Penny sat on one side of Ellen and Sam on the other. The three of them did not move from their chairs while they waited.

Sam sat as silent as Ellen. Off and on, she shook her head in disbelief and twisted her hands in her lap.

When the surgeon came out, Virgil and Ellen almost ran to meet him, with the others close behind.

"He's lost that leg, but he's sure got a lotta gumption, that one. I can't believe anyone would pack his own leg with gunpowder like that and blow his leg half off."

"No way to treat a rattler bite without you git the pizzen out," Ellen said. "He done what he had ta do."

"You his mother?"

"Yes. He gonna be okay, Doctor? I kain't lose another one." Ellen suddenly turned to Virgil and buried her face into his shoulder. Loud sobs erupted.

Over her shoulder, Virgil told the doctor, "We just buried her husband, my pa."

"Mrs. Carter, m'am, your boy's going to live. He'll be alright, but it'll be awhile."

"Kin I see my boy?"

The doctor nodded, and he led Ellen and Virgil to the ward where Hiram lay. A nurse stood beside his bed. With the side-rails up, the bed looked like a baby crib holding the child of a giant.

Hiram did not move when they approached. His glassy eyes stared straight up at the cracked ceiling.

"Hiram? Son?"

"He's still half asleep from the operation. I doubt he can even hear you now."

"Kin I sit here tonight?"

"No, Ma, you need to get on home. The nurse'll take care of him."

"Kin I stay, Doctor?"

He shrugged. "If you really want to, yes. All we've got here is that straight chair. You won't get any rest."

"I ain't staying here to git no rest. That-air straight chair will be jest fine. It'll hep me keep awake."

"Nurse? Will you get her anything she needs?"

"I ain't gonna need nothing but seeing my boy's awright."

"Yes, m'am," the nurse said. "But if you want some coffee, I'll have a pot up at the desk. Just let me know."

Virgil said goodnight to Ellen and walked back to the waiting room. "Ma's gonna sit with him tonight. I'll stay here awhile too. Charley, you need to get Penny to the house."

"I'm staying," Penny said.

"No, you go home," Sam said.

"Pa!"

Charley rose.

"C'mon, sweetheart. You can't be staying up all night like this. Think of our baby." He held a hand down for her.

She looked from his hand to her father, who nodded; to Virgil, who cut his lips down and nodded; and then to Charley, whose fingers wiggled for her to come on.

"Awright," she said and stood up. Then she put a hand on her belly and said, "I bet the young'un'd wanna stay iffen he had a choice."

"Well, he ain't got no say in the matter," Sam said. "Git on home and git to bed. I'll be here with Ellen and Virgil."

"And I gotta stay here too, seeing as Virgil's done made me sheriff and I gotta talk to Hiram about what all happened out there." Gus took a deep breath. He didn't want the load Virgil had placed on his shoulders.

Chapter 15

Sunlight seeping into the ward woke Gus, and at first he wasn't sure where he was. Remembering, he shuddered and looked over at Hiram. The boy was still in a deep sleep. That-air morphine sure did keep him knocked out.

Ellen slept with her head resting on her forearms on the bed beside Hiram. Sam and Virgil were gone.

Gus rose and walked to the nurse's desk.

"You still got airy coffee, m'am?"

"Sure do, Sheriff. How'd you want it? I got plenty of cream and sugar."

"Better load it up, m'am. Maybe one fer his ma, too, iffen you doesn't mind."

He carried the two mugs to the bedside and set one on his chair. He gently touched Ellen's shoulder.

"Coffee, Ellen?"

She lifted her head, sighed, looked up to Gus, and nodded.

"Thank-ee, Gus."

"It's pretty hot. Go easy. The nurse got plenty of sugar and cream in it. I figgered we needed some to git going."

Jake walked in, with Sam behind him. "Morning. He awake?"

"He been sleeping all night," Ellen replied.

"Likely he needed it. Miss Ellen. Gus. Virgil and Sam came by to see me last evening. Mind if I talk to the boy a minute?"

Ellen and Sam nodded. Gus shrugged.

The GBI agent placed a hand on Hiram's shoulder and gently shook   it.

"Hiram? You awake, Hiram?"

The boy moved his head and groaned. One hand moved down toward the missing leg.

" 'S'awright, son," Ellen said. "Don'tcha try to move none."

"Hey, Ma." Hiram turned his face toward his mother and smiled. "I done got that Perry man."

From across the bed, Jake bent over Hiram. As Jake's shadow fell across his eyes, the boy turned toward him. Hatred erased all pleasure from the boy's face as he focused on Jake.

"Why did you kill them?" Jake asked softly.

"I didn't know where you was at."

Jake breathed in hard and slowly exhaled. "Why did you want to kill me, Hiram?" he asked.

"You kilt Billy Jack. All-a y'all kilt him."

"Who helped you?"

"Ain't nobody done nothing to hep me. You and that-air judge, you done kilt him." He rolled his head back toward Ellen. "Ma, make him go away."

Jake stood erect, nodded to Ellen, and as he walked toward the nurse's desk, he waved Sam and Gus to come with him.

Out of earshot of Ellen and the nurse, Jake turned to Gus. "Too bad he didn't wait a day. BJ's a lot better off than Hiram." Jake shook his head. "How old is he? Virgil said last night he's not but twelve, but he sure is big enough to be twenty-five."

"He ain't but twelve year. We gonna hafta have him hung?" Gus asked.

Jake shook his head. "No. Like I said, I talked to Sam and Virgil, and we went to see Prosecutor Jenkins. We decided best thing is, if you want to, is send him over to Milledgeville to the asylum. He'd have to be there for life, though. But that's better'n going to the boys' training school over in Milledgeville. They beat up on the boys there. Leastways in the asylum, you can see him when you please, and they'll take care of him. You don't want in him jail when he don't have but one leg."

Gus thanked Jake and he and Sam headed back to Ellen.

As they approached, Ellen rose. "What'd he allow?"

"We kin put the boy over to Milledgeville," Sam said.

Weeping, Ellen leaned into Sam's chest.

At least this time there ain't gonna be no jail and no funeral.

PART VI: AUGUST AND SEPTEMBER 1946

Chapter 1

Dust thickened the air so that each breath tasted not only hot but also dirty. His leg healed, BJ had been transferred to the state prison only fifteen miles from home and assigned to a chain gang that worked on paving the roads in the next county. His attorney promised him and Virgil that the appeal was underway and would be approved.

His first day on the chain gang, he learned the prisoners' worker's incentive plan. He was put on a gang consisting of only Negroes, and when he told a guard, "I ain't working with no niggers," the guard called two other officers over. He handed his shotgun to one, told the other to hold the boy still, and set about hammering BJ with his fists.

That night, he asked to see the warden, but the warden did not come to his cell. He asked to see his brother, but Virgil did not come. He asked to see Matthew Rogers, but his attorney never showed up. BJ did not know that his messages never went beyond the guards. He knew only that he was alone and his family could no longer help him. The state chain gang was out of their reach.

He felt sure the warden, however, was within the reach of Lawrence Cunningham. BJ lay on his bunk and thought about whiskey. Pa used to sell to Cunningham, and Cunningham sold all over middle Georgia, to everyone in driving distance. Old Man Cunningham would take his anger out on anyone close to Charley now.

If only he could see Charley or Virgil. Anybody in the family. If only the lawyer would come by. Or Gus come check up on him.

Gus. Uncle Gus, who drove him to the prison, talked to Warden Williams in front of him. "This boy is my nephew and I want you to treat him right. Don't let the guards get rough with him. He means a lot to us all."

And the warden's words back. "Don't you worry none, Sheriff. I'll take keer of him like he's my own young'un."

But now he knew that Warden Williams belonged to Cunningham.

He flexed his muscles and felt pain ripple over him. He might be isolated and alone, but he would work to change that. Just give me time. Just give me time.

As his bruises faded, his anger grew, the blisters on his hands became hardened calluses, and his shoulders widened to the point of almost ripping through his shirt. He chopped his way along behind the bulldozer and dreamed of the day he would be elevated from the pack to replace the only other white man on the gang.

A white man had no business being forced to work beside niggers, especially niggers that were so uppity, too good to be respectful of white folks. The time would come when his only aches and calluses would be from sitting on that bulldozer. Besides, women didn't like rough, hard hands, and he had caught glimpses of the women who sat on their porches and watched the workers. He had no time to study them because when he could quit swinging his pick he sat on the ground in exhaustion.

He concentrated his anger into hatred for the bulldozer driver, a hatred that matched and then exceeded his hatred for the Negroes who worked beside him and the guards who jeered him day after day. The driver and guards were out of reach of his anger; he did not want another beating while a guard held him pinned. But he could jeer at the niggers. At least they couldn't bother him. He bunked on the white men's side in the prison, and not a nigger in the world would hit him in front of a white man. He swung his tools with more vigor each day, and each day his gaze lingered longer on the bulldozer.

One afternoon black-bottomed clouds split open from their own weight and dumped rain. Only steps from the dozer which had stopped with the first clap of thunder, he dashed to it for shelter rather than wade through the slick, fast-forming mud to the prison bus half a mile away.

He almost collided with the driver as he stepped down.

"Well, well, if it ain't the white nigger boy," Deke, the driver, said. "You scared you'll git too white iffen you stand in the rain, nigger lover?"

"You goddamn—!" BJ muttered, blinded with hate as he swung at Deke, who was at least five years older and outweighed him by thirty pounds. But BJ had been in hard labor while Deke's only job had been to move the controls on the dozer.

His fist only grazed Deke's shoulder as he dodged. Deke swung back and leaped at Billy Jack as the guard shouted, "Hey, stop it, you two!"

They had no intention of stopping. Deke fought with violent pleasure; both fought with the unleashed passion of males wanting the same female as they tumbled in the mud, gouged, bit, and kicked. They rolled under the dozer blade and back out. The force of their struggle covered them with mud as it carried them to the edge of the ditch. They plunged down and grabbed at each other and the mud to halt their fall.

Deke's body cushioned BJ as they slammed into a tree. A guard slipped in the mud behind them, his belly in the way of his legs. The pistol he clutched and his belly tried to be first to the bottom of the bank. The two tumbling, mud-covered forms looked identical to him as they began to pull themselves up to their feet. With bodies bent low and arms swinging free, they prepared to lunge at each other again.

All three froze at the over-loud thunderclap so close that the guard looked around to see what the lightning had struck. Only when the acrid smell of cordite hit his nostrils did the guard realize that he had fired. His mouth wide, he looked from his pistol to the two forms frozen in half-crouch.

Finally they began to move, one to stand erect, the other to plop face first into the mud.

Rain splattered down and the standing fighter rubbed his face partially clean and turned it up to let the rain wash it. Mud dripped from his face and hair.

"You done kilt him," BJ said, his voice steady although he was panting for breath. He felt strangely calm, as if he had stood by and watched everything rather than been involved himself. His eyes met the guard's, and BJ saw fear fill the man's face.

"You don't do like I tell you and I'll tell 'em me and him was having a friendly little tussle and you up and shot 'im fer no reason. But iffen you do like I say, I'll say he tried to run off and you had to shoot him to stop him. You think it over. We got till one of them-there other guards gits here and starts asking questions."

Someone shouted from the top of the bank. "What happened down there, Tommy? You all right?"

The fat guard looked at BJ's calmness and shuddered as a chill trickled down his back. Never had he seen such cold, calm calculation, such willingness to destroy.

"We're all right. Deke tried to escape and I had to shoot him. Wouldn't have known what was happening if Carter here hadn't hollered and gone after him."

The other guard came crabwise down the bank with short, quick, jumping steps and stood frozen. He stared at the expression on BJ's face and shook his head quickly, almost imperceptibly. He slopped through the mire to Deke and used his muddy toe to roll the inert form onto his back. Blood blended with red mud. Rain began to move the mud in streaks off his face.

"You shore stopped him good," he said softly. "Hey, Carter, grab his shoulders." He waved an arm at BJ. "We got to get him to the bus and outta this-here rain."

BJ glanced at Tommy and saw enough fear looking back. He knew that he would have no worry now. He could control the guard and through him the entire work gang. He might even be able to get turned loose because of this.

He sloshed his way to the body, seized Deke under the armpits, and hauled Deke into a sitting position. The guard turned his back, squatted, pulled Deke's feet up and around his waist. They started up the slippery climb back to the road, the guard in front.

"He shore do be mighty damn heavy."

"That's all this here mud," the guard said. "He must have been at the top of the road when he got it and rolled all the way down in the mud. God, but he's dirty."

The smell of blood, mud, and sweat mixed with the clean coolness of the rain. Wasn't any difference in the smell of a dead man and a dead cow. Both stank like iron rust and emptied gut.

As the wind whipped the smell of Deke's death into his face, BJ looked at the oozing, gaping hole in the naked chest and had to force back a smile of pleasure. He turned his thoughts to his future.

No longer would he hafta work with the niggers; no longer would he have aching hands and shoulders at night. He would ride the machine and command Tommy until he got his pardon. He would have to be sure to mention his pardon to Tommy as soon as they were rid of Deke.

Chapter 2: Three Days Later

As he sat on the bulldozer, BJ now had time to study the women, and he realized they all watched him. He felt energy and something else building up inside. He wanted a woman real bad.

A dark-haired woman, about his age he thought, rocked on the porch of a small, white house and watched him all day. Her gaze caught his and then dropped slyly. He decided he liked her, and when she looked up at him again, he smiled and winked, and, without taking his eyes from her curves, he stopped the machine.

As the bulldozer growled to a halt, he pushed his straw hat back, wiped his sweating face with a sweat-streaked arm, and winked again at the youthful figure, not caring that she now looked haughtily away. Girls always did when they knew they had gotten his interest. He grinned, jerked the hat down low again, flexed his shoulders and leaped to the ground. One quick jerk and he had broken a wire.

"Where do you think you're going, Carter?" Tommy strolled over to him as he started for the water bucket.

His grin widened. "That damn things busted. You oughtta do something about getting a good one while I'm visiting with a friend. You don't be fussy, Tommy, ole friend, or, well, you know." He did not need to finish.

The fat man shrugged. "Don't go far. Remember, the warden's gonna be by this afternoon and if you're not here you'll be in trouble that I can't get you out of."

He patted the guard's shoulder. "Don'tcha go fretting, old man. I'll be back. Besides, I'm gonna be a free man soon as that appeal gits through."

"We'll both be free, you mean," Tommy muttered.

BJ trotted to the water bucket, sloshed water over his head and shoulders, and let the sun and wind dry him. Fingers served for a comb as he jounced toward the small, boxlike house.

The girl looked beyond him as if she did not see him until he stood at the base of the stairs, rested one foot on a step, and planted both fists on his hips.

"And a good day to you, Miss," he grinned. Then he saw the

bundle in her lap was an infant. "The kid asleep?"

"Yes, he is, and I'll thank you not to wake him up." The girl sniffed and pushed her heavy curls back from her face.

He smiled and, without an invitation, mounted the steps, perched on the top one, leaned back on his elbows to look at the woman over his shoulder and to give her a good view of the length of his shirtless body. He crossed his ankles leisurely and let his hands slide up and down his smooth chest.

"You with the road crew?" the girl finally spoke.

"That's right," he answered. "I run the dozer. Only man with the company who kin drive the thing."

She grinned back a challenge. "Company? More like the county, ain't it?" Her black eyes sparkled.

He shrugged. "Want I should leave? It's mighty comfortable here in the shade."

She didn't reply immediately, and the only sounds were the soft squeaking of the rocker, the buzzing of a fly overhead, and the clacking of the tools on the road bed.

"My name's Alice," she finally said. "What's yours?"

"William John, but everybody call's me Billy Jack or BJ. I answer to either. Named for my old man's uncle." Another pause and he took advantage of the silence to stretch slowly and arch his back against the porch. He grunted faintly as he extended his hands over his head and flexed his rippling muscles.

She rocked and watched him, and her eyes softened to meet his smile.

"How about something to eat, honey?" he asked. "They don't really feed us over there."

She hesitated long enough for him to notice her hand tremble as she rearranged the baby to grasp the arm of the chair. "You go on to the kitchen. I'll tuck Eddie down for a nap."

He leaped to his feet to open the door before she reached it and with a grin dramatically bowed her in. Her answering smile told him that he wasn't fooling her for a minute.

He followed her into the baby's room, waited, and once the problems of the baby were behind her, he followed her toward the kitchen. But in the cool semidarkness of the hall, he grasped her arm and pulled her roughly against him so she was trapped against the wall.

He grinned down into her eyes, wide with expectancy, and slowly traced her profile with his finger, down her nose and lips.

"Anybody ever tell ya you is pretty? I've been watching you all day, wanting to come over and pay you a visit." His finger moved down her chin and around her neck, and he inched closer until their bodies touched. He felt her tremble slightly.

"Scared?" he grinned. "I ain't gonna hurt you."

"That's not what I'm worried about," she whispered and tilted her head for his hand to slide around her neck. "I was worried that all you really wanted was something to eat." Her breathing speeded up.

He brushed his lips across her cheek as his hand slipped inside her blouse. Her response was quick and demanding. Her lips seared his as she pulled him closer and rose on tiptoe to thrust herself hard against him. She moaned her need fiercely and unbuttoned her skirt. It fell. She was naked except for the loose blouse.

Billy Jack pulled his lips from hers as he lifted her, but she clung to him, pulled his lips down to her breast as he carried her to the bedroom.

*   *   *

The hot wind, pushed by a small fan on her dresser, cooled their sweating, naked bodies while they lay exhausted.

"Hand me a cigarette, honey," she muttered. He lit two, handed her one, and grinned through the smoke.

"You're okay, Alice."

She chuckled, rose enough to lean on her elbow, and puffed smoke into his face. Her breasts lightly brushed his chest as she kissed him.

He sighed with contentment; he would be free soon as the lawyer got the appeal back from Atlanta. Until he was free he would visit like this whenever he pleased. He snuffed out their cigarettes and stretched leisurely in the soft comfort of the mattress. His stomach growled at him, and she patted it. "You still hungry?"

"Starved," he admitted and sat up on the edge of the bed. He tickled her roughly through the sheet and sensed desire rising in her again. He pulled the sheet down, kissed her belly and rose. He slid on his trousers.

"You gonna fix something for me?"

They walked hand in hand to the kitchen where she prepared cold ham and fried eggs that he wolfed down as if he had not eaten in days.

She leaned her elbows on the table and watched with delight.

"Mighty good." He sighed, patted his belly, and wiped his mouth with the back of his hand. He leaned back in the chair until it tilted on two legs.

"It sure is good to see somebody eat like he likes it. My Edgar don't seem to care what he eats."

"That your husband?"

She nodded, her lips cut down in disgust. "Yeah, some husband."

"I don't want you to go worrying about him, now, you hear? I'll take care of all the worrying." He paused and then said, "And I'll take you outta here iffen that's what you want."

"You mean that?" Alice rose, circled the table and sat in his lap, her arms around his neck. "You really mean that?"

He lifted his shoulders casually. "Course I mean it."

"Oh, Billy Jack." She kissed him.

"Hey!" He pushed her back and grinned. "Save some of that loving, honey." He rose and his arms around her, said, "We'll figure it all out this week. Okay?"

She nodded eagerly.

Billy Jack squeezed her rump. "I got to git back to work or them-there guards'll be looking for me. I'll see you tomorrow," he promised.

*   *   *

He returned the next day while the rest of the work crew ate their lunch in a small spot of shade across the roadway.

"I'm really wanting to git outta here," Alice said as they lay together after making love. "I don't even like my old man."

"How come you married up with him iffen you don't even like him?"

"I got pregnant and the baby's daddy was married. At least, I think he was the baby's daddy. But I got with Edgar afterwards, and then I told him it was his'n. He don't know no better. Les do it again."

Moments later they were so lost in their lust for each other that they failed to hear the truck rattle to a stop outside or the footsteps on the porch stairs.

But the slamming back door had Billy Jack on his feet, pants in one hand and shoes in the other as he leaped from the window. He was behind the garage before the bedroom door opened.

He dressed as quickly as he could, delayed by the trembling of his entire body, his fear, and unfulfilled passion. He peeked around the garage.

Edgar leaned from the window and cursed, but when Alice, stark naked, appeared behind him and wrapped her hands around Edgar's chest, the shouting stopped and they both disappeared.

Angry, Billy Jack slunk through back yards until he reached the bulldozer. His mind churned with plans.

*   *   *

That night, Warden Williams came to his cell while BJ was eating his pork chops, greens, and cornbread. He had a table and chair in his cell.

"I asked to see you more'n a month ago. How come you took so long to git here?" BJ growled at the warden and did not bother to stand up. If Warden Williams belonged to Cunningham, he wasn't about to show him any respect. Not after the way the old man treated Penny.

Williams unhooked a large ring of keys from his belt, sorted through them, and unlocked the door.

"I found out what you got going, boy. You back up over to the corner."

BJ stood up and moved to the far end of his bunk. Williams stepped in and over to the table, picked it up, together with the food and the co-cola, and set it outside the cell. He returned for the chair.

"It's stopping right now, boy. No more special food. No more food tonight, neither. No more sitting on that bulldozer, neither. You going back on the pickax first thing in the morning."

"Who you been talking to?"

"I ain't gotta talk to anybody. I run this prison, not you. I don't know what you got on one of my guards, but it's over. None–a-them can change my mind. Don't you go trying nothing, neither."

"Old Cunningham shore must hate me and mine. He oughtta be glad I ain't told on him and got him in real trouble. I could-a done it, you know. You go tell him. Sounds like you still do what he tell you. How much whiskey you git from him since Charley taken his business away?"

"Shut up."

"You go tell Virgil I wanna to see him."

"I ain't your message boy. If he wanted to see you, he'd a-been here."

Williams locked the cell and left.

BJ sat on the bunk and seethed.

He'd have to get word to Virgil. Maybe Alice could go see him.

Long after midnight he lay awake. When he finally slept, he dreamed of beating up on Warden Williams.

Chapter 3

Morning found BJ standing by the bulldozer, a pickax in his hand. Another white man had joined the road gang and sat in the driver's seat.

"You know any thing about that-air machine?" BJ asked him.

The man shook his head. "They say you gonna learn me what I need so's I kin run it."

"I ain't learning nobody nothing."

He swung the pickax over his shoulder and strode toward the cluster of Negro men who chopped up the clods left from the day before.

Tommy came after him.

"BJ, come back here. We kin work this out, you and me. Ain't nobody gonna know accepting us. C'mon back. "

"You went and told the warden, Tommy. I ain't got no use fer you no more."

"I didn't. I promise I didn't. He'll fire me iffen you don't learn Lenny how to run it."

"Tell you what, Tommy. I'll show him how, and you still give me time over yonder." He nodded toward Alice's house. "Today and tomorrow, leastways."

"Okay. You go over in the middle of the day, while everybody's eating. I'll keep Sammy busy talking, and he ain't likely to notice."

BJ took the seat in the bulldozer, cranked it up, and proceeded with the lessons. By lunch time, Lenny could move the machine back and forth and push dirt around.

He headed to Alice's for lunch while Tommy kept the other guard too busy to notice.

She cracked the door as soon as he stepped onto the porch, and as he neared it, she grabbed him, pulled him inside, and shut not only the screen but also the wooden door.

"Gotta be sure Edgar ain't got time to git in afore you can git out," she said. "C'mon."

She led him to the bedroom.

*   *   *

Alice piled pillows up against the head of the bed and they half-sat up to smoke.

"I'm heading out today," he told her. "With you, I'm hoping."

"You gitting off the chain gang?"

"Yeah. I taking myself off. I ain't about to stay here and grub in the dirt with a bunch of niggers."

"You gonna escape?"

"I shore am. Gonna go to Texas. Wanna go with me?"

"I sure do. But how can we? You ain't got no money or no car or nothing."

"Don't you worry your pretty little head about that. You said your old man brings home his pay on Thursday. This here's Thursday. I seen him gitting home afore we break off work. And he got a truck. We'll take it and head off fer Texas."

She wiggled against him. "You sure think of everything, don't you, honey?"

"Uh-huh," he grunted, his fingers feeling of her as if for the first time.

*   *   *

Later that afternoon, BJ told Tommy he had to step into the bushes for a minute, and he went to Alice's house, around to the back yard where Edgar had parked his truck. A glance inside showed him the keys in the ignition. He looked in the tool box for a screwdriver, found one, and quickly removed the tag.

Keeping his head low, he slipped round the house. He heard Edgar in the baby's room, talking to the infant as a child talks to a puppy. He smiled.

The sound of a pot being placed on the stove told him Alice was in the kitchen. He eased the screen door open, and, with his forefinger on his lips, he hissed her to silence before she could speak.

"Got the money?" he asked

She nodded and pulled it from her apron pocket.

"Want the kid?" was his only reply as he took the money and shoved it into his pocket. She shook her head. "Come on, then. And be quiet so's he kain't hear us."

They eased out the door and toward the truck.

"Don'tcha slam that-air door," he said as they crawled into the seat.

He slipped the gear into reverse before he cranked the truck and then let the clutch out quickly so the truck roared backwards down the driveway. He smashed two bushes before they got to the road.

As he turned the truck to head east she asked, "Ain't we going to Texas?"

He looked in the mirror and saw Edgar run down the driveway, arms waving. Beyond the driveway, Tommy stood and stared after them. BJ grinned to himself. "Sure we are, honey. I jest want anybody seeing the truck to think we heading east. I'll swing off the first road we come to and circle west." He reached over to take her hand.

"Anything you say," she whispered back and snuggled against him.

Two miles down the road, he turned north. He had no idea how to get to Texas, but he knew they would soon be going west. He would get a job working cattle and never go back to jail.

PART VII: OCTOBER 1946-FEBRUARY 1947

Chapter 1: Late October

Sausage spattered grease onto her hand and Penny quickly sucked on the spots to relieve the burning pain. She felt good today and looked forward to breakfast.

"Them biscuits about ready?" she asked Ellen, who was peeking into the oven. The aroma of baking bread rose up to mingle with the smells of frying pork and coffee.

Penny's belly rumbled with hunger.

Charley poked his head into the kitchen door as he shucked into his old army jacket.

"I've got something to show you as soon as we finish eating. It's something you've talked about wanting."

"Oh, Charley, tell me. What?" Penny's voice rose with excitement as she turned from the stove. "Tell me. Tell me."

"Tell me, too, Charley," Buddy grabbed at his hand. "Tell me."

Charley grinned and shook his head. "I'll drive you to see it. After breakfast." He took Buddy's hand. "And you, my boy, will hear all about it later, too."

He backed out of the kitchen with Penny calling to him. "C'mon back here, Charley. Whatcha talking about? I kain't make this here pig cook any faster."

"I'll show you," he called back.

"Les git it on the table. I wanna see what he's talking about."

A few minutes later, the five of them sat down at the kitchen table, with Sam at one end and Charley at the other. As she did every day, Penny glanced at the empty spaces around her. Jack dead. BJ gone off somewhere with that married woman. Hiram forever in the asylum over in Milledgeville. But today, she wouldn't think about how times had changed this year. She'd think about the surprise.

"What's it, Charley?" she asked as she poured him his first cup of coffee.

"In a minute, sweetheart. Is there any more cream in the icebox?"

"I'm so excited I forgot," she said as she rose and went to the icebox. Sam and Ellen wanted cream for their coffee too, and they passed the pitcher around. Penny drank only milk with her meals, afraid of coffee since she threw it up several months ago. It smelled wonderful, but tasted vile to her now.

She thought he would never finish. Today of all days, with that surprise hanging out in front of her, he decided to have a third cup of coffee. And then he was ready.

"Okay, sweetheart. You need to get a pillowcase to wear over your head."

"I ain't wearing no pillow case." Her tone rang with determination and her shoulders shot back in defiance.

He only grinned. "That's my ruling today. Pillowcase, or wait another day. Which is it going to be?"

She smirked and dropped her shoulders. "Oh, awright. Les go."

While he waited in the front room, she went into her bedroom and came back with a pillowcase and the new sweater he brought her the week before. As they started for the front door, Ellen called from the kitchen where she was washing dishes.

"You going off now?"

"Yeah."

Ellen's laughter drifted ahead of her words from the kitchen. "He done bought you a house. Nothing else big enough to have to wear a pillowcase."

"Ellen! Why'd you have to go bust up the surprise?"

"Well, I ain't knowing what it looks lak. Y'all git along and then come back fer me and Sam so's we kin see it too."

She laughed as they hurried out the door.

Penny had no idea how long she'd worn the pillowcase or even where they were when the car slowed and finally stopped.

"Don't you peek," he warned her. "I'm coming around the car."

She felt the door open and then his hand on her arm.

"Come on out real easy," he directed. "I won't let you fall."

When she was steady on her feet, he told her to take off the pillowcase.

"Oh, Charley! It's beautiful!"

She tilted her head back and let her eyes wander up the front of her new home. Four columns rose from the lower porch to support an upper porch and then the roof. Wings spread out on each side, with tall windows and green shutters. Crepe myrtles, their trunks molted with shedding bark, gleamed with red leaves. Two magnolias with heavy curved limbs stood in the front yard and poked roots up through the soil. Leaves scattered beneath each had drifted over the lawn with the autumn breezes.

An arm around her shoulder, Charley beamed at her.

"Let's go inside." He took her hand and they walked up the steps side by side.

"It's the biggest house in town," Penny said as she tried to absorb everything.

Glass panels inset in the wall flanked the front double doors, and Penny stopped a moment to look at the etchings in the glass. She reached out to touch a panel, her fingers tentative.

"How'd they do this here?" she asked.

"I dunno. Let's go on in." He pushed open the front doors, and they entered a wide hall that rose overhead to the attic level.

"Oh, gosh!" Her gaze moved upward and followed the curve of the stairs. Then she turned to look at the hall, and at a pair of paintings to her left.

"Are those—? Didn't I see them at your daddy's house?"

"Yes. I went out there this week, after I bought this house, and got a lot of my mama's things. C'mon. Let me show you."

They entered the living room to their right, which was fully furnished with antiques. A sofa, a matching love seat, and two heavy armchairs, with several side tables—one with a marble top, and three of solid mahogany with curved legs. Before she was able to soak up everything, he pulled her on through the house, into the dining room, with a sideboard covered with silver pieces.

Beyond the dining room another room stretched the length of the house.

"It's big enough to pasture Doc Jacobs' cows in," she said.

"It's a ball room. We'll hold our parties here."

"Parties?" She wanted to tell him no, no parties. She couldn't stand it if nobody came. They might come to his party if he hadn't married her, but they'd never come to her home.

"Sure. We're going to be society here now, Pen. I'm gonna have the biggest parties in town, and everybody's gonna want to come here. We'll only invite people we like and people who treat us and Virgil right. We won't mess with folks who aren't somebody. C'mon. Let's go upstairs. There's a lot to see up there, too."

The winding stairway ended in another hallway, and off it to the right was a large bedroom with a tall black four-poster, the finish almost cracked with age, with its back to the wall opposite the door. Windows rose to the ceiling on either side of the headboard.

"It's big enough to plow for a garden," she said.

"Well, we'll be planting a lot here, only it won't be a garden." The smile he turned to her was almost a leer, and he waggled his eyebrows at her.

She giggled. Then the smile faded and she turned to him, her face a serious mask.

"Charley, I can't believe you done did this here for me. I love you so much."

"It's for us both. And the baby." He touched her belly.

"We ain't never gonna use up all the space. Must be ten rooms here."

"We will. When we have our parties."

"Won't nobody come, Charley. They think I'm trash. They'll remember BJ and Hiram."

"Oh, they'll come. Virgil runs the county now. And I control all the whiskey. You think they'll snub me when they know if they do, they'll have to go out of town for their bootleg? Or they'll never get their roads paved in from their farms? They'll come, and so will their wives. And they'll be polite. You'll see."

"Reckon I got time to talk better?"

"You already do, love. Janice's lessons have helped. You're going to be fine. I just know it."

"I ain't—won't hafta dance, will I?"

He circled her waist, pulled her against him, and kissed her cheek. "We'll keep on practicing." He began to hum and led her off into a slow waltz.

She closed her eyes and tried to keep from stepping on his toes. The wonder of life with Charley seemed to overpower her as she tried to merge into him, but her belly was pushing her away.

He waltzed her to the side of the bed and stopped beside the head. "Hold on a second," he said, and reached under the pillow. He pulled out a folded set of papers and handed them to her.

"What's this?"

"The deed. It's yours. The house, I mean. See here?" He took the papers back and unfolded them. "Right here. Here's your name. 'Penny Carter Cunningham, my beloved wife and soon to be mother of my child.' "

"Oh, Charley, you ain't really giving it to me, is you?"

"Course I am. It's done already. All legal down in the courthouse."

Oh, Gawd, she thought. It jest kain't be Jeff's baby. Be better iffen it never got born.

Chapter 2: Three Weeks Later

Penny daily thanked Janice for the lessons on speech, and slowly began to learn to say "if" instead of "iffen" and "isn't" instead of "ain't." She learned new words to use in place of many that were automatic to her. Penny thought the lessons would never be over, and she feared the days when she would be have to face the ladies of town. Every lesson with Janice told her more and more how little she had learned at school. If only she'd gone every day. And every year. And had listened to the teachers instead of dreaming about Charley. But thinking on what she oughtta have done didn't help now, she reminded herself.

"I'm scairt, Janice. Suppose people do come. What'll I do? What kin I say to 'em? People I don't know." The party was less than a week away.

"You talk to them, same as you've been practicing with me since back in August. They may talk fancier and be richer than you're used to, but they're still just people. And the ones who'll come to the party want something from either Charley or Virgil, so they'll be respectful. When they arrive, you go up to them and hold out your hand and say, 'Welcome to my home.' "

"Welcome to my home," she said back.

"And if they ask how you're doing, say, 'Very well. And you?' "

"Supposing they ask more'n that?"

"You can always say, 'Excuse me, I must welcome someone.' Try it a couple of times."

Penny did. She surprised herself when she realized she could say those words without sounding too country.

"That's good," Janice encouraged her.

"I ain't sounding countrified with them words, am I?"

"No," Janice said. "But try to avoid 'ain't.' For example, you could say 'Am I sounding too countrified?' Okay?"

*   *   *

The morning of the party, Charley took her to get her hair done at a beauty parlor. She felt important as the woman washed and curled her hair and talked about the party. The hairdresser seemed to know everybody in town, and she told Penny their party was the talk of the town. Some people who weren't invited wondered what they had done to slight Charley.

Penny went home with more confidence.

That evening, Janice came over early and helped her dress in her floor-length maternity dress and to exchange the plain barrette from the hairdresser's to the silver one Charley bought her. As she walked down the stairs, she felt an unfamiliar softness on her bare shoulders as her hair caressed her.

Penny felt relief that Charley had someone from over in Macon to attend to everything for the party—from the punch to the maids to the strange food.

Three Negro maids wore black dresses with white aprons to answer the door and keep food on the long table in the ballroom. One of them stood all night by the punch bowl and used a silver dipper to pour punch into tiny crystal cups.

Penny didn't know what most of the food was. Small, green, bitter-sweet-tasting balls with red something sticking out of one end. What looked like potted meat that people spread out on crackers, but didn't taste at all like potted meat. Maybe a little bit like liver. Funny-looking cheeses—one she thought had gone bad cause it looked like it had spots of mold in it, and one that looked like it would pretty soon melt all over the plate.

Each end of the table held drinks: A punch bowl of sherbet floating in ginger ale for the ladies at one end, and wine bottles of Charley's whiskey at the other end for the men.

She decided to limit herself to the plain, familiar, yellow cheese and the punch. The company could eat the rest of that stuff. If she was hungry when everybody left, she'd find something in the kitchen. She wondered if she would ever get used to living like this. She'd never seen flowers this late in the fall, but Charley had gone over to Macon and come back with vases of what he called hot-house flowers that morning, and these lined the center of the table.

At one end of the ballroom, three men sat in straight chairs and plucked and tooted their instruments. The fiddle she knew, but the long curved horn she had never seen before. And the buttons down it! How in the world would that man ever know what buttons to push to make the right sounds? The other horn looked like it might come in two, the way the man moved the front end of it back and forth.

She hoped she could remember the dancing steps Charley had been helping her with. She didn't want to embarrass him by stomping his feet—or anybody else's feet if she had to dance with anybody else.

When the doorbell rang, Virgil and Dr. Jacobs entered and the trio began to play.

And people came. The men wore dark suits, white starched shirts, and black ties; the women, long lacy dresses that dragged the floor. Some in pale blue, some in pink, some in what looked to Penny like the colors of the wild roses that ran along Dr. Jacobs' fences. No one else wore a gold gown like hers.

The first couple she welcomed, with Janice beside her, were the solicitor and his wife, and then she quickly moved on.

"Perfect," Janice reassured her. "You're on your own now."

Penny tried to hide her fear as she moved around the room. These were all Virgil's and Charley's people. People who voted for Virgil, people who worked for the county, people who bought Charley's whiskey.

Relief brought a smile when Charley came up to her. But that relief faded into fright at his words.

"Let's dance." He took her hand and led her to the middle of the floor, and the trio began another slow song as Charley took her into his arms and pulled her close. She closed her eyes, lowered her head onto his shoulder, and allowed him complete control of her movements. Not once did she make a misstep.

"You've learned beautifully," Charley whispered in her ear.

She pulled her head back, opened her eyes, and smiled up at him. "Thanks, Charley."

She saw other couples dancing, and the night became a pleasure, not something to fear.

The tall clock in the hallway striking midnight seemed to be a signal for everyone to leave. With Charley, she stood by the door to say goodnight, and one by one the ladies smiled at her and thanked her for inviting them into her home. When the door closed behind Virgil, Penny walked to the living room and sank down onto the sofa.

"You were wonderful," Charley said as he strode in from the front door. "You were a big hit. Everybody wanted to dance with you. Are you worn out? You didn't do too much, did you?"

"I ain't plum wo' to a frazzle, Charley, but I am a mite tired." She grinned up at him as she pulled off her shoes. "It would-a been easier if I could-a taken them off a long time ago."

He laughed. "C'mon, let's go to bed. It's a cold night, and I need warming up."

Chapter 3: February 14, 1947

Penny held one hand over her mouth as the bacon sizzled and its smell triggered the bile in her stomach. She wasn't supposed to get sick to her stomach with the baby due any time now. She shivered. The gas heater hadn't been on long enough this morning to warm the kitchen good.

She still didn't like this new-fangled electric stove, which didn't heat up the kitchen the way Ellen's wood-burning stove did.

It didn't use any wood and she couldn't leave a pot of coffee on it all day or even a pot of water for the dishes. She still hadn't gotten the hang of it. Turn a knob and it got hot. Nowhere to push a pan of cornbread back to keep it warm. It was either hot or not.

If only she had one of those party maids here today to do the cooking. Her stomach continued to tell her to leave the kitchen and its rich smells.

She flipped the bacon, noted the deep brown, almost black, upper side, and sighed. Almost burned. A wave of grease smell rose, and she had to swallow bile again.

"OhmyGawd," she said aloud and yanked open the oven. The warm damp aroma of baking biscuits rose into her face, and she squinted to see past the heat. The bread was beginning to brown. Time enough to fry up Charley some eggs.

She turned away from the stove to the Frigidaire. Like the stove, it was different from the icebox. Just run a plug into the wall; no need for the ice man to come around twice a week. Four eggs. No. She wouldn't eat one. Probably couldn't keep it down anyhow. Three for Charley.

After cracking them one by one into a bowl, she took up the bacon, laid it out on a paper sack from the Piggly Wiggly, and poured the eggs into the bacon grease. She shook pepper until it showed over the yellows.

As Charley walked in, he pulled his suspenders over the shoulders of his flannel shirt. An undershirt showed at his throat. He'd be warm out there today, in spite of the ice hanging from the trees.

"Smells wonderful," he said, kissed her neck, and pulled a chair up to his end of the table.

His face looked tired, but his eyes smiled love at her. All these months he hadn't tried to love up on her but had laid beside her night after night, one arm under her shoulder and his other hand rubbing her the way she rubbed the kitten's back—long, slow caresses that soothed her into sleep. And with the cold, his body had been like a heater that warmed her back and the whole bed. He even let her put her icy feet on his side of the bed to soak up warmth.

He smiled. "How you doing today, sweetheart?"

She shook her head. "I feel poorly, Charley. So tired of toting this baby in my belly. Leastwise, Dr. Jacobs said it ain't—it won't be long now."

"You hurting more'n usual?"

She shook her head as she laid his plate in front of him.

"Naw. Jest the same like the past couple-a days." She returned to the stove, poured one cup of coffee, and set it beside his plate. Then she sat down at an empty place.

"You not even having coffee?"

"No. My stomach's got the kain't-hep-its. I'm not gonna mess with it today. Whereabouts you heading out to?"

"Over to Noah's. I shoulda picked up last night, but the rain was too bad. I gotta deliver to the solicitor today for his wife's birthday party. That's all I gotta do, so I won't be gone long. Your time's getting close and I wanna be sure to get you to Dr. Jacobs with plenty of time to spare."

"Janice has been good to me, her asking me to stay with them when the baby comes. I wanna be home with Ellen, though."

"Ellen doesn't have running water, and wind whups through that house like it hasn't got walls. Doc's promised plenty of wood for the fireplace if this cold keeps up. Long as you're needing somebody with you, his place is the best."

She nodded and propped her chin in one palm as the other hand rubbed her belly through the plush wool bathrobe Charley had bought her. They sat in silence as he finished his breakfast, wiped his mouth with a napkin, and rose.

He came around the table and reached his left hand over her shoulder to rest on her belly.

"He kicking today?"

She shook her head and smiled up at him. His freckles were as close and sharp as the stars on a bitter cold night. He smelled of Ivory soap. She had learned real quick to love the smell of Ivory soap when he insisted she not make soap any more. She touched his hand on her belly, and then reached up to lay it against his cheek.

"I love you, Charley."

"And I love you, Penny. You gonna be alright for a few hours?"

"I'll be okay. You come in so late last night, I didn't git a chance to tell you. Doc said it won't be long and—." She smiled up at him and quickly cut her eyes away as if shy about telling him.

"Well? What else did he have to say?"

She pulled herself up a little. "He said I'm built better'n my mama, that I got wider hips and that—"

"Well? Go on."

"That my hips is made for having babies."

"I agree, sweetheart. We'll have fun making ourselves a passel of children."

"Promise?"

He nodded, leaned over, and kissed her cheek.

"I'll be going." He took his coat off the hook by the back door, shucked it on, and reached for the door knob. "I'll get back quick as I can."

He pulled the door open and a harsh wind snapped into the kitchen as he hurried out. Penny shivered again as the lace curtains lifted from the windows to show ice outside on the panes. Just like the school bus windows, she thought, when we would put our bare hands against the glass to melt our hand patterns into the frost.

Hope he don't go sliding in the ditch with all that-air ice everywhere.

She continued to sit at the kitchen table, rested her head on her folded arms, and wished for the back pain to go away. And for the smell of bacon to leave the room.

If only she felt like getting up, or eating. But the last few days all she wanted was to sleep, to escape the dull aches that seemed to have swallowed up her whole body. Even her legs, which used to carry her miles across the country, now ached when she walked through the house. If the baby would just be born.

The calico cat jumped onto the table, purred, and began to lick at the remains of egg on Charley's plate. She needed to clear the table, but decided to let the cat lick that plate clean and then all she'd have to do was put a little soap on it.

With a sigh she pulled herself upright and rubbed her hand down the cat's back. It turned golden eyes to her, arched its back, and purred louder as it returned its attention to the food.

Last night's dishes lay in the dish pan, covered with cold water that floated the grease from the steaks. She would have to do something about them to get rid of the smell that was making her sick.

Still, however, she sat, her chin cupped in both hands and her elbows braced on the table. Weight seemed to push her down. Weight of the baby in her belly. Weight she had put on all over her body since she quit walking all those miles to go home to visit with Ellen and Pa. With the baby so close, it was too far to walk home or to Dr. Jacobs' house.

Lonesomeness overwhelmed her. Loneliness and the worry that never seemed to leave her mind. Would be baby be black like Jeff? Was Ellen right that it was Charley's? She shivered again, and this time the fear overcame her ability to swallow the bile. It rose, and she jumped to the sink to heave mucous and fear.

When the spasms subsided, she splashed icy cold water on her face and dried herself with her skirt tail. She sat back down, folded her arms on the table, and laid her head down so her forehead rested on her forearms.

Her mind churned over the past couple of weeks that she had felt so trapped in the house. Christmas had been warm, and she and Charley had visited with Ellen and Sam, and the Carters had called on them. They had not gone to see Charley's daddy over the holidays. Charley said he didn't want to go back to the house again, and anyhow his daddy had gone to drinking. Only his woman came to town now, driving that new Packard to pick up groceries.

But the past couple of weeks, the weather had soured and turned cold and rainy. With the cold wrapping itself around them, people stayed home except to work and bring home groceries. No one came calling. No one even went outside except for firewood. At least we've got those gas heaters and Charley gets up first every morning to light the one in the bedroom and in the kitchen, she thought.

Even with the kitchen heater on all morning, she felt chilly. Ice dripped along the eaves, lay like icing on the oak limbs, and glittered everywhere. It was too cold out for the little heater to warm the kitchen.

Her baby stirred, and she looked down at her swollen belly sitting in her lap. She chuckled at the thought of her belly sticking through the front of her skirt. Funny clothes now for girls with big bellies.

When Ellen had a big belly, she made her dresses bigger and never cut a hole in front. And Ellen was swelling up again, this time with Pa's baby. Gonna seem funny to have a brother or sister of my own, one younger than my own baby.

"Oh Ellen, I do want to come home."

But home wasn't the same anymore with BJ gone off with that woman to who knows where and Hiram in the asylum, and Virgil moved in forever at the Jacobs place since he married Janice.

Leastways here in town she didn't have to walk across the back yard to the outhouse, to pull her undies down in the cold, and sit on a plank that bore frost this time of year. And she didn't have to smell the constant stench of the outhouse, or walk across the cans and bottles the boys always threw out in the back yard.

At least here in town, the outhouse was inside, it flushed, and she didn't have to freeze her backside. Or have the rooster peck at her bottom.

When she burst into laughter, the cat jumped from the table and ran into the front of the house. Her smile remained as she rose, stacked the dishes, and walked to the sink.

The cat returned to the kitchen and hunkered down by her bowl with hope of getting something to eat that she didn't have to chase.

Before Penny finished the dishes, pain moved down her belly like a ripple across a pond. Her baby was trying to be born, like Dr. Jacobs said, with that little pain. She smiled. Then the pain erupted inside, like a smashed watermelon, and she bent forward to fold it up. She had to grip the edge of the sink for balance. The baby must wanna be born real bad, she thought, and then her water broke and flooded warmth down her legs. It spread across the floor, and she looked down at it in dismay. How in the world was she going to mop up the floor with this pain sweeping down on her?

She continued to cling to the edge of the sink, and after what seemed like forever, the pain began to fade to bearable. Clean up the floor, she told herself. Can't have Charley coming home to that all over the place. Get the mop. Don't have the energy to really mop. At least try to get the floor dry.

When she opened the door to the back porch to go into the outside pantry for the mop, the cold slapped at her face and through the bathrobe. She cringed as her fingers touched the handle of the metal bucket; the mop's handle didn't seem to be as cold. She kicked the door to as she came back into the kitchen.

Four swipes across the floor and she decided that was enough mopping. After sticking the wet mop into the bucket and leaning it against the wall, she went to the stairs and considered going up to bed. One foot rested on the bottom step and her right hand on the banister rail for a long minute. Her mind was blank, not actively thinking about the climb upstairs, but she turned away with a muttered, "No."

I'll go home. I can make it. I know I can. I'll get me Charley's army coat and one of his hats outta the hall closet. And iffen I wear his brogans I can keep my feet from freezing off. I can walk out to the house in less'n an hour if I keep on steady.

She was pulling on the left shoe when she heard the car. The silence outside was so intense she wasn't sure if it was in the driveway or on the road. She dropped her foot to the floor and waited. Was it Charley?

The car went on by. She put the shoes on, gave the laces an extra tug, rose, and walked to the back door. When she pulled it open, the wind flung icy melt into her face. She backed up and closed the door.

Another pain hit, and she sat down in the chair she had just vacated while the pain rolled over her. She gripped her belly and tried to think. But all her mind could grasp was the pain and the need to reach Ellen.

She had to get some help. Had to get to Ellen and Dr. Jacobs. She didn't know enough to do this by herself and Charley would be gone at least another hour. Maybe two. Home was seven miles in the ice, and with the bulldozers getting the road ready to be paved, it was all mud, ruts, and ice.

Uncle Gus. He was up the road, in the house behind the jail. I can get over to the jail, she told herself. No, wait. I can telephone him. I ain't never used it, but I can try. Maybe I can call over to the jail and Gus can come take me home to Ellen.

She rose, removed her coat, laid it on the chair, walked to the room Charley used as an office, and lifted the ear piece. She'd seen him use it and knew all she had to do was jiggle the hook the ear piece hung from, pick up the stand, and talk into it.

She listened to a vaguely familiar voice. "May I help you?"

"I need to talk to Sheriff Carter."

"Mrs. Cunningham?"

"Yes?"

There was no answer. Only a click and silence.

She jiggled the hook again. Still only silence.

I gotta walk over to the jailhouse, she told herself and returned to the kitchen for her coat.

As she put it on, the back door opened with a blast of cold, and Charley stepped quickly in and shoved the door closed.

"What the hell're you doing?" he asked as he stared at her.

"It's the baby. I thought you'd be gone a long time. It's trying to be born. I'm scared, Charley. I been scared you wasn't gonna git here. I was gonna walk over to the jailhouse and git Gus to take me out to Ellen's."

She erupted into tears.

He pulled her close.

"Shhhh. I'm here now. I'll get you to Dr. Jacobs. How come you didn't use the telephone and call Gus?"

"I did. Only the woman wouldn't help me."

"Damn it. Karen's working for the telephone company. She had no call to do that. It won't ever happen again." He caught sight of the mop and bucket. "You haven't been mopping the floor, have you?"

She shook her head. "My water busted all over the floor."

Charley's hands began to shake.

"I gotta get you to Doc's house right now. Can you walk to the car? You need me to carry you out?"

"I kin walk iffen that-air pain don't come back on me."

"Let's go."

He held onto her as she stepped onto the porch. The ice had begun to melt as the sun climbed higher and the wind rose. But the over-sheet of water made the steps even more slippery.

"Let me in front, and you hold onto the banisters with both hands," he said.

He gripped the banister with his right hand and held his left hand up and under her armpit to give her support if she slipped. One foot down and then bring the other foot even, and then down the next step. His earlier going out and walking back in across the yard had broken the sheet of ice from the grass, and she walked steadily to the car. He opened the door and helped her inside.

The drive out became erratic. Charley became so nervous that

Penny finally said, "Charley, please. Slow up. This here baby ain't gonna git born before we git there. I ain't had a pain in forever now."

When they reached the area being worked by the bulldozers, Charley studied the road and decided to straddle the ruts. His Buick, the trunk heavy with whiskey, sat low to the ground, too low to ride the ruts. And if they slipped into the ruts, they'd have to walk the last quarter mile.

He shifted into second after only a few yards and kept his foot steady on the accelerator. If he slowed down, he might never get through. The car slipped and slid but did not fall into the ruts, and they were soon across the worst part of the road. He'd have to talk to Virgil about the workmen going off and leaving the road in such a mess.
Minutes later, he parked by Jacobs' back porch.

As soon as Charley had Penny inside with Dr. Jacobs and Janice, he drove off to get Ellen. When he got back with her, he was pushed out of the room. Only Dr. Jacobs and Ellen stayed with Penny. Even Janice sat in the living room with him and Virgil.

For Penny time became pain and fear and Ellen's hand in hers. The wind rose and broke an ice-heavy limb that crashed onto Jacobs' generator and put out his electricity. Janice pulled out the oil lamps and put a pot of water to boil on the fireplace.

Penny tried to swallow her pain and not scream at it. She wanted everything over, all the doubts gone.

"I'm so scairt, Ellen," she muttered.

Dr. Jacobs responded, "You're doing fine, Penny. You're built to have babies. Don't worry."

"It ain't nothing to be scairt about, Pen."

"Your baby's almost here," Dr. Jacobs said. "Here comes its head now."

"Aunt Ellen?" Penny's voice broke. "Is it—?"

Ellen released her hand and went to stand behind Dr. Jacobs. "Hit ain't got Charley's red hair, but hit looks like the Carter men's hair, black and curly."

Penny closed her eyes. Oh dear Gawd. Jest like Jeff's too.

A FEW WORDS ABOUT WORDS

This novel contains a few words that are not in common usage today, but that I heard frequently, and used, in my childhood.

I don't know the source of the term "**brinjin hot**." It was commonly used in my family circles—among cousins in distant states. My personal definition is "hot enough to singe off the eyebrows and to burn water."

The **barn owl** scream does sound like a wildcat (or to some, like a frightened woman) screaming. The first time I heard one, I tried to sneak up for a look at the wildcat, only to spook the owl.

The **barred owl** call is quoted by hunters, especially turkey hunters, as sounding like "Who cooks for you, who cooks for you all." Wild gobblers will often respond to it with their own gobbling from the roost. And crows flock to the owl's call to harass the larger bird.

The **boys' training school** was located on the outskirts of Milledgeville. From the school bus, I did see a staff member slug an inmate.

A **cat saddle** is made by two people gripping each other's arms or wrists to form a support. The grip changes to fit the object to be carried.

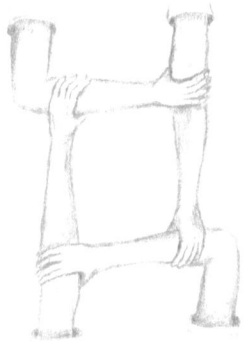

The call of the **chuck-will's-widow** is often confused with that of the whip-poor-will. The former call is a four beat sound, beginning with what sounds like a hiccup. The ranges of the two birds overlap in Georgia's Piedmont.

Croaker sack is the term used in my rural South for "burlap bag."

Haint is a "haunt " or ghost. It's been in use for several centuries in the South.

Harness and plowing terms terms:

Breeching is the band that goes across the mule's backside

Middle buster is the plow point that is used to make a furrow and throw dirt off to both sides.

Bottom plow: A shovel-shaped blade that lifts soil and turns it over, so that it brings an under layer of soil to the top.

The **Jacobs place** is used without an apostrophe. If the article "the" is omitted, the possessive form is used, as in Smith's house. "Smith" becomes an adjective, however, in our Georgia lingo when we say "the Smith house ."

The **northern lights** seldom flare as far south as middle Georgia, but I saw them in my growing up years outside Milledgeville. They became the talk of the community.

Klu Klux is local pronunciation for Ku Klux. For some reason the "l" sound is added.

Light'erd is the local term for "light wood" or pine kindling that is heavy with resin.

Lucifer was a common name for "kitchen matches," that is, wooden matches that would strike on any rough surface.

Painter for panther or wildcat is still is use among some groups.

Sick the dog means to instruct the dog to attack or to find. "Sick'em" is still used by possum and coon hunters, and even at times by a homeowner who believes a prowler is in the yard and wants the dogs to chase him off.

Scattergun is another name for a shotgun.

"Screens held up windows" in my youth. Antebellum homes had no screens over windows, but expandible screens were available. They had a light-weight wooden frame that could be adjusted to fit the window and was strong enough to support the lower sash.

The stallion **"shot one hip."** That is, he took weight off that leg, rested his hoof on its toe, and relaxed. Horses sleep standing up, with one hip shot.

Worth shucks is a short version of "not worth shucks in August," that is, there was no value to corn shucks.

The **state hospital** for the mentally ill was located on the south side of Milledgeville. At one time, its chefs cooked for 12,000 people daily. In the 1940s, it was a simple matter to have someone committed. I saw one lady come into the courthouse to the Ordinary's Office and state that her husband beat her again. The Ordinary assured her that she'd have him placed in the state hospital.

ABOUT THE AUTHOR

Susan Lindsley was reared on an ante-bellum plantation. Her rural life was influenced by scientists and writers such as her neighbor Flannery O'Connor and her aunt, Sue Myrick. Her work has been published in a variety of magazines and anthologies. Among her other books:

Susan Myrick of* Gone With The Wind*: An autobiographical Biography, hardcover with dust jacket, $29.95, ThomasMax Publishing. The story of Susan Lindsley's aunt, Susan Myrick, who served as technical consultant for Southern authenticity in the making of the movie "Gone With The Wind," contains letters, including correspondence between Myrick and Margaret Mitchell, clashes with David O. Selznick, Myrick's diaries and dozens of photographs. Also available on Kindle for $9.99.

Margaret Mitchell: A Scarlett or a Melanie? Trade paperback, $14.95, ThomasMax Publishing. Lindsley presents works by her aunt, Susan Myrick, in answering the title question and also explores other articles by Myrick, including three feature stories about survivors of the War Between the States. Also available for Kindle or Nook for $4.99.

Blue Jeans and Pantaloons in Yesterplace, Trade paperback, $16.00, ThomasMax Publishing. A slice of rural life in the "Old South," Yesterplace inhabitants included Flannery O'Connor, Susan Myrick, cattle rustlers, shady politicians, world-renown scientists, murders and a conjure woman. With neither TV nor telephone, Susan and her sisters made up their games and songs, rode horses to the picture show, and played at Roy Rogers and Jesse James. Kindle/Nook, $5.99.

Christmas Gift, Trade paperback, $10.00, ThomasMax Publishing. Lindsley has created a classic collection of family-friendly Christmas poetry with illustrations, including "A Deer with Funny Feet" and twenty other poems. Kindle/Nook, $3.99.

Myrick Memories, Trade Paperback, $10.00, ThomasMax Publishing. Learn about race relations, including interracial marriages, in the early 1900's. Explore courtrooms and visit an old-fashioned prom. Learn about housekeeping and child care in the late 1800's. Read Susan Myrick's only published short story. Kindle/Nook, $5.99

All books shown are currently in print and available virtually everywhere books are sold. If your favorite bookstore doesn't have a copy, ask them to order it for you. Also available through Amazon.com and other online book sellers, including Barnes & Noble, Books-a-Million, and many other websites. To purchase autographed copies and see or purchase other works by Susan Lindsley, contact the author by email at yesterplace@earthlink.net or by mail at P.O. Box 33536, Decatur, GA 30033.

www.ingramcontent.com/pod-product-compliance
Lightning Source LLC
Chambersburg PA
CBHW020441270626

47155CB00022B/791